Jane Costello was a newspaper journalist before she became an author, working on the *Liverpool Echo*, the *Daily Mail*, and the *Liverpool Daily Post*, where she was Editor. Jane's first novel, *Bridesmaids*, was an instant bestseller. Her second novel, *The Nearly-Weds*, won Romantic Comedy of the Year 2010, and her latest novel, *Girl on the Run*, was a *Sunday Times* Top 10 bestseller. Jane lives in Liverpool with her two young sons and she is currently working on her next novel.

Also by Jane Costello

Bridesmaids
The Nearly-Weds
My Single Friend
Girl on the Run

Jane Costello

All the Single Ladies

**SIMON &
SCHUSTER**

London · New York · Sydney · Toronto · New Delhi

A CBS COMPANY

First published in Great Britain by Simon & Schuster UK Ltd, 2012
A CBS COMPANY
This paperback edition published 2012

1 3 5 7 9 10 8 6 4 2

Simon & Schuster UK Ltd
1st Floor
222 Gray's Inn Road
London WC1X 8HB

www.simonandschuster.co.uk

Simon & Schuster Australia, Sydney
Simon & Schuster India, New Delhi

A CIP catalogue record for this book
is available from the British Library

PB ISBN: 978-0-85720-553-7
EBOOK ISBN: 978-0-85720-554-4

Typeset by M Rules
Printed and bound by CPI Group (UK) Ltd, Croydon, CR0 4YY

For Mark

Acknowledgements

It's been five years since I signed my first book deal, an ambition to which I'd aspired for as long as I can remember.

For that reason, I'd like to extend a special thanks on the publication of *All The Single Ladies* to Darley Anderson and Suzanne Baboneau, the two people who agreed that deal and launched a career that's fulfilled dreams I didn't even dare contemplate.

Thanks also Clare Wallace and Maddie Buston at the Darley Anderson Agency, the brilliant Maxine Hitchcock, Libby Yevtushenko and Clare Hey at Simon & Schuster, and my copy editor Clare Parkinson.

Finally, a mention to my incredible friends (you know who you are), my lovely boyfriend Mark O'Hanlon, my mum and dad, and my two gorgeous children, Otis and Lucas.

Chapter 1

There's a time and a place in which to have an emotional break-down – and the edge of a bus lane while the AA man twiddles with your spark plugs isn't it. Sadly, the knowledge that my hysterical short breaths and raging tears are woefully misplaced does nothing to quell them.

He's pretending not to notice, instead peering into the depths of the bonnet, preferring to risk setting his head on fire than confront a woman in my state of disquiet. He knows what's happening, though. It'd be impossible not to. Every time the traffic on the busy dual carriageway dies down and I fail miserably to compose myself, the whine of passing cars is replaced by my frenzied snorts, which would rival those of a wild boar at the height of the mating season.

My mobile rings and I take it out of my jeans pocket and answer it. Except I can't answer it, not with words. A whimper is as articulate as it gets.

'Where are you, sweetheart?' my best friend, Ellie, asks with the urgency required for the Code Red status of this crisis. 'I expected you half an hour ago.'

I sniff, attempting to restrain the runny nose that's chosen this moment to unleash itself. 'My car broke down.'

'Again? You'd be better in a horse and cart. Get a taxi. Seriously.' This is an instruction, not a suggestion. 'You can't be by yourself.'

'I'm not.'

'Who's with you?'

'The AA man.'

'Sam,' she tuts. 'Being the fourth emergency service doesn't stretch to psychological support.'

The comment makes me wince. This isn't like me at all. I am unflappable in a crisis; I keep my head when those around me lose theirs. I'm a person who sees solutions, not problems, who's unfazed by unpredictability and immune to near-catastrophe. Not that you'd know it to look at me. My composure remains as intact as my mascara and, as the charcoal mess on my cheeks indicates, that's . . . not at all.

'Nearly done,' says Mr AA, momentarily popping up his head, before dipping it again fast enough to absolve me of the need to respond.

'He's nearly done,' I inform Ellie numbly.

'Good,' she replies. 'Though if "nearly" means ten minutes then fine. Any longer and you must get a taxi.'

In fact, it's less than ten minutes – and would probably be even less than that if the AA man didn't obviously have to wait for a pause in my weeping before conversing with me.

'That should be fine for you now,' he says, wiping his hands with a rag and refusing to make eye contact. I'd guess he's in his fifties, though he could be older, with hair that was once ginger but has aged to blond.

He looks solid and dependable, the sort of man who, after his shift, will have a single beer while he watches a repeat of *Midsomer Murders*, then pull on his M&S pyjamas and slip into bed in the hope that Mrs AA hasn't got a headache.

I feel a swell of admiration for this man whose low-octane existence is quite enough for him, who sees the uncomplicated pleasures of suburban living as the source of nothing but happiness.

'I've done enough to tide you over, but you need to get this car to a garage in the next couple of days,' he says, before reeling off a list of problems that sounds like the index in a Haynes manual.

'Thank you,' I mutter, instantly forgetting everything he's said.

'Sign here.' He hands me a clipboard and I'm halfway through my signature when emotion hits me again in another thrashing wave. As the sting of tears bites my cheeks, the AA man shifts uncomfortably.

'Are you okay, love?' he asks gently.

The blindingly obvious fact that I'm not okay doesn't matter. There's a part of me that's glad he's asked, because I want to explain. About the fact I'm not some emotional jellyfish who regularly contemplates throwing herself off a cliff. About this behaviour being unheard of – for me. About my world having been turned upside down so violently I feel dizzy. But, most of all, I want to explain about Jamie. Only, I'm not in such a state that

I don't recognize a man who wouldn't appreciate a conversation of that nature.

'I've been dumped,' I say simply, feeling immediately exposed by publicizing this infinitely personal matter.

'Ah,' he replies sympathetically. 'I don't know what to say. It happens to the best of us.'

He hands me the keys and his mobile rings. I head to the car as he begins discussing an instruction to pick up some margarine on the way home. 'Yes, sweetheart, the slimming stuff – I know.'

He's keen to get off the phone – she's obviously one of life's talkers – but the fondness in his voice is unmistakable. As he ends the call, I ponder why it is that some men spend years with a woman – existing in a state in which a lack of drama and excitement is more than compensated for by quiet content-ment – while others can't last the distance. Others need more than just contentment.

'Your wife?' I ask, as he puts away his phone.

'Boyfriend,' he corrects me and heads to his van.

I slide into the car and throw my handbag on the passenger seat, where it joins a handful of letters I picked up yesterday on my way out. I gaze at the one on top: my welcome pack after sponsoring a child in Eastern Europe. I pick it up and it strikes me how, twenty-four hours ago, when I first looked at this simple, pedestrian thing – an envelope – my life was completely different.

Now, for the first time in six years, I'm alone.

And it's the worst feeling in the world.

Chapter 2

I arrive at Ellie's house shortly afterwards and she opens the door with the sort of expression you'd use to gaze upon a tortured kitten. She lives in Woolton, a couple of miles from me in south Liverpool.

'Oh don't,' I groan.

Not that I'm surprised at her reaction; I could barely bring myself to glance in my car mirror on the way here.

Despite last week's cut, my long, dark bob, which usually has a passable amount of va-va-voom, is scraped into such a haphazard ponytail that it'd shame a Blackpool donkey.

My skin, usually the tans-easily kind, has developed a pallor comparable to that of someone recovering from the Black Death; it's a fetching shade of grey offset by red neck blotches that appeared at the start of my weeping marathon at six o'clock this evening.

And despite the fact that I've been on a health kick for the last six years (in which I've counted an infinite number of calories and plummeted from a size twelve to a . . . erm, size twelve), my jeans already feel baggy and shapeless as if just a hint of the now-inevitable Heartbreak Diet has shrunk me.

'Don't what?' She pushes her glasses up her nose.

'Look at me like that. With such . . . morbid pity.'

She frowns. It's an expression you'll rarely see on Ellie because she's permanently in a good mood. At five foot three, my best friend is four inches shorter than me and has porcelain skin, full lips and a pretty-geek look that – despite being twenty-eight, the same age as me – means she still has the air of the girl everyone fancied in chess club. She also has the best hair in the world, bar none. I cannot describe how much I covet Ellie's hair. It's long, mahogany-coloured and so lustrous and glossy that the first words out of her mouth every morning could reasonably be: 'Because I'm worth it.'

She teaches English Literature in one of the roughest comprehensive schools in the city, a job which requires her to be one tough cookie and no mistake. Although I'm pretty sure that it's her permanently upbeat disposition that wins them over, rather than the karate skills she honed on a six-week course in 2006 and has since used precisely never.

'What else do you expect, gorgeous?' she says softly. 'I'm hardly going to congratulate you on the wonderful evening you've had.'

The fact that Ellie can still call me 'gorgeous' when I look as attractive as road kill is yet another reflection of my best friend's generous personality. I press my back against the wall and feel my face crumple, without having any control over the matter. 'I've turned into a crying machine. I hate that.'

She shakes her head and opens her arms wide, wrapping them round my shoulders and pulling me in. 'Stop being silly. And cry. That's what you're supposed to do.' I bury my head in her hair and breathe in the full force of her Herbal Essences.

'Tell that to the AA man,' I manage. 'I don't think he was counting on Gwyneth Paltrow's acceptance speech when he came to look under my bonnet.'

She snorts with laughter, but I know it's the last coherent sentence she'll get out of me for a while, as a twist in my stomach prompts another violent wave of tears.

We make it into Ellie's living room, where she sits me down on one of her sofas, the big one she's had since we were students, with huge, squashy seats and gaudy, mismatched scatter cushions.

I don't know how Ellie's house manages to look stylish when it's full of such unapologetically eccentric stuff. The stripped floors and ceiling-high bookshelves help, but she and Alistair – her boyfriend – wilfully turn their noses up at anything trendy and opt simply for what they like.

The result, thanks to the weird trinkets from the Gambia, the Queen of Hearts door knobs and the debris of toys courtesy of her two-year-old, Sophie, is a home that has their individual stamp on it, and no mistake. It's lovely.

She disappears from the room to get some wine and I find myself gazing at the screensaver on my phone – a photo of Jamie and me in Abersoch last year. It isn't a great shot of me, in all honesty. My bright green eyes, which can be one of my best features, look nearly grey in the sallow light and the wide smile I'm often complimented on just looks wonky. But I still love the photo. I love the way Jamie's squeezing my shoulders, the way he's gazing at me proudly as if telling the world: 'She's mine.'

Ellie returns with a bottle of Sauvignon Blanc and a glass for me. She tops up her half-empty glass and pours another so full to the top I almost spill it as I lift it to my lips.

'Start from the beginning,' she instructs, tucking a maroon-legginged limb under her backside as she sits on the sofa opposite. 'What did he say? And what did you say? And when did he leave? And how did he leave?'

I take a deep breath and my lip wobbles. Recounting how the love of your life has left you isn't easy, no matter whom you're telling.

'We were supposed to be having a romantic dinner tonight,' I reply, hearing the tremor in my voice. 'I had it all planned. I was making chicken cacciatore.'

'Nice choice.'

'I couldn't tell you,' I shrug. 'It was never eaten.'

I take a mouthful of wine. 'When he came in he had a funny look on his face. Nothing over the top. Nothing that gave me a clue as to what he was about to say. He looked like he'd had a bad day, that's all. You know what men are like when they've had a bad day.'

'A bear with haemorrhoids,' Ellie nods.

'I just assumed he'd had a bollocking from the boss, or failed to hit his monthly targets or there'd been an unpleasant customer in the shop or . . .' My voice drifts away, bereft of steam.

'When did it become clear something was really wrong?' Ellie asks.

'He said nothing at first. I walked around babbling about the tennis event we're organizing and what Natasha Munn in accounts did today and . . . I didn't see it coming.'

She bites her lip.

'Then I realized he hadn't said anything for ages. So I asked if everything was all right. And as he started speaking . . . I wasn't taking in what he was saying. All I could hear were words going round the room and . . . urgh!' The memory makes me shudder.

'What words? What did he say?'

'That he loves me more than anything. That it would kill him to be apart from me. That he'd do anything for me and I'm everything he could ever want in a woman.'

She scrunches up her nose. 'Are you sure you've been dumped?'

'He added that sometimes he thinks he'd rather die than be without me.'

'Wow. I mean . . . what? I don't get it.'

'Me neither. Well . . . except I do.'

'I'm lost,' she continues, shaking her head. 'How can he think all that and then split up with you?'

I frown, and for some unfathomable reason feel the need not just to explain, but to defend his position. 'Because of what I've known about Jamie since the first day we met.'

'What's that?'

'He's a free spirit. He doesn't want what I want. He doesn't want the marriage, the kids, the Victorian terrace with sash windows and hanging baskets. He might want me . . . but he doesn't want that.'

She closes her eyes at this moment of clarity – one that makes perfect sense to both of us, horrific as its consequences are.

'But you've never been one of those women obsessed with marriage and kids and all that stuff,' she argues. 'I don't think I've ever heard you mention it . . . not to him, anyway. Clearly, what goes on between you and the girls on a Friday night is another matter. Besides, you're perfect for each other. I've never met a couple so made for each other. You sparkle together. I know that. Everyone else knows that. It even sounds like Jamie knows that.'

'Well, it hardly matters,' I sniff. 'I've little choice on this issue.'

'Oh I don't believe that,' she says dismissively, leaning over to grab the bottle and top up our glasses again. 'He'll be back in days. I know it. He'll move into one of his mates' houses and within a week of eating slimy takeaways and living with each other's farting and dirty pants on the bathroom floor, he'll be on the doorstep. I guarantee it.'

I gaze into the middle distance, feeling my tears well up again. 'He won't, Ellie.'

'How do you know?' she challenges.

'Because he's got a ticket to South America. And it's not a return.'

She opens her mouth wide. 'What? When?'

I swallow. 'He flies out in five months. To Peru, apparently.

He's got some job with an environmental monitoring project that starts in December.'

'But he's dumped you now?'

I shrug. 'I guess if you know you're leaving someone it'd be difficult to live a lie for such a long time.'

Ellie shakes her head incredulously. 'Has this come totally out of the blue? He gave you no indication before tonight that he was planning this?'

I let out a deep breath. 'Things weren't perfect. But are they in anyone's relationship? Honestly, Ellie – I never expected this.'

She goes to answer, but the beep of a text interrupts her. I pick up my phone with trembling hands.

I love u, Sam. I'll always love u. But I have to do this. I'm so very, very sorry xxxxxxx

Chapter 3

I know how it sounds. The man's dumped me. So, assuming there's nothing fundamentally wrong with me (and you'll have to take my word for that), he must be a selfish prat, a loser or an emotional fuckwit. Or – worse than all those – a wonderful guy who happens to have fallen out of love with me.

The stupid thing, though, is that none of those apply.

Despite the circumstances, I know he loves me – and not only because he's told me. That's not to say that I don't feel like throttling him, because I do. But more than anything I want to kiss him. The thought of never kissing that man again makes my insides ache.

I knew within a week of meeting Jamie that he was 'the one'. It was a fact so obvious it practically leaped out and grabbed me by the heart with both hands. I never thought he was perfect, although he was without question the most charismatic and unique person I'd ever met. I simply thought he was perfect for me – which is all that counts.

Even after six years together, we had that indefinable

something, the X factor that makes couples live with their differences, put up with the odd row and know that they're simply meant to be together. We had chemistry, at least as far as I was concerned.

Six years. Quite a while by the standards of some relationships. Yet, now he's gone, it feels as though that time has passed in a flash. I can still conjure up a replay of when we met, as agonizing and gorgeous as it is to do so. We were in Koh Samui, Thailand, and it was January 2006 . . .

I'd been an irrepressible tomboy when I was little and even now, when I should know better, there's a part of me that fancies myself as an Action Girl type. I love the idea of being sporty, adventurous – capable of everything from mountain climbing to white-water rafting.

Sadly, the notable lack of mountains and fast-flowing rivers in south Liverpool, where I grew up and still live means this image has never been fully tested. Plus, as I constantly discover whenever I give such things a whirl, they're harder than they look. Still, I'm bloody good at Boxercise, if I do say so myself.

During my gap-year trip round the world with Ellie and our friend Jen (which turned out to be a gap seven months round Asia thanks to our less-than-meticulous financial calculations), I leaped at the chance to unleash the go-getter side of my personality.

I'd have loved to scuba dive. But not being in possession of a PADI diving qualification, or the trust fund required to gain one, we went for second best: snorkelling. What was good enough for Ursula Andress was good enough for us.

'God only knows where this has been,' said Jen, glaring at the end of her mouthpiece. It looked as though it had been chewed by a Rottweiler.

While she grumbled, those in Jen's presence, as ever, gazed upon her with expressions that fell into one of two camps: mild envy (in the case of the women) or unrestrained lust (in the case of the men).

That remained the case even though her hair – usually cheerleader-blonde to bring out her Coppertone-advert skin – wasn't looking its best. The dreadlocks she'd had installed on Chaweng beach a week earlier now resembled the rotting intestines of a dead squirrel – and were starting to smell similar too. Not that anyone was looking at her hair. When Jen's in a bikini, nobody looks at her hair.

'You worry too much,' I said, pulling on my flippers and plunging into the water. The manoeuvre was delivered with less aplomb than I'd hoped and I spent the next ten seconds adjusting my bikini top so that the triangles were covering the correct appendages instead of my armpits.

Ellie, in a polka dot bikini like the ones on old-fashioned postcards, tore off her oversized glasses and jumped in. 'Come on, Jen! It's lovely in here.'

We'd arrived at the secluded beach on one of those traditional Thai fishing boats – the wooden ones featured in every brochure, resplendent with ribbons at the front. The scenery was breathtaking: a crystal sea, verdant landscape and sand so fine and white it looked like something you'd sprinkle on a baby's bum.

Aside from our guide, the boat's captain and the five other tourists, there wasn't another soul. Not another person, not another boat. It was just us, a coastline full of coral and total tranquillity.

We dipped our faces underwater and began swimming above the coral, overwhelmed by what we saw. There were fish of every colour imaginable, coral in every shape and size, and as sunlight streamed through the water, we were dazzled. The further we swam along the coast the brighter and more beautiful everything was.

I was vaguely aware of the growing distance between us and the boat, but it would be impossible to lose our way: all we had to do was follow the coast back to where it had been anchored.

That was the theory. The practice, nearly an hour later, diverged somewhat.

I don't know why Ellie popped up her head at that precise moment; frankly, it doesn't matter. All that matters is that she thrashed her arms and legs, walloping my back until Jen and I looked up. The issue was immediately apparent.

The distance we'd covered couldn't have been more than a mile, but as we'd swum along in blissful ignorance, a crucial factor had changed: we were no longer alone.

Stretching the length of the coast were so many boats they would have made the Spanish Armada look like pedalos at

Center Parcs. They were all identical. What followed was a frantic few hours of splashing, panting and panicking, all of which did precisely nothing in the quest to locate our vessel.

We couldn't get anywhere near the island because of the coral and, of course, there was no way we were going to ask anyone on the other boats for help. We might have been desperate, but we were also British. The embarrassment would've been too much. But there comes a point when your sense of hopelessness overtakes your sense of self-respect – and it came to us in a flash.

Our thighs and our arms ached. Our eyes and our skin stung. Our stomachs cramped, our feet hurt and our heads throbbed.

More than all that, though, was the now overwhelming conviction that, if we didn't take drastic action, we were going to be left there, abandoned and destined to live a *Lost*-style existence. With no food, water, Factor 25 or Matthew Fox, I didn't like that prospect one bit.

In short, in the space of ten minutes we'd gone from not wanting to bother anyone with our troubles to being so desperate we'd have stowed away on a white slave ship.

Unfortunately, that point came at the exact moment when the boats fired up their engines and prepared to do the one thing we were keen for them not to do: leave.

'Surely they won't go without us. Surely,' said Ellie, breathless. 'What do you think, Sam?'

'No, they won't,' I replied with a conviction totally at odds with how I felt. 'Surely.'

'Yep, I'm sure too,' added Jen.

'As sure as sure can be,' Ellie said for good measure.

As the boats started heading back one by one to the main island, there came a point – with about three left – when there was only one thing to do.

Scream.

I'd thought I was loud – until Jen opened her gob and emitted a noise like the wail of a demented banshee on her way to the seventh circle of hell. But no matter how loud we shouted, how pathetic we looked, how blue in the face we turned in our attempts to catch someone's attention, we were ignored by all but one.

His voice swam across the Indian Ocean and swept me up. It had the lilt of an accent I recognized immediately, and although it said a dozen things it meant only one: we were going to be saved.

Chapter 4

Jamie had taken the job with the long boat company four weeks earlier and he told us that night that 'incidents' like ours were common. Very common. In fact, the more pressure Ellie put on him to reassure us we weren't imbeciles, the more common they became.

I often reminisce about that first evening, when we ended up alone, drinking cold Singha beers on the beach and sharing stories beside a fire we'd built, its flickering flames reflected in our eyes. It was terribly romantic – apart from the fact that chronic sunburn had left my shoulders, nose and forehead looking like a walking strip of pancetta.

I had a sense even then that it was one of the defining moments of my life, an unforgettable snapshot that would remain with me for ever. But it wasn't the setting that made such an impression. It was Jamie.

He was beautiful in a way I'd rarely seen up close. Lean and tanned, his body was the equivalent of a gorgeous, gooey cream cake I was never going to be allowed. So why did I think I wouldn't be allowed him? For a start, with his blue, cool-water eyes and a heart-stopping smile, he was too good-looking for me. I was punching above my weight and I knew it.

Yet I wanted him so badly it made my head spin.

He was well-travelled and well-read, intellectual and thoughtful. He talked about books by John Fante and Bukowski (no, I'd never heard of them either) and had a CV of exotic jobs ranging from tour guide in Borneo to jobbing guitarist in Sydney.

But with that Liverpool lilt betraying the fact that we'd grown up less than ten miles from each other, his dazzling experiences weren't intimidating. He and I shared a history and sense of humour that created an instant connection.

'Isn't it difficult constantly moving round? Maintaining friendships must be hard,' I said, pushing my feet into the warm sand and feeling it run through my toes.

'I make new friends. You get used to it,' he shrugged, letting a handful of sand slide through his fingers. 'Though I must admit . . .'

'What?' I asked, sensing his hesitation.

'I miss having a girlfriend.' He looked into my eyes and smirked. 'It's been . . . a while.'

I raised an eyebrow. He laughed. 'Oh I don't mean sex – I've not struggled with that . . .' Then he widened his eyes. 'Oh God! That came out wrong!'

It was the first sign of self-consciousness I'd detected.

'What I mean is –' he took a gulp of beer – 'I'm not saying I've been an angel . . . but sleeping around holds no interest for me. I want intimacy with someone on every level.'

I sipped my beer. 'Good for you.'

'Does that surprise you? Given that I'm bumming my way around the world, I mean. The thing is, there's a big part of me that wants to find someone to spend, well, forever with.'

I peeled off the label from my beer bottle. 'Forever's a long time. And that might be tricky given that you are, as you say, bumming your way around the world. Maybe you can't really decide what you want in life.' I flashed him a challenging grin and he laughed.

'Oh I know what I want. I have a list.'

'A list?' I laughed. 'What's on it?'

'Let's see . . . adventure. Love. Happiness. Fun . . .' His eyes twinkled as he was unable to suppress a smile. 'Lust.'

We both giggled. He'd moved closer to me, so close I could feel his breath on my face.

'That's a great list,' I whispered, my heartbeat thundering in my ears.

'It is, isn't it?' he replied as his lips melted into mine.

The girls and I were supposed to be staying on Choeng Mon beach for only a few days. But, for one reason or another, we stayed two weeks. What I really mean by one reason or another is Jamie. He was the reason. And my friends, loyal and lovely as ever, indulged the holiday romance they could see developing. Even if it did involve remaining in the 'luxury beach hut' whose shower facilities consisted of a tap that intermittently vomited dirty water and more wildlife than a David Attenborough box set.

Jamie and I couldn't stay away from each other. It was one of those intense relationships that felt like a drug addiction. When we were apart, all I could think about was my next hit. When we were together, the pleasure was so sweet it made me glow.

I told him every day of the last week on Choeng Mon that it would be my last. I had to move on. My friends were getting restless and I owed it to them to continue with the trip. Yet the thought of leaving him was unbearable.

On the day we were due to sail back to mainland Thailand, I felt like I was being ripped in two. We'd exchanged numbers; we'd promised we'd email; we'd agreed that, if he ever came back to the UK, we'd go for a drink. A drink. It sounded so small and unsatisfactory compared with the explosion of emotion I'd experienced in the last fifteen days.

'Come on, gorgeous – I'm sure your paths will cross again,' Ellie said, as we loaded our backpacks onto the taxi and climbed on. It was one of those open-air Thai ones easily mistaken for a milk float. 'Besides, it's never the same when you get home. Without the sunsets and the tan you don't get that rush of blood to the head.'

'It would have been different,' I insisted, as Ellie squeezed my hand.

And I meant it. I knew it. I could feel it in the sting of my tears when he kissed me for the last time outside his hut and told me he'd never forget me.

I often wonder how fate would've played out if our taxi hadn't broken down on that dusty road to the harbour. If we'd set sail on time. And if I hadn't looked up as the driver stood at the side of the road gesticulating – and seen a motorbike racing in our direction.

It was only as it skidded to a halt, dust billowing around the driver, that I realized who his passenger was. As Jamie stepped off the back of the bike and strode towards me, I was alive with anticipation.

'What's up?' I managed.

Then I noticed his backpack, his guitar. He put them on the ground and held my face in his hands, kissing me slowly, as if we had all the time in the world.

'I had a moment of realization,' he said eventually.

'Oh?' I replied, holding my breath. 'What did you realize?'

He smiled. 'That I've found someone to share my list with.'

Chapter 5

When I first heard the name of my new client, Lorelei Beer, I pictured a vaguely slutty type whose main talent is giggling.

I've only once met Lorelei in person – during our kick-off meeting for an event I'm organizing for her company – but she's nothing like I'd imagined. A large, loud redhead of indeterminable age, with a thick Cardiff Bay accent, she isn't remotely slutty (as far as I know). And there was no giggling.

'I've looked at the celebrity guests you're proposing,' she booms down the phone, almost setting my earlobes on fire.

'Right,' I say, as brightly as I can. Despite being confident about the quality of my guest list, I'm struggling with work today like never before. 'What do you think?'

She doesn't miss a beat. 'They're a shower of crap, my love.'

I take a deep breath and attempt to compose a lucid response, even though there's only one thing on my mind – and it isn't work. She beats me to it.

'That's a generous assessment, by the way. A kind one. I should get a frigging OBE for not having torn up that list and spat on it.'

I open my mouth to speak.

'I said I wanted A-LIST, my darling.'

Lorelei, I discovered early on, has a unique ability to combine terms of endearment with insults as toxic as nuclear waste. 'Some of these soap stars wouldn't go to the opening of a Netto, my lovely. And where's Coleen? You promised me Coleen.'

Lorelei is the Marketing Director for a massive charity that was launched in Liverpool nearly a century ago to help vulnerable young adults. Despite the fact that the charity now helps teenagers in need in several corners of the world and its main HQs are in London and New York, it continues to have a major office here, and the local connection means that they still have the odd event in the city.

The event I'm in charge of is one of a string of parties marking the charity's centenary in November. The others, including a black-tie ball, a networking event for suppliers and a staff shindig, are all in London. But they wanted to throw the hundredth-birthday party itself in the place where it all began.

Which is where I, as Events Director (Liverpool) for BJD Productions, come in. If the grand title gives the impression that I have scores of minions to jump to my every creative whim – be it a chocolate fountain the size of Victoria Falls or Bill Clinton as an after-dinner speaker – don't be fooled.

It's not that we don't do ludicrously proportioned chocolate fountains or former presidents, because we do and we have. It's just that, despite BJD being a big London-based company with several sub-branches, there are only a handful of us in

Liverpool – and, far from being minions, one or two of the staff like to think of themselves as only slightly lower in status than the Sultan of Brunei.

'Well, the list's a work in progress,' I say, attempting to placate her, at least until I'm feeling my usual efficient self again – which I sincerely hope will be soon. 'I'll review it this afternoon and add some more, erm, brand-appropriate names.' I hate that term with all its contrived David-Brentness. The clients are universally orgasmic when you use it, though, and who am I to argue? 'Plus, if you feel Coleen is central, you have my word that we'll do our best. We have good contacts with her people and I'm confident that the celebrity turnout will be second to none. But bear in mind that the bigger the name, the less likely they'll commit until closer to the time. They see what's on their schedules and—'

'Listen, luvvie,' she snaps with a voice that makes my root canals tremor. 'Don't give me that crap. Have I told you Kevin S. Chasen might be coming?'

Kevin S. Chasen, by the way, is God. In fact, he's more important than God as far as Lorelei's concerned because he is the CEO of Teen SOS (whose name is the result of a relatively recent rebranding of the charity that one hundred years ago was simply called Buffets).

Despite the high-profile job, he's a shadowy figure, keeping himself relatively out of the public eye; when I Googled him I discovered only two blurry pictures taken several years ago.

The fact that he may grace an event Lorelei has commissioned is a prospect that's got her knickers in such a twist it's a surprise she can walk properly.

'If Kevin S. Chasen is there this event has got to be show-stoppingly brilliant and nothing less. So don't feed me any crap. Because I've been around the block enough to know when I'm being fed crap and this is such blatant crap I can virtually smell it.'

I take another deep breath. 'Ms Beer—'

'Lorelei, my gorgeous,' she corrects me. 'We agreed to dispense with all that surname crap.'

'Lorelei. All I can say is that everything is in hand—'

'Soz, luvvie – another call's coming through. Just sort it for me, won't you?'

She slams down the phone and I'm left gazing at the handset.

I look at my to-do list and add to it a review of Lorelei's invitees. My to-do list now runs to six pages. Any more and I could wallpaper my downstairs toilet. Under normal circumstances, I'd whizz through it, picking off tasks and doing my best to demolish them. However, my brain feels as though it's made of butternut squash soup this morning. And I hate it.

I look around the office; the place is quietly buzzing. The BJD team occupies one floor of a large, overly expensive building that we share with several other companies. The fact that my bosses pay over the odds for impressive views and top-of-the-range furniture is a reflection of how important image is to them. It does, however, mean that we have to work very hard at keeping our team as profitable as it is. Which can be a challenge given some of the staff members I inherited, as anyone who's come across Natalie and Deana would testify.

Natalie and Deana work here, but only in the technical rather than the literal sense. They turn up (usually). They remain in the office for eight hours (if you're lucky). They leave (hastily). And they get paid for all of this. Whether this constitutes work is a moot point, particularly since they rarely engage in activity even vaguely beneficial to their employer.

'I asked Ged for flowers the other day,' announces Natalie, our Administrator, pausing briefly from reading her *Take a Break*. Both she and Deana are about the same age as me, but that's where the similarities start and end. 'He started banging on about it being the twenty-first century and it should be me bringing him flowers. I said to him: "If you're such a sodding feminist, get your Marigolds on and scrub that bog for a change." That shut him up.'

Deana, our Junior Events Coordinator, pouts. 'You'd think it was hard, wouldn't you?' Her distinctive, high-pitched whine is comparable to that of a metalwork drill. 'That bloke I went out with from Plentyoffish.com was like that. He wanted me to pay all the time. Talk about taking the piss! Hey, have you seen Katie Price's new extensions? Gorrrrgeous!'

Deana and Natalie have but two topics of conversation: celebrities and men. The latter, as a breed, are considered to be a bunch of useless reprobates but still provide endless opportunities for analysis and discussion.

I turn to my laptop and focus on my inbox but the screen makes my eyes hurt. It was gone three o'clock before Ellie and I retired to bed last night. And, unlike my friend, who seems able to function no matter how late a night she's had, I'm wrecked – emotionally and physically.

'You look pale, Sam,' says Deana, in between her stream of abuse about the Plentyoffish.com man.

I look up, taken aback. I must look bad for Deana to have noticed. Under normal circumstances it'd take a tidal wave to tear her away from *Closer*. Natalie leans in and narrows her eyes in the same way she does when she's examining her blackheads at her desk. 'Ooh, yes, you are . . . Are you coming down with something?'

'I'm fine,' I reply through a forced smile. 'A lot to do, that's all. Any chance you could do some of that photocopying I gave you, Natalie?'

She stiffens. 'Piers said I didn't have to do as much of that sort of stuff any more.'

I frown, but can't be bothered arguing. Not today.

Piers is my boss. And, despite the fact that Deana and Natalie are actually in contact with him for about one and a half hours per year, he insists that they, along with everyone else in this office, report directly to him. I strongly suspect that the reason for this insane state of affairs is his appreciation of the length of their skirts – and the fact that he's such a power-crazed oligarch he'd feel at home running North Korea. But my attempts to address the issue continually fall on deaf ears.

'Fine.' I shrug, and she frowns suspiciously. They continue with their conversation as I sit, staring numbly at my laptop. I log on to my Hotmail account, reopening the draft of the only email I've written all day.

> Jamie,
> I've got a million things I want to say, so many things that putting them all down here is impossible.

I pause for a second, rereading the sentence. Impossible? Really, Sam? Have you ever really been the sort of woman who struggles to express her feelings?

The message I proceed to write to Jamie is of such length and eloquence Tolstoy couldn't match it. It dissects our relationship in meticulous detail: where it went right, where it went wrong. What we could have done differently. What we should have done differently.

But there's one overriding message: we should try again.

The psychoanalysis I put into practice so thoroughly cathartic that, before I know it, two and a half hours have passed and the email runs to 5,389 words. I end with one sentence, from the heart.

> I love you and I will always love you. I will change, I promise. So don't go. I beg of you. Please.
> Love,
> Sam
> xxxxxxxxxxxxxxxxxxxxxxxxxxxxxxxxxxxxx

With tears pricking my eyes, I hit the send button, feeling a rush of emotion – and a swell of positivity.

This is going to work. I know it.

Chapter 6

After ten minutes, I've heard nothing, at least nothing from Jamie; there have been just several calls from my mum, which I deliberately miss.

After thirty minutes, the situation is unchanged.

And when I look at my clock and realize it's been an hour, panic sets in. So I send him a text asking if he's checked his emails – and follow it up with an email asking if he's checked the earlier one. I leave a message on his answer machine – both at home and on his mobile.

The response amounts to nothing except three torturous hours, during which my stomach churns as if it's attempting to make butter out of the five cups of coffee I've thrown down my neck.

Meanwhile, my to-do list experiences a growth spurt of explosive proportions. There are phone calls, messages and a million people to chase up. But I'm incapable of doing anything productive.

Each time I try to respond to an email or pick up the phone, my mind is yanked violently back to a replay of yesterday evening. To things I should have said or done. I turn to my laptop and open the email in my sent box, cringing as I reread sentences that could be misinterpreted, words that aren't quite right. Bits I wanted to say but have somehow missed out.

I whip myself into a fireball of nervous energy. I'm convinced that the email I'd thought was brilliant only hours ago is nothing less than a disaster.

There's only one thing for it: to email him again. I start composing another tome – not quite as long; in fact, it's relatively succinct at 3,876 words.

Throughout all this, all I can hear is the buzz of Natalie and Deana's conversation about how the former's sister-in-law's second cousin is about to feature on *Jeremy Kyle*, and how the latter once got caught in a thunderstorm after a spray tan – resulting in her attendance at a wedding looking like she had scabies.

Once I've sent the third email, I stand up to go to the toilet and am five steps from my desk when my phone beeps with a text message. The movement I employ to reach it starts off with a spectacular Jackie Chan-style flip, progresses to a *Matrix*-style dive and ends with a near impaling on a jar of blunt pencils. I juggle the phone with trembling hands, scanning the message as fast as my eyes allow.

Hey – been mad busy in the shop today. Just got your emails. I think we need to talk.

Jamie's staying with Luke, who's been his friend since primary school, despite the fact that they appear to have as much in common as Meatloaf and Jane Asher.

Consumed by nerves, I walk up the path of Luke's terrace cottage in Rose Brae, passing an array of lovingly tended hanging baskets, which are spilling over with begonias and ivy. The cul-de-sac is quaint and quiet, within spitting distance of Allerton Road with its trendy bars and their attractive clientele – a factor which, I have no doubt, swung Luke's decision to buy the house.

I ring the bell with a thrashing heart, and when Jamie answers I experience a weird and fleeting sensation in which I've forgotten that we're no longer together. I gaze into those pale blue eyes and it feels exactly as it has done for six years. Until last night.

'Hi,' he says softly, looking unhappier than I've ever seen him.

'Hi,' I reply in a strangled voice.

We stand a foot apart yet it feels like a mile. All I want to do is reach out and touch him – except I know I can't. I shift awkwardly, hyper-aware of my shallow breaths.

He coughs, breaking the silence. 'Come in.'

The first thing that strikes me every time I enter Luke's house is that it must be the most fabulous abode ever to be inhabited by a straight man. It's all gorgeous wallpapers, Jo Malone candles and exquisitely coordinated soft furnishings.

All, however, is not what it seems. I've known Luke long enough to know that his cupboards boast a porn stash that could single-handedly fund one of Hugh Hefner's yachts; plus, he recently turned his spare room into a gym, where he spends hours inflating the muscles he tells women he was simply born with.

And women there are – because Luke is not just straight, he's unstoppable. On Facebook, he has 876 friends (and counting), 710 of whom have two X chromosomes. He is a project manager for a construction company but goes out with women from all walks of life: barristers, hairdressers, doctors, air hostesses. They have one thing in common; they throw themselves at him as if he's the last man in the northern hemisphere.

I sit on the edge of a lilac velvet sofa and expect Jamie to head to the armchair on the other side of the coffee table. Instead, he sinks next to me, so close that the familiar smell of his clean skin whispers into my lungs and makes me faint with longing.

'I read your emails,' he says.

'Did what I said make sense?' I ask anxiously.

He nods. 'It did.' Although he's agreeing with me – technically – I can't read his expression. 'You're right . . . in so many ways.'

I hold my breath, waiting for an explanation. It isn't forthcoming. 'Which ways?'

He sighs. 'About me waving goodbye to the best relationship I've ever had. About you being the only woman I've loved. About you being my best friend. About me . . .' His voice breaks up again. 'About me still being in love with you.'

As the last words fire through my head, I feel the stab of tears in my eyes. 'Are you still in love with me?'

With his elbows on his knees, he puts his head in his hands

and lets out a quiet sob. Jamie's never been afraid to show his emotional side. He's regularly in floods at some of the obscure foreign films he has on DVD (although he insisted he was just getting a cold when I put on *Marley and Me*).

But when he lifts up his head and looks at me directly, even I'm not prepared for how devastated he looks. Fat tears cascade down his cheeks as he reaches out and grips my fingers. 'You know I am.'

The sentence brings a swell of emotion in me too. But the tears soaking my cheeks don't just represent my hollow sadness. They represent something else. Frustration.

'You say that, Jamie, but how can you love me?' I sniff. 'How could you leave me if you loved me?' I'm trying to keep my voice level but it's impossible not to betray my exasperation.

He shakes his head. 'I don't know. I'm confused. I've been confused for such a long time. My feelings about you, Sam, are the only things that have remained clear. I love you. But I've been living a lie for the last six years.'

My eyes widen. The last time I heard something like that was on *Jerry Springer* and it was the prelude to a confession involving exotic mail-order underwear and a penis transplant.

'What do you mean?'

'I mean . . . that,' he says, as his eyes dart in disgust to a stack of foolscap folders on the coffee table. 'I mean . . . this,' he adds, angrily pulling off his tie. 'I mean being a salesman for a bloody mobile-phone company, Sam.'

I bite my lip and sniff back my tears. 'I thought you'd started enjoying work a bit more,' I try, but I know this conversation is futile. I'm talking to a man who reads Kafka in his spare time and who learned to catch fish with a spear in the Cook Islands. Despite any enjoyment he's had with me, and despite all the fun during his stints as a guitarist in various bands over the last few years, his job is a long way from his definition of mentally stimulating.

Ironically, Jamie's very good at his job. This is a situation with which he feels distinctly uncomfortable. They've repeatedly tried to promote him, but he's refused, turning his back on the increased responsibility and pay rise, presumably because it would involve admitting that this was his career. That's a prospect about as appealing to him as genital warts.

'Then how about I put a proposition to you?' I begin firmly, with a racing heart. I have an overwhelming sense of what I've got to do, and say, to secure my future happiness. He looks up.

'How about we both give up our jobs and I come with you?'

For the past twenty-four hours I've thought over and over again about saying this sentence, yet I surprise even myself when I actually go through with it.

The truth is that I thought I'd done all the backpacking I ever wanted. I thought what I now wanted was some roots: a house, a career, my friends and family. Plus, while I've never allowed myself to even think about marriage and kids, deep down I know that that's only because I've never dared.

Now, though, all those things are irrelevant compared with the one, overriding thing that I want. Jamie. If I have to give up everything else for him, I'm prepared to do it. My lips tremble as I await his response. It isn't the one I'd imagined.

'Sam,' he says, shaking his head. 'Every part of me wants to say: let's do it. But I can't. And I can't for the best of reasons.'

I frown. 'What reasons?'

'Because you'd be doing it for me and not because it's what you really want. You want the house, the career . . . your friends and family. You want to drink cocktails and go shopping.'

I sit back, stung by the implication that I'd prioritize such shallow luxuries.

'And why the hell shouldn't you?' he continues hastily. 'Not everyone wants to live in South America. In the jungle. With no running water or shops or insect repellent.'

I pretend I haven't heard that last bit. 'I . . . might,' I reply weakly.

'You don't,' he whispers, pulling me towards him, burying his wet face in my hair. It's the saddest embrace I've ever known.

Chapter 7

Returning home for the first time after the upheaval of last night is the emptiest experience of my life.

The Victorian terrace house Jamie and I have shared for three years is one I've spent endless amounts of time and energy getting right. Despite the expensively restored fireplace, lovingly sourced flooring and the Moroccan rug I almost broke my back carrying home (admittedly from Ikea, as opposed to Morocco), the rooms aren't welcoming tonight.

The house is in my name, but we always considered it as much Jamie's home as mine. And, while most of the decor was chosen by me, it was with both of our tastes in mind. There's only one thing that Jamie actively didn't like and that's the huge pop-art print of New York's Times Square on the living-room wall.

It was the source of some debate over the years. Jamie thought it was naff, a gaudy image too ubiquitous in home-furnishing departments.

But he never loved New York like I did. I've visited four times and have never been disappointed. It has held an endless fascination for me since I first watched *Breakfast at Tiffany's* as a teenager.

Besides, this is different from other Manhattan prints I've seen; its vivid colours against the black of night make me feel alive; it is a reminder of a place that makes the blood in my veins buzz as soon as I step off the plane.

Tonight, I can't bear looking at it. It's a symbol of my failure to compromise, to make him happy, to make him love me enough to stay. I walk to the wall and lift it off, carrying it awkwardly up to the spare room, where I slide it under the bed.

Then I walk silently around the house, going from room to room, but soon realize that the picture isn't even half the problem. Jamie is everywhere.

He's in the bottle of beer abandoned on the patio table, the blurry pictures of his travels on the kitchen wall. He's in the T-shirt lying on the bathroom floor and the faint smell of deodorant on our sheets.

I flop onto the sofa and, with blurred eyes, put on my iPod, feeling an instinctive pull to a song I've always loved but which has never before meant so much.

Adele's 'Someone Like You'.

Her words make my stomach clench as a downpour of tears soaks my cheeks in the bitter realization that these things – the bottle, the T-shirt, the pictures – will shortly be gone.

Jamie was everywhere in this house. Soon he'll be nowhere, nowhere at all.

Chapter 8

Having a sister ten years older than me is great in every way but one: people can never tell which of us is the younger.

Although she is thirty-eight, Julia's results on a Ten Years Younger survey would come back at twenty-five – and that's without Botox, veneers or questionable fashion overhaul. If it wasn't for another factor, people might think we were twins. The other factor being that she is mixed-race and I'm not.

If you want the whole story, Julia isn't my real sister. She was adopted four years after Mum and Dad married because they had such a horrendous time trying to conceive a baby that – although doctors could find nothing wrong – they became convinced they'd never have children naturally.

That was eventually disproved by my existence, but, after suffering five miscarriages, you can see why my parents had their doubts. Not that me coming along any sooner would have changed their decision; they love Julia and me exactly the same and there's never been a shred of evidence to the contrary.

'You're going to hate me for saying this,' says my sister, coolly scanning her menu, 'but there may be some sense in what Jamie's saying.'

I throw her a look that stops just short of my eyes turning red and me breathing fire in her face.

We're in the Monro, a gastro-pub on the edge of the city centre that serves good, simple food and is big on atmosphere. It's Friday lunchtime and so busy that we were lucky to get a table, particularly one in a relatively private corner.

'Look,' she says, in that uniquely serene way my sister does so well. 'I know you're upset. Of course you're upset. Your whole life has been turned upside down. Plus, you and Jamie were great together. But there always was that small issue hovering in the background.'

'What small issue?'

'His itchy feet.'

'What?'

'He's always had them, Sam. No matter how much you adored each other, his feet were blatantly itchy.'

'Great,' I mutter. 'The most significant relationship of my entire life can be boiled down to a conversation we could be having at the chiropodist.'

A waiter arrives and we place our order. I change my mind twice and mispronounce the name of the wine. Then he turns to Julia, and although she asks only for a smoked chicken salad, he's left gazing in her eyes as if she's read him a sonnet.

Which brings me to the other reason we'd never be mistaken for real sisters: Julia oozes grace and elegance. When she enters a room, she glides, turns heads along the way. The last time I turned heads as I entered a room, it was because I'd tripped over the carpet. And that's probably why I could never do her job, preferring a vocation which keeps me firmly behind the scenes.

Julia is a professional musician. I know that when most people over thirty describe themselves thus, they're either one of those ageing club acts that none of the X *Factor* judges wants to mentor, or a tortured, too-serious-for-their-own-good type trying to avoid a proper job.

My sister falls into neither category. She is a cellist with the Royal Liverpool Philharmonic Orchestra, and a talented one as far as I can work out. I'd like to say her musical skills have rubbed off on me, but in a round of Singstar I could lose to a squeaky door.

'You know what I'm saying, Sam,' she continues. 'You can't change a man. It's pointless even trying.'

'I never tried to change him,' I hiss. 'I love him as he is.'

'I know,' she says softly. 'But by staying in a job selling iPhones, he's hardly being true to himself, is he?'

I'm getting annoyed now. 'What about love conquering all? And he does love me, Julia. I'm not deluded. He's told me.'

Tears spring to my eyes and it strikes me how unbelievably sick I am of them being there. I've spent more time checking my make-up in the Ladies in the last two days than I have in the last six months. I can tell without looking that my eyeliner's starting to run again.

'I believe you,' she whispers, reaching over and squeezing my hand. 'And I know you're right: he does love you. Oh look, I hate seeing you like this. Why don't you move into my place for a bit? It'll be just like old times. I'll even let you borrow my make-up this time. Plus, I've got a date next week so you can cover for me,' she winks.

The reference is to the fact that when Julia was growing up, despite never inviting male attention, she got it. Tons of it. I've tried to conceptualize her appeal over the years, though these things are difficult to pin down when it's your own family. Julia is pretty, of that there's no doubt; she has a slender figure, generous smile and a gorgeous cappuccino complexion. But this isn't a looks thing; it's more than that. Men find her mysterious without being unapproachable. She doesn't throw her charms in anyone's face and yet, between her instant likeability and quiet confidence, they're there all right.

'Is your car fixed now?' she asks.

'Just about.'

'Are you going to get a new one?'

I sigh at the mention of this, because the fact is I love that car. I know it's nothing special, and it has some way to go on the reliability stakes. But I bought it only a year and a half ago; and on the day I picked it up Jamie and I went on a long, sunny drive out into the Cheshire countryside. It was one of those beautifully perfect days that you know you'll remember for ever.

'I'm sure it'll be all right now,' I say, then change the subject. 'Has Mum said anything about Jamie and me?'

She raises her eyebrows. 'Of course. She's worried about you.'

I squirm. I've never been one for maternal heart-to-hearts. Despite what I've discussed with Ellie and Jen – with each of whom I spent an hour on the phone last night – I'd prefer to spill the details of this break-up to *Heat* than to my mother. This isn't because she's not sympathetic; the problem is that she's too sympathetic. Also, I hate the thought of her worrying about me. That said, I can't pretend my reluctance to share anything vaguely personal with her is entirely altruistic. It's a characteristic I was born with. The day she sat me down to discuss the birds and the bees I feigned a sudden onset of food poisoning and locked myself in the bathroom until she'd found something else to occupy her. Sorry, but sex education was for biology teachers, *Just 17* and Claire Tunney (whose extensive rear-of-bike-sheds experimentation was the subject of endless interrogation), not my mother.

'You need to go round, Sam. I know it's probably the last thing you want, but you're going to have to face her. Besides, it'll give her something to talk about other than my biological clock.'

I catch her eye and smile softly.

Julia has never wanted children and is determined that she never will. Maybe that's why she's never married or settled down, although she has had a couple of relationships lasting three or four years. How much of this has to do with her own background, I've no idea; but I'm sure a psychotherapist would have a few theories.

Julia was taken in by my mum and dad when she was a tiny baby, after being rejected, essentially, by her birth mother, for reasons that only that anonymous woman knows. Yet Julia's never expressed anything more than a mild interest, and certainly not enough to go on a *Who Do You Think You Are?*-style hunt for her biological parents.

You might think this is because she's worried our mum and dad might be upset, but that isn't the case. Both say they'd understand. But Julia genuinely doesn't feel a need to know more than she already does.

'I'm going to the Ladies before our food arrives.' Julia pauses and puts her hand on mine. 'You okay?'

'Of course,' I reassure her. However, I can feel my eyes getting hot again before she's even a foot away. For some reason, my frustration at the semi-permanence of these tears seems to make them all the more determined to reappear. I sniff and try to pull myself together, keen to avoid yet another trip to the toilet. Instead, I pick up my bag, rooting through it for my compact mirror.

I have no idea how long I spend looking for it, but it quickly becomes evident that I'd be more likely to find a haul of buried Inca treasure than my mirror. And all the while I continue attempting – and failing – to compose myself. Certain my cheeks are by now covered in mascara, I'm willing Julia to return so I can go to the toilet myself.

I finally lay my hands on my mobile phone and ingenuity strikes me. Checking that my fellow diners are suitably distracted by their food, I hold out my phone, spin it round and take a photo of my weeping self – the idea being that I can see what I look like without any requirement for a mirror.

Unfortunately, at the exact second that the flash goes off, I glance up to see the waiter, plate in each hand, looking at me as if he's discovered his mother in bed with the milkman. 'Would you like me to take one for you?' he offers, as if this is a moment I want to keep for posterity.

Chapter 9

I have never felt less like going on a night out. I want to stay at home sobbing to 'Nothing Compares 2U' and inhaling the neckline of one of Jamie's T-shirts. Ellie, however, has other ideas. My best friend has never respected anyone's right to a quiet night in, and she is treating this evening's recreational activities as if she's organizing my hen do.

'Okay, fish face, give us a smooch,' she grins, standing on her tiptoes to kiss Alistair, her darling boyfriend. He is on the threshold of their Victorian semi, dodging an explosion of overgrown wisteria. Given that he's six foot four, my friend has to stretch, even with her spectacular suede heels.

'Thanks, fatty,' he replies, smacking her tiny backside. 'Don't I get a proper snog since I'm stuck in babysitting?' He rolls up a sleeve of one of his ubiquitous checked shirts (in the four years I've known him, I've never seen Alistair in anything else).

'Babysitting?' blusters Ellie. 'It isn't babysitting when it's your own child, my friend. And to think I used to consider you a metrosexual.'

He laughs and she tootles down the driveway, hair swishing as she hops into the taxi.

'Right,' she says firmly, clapping her hands. 'We, ladies, are on a mission.'

'I can tell,' I say, feeling worried. When Ellie's on a mission, all that the rest of the world can do is run for cover.

She clutches my hand. 'Getting out tonight is absolutely the best strategy, Sam. The worst anyone can do after they've been dumped is sit around moping. You need men lusting after you. And you need alcohol. In copious amounts.'

I roll my eyes and smile. 'The men or the alcohol?'

'I'd recommend both,' grins Jen, pausing from her frantic texting.

Jen is wearing a small, sexy, printed dress with a slashed neck and the sort of hemline that can only be carried off by somebody who models tights for a living. Fortunately, Jen could easily model tights for a living, though she's in no hurry to pack in her job as an A&E doctor, especially since she was recently promoted.

'You both know I can't even think about other men,' I point out.

'Of course we know that,' says Jen. 'How are you feeling, Sam?'

'Oh . . . I've got all night to bore you with that again. Who's the man?'

She innocently suppresses a smile. 'What makes you think there's a man?'

Ellie sniggers. 'A, because there's always a man, and B, you've texted so much since you got in the taxi, your fingertips are almost on fire.'

Jen begins to tell all about her latest squeeze, who can be summarized thus: he is gorgeous, he texts her five hundred times a day – or thereabouts, he's a fireman, divorced and lives in Mossley Hill. Oh, and he is gorgeous (in case we didn't get that the first time).

Essentially, this means he has muscles, lots of them; for this characteristic is non-negotiable as far as Jen's concerned. Any bloke who doesn't look as if he could wrestle a rhinoceros and emerge unscathed isn't worth considering. She proudly pulls up his Facebook profile on her phone.

'I'll give you one thing, Jen,' says Ellie. 'You never deviate from your type.'

'If my "type" is highly attractive, I admit it,' she grins, putting her phone back in her bag. 'What's wrong with that?'

'Nothing at all,' Ellie shrugs. 'Only I do wonder if the muscle fixation might be the source of some of your troubles. Maybe you should try a bloke without them. You might discover other qualities.'

'I want muscles and qualities,' she replies. 'Is that too much to ask?'

'Muscles and qualities is Daniel Craig,' I tell her, 'and if you pull him in a bar in Liverpool, I'm afraid you're going to have to share him with the rest of us.'

The 'troubles' to which Ellie refers is putting it mildly. We've seen Jen at the top of this spiral so many times we ought to buy her a crash helmet. It's not that she's short of a date. That never happens. What she's permanently short of, however, is a boyfriend. At least, one that sticks around for longer than three or four months (and that's if she's lucky).

I've never been able to work out the issue. She has more admirers than Carrie Bradshaw has shoes. Plus, you couldn't accuse her of not being enthusiastic: she throws herself into each new relationship from day one. The fact that none of them appreciates her efforts is a mystery.

'Lee's different,' she insists, as her mobile beeps and she plunges into her clutch bag.

We start with French martinis in Blue at the Albert Dock, then move on to margaritas in Alma de Cuba. We then go to the Living Room, where Ellie keeps daquiris flowing in a selection of flavours more varied than you'd find in a pack of Wine Gums. Unsurprisingly, it becomes a bit of a blur after that.

We end up in Mojo's, which I usually adore; it's a place with an electric atmosphere and dance-like-no-one's-watching music. But the more I try to enjoy myself, the harder it is. When I look at my watch at one thirty, I'm suddenly desperate not to be here.

I take a sip of my umpteenth cocktail in an attempt to numb my pain, but it's sickly and sweet and there's now so much alcohol running through me that my brain feels pickled. Weirdly, though, I hardly feel drunk any more. I hardly feel anything.

I gaze into the middle distance as Ellie perches on the bar doing her well-rehearsed *Dirty Dancing* routine with a guy who looks like Ron Weasley. Jen, who's been fighting men off all night, has her mobile out again and is looking worried.

'What's up?' I ask.

She frowns. 'I'm very concerned about Lee.'

'Why?'

'He hasn't texted.'

'But isn't he the one you were texting in the taxi?'

'That was ages ago,' she protests. 'I've heard nothing for an hour and a half.' I'm about to laugh but realize she's being serious.

I scrunch up my nose. 'He's probably in bed.'

'He's out tonight,' she tells me anxiously. 'Do you think there could be someone else?'

At that, her phone beeps and she breathlessly reads a new message, her face breaking into a wide smile. 'Crisis over,' she declares. 'Hey, are you okay?' I open my mouth but don't know how to answer. 'You're not, are you?' she replies for me. 'Come on, we need to get out of here. Wait while I drag Dita Von Teese away.'

Jen grabs Ellie by the arm and directs her through the crowd while her dancing partner pouts disappointedly. The air is thick with sweat and pheromones as we reach the door.

Ellie's slurring her words slightly, but – despite the dodgy dancing – generally looks less drunk than me. We march across the city centre until we end up in the subdued bar of The Racquet Club, a boutique hotel and one of the best-kept secrets in the city. Jen and I order a coffee while Ellie has a glass of wine.

'Awww,' she says, sticking out her bottom lip. 'We didn't manage to cheer you up. I consider myself a failure.'

'Oh I'm sorry,' I frown. 'You have cheered me up. Well, sort of. I was un-cheer-up-able.'

She rolls her eyes. 'You know what I hate about your boyfriend's decision?'

'Ex-boyfriend,' I correct her. 'What?'

'Well, this,' she says, gesticulating in my general direction. 'The fact that it's made you so . . . not yourself.'

'You mean I'm miserable and crap company,' I sigh.

'Don't be ridiculous,' says Jen, putting her arm around me. 'You wouldn't be normal if you didn't react like this.'

'Besides, you're never crap company, gorgeous. You know that,' insists Ellie, sipping her drink. 'It'll take some time before you get back on your feet, that's all. But you need to remember something.'

'What's that?'

'That you are a beautiful, clever and wonderful woman,' she says intently.

'Plus,' adds Jen, 'you functioned perfectly well before Jamie, and you will function perfectly well without him.'

'That sounds familiar,' I say, impressed.

'It's what Ellie tells me every time one of my men disappears,' Jen shrugs. 'She's on to something, believe me. And remember that at least you've got a six-year relationship under your belt. You've come close to being "the one". I've never been anyone's "the one". I've only ever been "the one they want to shag".'

Ellie laughs. 'Bloody men.'

Jen grins. I suspect she can laugh about this because her

relationship with the new Mr Muscles is on an upward curve. In two weeks it could be different.

'I know I never buy it at the time, but it is right.' She squeezes my shoulder. 'And while my flings don't compare to what you and Jamie had, I know you'll come out of this absolutely fine. Stronger than ever, in fact.'

'Maybe,' I reply flatly. 'It just doesn't feel like it. Plus, I can't help thinking that there's still hope.'

Ellie looks sceptical. 'Hmm.'

'I want him back,' I confess.

'Hmm,' she repeats.

'And . . . I think part of him wants to come back.'

'Hmm.'

'I just . . . don't know how to reach out to the bit of him that wants to come back – and tell the other part to sod right off.'

Ellie looks strange.

'Why do you suddenly look less than convinced? A few days ago you were saying he'd be back like a shot.' I get a horrible feeling that what Ellie said on the night he left wasn't a sentiment that's lasted. As if that was her spur-of-the-moment reaction, driven partly by an instinct to make me feel better, and after several days of sober thought she's far less sure.

She shakes her head. 'No, you're right. And I'm not unconvinced,' she replies, completely unconvincingly.

'Well, I'm certainly not,' adds Jen. 'Ellie, you and I have always said that we'd never seen a couple with so much magic. I think there's hope, no doubt about it.'

Just hearing those words sends elation running through my veins. Ellie leans forward and puts both elbows on the table. 'Tell me again his exact words the last time you spoke.'

I recount the story in fine detail and Ellie says nothing until I've finished.

'You know, in some ways it goes against all my instincts to say this,' she begins. 'I've always said that if a man wants to leave, you should let him go quietly. But maybe Jamie's different.'

'Go on,' I urge.

'Maybe some relationships are worth fighting for. Maybe yours and Jamie's is. He's an idiot for letting you go. I also happen to think he'll regret it when he gets to the other side of the world and has nobody but a load of insects biting his ankles to keep him company. You know, I'm convincing myself, the more I think about it . . .'

'Convincing yourself of what?' I reply breathlessly.

She pauses. 'Do you really want Jamie back, Sam?'

I look into her eyes and have no hesitation. 'You know I do.'

She takes a deep breath. 'Then come over tomorrow morning. Not too early, obviously. It's time we started getting practical about this.'

Chapter 10

I arrive at Ellie's place the following day feeling as though the principal ingredient in last night's cocktails was Jeyes Fluid. Ellie, on the other hand, doesn't look remotely hungover.

'Bright-eyed and bushy-tailed?' she grins, looking me up and down.

'You are a freak of nature,' I grunt. Her skin is only slightly duller than usual and there isn't the hint of a dark circle under her eyes.

Unlike mine. Mine have puffed up in the manner of a bullfrog undergoing a vigorous colonic irrigation.

'Years of practice,' she laughs. 'Besides, my amazing other half got up with Sophie so I could have a lie-in.'

'He's not all bad, is he?' I tease, grinning at Alistair as I head to the kitchen.

'I think you'll find I'm a model partner and father,' he replies, scooping up Sophie and carrying her over so she can plant an enthusiastic, if distinctly sloppy, kiss on my lips.

Ellie prepares two strong coffees before we head to the living room, while Alistair buttons Sophie into her coat to take her to the park.

'About what we discussed last night . . .' says Ellie, plunging onto the sofa opposite me.

I immediately suspect what's coming. 'Look,' I sigh, 'I know you're going to tell me to forget about it . . . to forget about him. But I can't. I want him back and I'll always want him back.'

She frowns. 'What makes you think I'd say that?'

I pause, slightly surprised. 'You say it to Jen every time she's been ditched.'

She rolls her eyes. 'Jen and her alpha males hardly compare with you and Jamie. Plus, there's a crucial difference. Like you, like Jen, I also think, on balance, that there's hope.'

Her words set my heart racing. 'Really? Then what do you think I should do?' I ask urgently. 'I should phone him again, shouldn't I? And it's been a whole day since I emailed him. If only I could sit down and reason with him, get across how much I want him and need him and—'

'Sam, stop!' she snaps, and I nearly drop my coffee.

She takes a deep breath then says softly, 'You're going to do none of those things.'

I look at her blankly.

'You're going to win him back,' she continues. 'At least, you're going to give it your best shot. But if you're going to do that, you'll also have to get a lot smarter about it.'

Ellie and I met when we studied English Literature at Manchester University and it was there that I became familiar with her counselling skills. Maybe it was the influence of her mum, who'd volunteered with the Samaritans for years. Whatever it was, she became the unofficial agony aunt of our halls of residence, and this was something that gave her and Alistair a lot to talk about when they met years later, because he basically did for a living what she considered a hobby. What gave Ellie's brand of sympathy the edge, however, was the fact that it had something nobody else's had: practicality. She wasn't a mere shoulder on which to cry; she dissected issues methodically and gave advice that was totally constructive.

'The most important thing you need to do, Sam, is also going to be very hard,' she tells me. 'You've got to stop being miserable.'

I screw up my nose. 'I've been dumped. Aren't I meant to be miserable?'

'Let me rephrase that,' she concedes. 'You need to pretend to stop being miserable. Bawl your eyes out as much as you want in front of Jen and me, gorgeous – but nobody else. And especially not Jamie.'

'But it wasn't just me crying this week; Jamie was in a complete state,' I argue. 'Besides, is it really going to make him feel better if I sit there like an ice maiden, pretending I'm not fazed by anything?'

She leans forward on her sofa. 'Sam, Jamie fell in love with you because you were the happy, go-getting, easy-going girl you are. You need to remind him who that girl is. That being with you is fun, not a ride on an emotional roller coaster, even if that roller coaster is one he put you on.'

'But if you'd seen what he was like—'

'Sam,' she interrupts, 'I don't care if he's an emotional wreck; you can't be anything other than composed. As hard as it may be . . . don't cry. I'm not saying this to try to make you repressed. I'm saying this to empower you.'

My bottom lip starts wobbling. 'I don't feel empowered. And I don't see how going round grinning like a lunatic will change anything.'

She smiles. 'Trust me. Besides, it could be a self-fulfilling prophecy.'

'That I become a lunatic?'

'I'm talking about acting happy. But we're getting ahead of ourselves. First, let's concentrate on making him think you're doing just great without him. On showing him the amazing, happy girl he's missing out on. He mustn't see that he's made you crumble because, believe me, Sam, there's nothing less attractive than a needy woman.'

'You think I've looked needy?' But I don't need her to answer. 'God, I have, haven't I? Those emails . . . the begging . . . urgh!'

'Forget what's gone before,' she says diplomatically. 'Concentrate on the future. And for that, you need to put a lid on the emotional stuff.'

By the end of the afternoon, and copious cups of coffee later, Ellie and I have composed a plan. A brilliant, multi-layered and totally practical one; one that's utterly focused on winning Jamie back.

The first step involves pulling myself together, not just emotionally, but physically. I've already lost weight in the few days he's been gone and it's time to make the most of it.

The second step involves manufacturing an excuse to see him again as soon as possible, an occasion I hope will be the first of many. Except that now I'm not going to cry, and I'm not going to beg him to come back. I'm going to make him want me for entirely different reasons. My modus operandi is going to change drastically – and if what I've got planned works, he's not going to know what's hit him.

The third step involves a tactic that's worked in matters of the heart ever since the time of Henry VIII and his court. I'm going to influence those around him in the hope that they influence him. If Ellie has her way, everyone from his best friend to his sister is going to be telling him to get back with me.

And the fourth step . . . well, the fourth step I'm putting on hold. Not because I don't think it could work – and Ellie is determined that it would – but because the thought of it sends a shiver down my spine. Going out with another man to make Jamie jealous is the last resort to end all last resorts. A step too far, and one I seriously hope I'll never have to take.

Simply knowing that I'm actively taking measures to solve this problem makes me feel less upset. Not least because I genuinely think this could work.

'Exactly how much coffee have you two drunk this afternoon?' asks Alistair, picking up our cups from the table.

'We've been hard at work,' says Ellie.

'What are you up to?'

Ellie flashes me a glance. Then, to my acute embarrassment, she starts to fill him in. She insists that he is qualified to contribute to this exercise on two levels. One: he's a psychotherapist and understands the workings of the human mind better than most. And two: he's a man.

He says nothing while she talks, simply looks at me with something between concern and pity.

'So . . . what do you think about the plan, Alistair? Would Ellie's advice get her a job in your clinic?' I smile nervously.

He frowns. 'There's no doubt that it could help. It could be decisive. It could remind Jamie of what he's missing. It could restore the status quo, exactly as you want, Sam.'

'I can sense a but here.'

He smiles uneasily. 'Look, I hope it works. In fact, I think it might. But sometimes you can do everything right and life still doesn't go your way. That's the problem with people. They can be very unpredictable.'

Chapter 11

For the first time since Jamie left, I no longer feel as though there's a vacuum in the house. I have no idea why, but the belongings he left behind don't seem as redundant as before. Following my afternoon with Ellie, I have a feeling that maybe the small paraphernalia of his life may just stay after all.

I pad into the bathroom and open the cabinet, then pick up Jamie's only aftershave – a bottle of Armani I bought him last year – and hold it to my nose. It's not quite the scent of him; it's too sharp, without the warm undercurrents of his skin. But it still provokes a gush of thoughts, fantasies, memories.

Memories such as our holiday to Cuba, when he kissed my neck in the swimming pool as I wrapped my legs round him and forgot the rest of the world existed. Our picnic in the shadow of Speke Hall, when we got hopelessly tipsy and rolled round under an oak tree until the sun set. Or that Christmas Eve when we made blissful love under the tree . . . until the fairy lights caught my ankle and short-circuited the ground floor.

I put the aftershave back in the cabinet and the door wobbles precariously. Jamie and I have always been awful at DIY; it was one of the main things we had in common. Hence the fact that the television is strategically positioned to disguise a dodgy piece of wood flooring and the way that one end of the curtain rail is held up by Blu-Tack.

For my part, the issue is down to the chronic time poverty that's a necessary result of my twelve-hour working days. And, all right I admit it, general incompetence. Which I hate confessing. I consider myself intelligent and capable when it comes to most other elements of my life, so why I should be so catastrophically feckless with a Black & Decker is anyone's guess.

Jamie's reasons are different. He's always argued simply that life's too short to worry about fixing broken shelves. And while I'd certainly never assume that, as a man, this domain was necessarily his, I can't help thinking feminism left us with a raw deal on this issue: it meant he could put up his feet and watch the house crumble with a clear conscience.

I chuckle to myself as I close the cabinet door – and get the shock of my life. The face that stares back at me is a scrap heap of womanhood. My hair is dragged back in a greasy pony tail, my eyebrows are unplucked, my skin unexfoliated and my lips unmoisturized. My nails look as though they've been filed by something used in a prison break.

No wonder nobody tried to pull me last night. And I expected Jamie to stay with this!

I cast my mind back to Ellie's words: about behaving as though life goes on. Looking happy . . . carefree . . . giving the impression

I'm having the time of my life. And, above all, reminding him of what he's missing. On current evidence, all he's missing is a woman whose split ends haven't been tended to in months and legs that could've been knitted from mohair.

Well, not any more. There is a gorgeous siren under this grooming catastrophe and I'm determined to unleash her.

I set about tackling the worst offences. I wax my legs, appalled by the resulting strips, which I could flog to a toupee manufacturer. I give myself a pedicure, a manicure, then apply a face mask I bought a year ago but never got round to using.

I negotiate the stairs and hallway in toe separators until I reach the living room, where I examine my iPod, scrolling through the 'recently played' list disapprovingly.

'Everybody Hurts' by REM. 'Goodbye My Lover' by James Blunt. 'Teardrop' by Massive Attack. 'In My Life' by the Beatles.

No wonder I've been depressed. If anyone came up with a compilation called 'Now That's What I Call Music to Slit Your Wrists To!', this lot would be on it. I head to my study, log on to my laptop and set about deleting them one by one. It's not easy – I love some of these songs – but it's for the best.

However, as my iPod is purged of misery tracks, I realize that I'm barely scratching the surface of my cultural influences. Between *The Bridges of Madison County* and *Ghost* and *Truly Madly Deeply*, there are so many weepies in my DVD collection that I'm surprised the emotional strain didn't lead to me being committed years ago. There are a lot of romcoms too, of course;

except now isn't the time for those either. I'm not ready yet to spend an evening watching other people falling in love.

I place anything remotely controversial in a box and hide it under the stairs, telling myself it can re-emerge when I'm good and ready. Which a part of me hopes is soon, because the only DVD left is *Belly Dance Abs Blast* (a Christmas present from Aunt Jill), whose wrapper remains as intact as the rolls on my stomach.

Next, I wander upstairs and open my wardrobe doors, examining its contents and assessing their ability to make me look desirable. Desirable to Jamie, that is, which is a specific ask.

If you asked most men to define a sexy outfit they'd say high heels and short skirts – something significantly more frou-frou than the average woman would opt for. Not Jamie. Jamie likes combat shorts, slouchy jeans and retro T-shirts. He likes outfits so low-key that, without careful handling, they can look as though they've been fished out of a skip.

I'll admit that when we first met, despite being entirely confident in my tastes, I enjoyed dressing in a way he found attractive; and, at least for a while, my wardrobe took on some distinctly grungy overtones.

It didn't last, of course. When you're a girl who loves high heels, minidresses and slinky black jeans, eventually not even a man will keep you out of them. Still, while ditching them now would be a travesty, needs must in the short term.

So I set about organizing my wardrobe. My favourite clothes go on one side; on the other go the clothes devoted to attracting Jamie.

And while the vintage hoodies and vest tops have previously been held in little esteem, now I love them more than anything else in here, simply because these are the clothes that are going to win Jamie back.

Look, you might think this is shallow, or that I'm not being true to myself. But there's a loftier cause at stake – temporarily, at least – than my addiction to three-inch gladiator sandals.

Of course, there's another big difference between the me of today and the me of six years ago: about a stone. I don't know how or why that weight crept up on me, but it did. The legs that used to be my best asset are now distinctly blancmange-like around the top and my belly is about as hard as the questions on *Family Fortunes*.

I head to the fridge and survey its contents. The diet had a kick-start the day Jamie left. But while I've inadvertently been given a helping hand by my sheer misery, my mission to become Ms Irresistible is going to start in earnest right now.

I might be thinner but, given that until a week ago I had more orange peel on my legs than a Christmas potpourri, I've still got a way to go.

So I throw the Ben & Jerry's ice cream in the bin, followed by the Camembert, the squirty cream, the bacon, the chocolate bites and the sausages that individually contain enough fat to see a herd of camels across the Gobi desert.

Then I head back to my laptop and call up the last email I sent to Jamie.

It's the longest yet: over six thousand words.

The one I compose now is barely more than sixty . . . and that's the way it will be from now on. Succinct, easy-going, polite. To the untrained eye, you'd never guess it was an email between two people who'd just experienced a devastating break-up.

Hi Jamie,
Hope you're okay. I'm feeling an awful lot better – think I was in shock before. I wondered if you'd be able to pop over on Tuesday night, so I can sort out some practical matters – bills and stuff. It won't take more than five minutes. And could you make it before 7.30 because I'm going out straight afterwards?
Sam x

He sends his email from his phone seconds later.

No problem. About 6.30 then? Who are you out with? xx

I study the two questions and compose my response.

6.30's fine. See you then. x

As I'm certain Ellie would counsel, sometimes it's better to leave them wondering.

Chapter 12

Despite the intensity of my feelings for Jamie soon after we'd met, my bliss never felt anything but precarious. As he joined Jen, Ellie and me on the trip, stopping in Hong Kong and Kuala Lumpur, I was still aware that our respective destinies were both sealed – and separate. Mine was to return home and win the job of which I'd dreamed for years. His was to continue his nomadic existence on the other side of the world.

But with three weeks until the end of the trip, Jamie did something that stunned me: he booked a flight home to Liverpool. It was only for a couple of weeks, and to catch up with his family, whom he hadn't seen for a year. But I couldn't help thinking of the one thing I daren't hope for.

I was experiencing two urgent, aching desires that were violently opposed.

On one hand, there was my imminent interview for a junior events executive position at a big marketing agency in Manchester.

That job was so close I could almost feel the fabric of my

slick new work suit, the one I'd splash out on with my first pay cheque. I could almost hear Donna Summer singing 'She Works Hard for the Money' as I strode along King Street to the office. I could taste the first sip I'd have from the water cooler and feel the chill of air-conditioning against my cheeks. I was Melanie Griffith in *Working Girl*. I was SJP in *SATC*. I was Ally McBeal and a dozen other glamorous overachievers entering a world of plush offices, takeaway cappuccinos and white wine after hours.

What made it even more exciting was that the environment I was entering wasn't any old office job: I was going to work in events. Which meant parties, champagne bars, travel. (What I didn't know then was that the first few years, before I got a more senior job at BJD Productions, would involve everything from picking chewing gum off floors to manning cloakrooms – but that still wouldn't have changed my mind.)

Yet, on the other hand, fixated as I was about fulfilling my ambition, there was also the tornado that had entered my life in the form of Jamie. A man who made me feel like nobody else did. A man with whom I felt a bond, an intense passion, a raw need that ran so deep it was as if I'd known and loved him all my life.

It was at the homecoming barbeque that Jen's parents threw for her that everything changed. The air was filled with the scent of jasmine as a hot sun sparkled on our shoulders and a hog roast sizzled on the lawn to the sound of clinking glasses.

Jen had a new boyfriend. I can't remember who, but he was undoubtedly gorgeous, undoubtedly had muscles and undoubtedly was 'the one'. Ellie, on the other hand, was resolutely single; this was before she and Alistair had even met, let alone had Sophie.

'You and Jamie really are smitten, aren't you?' she marvelled as we stood outside the bathroom, in advance of the wee/gossip combo no trip to the Ladies went without. She was wearing Capri pants with polka dots, and looked like one of those Pink Ladies in *Grease*.

'He's amazing,' I gushed tipsily. 'Beyond amazing.'

She rolled her eyes. 'I'll take that as a yes.'

A voice piped up from behind us. 'If it means anything, I know the feeling's mutual.'

I'd heard a lot about Dorrie, but that day was the first time we'd met. She represented a link between Jen and Jamie – having attended ballet classes with the former when they were twelve and been friends with the latter since they'd lived next door as two-year-olds.

I'd seen a picture of them in a paddling pool; she'd been a skinny and not overly cute child, a description that didn't still apply. As an adult Dorrie was – is – tall, Amazonian almost, with clear olive skin and ludicrously long legs.

'You know,' she smiled broadly, 'I've known Jamie a long time and I've never seen him like this. I don't know what you've done, but he's a gonner!'

As darkness fell on a warm evening and the sound of laughter was replaced by an impromptu disco, Jamie and I sat on the grass in a quiet corner of the garden, spectators to a party that would be talked about for months. I can remember the lead-up to the conversation that would come to change my life . . . it was about fried eggs.

Three nights earlier we'd spent our first night together since we'd returned to the UK; Luke had been away and he'd let us use his spare room. It was quietly spectacular: we stayed up all night, talking in between slow luxurious kisses . . . and other things.

We slept in until twelve thirty, when I woke lazily to make breakfast. I'd hoped my culinary efforts might produce something resembling those New York breakfasts, with sumptuous French toast and orange juice so fresh the pips get stuck in your teeth.

Sadly, I was never a master of the fry-up. So while my tomatoes, mushrooms and burnished toast were passable, my fried eggs looked as though they'd been involved in a drive-by shooting. I was about to bring the plate up to Jamie when he appeared at the door, laughing at my efforts. Then he threw his arms around me.

'So you weren't impressed with my eggs this morning,' I giggled eight hours later.

He grinned. 'I was totally impressed with your eggs. No woman has ever cared enough about me before to go through an entire carton of eggs to try to get a single one right.'

I shook my head and slapped my hand on my forehead. He peeled it away and kissed me on the lips.

'You know what those eggs made me realize?' he added.

'That I'd never get a job as a chef?'

'Precisely,' he smiled, then he looked at me intensely. 'Not only that, though, Sam. They made me realize that I'm in love with you. And that there's no way in the world I can leave you.'

Chapter 13

It's funny how different attitudes can be to the old-fashioned concept of charidee. At one end of the spectrum, you've got the Bob Geldofs and Annie Lennoxes of this world, those who put their heart and soul into making a difference. At the other end are the natural-born misery guts, who'd prefer to saw off their foot with a cheese knife than give their last fifty pence to a *Big Issue* seller.

And somewhere in the middle you've got me. Although I hope I'm closer to the former than the latter . . . at least I try. Sadly, while I've got the conscience, what I haven't got is the time, connections or money. So instead of rolling up my sleeves and really getting stuck in, I make the small sacrifices at my disposal. Which in reality means one pair of shoes fewer every couple of months . . . and more monthly standing orders than I could possibly reveal without giving the impression I'm an unmitigated sucker.

It's the source of some amusement in certain quarters.

'What's this I've heard about you signing up to sponsor

another kid in Africa?' cackles Lisa, Jamie's sister, before I've even entered the house. I've popped in to see her on my way home from work, because if anyone knows the way to Jamie's heart it's her.

'Oh that was a while ago,' I mumble. 'And it's Eastern Europe.'

'Foo-eee! You're like Angelina Jolie, you are. You can't save the world personally, you know! Aw, look – good on you. You've got no kids of your own, after all. I remember those days well,' she mutters, surveying the devastation before her.

I consider myself relatively easy-going when it comes to house-work. I've never been one of those women whose kitchen cupboards resemble the filing system of the British Library and whose toilet pan needs to gleam like Simon Cowell's dental veneers. But even I feel a twitch of unease on entering Lisa and her husband Dave's living room.

Neither has ever been particularly house-proud, but even if they had, the number of children they've produced in the last ten years would have decisively put paid to any prospect of an *OK!* spread. The lounge looks as though a category five hurricane has swept through it. That said, the couple's four boys and one girl have the capacity to create more havoc than most extreme weather conditions – despite being as cute as they are.

'TWO SUGARS, ISN'T IT?' she shouts from the kitchen as a three-foot plastic Tigger is torpedoed across the living room and ricochets off the patio window.

'NONE THANKS, LISA,' I yell, but I'm drowned out by

four-year-old Suzuki employing enthusiastic karate moves against her little brother, Elvis.

'Right – OUT!' hollers Lisa as she appears at the doorway with two teas. 'In the garden. Auntie Sam and I have things to discuss. And she'd prefer to do it without two demonic kids trampolining on her.'

The children leave in a fireball of martial-arts moves, intercepted en route by their mother, who smothers each in so many kisses you'd think she hadn't seen them for a week.

At thirty-three, Lisa's five years older than Jamie, but you'd never guess they were siblings. It isn't only their physical differences that are marked (though she has a three-stone advantage on him). It's also their personalities. She's as naturally personable as Jamie and makes friends as easily – but, unlike him, her tastes are about as bohemian as a Marks & Spencer ready meal. Today's outfit sums it up: jeans with a Sunday-supplement waistband and a T-shirt in an eye-watering shade of orange that precisely matches the awning on their caravan.

Not that it matters. Particularly because, in her husband's eyes, Lisa is the most irresistible woman on earth.

'Is Dave back at work after his throat infection?' I ask.

'Oh Dave's grand. More than grand, actually,' she winks. 'I've just had my latest *special manual* delivered.' The words *special manual* are accompanied by exaggerated air quotes, which alone are enough to make me feel slightly queasy: I know what's coming next.

She checks the kids are out of sight before grabbing her

handbag and producing a small hardback book which she thrusts into my hands. It's called *Ready, Steady, F***! Aphrodisiac recipes guaranteed to spice up your sex life.*

I attempt to keep my eyeballs in their sockets as I flick through the pages; they boast a selection of exotic recipes, positioned next to a selection of exotic . . . well, positions.

'Baked oysters and spinach . . . hot buttered lobster . . . chocolate cognac truffles. Sounds like a lot of washing-up for a roll in the hay with your husband, Lisa,' I smile awkwardly.

'Why do you think I bought a dishwasher?' she grins. 'But enough about me and my libido. Let's talk about my brother and what he's playing at.'

I take a deep breath. 'He must have told you what's happened.'

She rolls her eyes. 'I've heard about him wanting to discover himself. I've heard about him flying to the back of beyond to build mud huts and eat beetles for his tea. I've heard about him still being in love with you, apparently.' My heart rises as she says this, but she doesn't pause for breath. 'And in all bloody honesty . . . I've never heard such bollocks.'

I open my mouth to speak.

'Sam . . . you know I love Jamie and would do anything for him. Nevertheless, he's being a grade-one arse. If they gave prizes for being a tosser, he'd have a cupboard full. He is King Knobhead in my eyes. And I've told him as much.'

I realize I'm a tad shell-shocked by this diatribe. 'You think he's doing the wrong thing, then?'

'Wrong thing?' she blusters, throwing up her hands. 'Look. We know that Jamie was cut from a different cloth from you and me. He's always been a bit different. We knew that when he was nine and he announced to Mum – on mince and chips night, no less – that he was becoming a vegan and he wanted her to make his Angel Delight out of soya milk. And, look, it's great that he's different. In fact, it's lovely. It makes Jamie who he is.'

I frown, taking this in. 'You're almost convincing me he's doing the right thing, Lisa.'

'I hadn't finished,' she says decisively. 'What's as important is that Jamie honestly and truly believes that he's met the love of his life: you. And I believe that too. The whole family does.'

I feel a swell of gratitude.

'I just can't help thinking, Sam, that while he's entitled to never settle down, that won't make him happy. He's setting himself up for a life with no kids, no proper family, no ties. And I know Jamie. Ultimately, that's not going to make him satisfied. He loves kids too much.'

'But he doesn't want kids. He's always said that,' I point out.

'He was playing with our Suzuki yesterday and didn't even mind when she wired up his nipples to the Operation tweezers. The boy's a natural,' she says, thumping her hand on the coffee table. 'He just doesn't realize it.'

I suppress a smile.

'At the end of the day, this big adventure isn't going to make Jamie happier or more content,' she adds. 'Only you are, Sam. If only the idiot would recognize it.'

I close my eyes and put my head in my hands. 'So what you're saying is that I need to let him go to South America, do what he needs to do, and then realize he misses me?'

'You can't wait around for ever,' she says, wide-eyed. 'We need to stop him going.'

'You think that's possible?'

'I'll do my best, Sam,' she replies firmly. 'That's all I can promise. I'll do my absolute best.'

Chapter 14

'When you said, "Let's grab a late lunch", I thought you meant a couple of toasties at Costa Coffee,' I tell Ellie as she orders a large glass of wine in San Carlo. The restaurant is bustling with a suited-and-booted crowd talking costs, opportunities and a host of other corporate concerns. In other words, not what Ellie and I are about to discuss.

'Make the most of it,' she replies, flicking her napkin on her lap. 'When your friend wants to buy you lunch, don't complain.'

'How come you're able to do lunch anyway? You haven't broken up for the holidays yet, have you?' I ask.

'No, but I've spent the morning at another school for a moderating meeting. I was meant to be there all day, but it finished early.'

'Right. I haven't got long though, I warn you. I've got a million things to do when I get back to the office, especially as I need to leave early.'

She pours me some water. 'How are you feeling about seeing Jamie tonight?'

I hesitate. 'Fine.' The reality is that as much as I'm desperate to see him, I'm also terrified. Which is ludicrous. This is a man in whose presence I've been almost every day for the last six years. Feeling nervous around him is wrong. 'I just want to play this right,' I add.

She pops an olive into her mouth. 'Well, remember: act cool. You might not be feeling cool, but act it.'

I nod and take a sip of water to alleviate my suddenly dry mouth.

'And don't – no matter how tempted you are – start discussing your relationship. Even if he brings it up, change the subject. We don't want you saying anything that could be interpreted as putting pressure on him. He's got to decide things for himself. And we definitely don't want you crying. So keep things . . . light.'

'Light. I can do that,' I say earnestly.

'Don't look so worried, Sam. Remember, you're not there to analyze. You're there to seduce.'

My eyes widen. 'You never mentioned that before.'

'I don't mean sex,' she says dismissively. 'At least not tonight. But, absolutely you're seducing him. You're making him want you. The more desperately the better.'

I nod.

'Also—'

I groan and she smirks. 'I was simply going to say . . . look amazing. Not that I've any doubt you will. You've lost weight, Sam. Don't lose any more, will you?'

'It's my *Belly Dance Abs Blast*,' I tell her.

'What?' she frowns.

'It's the only DVD I've got left. I've only been doing it for a couple of days and it's phenomenal.'

'Never heard of it.'

'It's presented by an instructor called Princess Karioca. The thick Glaswegian accent is hard to follow at times, but she's my new best friend . . . despite the fact that my stomach muscles feel as though they've been attacked with a meat tenderizer.'

'But you hate dancing,' she points out.

I can't argue with that. Dance floors are, to me, dens of evil inhabited by those whose coordination needs only to match that of a penguin in the throes of a psychedelic trip to show me up. But it seems there's an exception. 'Not belly dancing,' I shrug.

She raises an eyebrow, dipping her bread in some olive oil. 'Is that a spray tan?'

I gasp. 'Can you tell?'

Knowing I was seeing Jamie today, I slipped this into my schedule yesterday after work, requesting that the coating applied was in the most subtle shade possible. Unfortunately, given that my 'tanning technician' was herself the colour of a teak sideboard, it's little wonder she ignored me, instead spraying so enthusiastically that she should really be moved on to the production line of a Xsara Picasso.

'I can tell – but he won't be able to. Men have hardly got a trained eye for these things. So what are you wearing?'

'Combats, Superdry shirt – the first thing I threw on,' I wink.

'Ha! All brand new?'

'Obviously,' I grin. 'Plus, a little help in the bra department.'

'Chicken fillets?'

'Even better. A little something I saw reviewed in one of the Sunday papers.' A waiter appears at our side with our pasta dishes, so I never get the chance to tell her.

'Another large glass of wine, please,' she instructs him. 'Oh come on, have one with me. I hate drinking alone.'

'That's never stopped you,' I point out. 'And no, thanks. Honestly, I've got too much on.'

'Fine,' she pouts. 'But I'm having another.' As the waiter disappears, she raises her glass, and the drop that's left in it, to ping it against my water.

'Here's to winning him back, sister,' she grins. 'You can do it. And if you can't . . . then he's not worth having.'

When I get home, I set to work on my appearance. I spend twenty-five minutes blow-drying my hair in a style that has the appearance of having taken twenty-five seconds. I apply a mountain of make-up designed to look as if I'm wearing none. And I smear on a volumizing lip gloss bought this afternoon on the basis that, although I've never really thought my lips needed volumizing, it can't do any harm.

But what I'm most excited about is the 'little something' I never got to tell Ellie about properly: my Miracle Cleavage Air Pump Bra.

This state-of-the-art boob-enhancing contraption makes my

Wonderbra look terribly last century. It works on the same principle as an inflatable camp bed, but on a smaller scale and without any need for a foot pump.

To look at, it's simply an attractive, lacy, black bra; but it has an important twist. I put it on and follow the instructions.

'With your thumb and forefinger, simply inflate your Miracle Cleavage Air Pump Bra to the desired level of volume.'

I give it a squeeze and examine the results in the mirror. Not bad . . . but could do better. I try the other one and decide that's almost it . . . but not quite.

I take a deep breath and, with my hands in both cups, give a series of sharp, convincing bursts. Then a few more. And a few more for good measure.

I stand back and look at the results, which are . . . bloody magnificent, if I say so myself.

I've always fancied having bigger boobs. It's not that I'm devastatingly flat-chested, but something vaguely in proportion to my bum would be nice. And much as I warm to men who say they prefer women who are 'natural' – with no implants, no pads or indeed anything except the real deal – I can't help thinking that what they really mean is they prefer women who are natural Kelly Brook lookalikes.

Sadly, nature did not furnish me with Kelly Brook curves; it saved those for Kelly Brook.

Next, I remove my new Figleaves underwear from its box and unfold it. I marvel at its lacy underwiring, and the fine balance it strikes between good taste and outright sluttiness. But I don't put it on. Oh no. Tonight, these particular undies have a different function.

I take my two bouquets of flowers – bought this afternoon – and merge them into an impressive arrangement on the living-room table.

I plump up cushions, spray perfume around the room, and set the iPod to the playlist I compiled last night, the contents of which are from a website dedicated to songs 'to get jiggy to'. Not that I want to get jiggy tonight. I simply know it won't do any harm to get Jamie thinking about it – because my aim tonight is for jigginess to be uppermost in his mind as he leaves.

Jamie is almost always late. It's a side effect of his resolutely laid-back personality. Yet, tonight, at 6.20 p.m., the doorbell rings. I leap up from the sofa with a racing heart and – channelling Sigourney Weaver in that *Ghostbusters* scene when she's transformed into a sex-mad demon – I open the door slowly, deliberately, seductively.

My hand is on my hip. My shirt is open enough to display my cavernous new cleavage. My lips are so goddamn volumized they're almost visible from space.

'Windows, love! 'Fraid you owe us for two weeks . . .'

Jimmy, my fifty-five-year-old window cleaner, trails off as he takes in my lap-dancer décolletage and porn-star pout.

He looks as though he's experienced a mild cardiac arrest. And this from a man who Sylvia, my neighbour, once told me popped up to squeegee her bathroom window at the exact moment she was wiping her bum.

'Ooh, er, sorry,' I say, scuttling into the house to find my purse. I've paid Jimmy and am about to head back in, when I hear footsteps coming up the path.

It's Jamie. Looking almost as nervous as I feel.

Chapter 15

The thing about being a seductress is that all you have to do is get into the mood. And I'm determined to do so. Not in the mood for sex – as Ellie said, that's out of bounds tonight. I'm in the mood for seducing. Despite the setback with Jimmy.

Admittedly, I'm not wearing the traditional get-up for such an exercise. I'm not perched on a chaise longue in a negligee and marabou heels. But I'm also confident that this is the sort of gear Jamie finds irresistible, unlikely as it seems. Not that his tastes are one hundred per cent left field – hence my efforts with the underwear.

I have high hopes for the combined effect. If I let myself, my state of agitation would be all-consuming – but I'm not going to let myself. I'm going to pretend my palms aren't sweating and my heart isn't thrashing, and in sharp contrast to reality, appear as serene and magnetic as possible.

It becomes apparent the second Jamie walks in that my plan is off to a flying start. He can't take his eyes off me – or, more specifically, my boobs.

In fact, he moves towards the living room barely able to focus on anything else, and as the opening bars of Kings of Leon's 'Sex on Fire' kick off he stumbles across the threshold. I pretend not to notice; instead I smile sweetly, flicking back my hair flightily and giving my eyelashes a flutter.

'How are you, Jamie?' I ask breathily.

He coughs and drags his eyes from my chest, running his hand through his hair. 'Hmm . . . me? Oh fine. Yep . . . fine. And you?'

'Fine too,' I say smoothly as I perch on a sofa arm. 'I was in shock the other day. I totally understand where you're coming from now. And I'm fine about it. Really. Hey, take a seat.'

He hesitates before sitting on the sofa opposite. I don't know why but I suddenly feel the need to bend forward and start rearranging one of my shoes, showing off my cleavage to its full effect. After a couple of seconds I look up and smile cheekily. He glances away.

'Um, so . . . you're fine,' he says. 'About us splitting up?'

'Oh completely,' I reply in a manner designed to give the impression I'm reassuring him. 'This is how I see it: we had six fantastic years together. And you know I never wanted this. But it's happened and I'm dealing with it. It's not as if I'm never going to have any man interested in me again, is it?' I laugh lightly. 'It's not as if I'm never going to feel a man's arms around me. Or be kissed by anyone . . . or . . . well, you know.' I raise an eyebrow.

He looks like he's stopped breathing.

'The point is,' I continue softly, 'that life goes on. So, honestly, you don't need to worry about me.'

'Don't I?' he frowns.

'Course not. But we've done enough talking about us. It's time to move on from all that heavy stuff, don't you think?'

I suddenly notice Jamie is glaring at the radiator behind me.

'Oh!' I laugh, leaping up. 'How embarrassing. Can't believe I left those out to dry when I've got company.'

I head to the radiator and pick up the black lacy Figleaves bra – the one that has neither been washed nor is drying, but has been strategically placed to give the appearance of both.

I pick it up slowly and start folding it as I walk towards him. Actually, that's not strictly true: I am not so much folding as caressing the damn thing, before placing it on the table. Then I demonstratively pick up a teeny pair of knickers so sheer they almost qualify as invisible. I sit them on top and turn back to Jamie. He gulps. Twice.

'Drink?' I smile.

He snaps out of his daze. 'Um . . . I shouldn't. I know you've got to go out soon.'

'One won't do any harm,' I reply, gliding into the kitchen.

I turn the corner into the kitchen and have a surreptitious peek at my boobs. Somehow, they don't look as spectacular as when I last looked.

Checking the coast is clear, I shove my fingers in either side of the bra and give it five or six vigorous pumps. This has an instant and thoroughly impressive effect. Then I pour two large glasses of wine, take a character-building slurp and serenely head through for round two.

Jamie looks troubled.

'So, about the bills we need to sort out,' he says. 'Which ones are they? Obviously, I'm not going to leave you high and dry. I feel really bad about the house thing . . . Have you thought about whether you'll stay here or go?'

I gaze into his eyes and hand him his wine, deliberately brushing against his fingers.

I consider sitting on the chair opposite him, but instead make a split-second decision and slink onto the sofa next to him.

We're so close I can feel the heat from his body – and, let me tell you, there's a lot coming from him; it's like sitting too close to a four-bar fire. He looks deeply unsettled – in a good way. A very good way. He leans forward with his elbows on his knees, nursing his wine. I lean casually into the cushions and rest my arm lazily on the back of the sofa.

He turns and glances at me, then at my boobs, then at his wine, which he knocks back fast. There's a moment of silence as he fixes his fly, as if something untoward is happening in his gentleman's region, causing an unexpected tightening of his undergarments.

The iPod moves on to its next song. 'Ooh La La' by Goldfrapp. The closest you'll get to an orgasm in four and a half minutes. Jamie swallows again.

'Look,' he says, putting his glass on the coffee table. 'I know you didn't want to talk about our relationship, but perhaps we should.'

'What's there to say?' I ask innocently.

'Well,' he blusters, 'a lot, I would say.'

'Oh Jamie, forget it.'

He's torn between anger and lust.

'Sam, you might be able to instantly forget six years of the biggest relationship I've ever experienced, but I sure as hell can't.'

'Can't you?' I pout, gazing into his eyes.

'No, I can't!'

I reach out and grab his hand. 'Jamie . . . I hate to point this out, but you ended the relationship. And you seemed very sure that it was the right thing at the time.'

The reminder jolts him.

'Well, I . . . I wasn't sure. If I gave the impression I was sure, then I gave the wrong impression. I was confused . . . I am confused. I . . .'

'What are you saying, Jamie?'

The reply for which I'm desperate is that he's changed his mind. If we were in a film, that's what he'd say. That's what Richard Gere would've said if this was *Pretty Woman 2*. Or Billy Crystal if it was *When Harry Dumped Sally*.

'Jamie . . .?'

I consider asking him outright if he wants me back, but suppress the urge. Tactically, Ellie's right: I have to let him come to me.

'Sam – things weren't right near the end . . . you've got to have noticed that,' he says. 'And, for the record, I know I'm to blame for a lot of that. I know there were times when I let you down. I know there were times when I put my friends before you, myself before you. I did things that no girlfriend would appreciate. And I'm not proud of that.'

'Jamie, we don't need to talk about this,' I squirm, astonishing as it is to hear Jamie concede some of the issues that used to wind me up no end. I'm determined to keep the tone of this conversation light and seductive, not like a Relate session. I move closer to him as our eyes lock and the blood running through my veins heats up several degrees.

Suddenly, whatever's happening is as electrifying as the first time we kissed – if not more so. Jamie's expression is overcome with desire . . . and that's before we discuss the action in his trousers.

He moves forward slowly, tantalizingly, as if we know this shouldn't be happening, but can't stop it. I edge to him, exploding with longing. As his lips go to touch mine, I lean against the sofa and close my eyes, submitting to the moment. Only the moment holds more surprises than I'd thought.

'SSSSSSSSSS!'

Jamie pulls away and my eyes flutter open hysterically.

'What was that?' he frowns.

I blink. 'What was . . . what?'

'SSSSSSSSSS!'

I freeze, taking in what sounds like a Pirelli tyre being harpooned with a kebab skewer.

'Oh . . . erm . . .' My mind whirrs with possibilities. 'I was simply going to say, "Sssssssssooooo – how've you been?"'

Jamie looks at me as if my mental faculties must be in a lost-property department somewhere. 'I thought we'd discussed that.'

'SSSS!'

I straighten my back and look up to the window, hoping to give the impression that the noise is outside. How I think I'll pull this off I don't know; it's not as though we get many passing boa constrictors around here.

'SSSS!'

'What's that funny noise?'

I know the worst thing I can do is look at my cleavage, but something compels me to do so – and a split-second glance reveals that my right boob resembles a pillow that's lost its stuffing.

'Oh . . . nothing!' I say, grabbing the remote and turning up the volume on the iPod as I lean strategically into a cushion to divert attention from my anatomical imbalance. 'Where were we?'

Jamie's eyes blur seductively. Again, his mouth moves to mine as I close my eyes. I can feel his breath on my face, sense the throbbing in his trousers, almost taste his kiss, when suddenly . . .

POP!

He leaps back in shock and I look down at my now entirely lopsided cleavage. I grab a cushion and cling to it.

I am about to make my excuses to go and swap the bra for something more reliable, when he beats me to it.

'I need to go,' he says urgently, standing up. 'The gas bill. Why don't you email me?'

He heads for the door and opens it, while I sit nodding manically and gripping the cushion.

'See you later,' he waves, closing the door behind him.

I breathe in deeply and take stock. Okay, it wasn't perfect. Wonky boobs hadn't been part of the plan.

But that doesn't change how I managed to make Jamie feel. And as I slip into something more comfortable and slot my *Belly Dance Abs Blast* DVD in the machine, it strikes me that tonight I got something back that was rightfully mine. My mojo. And I'm not intending to let it go.

Chapter 16

For a feminist, my mother can be a terrible bimbo sometimes.

'What do you think of the pattern?' she asks airily, perching on a step ladder in combats that look genuinely war-ravaged, a stretch of wallpaper pinched between her fingers.

'Nice,' I reply truthfully, even though it's not to my taste.

'I wouldn't normally go for floral,' she muses. 'But I thought it'd be okay in the breakfast room. It was a choice of rose, lavender, jasmine or this – listeria.'

I frown. 'You mean wisteria. Listeria's in uncooked chicken. I'd be surprised if Linda Barker named her new range after something that gives you diarrhoea.'

'I'm certain that's what they said in the shop,' she replies hoity-toitily, brushing down the paper and stepping back to examine it.

Even at fifty-seven, Mum never needs more than a smudge of make-up and, with her wispy dark-blonde curls and slim build, she'd still look and sound like the sugarplum fairy if she wasn't so uncomfortable with the idea of wearing skirts. She never puts on any weight. Even in the pictures I've seen of her when she was seven months pregnant with me, she looks as though she's just had a big roast dinner.

Today, her look has been accessorized with splatters of white paint – a by-product of her ceiling decoration. You could read Braille off her forehead right now.

'Right,' she says, turning her attention to me, 'I think you and I need to talk, don't we?'

The words send a shiver down my spine. Don't let my mother's floaty demeanour fool you; when she sets her mind on something, she can be difficult to argue with, as my father discovered a long time ago. 'Frank, some tea would be nice.' This is not a hint but an instruction.

My dad looks up, expressionless, from the financial section of the *Sunday Telegraph*. I never know whether he's actually reading it or pretending to for a quiet life. 'Of course, my little Terminator,' he replies sweetly. 'Your usual, I take it?'

As Dad heads dutifully into the kitchen I notice that he's in his weekend attire: a buttoned-up short-sleeved shirt, boat shoes polished to a Queen's Guard-standard shine and . . . jeans. Which means he must have woken in a particularly devil-may-care mood today, for denim is rarely worn by my father.

The first time he ever bought jeans was in the late 1990s, and then only on the condition they boasted a crease down the front that could've been administered by a Savile Row tailor. Obviously, no evidence of stone-washing would be tolerated; in his mind that is two steps from crystal-meth addiction.

'Now,' begins Mum, as she sits at the breakfast table. 'About Jamie . . .'

Until the moment she delivers her verdict, I am struggling to predict it, simply because, from the first minute she met my ex-boyfriend, she was his biggest fan. They hit it off so comprehensively she was even one of those rare beings who thought his music sounded good.

'Jamie,' she says serenely, 'is a bastard.'

'Mother!' I splutter.

'Oh don't get me wrong,' she protests innocently. 'They all are. Men, I mean. Didn't I teach you anything, Samantha?'

'I see you still hold us in high regard, dear.' Dad reappears and catches my eye, winking. I suppress a smile.

He puts down two mugs, including Mum's favourite. It is plain white with the words 'Well-behaved women rarely make history' on the side.

'I don't mean you, Frank,' she tuts softly. 'It's the rest of them that are the issue.'

'I do love a sweeping generalization, dear,' he replies, heading back to his chair on the other side of the table. 'Jamie . . . the Yorkshire Ripper . . . Ghengis Khan . . . all bastards.'

She rolls her eyes. 'Frank, do I need to remind you of the statistics? Two-thirds of the world's work is performed by women. Only ten per cent of the world's income goes to them. You do the maths. Obviously, it doesn't mean we don't love you. We can love you but recognize you're all bastards.'

Dad picks up his paper again and opens it as Mum stands to

stir her wallpaper paste. 'I've learned over the years, Samantha,' he mutters, 'that this is an argument I can't win. I don't even try.'

Mum kisses him on the head. 'Which is why, of all the bastards in all the world, Frank, you're my favourite.'

My mum and dad are one of those rare couples who haven't only stood the test of time, but they've blossomed. Like those pukesome people on Steve Wright's Sunday Love Songs (in fact, Dad once attempted to make a request for Mum, but the producers didn't feel 'Mad, Bad and Dangerous to Know' was in keeping with the tone of the show).

They couldn't be more different, though – even in their working lives. As well as being a part-time boil on my dad's bum, Mum works full-time at the Liverpool Women's Hospital Maternity Unit. She's a midwife – head of her department, in fact – and, I'm led to believe, is brilliant at her job. She hasn't always worked there; she's done stints in London too, although that was years ago.

I find it difficult to imagine my mother being present at the most excruciating, terrifying and monumental event of my life. But she has her fans, to which the scores of flowers and cards from grateful new parents testify.

My father has a senior position at the Highways Agency, but beyond that I couldn't tell you a great deal about his job. He's not the sort of man who comes home and regales us with riotous anecdotes about what's gone on at the office. He could have spent eight hours doing the can-can and shooting passers-by with water pistols for all we know.

'I only say this, Sam, to remind you that no man is worth shedding tears over,' Mum continues. 'Not Jamie, not anyone. We might adore them . . . we might not have discovered a way to keep the human race going without them . . . but we must always remember we are worthy and beautiful people, whatever misery they cause us.'

She isn't joking about the misery. In the five days following Jamie's visit to the house, my mood has swung so dramatically it almost qualifies as a bipolar episode. Dazzling him with that combination of my blow-up boobs and fake drying of laundry on the radiator was thoroughly empowering. The feeling continued the following day. But the day after that, when I still hadn't heard from him, a gnawing started in my stomach. I thought nothing of it. Jamie's always been unpredictable; not hearing from him for a couple of days is something I'd got used to over the years, even when we were living together.

On day three, we exchanged a couple of texts, but they were confined to discussing the gas bill, so my unease became more pronounced. By day four, it was less like a knot in my stomach and more like a melon-sized peptic ulcer. And now . . . now I don't know what to think.

'I'm not sure this is helping, Mum,' I mutter, in the absence of anything else to say.

Dad looks at his watch. 'Right – I'd better run. I have an important appointment with twelve men dressed in red.'

My dad is a lifelong Liverpool fan and they're playing Chelsea today.

'Well, good,' says Mum. 'Sam and I can have a proper chat.'

'What makes you think I want a proper chat?' I squirm.

'Of course you do,' she pouts. 'I'm your mother. You're meant to discuss these things with your mother.'

'Well, we've discussed it,' I reply, drinking my tea as fast as I can. 'I've told you what happened and you've told me not to cry. Which is excellent advice and I promise I'll take it.'

'Now you're being sarcastic,' she says as Dad heads for the front door. 'I'm only trying to help. And what I say is true. If you spend too much time thinking about it, you might go and do something stupid like try to persuade him to come back.'

I look at my shoes. She looks at me.

'You haven't!'

'Hmm . . . no,' I reply, my face flushing. 'But . . .'

'But what?'

'Oh Mum! I haven't done anything,' I protest. 'If, for argument's sake, Jamie and I were to get back together . . . and I do mean if . . .'

'Yes?' she asks suspiciously.

'You can't give him a hard time.'

'As if I would! I've always loved Jamie.'

'You've just called him a bastard.'

'I'd never hold it against him. I explained that,' she argues, taking a sip of her tea. 'All I'm saying is this: don't waste time and energy thinking about a man who doesn't want you. There's only one thing you should be saying in this situation.'

'What's that?'

She flutters her eyelids. 'Next!'

I roll my eyes.

'I'm serious,' she insists. 'And you should go out and treat yourself a little. Go and have one of those spa days you like. Or buy yourself a new outfit. I heard they had a sale on at Ted Bacon.'

'Ted Bak— Oh it doesn't matter, the point is—'

I'm interrupted by the slam of the front door and when I look up Julia walks in. But my sister doesn't look quite right. I can see that immediately.

'What's up?' I ask.

She swallows, clearly troubled as she clutches something in her hand, glancing between Mum and me.

'Um . . . I got a letter. It arrived on Friday, but I've been so busy I forgot it was there. I only opened it this morning.'

'What sort of letter?' Mum asks.

Julia takes a deep breath. 'It's come totally out of the blue. I don't quite know what to make of it. Or what to do about it. Or . . .'

'Julia, what is it?' I ask.

Julia looks nervously at Mum. 'It's my birth father.'

Blood drains from Mum's face so rapidly it's as if someone's opened a valve at the back of her neck. 'Your birth father? What about him?'

Julia looks at the letter and whispers, 'He's found me.'

Chapter 17

Mum has always said she'd be fine about Julia finding out about her birth parents if she chose to do so. I know other adoptive parents can't always see things like this, but Mum seemed to have total conviction, even if Julia insisted she had no desire to follow that path.

As far as my sister's concerned, her parents are the ones she shared with me. Blood is irrelevant. Even though it's obvious, as my mum and sister sit together at the table, that they're hardly two peas in a pod.

Julia is clearly mildly numb with the shock. Mum's approach to being stunned is a little different.

'Jesus Christ Almighty on a pushbike,' she babbles. 'What the hell does the letter say?'

Julia stands. 'I'll put the kettle on. We'll all have a cup of tea and I'll read it to you.'

'Forget about the tea, Julia! The letter!'

'Sit down,' I tell her gently. 'I'll do it.'

I fill the kettle and listen to Julia as she reads the letter, handwritten on thick, ivory paper.

Dear Julia,

My name is Gary Collins and I am your father.

I have written what feels like a hundred versions of those words and have so far failed to come up with one that doesn't feel either horribly blunt or wholly inadequate.

But I hope you will bear with me on the basis that one day you may perhaps consider meeting me face to face, to give me the chance to talk to you directly and to explain why I decided, after a huge amount of consideration, to get in touch.

I pour the boiled water and scrutinize Mum's expression, which becomes more and more unsettled as Julia continues reading.

It turns out that Gary Collins read a recent interview with Julia in a classical music magazine to which, as an avid but purely amateur violinist, he subscribes. In it, Julia spoke extensively of her background, even naming the hospital in which she'd been born, and the month and year in which she was adopted. More than any of those jigsaw pieces fitting together, however, Gary says he simply knew the second he saw her that she was his daughter. The family resemblance was unmistakable; plus, the single photograph he has of her as a baby was proof enough. In it, the tiny Julia sported the distinctive butterfly birthmark on her arm that she still has today, and which was clearly visible in the magazine photograph.

'This is unbelievable,' I say, going over to Julia as she folds up the letter and places it carefully in her bag. I rub her back soothingly. 'Are you okay? You must be totally in shock?'

She takes a deep breath but glances over to Mum. 'A little. Are you okay, Mum? How do you feel about all this?'

Mum swallows, clearly attempting to compose herself. 'I'm a bit surprised, obviously. But . . . you've always known my views. I've always said if you wanted to try to make contact with your biological parents, then I'd understand. Completely.'

Julia hesitates. 'Do you still think that, Mum? Now that this has happened? You know I'd never have sought out my birth dad. But . . . I suppose I never expected this either . . .' Her voice trails off.

Mum's jaw tenses. 'So you're going to write back? You're going to see him?'

'I'm not saying that,' Julia says awkwardly. 'I must admit, though . . . I'm intrigued. And I suppose I'm not ruling it out. As long as you're okay with that, Mum?'

Mum swallows and smiles thinly. 'Of course I am.'

'I'm not saying I definitely will,' adds Julia. 'Although I think it'd be rude not to at least acknowledge the letter. I need to think about it. I'm not going to make any hasty decisions. What do you think, Sam?'

I bite my lip, wondering if I should keep my mouth shut. I quickly decide I owe it to Julia to speak the truth, even if I suspect it isn't what Mum wants to hear.

'If it was me,' I say hesitantly, 'I don't think I'd be able to resist finding out more. I wouldn't have it in me not to respond.'

I glance at Mum and am certain she's holding her breath. Then she looks up and tries to smile reassuringly. She's fooling nobody.

Chapter 18

I'd never bought the idea, perpetuated by sitcoms such as *Friends* and *Frasier*, that there are cafes a person can love so much that they hardly set foot elsewhere. That was, until I got my own.

The Quarter in Hope Street has been a second home to Ellie, Jen and me for the last few years. Frequented by a mix of performing arts students from nearby LIPA (or 'Paul McCartney's Fame School'), professionals from surrounding businesses and bohemian types from . . . God knows where, actually (but here they are).

The bistro-cum-cafe is located amid the quiet splendour of Liverpool's Georgian quarter and is the epitome of understated style, with its simple tiled and wood surfaces and bold original art. The staff are friendly, young and ludicrously attractive. While I have no idea if it's company policy to only employ people with the latter quality or simply a happy accident, it undoubtedly adds another dimension to grabbing a coffee.

The real draw, however, is the food, particularly the cakes.

They sit in a spectacular display at the front like an edible version of the Crown Jewels. For the first time ever, though, my stomach's so tense that not even the Lumpy Bumpy cake can tempt me. Still, at least it's a good day for my cellulite.

'I can only stay for a quick coffee,' I tell Ellie and Jen as I join them. It's a gloriously sunny Tuesday lunchtime and they've managed to get a table on the cobblestones outside. 'The tennis tournament we're involved in starts tomorrow and I've literally popped here on the way there to check the place over. I shouldn't really be here. But . . . God, I need to talk.'

'Jamie?' asks Jen.

'Have you still heard nothing from him except a couple of texts about the gas bill?' Ellie asks, sipping espresso.

'Not a sausage. I'm going to text him again today,' I add defiantly. Enough time has passed for me to be confident that Ellie's theory about playing it cool isn't working. I don't care if I'm challenging his 'hunter-gatherer instinct'; besides, I'm coming to the conclusion that Jamie's hunter-gatherer instinct is about as finely tuned as a Barbie doll's.

'What are you going to say?' asks Jen. Her mere presence has prompted a collective bout of giddiness among the young male waiters, who are falling over their trendy black aprons to serve us.

Her Karen Millen jeans – or 'Jen's lucky jeans' as they're now officially christened – often have this effect. She never fails to pull in them; they're capable of such supreme sexual magnetism you'd think they came with handcuffs.

'I don't know yet,' I sigh. 'I honestly don't. But I need to make contact with him and see how the land lies. Oh Ellie, don't look at me like that!'

She raises an eyebrow and glances away pursing her lips. 'I'm saying nothing.'

Jen frowns. 'Am I missing something? Why wouldn't you text someone when they've got a perfectly good mobile? That's what they're for. I can't stop myself, personally.'

'We know!' Ellie says pointedly.

Jen goes to respond, then realizes where this argument might lead. She knows it's unlikely to be to her outstanding practical knowledge of how to handle men.

'How's your fireman?' I venture, partly to change the subject and partly in the hope that she'll have some good news. I shouldn't have bothered.

She scrunches up her nose and pretends to weep. 'Did you have to?' she says, clearly resigned to another romantic false start.

I squirm. 'Oh . . . sorry.'

'I haven't heard from him. I mean, obviously I haven't heard from him. It was going far too well for me to have heard from him.' She's on a roll and even the dishy waiter who approached to top up the sugar bowl has backed away. 'This is one thing I don't like about the digital age. There are a million ways for a man to ignore you.'

'Oh Jen, I'm sorry. I really thought things were looking good with that one too,' I lie.

'So did I!' she huffs, shaking her head in bewilderment. 'I was planning a weekend to Paris and everything. God, I had some good outfits lined up.'

'Jen,' says Ellie despairingly, 'you'd only known him a couple of weeks.'

'So?' says Jen innocently.

'You'd only known him a couple of weeks and you were planning a weekend to Paris,' she states. 'Do you not see something a little . . . wrong with that sentence?'

'I'd offered to pay, if that's what you mean,' replies Jen, sipping her coffee.

'Of course that isn't what I mean!' says Ellie with gentle exasperation.

'I think what Ellie's trying to say is that it might have been a little early for you to be planning European mini-breaks,' I point out.

'Ohhh . . . Well, I know it looks bad on paper, but I really felt as if he was "the one",' she insists. 'He was perfect. Intelligent, bags of charisma, good-looking, plus . . .'

'Muscles?' offers Ellie.

'Well, obviously,' sighs Jen.

'Jen,' says Ellie, reaching over to clutch our friend's hand as if she's her counsellor. 'We're going to have to have "the talk" again, aren't we?'

Jen laughs and rolls her eyes, knowing what's coming.

'You are beautiful, intelligent and charming,' Ellie reassures her. 'But there is one thing you've got to get into your head. And that's to stop being so bloody full-on after knowing someone for about five days.'

'They were five very intense days,' Jen replies weakly.

'Jennifer, if you want a man, you need to stop texting every minute of the day. Stop chasing them with phone calls. And, above absolutely everything else on this list that's making you look like a bunny boiler . . . don't even think about Paris! Not until you've known him for at least three months. And even then let him suggest it, not you.'

'You're such a spoilsport,' says Jen, as a waiter with Malteser eyes and biceps that would probably be visible on Google Earth removes the coffee cups. 'I love the Louvre in summer, too.'

Twenty minutes later, as I leap into my car to head to Sefton Park to check the arrangements for tomorrow's tournament, I experience a strange sensation with regards to my mobile phone. It feels like I've been walking round with a Galaxy Ripple in my handbag on day six of a fast.

For the first time in my life, I sympathize with Jen on this issue. The phone is a miniature siren; it's beckoning me, tempting me to its glistening keypad. And having spent all morning with my fingers twitching over it, fighting the urge to do what my instinct tells me, I can hold back no longer.

Once I've made the decision to text Jamie, I approach the enterprise like a junkie who's stumbled across some crack: breathlessly, my hands fumbling in frenzied anticipation. It's unbelievably hard to edit down my first three drafts to anything less than seven screens. Winston Churchill's chief speech writer didn't sweat as much as this.

I'm midway through deleting some of the vaguely repetitive stuff, when my phone beeps, leaving me juggling it as if it's on fire. I save a draft and flick to the new text. It's from Jamie. It is four words long.

Hey. How u doing?

They don't declare his undying love. They don't even ask to meet up again. But one thing's certain in my mind: I am back in business!

At least . . . for about an hour I think I'm back in business. But it turns out to be a fleeting sensation because, after abandoning my lengthy drafts and going with a 'Good, thanks – and u?', no response is forthcoming.

And after sixty torturous minutes this is too much to bear, so I dig out draft four.

Jamie, have been thinking about you and me and the reason 4 your decision. I know we weren't perfect and there are a million things I'd do differently. But if you'd give me another chance then I am absolutely certain I could make u realize that staying here and with me isn't such a terrible option. I know u need to be true to yourself and I know

I am halfway through the sentence when the phone beeps again and I inadvertently delete the tome that's taken me fifteen minutes to compose.

Bit low actually. I miss you.

My heart does a backflip as I continue reading.

Maybe we could have another chat some time.

Great idea – when? x I reply eagerly.

He texts back straight away.

Shall I give you a shout next week?

I frown, disappointed not to have pinned him down to an exact day, and I am about to fire off my 'No probs' reply when a kind of romantic madness grips me. I add a kiss, followed by six more. I gaze at the phone after I've sent it, longing for him to send back some kisses.

That's all I want. A small but significant gesture.

But they never arrive. Which sends me into a whirlwind of analysis about the reasons for the lack of them: he feels nothing for me any longer? Or: he doesn't want to get my hopes up? Or: he's trying to suppress his feelings? Or the wackiest theory of all – which comes from Alistair, who I bump into in Tesco later that night: he's a bloke, so it never occurred to him to send some and it is no big deal. And this measly interpretation from a psychotherapist!

I'm aware that all this thinking about the situation is no good for me. It'd be no good for anyone. I'm convinced Stephen Hawking thinks less than this. Besides which, nothing remotely productive seems to come of it.

Chapter 19

The Liverpool Lawn Tennis Masters has become one of the big dates in the city's lively sporting and social calendar. It's a four-day extravaganza in the third week of July and BJD Productions have been commissioned to help organize it for the first time.

The part we're looking after is corporate hospitality – and very important it is too, given the profit involved. However, with cash comes responsibility, and it's therefore essential that every detail is right.

'Deana, could you give me a hand?' I puff, attempting to screw a wobbly leg back onto one of the tables while on my hands and knees, my new Reiss skirt hoisted round my thighs.

The fact that neither Deana nor Natalie was born overburdened with a sense of urgency is painfully evident this morning. While I've been here since six, zipping round like a blue bottle whose wings are on fire, my assistants rolled in an hour ago and have barely moved, except to check on their eyelashes.

'Deana?' I repeat.

I look up, but she's deep in conversation with Natalie, who is indignant about something.

'DEANA!'

She looks at me and screws up her nose like someone's shoved a dirty sock under it. 'What?'

'Can you help me, please?' I ask as evenly as possible.

Despite the wobbly table leg, I'm pleased with the marquee: it seats four hundred and is gloriously positioned in the heart of the park, surrounded by hydrangea and blue mist, which look particularly stunning given that the sun has made an appearance.

Inside is an English country garden theme, with peonies and delphiniums on the tables and ivy across the doorway. My client's pleased too, judging by the feedback; though, admittedly, no one's sampled Deana and Natalie's unique brand of customer service yet.

'Did we have to wear these crap uniforms?' Deana pouts as she finally turns her attention to my request.

I rarely use the terrible twosome at events, preferring to keep them apart when inflicting them on members of the public. But we are short on staff so it's all hands to the pump.

'I'm afraid you did,' I reply firmly, twisting the leg so frantically I nearly sprain my wrist.

'I don't see what harm it woulda done for us to get a bit tarted up. Did Piers authorize this? I mean, look at this jacket. It's –' she pauses to search for the precise adjective, like a sommelier describing fine wine – 'shite.'

The uniform to which she refers consists of cream trousers, flat shoes and a tailored jacket with pistachio stripes. Not green, you understand. Pistachio. Which may or may not be one of the factors that gave the manufacturers carte blanche to charge an arm and a leg. Not that they're not worth it; in spite of Deana's damning verdict, they're perfect for this event. And even with the overdone fake tan, overdone fake nails and overdone fake eyelashes, she and Natalie look the part.

'I look like I should be selling bloody ice creams,' shrieks Natalie. It's how they sound that I need to work on.

Deana and I heave the table back into place. 'Now, ladies,' I begin, thinking a little pep talk might generate some enthusiasm, 'I really appreciate the effort you're both putting in today. I'll make sure head office knows all about it in your next personal development reviews.'

They gaze at me with lobotomy eyes as if wondering why they would give a toss about their next personal development reviews.

I continue, unperturbed: 'I need you both to remember what I said about smiling, and being aware of the guests' needs. If I'm called away to another area it's you two who'll make sure the champagne isn't running low and everyone's happy. I know I can count on you.'

Deana raises an eyebrow as if to say: 'What gave you that impression?'

'And if you do a good job I'll give you both the next set of VIP tickets I get hold of for a new bar opening.'

'Oooooh,' they reply, perking up.

As the guests arrive, two hours before the sporting action

begins, my tempo steps up a gear. Between checking on the catering, answering queries from the groundsmen and trying to persuade the sporting VIPs to strike a variety of naff poses for the local press, it's non-stop.

Fortunately, everyone seems to be having a fantastic time, and as dessert is served I begin to relax – always a bad sign.

'Ewwwwww,' I overhear Deana exclaim to Natalie.

My ears prick up. 'What? What's the matter?'

'It was a mistake having this in a park,' tuts Natalie, as if she has any expertise in event coordination beyond purchasing the office paper clips.

'What is it?' I repeat.

Natalie purses her lips. 'Poo.'

'Look,' I say, starting to get annoyed. 'We're in the middle of this event now. Please stop complaining about your uniforms.'

Natalie looks baffled. 'Warraya on about?'

I frown. 'Warra— What are you on about?'

'There's a big dog poo near the entrance. I saw it when I nipped out for a ciggie,' Deana informs me matter-of-factly.

I start to hyperventilate – and not only at the thought of Deana standing at the entrance with a fag hanging out of her mouth. 'This place was supposed to have been cleared and inspected this morning. Did you get rid of it?'

Their faces nearly implode. 'Ewwwwww. You are joking,' splutters Natalie.

I've always lived by the motto that says if you want something done, do it yourself; but right now it's never sounded more hideous.

I scuttle between tables and out of the marquee, heading for the kitchens, where I elbow my way through catering staff until I locate the head chef, who furnishes me with the closest thing to a poop-a-scoop bag we can find: the ziplock bags he uses to keep the Camembert fresh.

The non-corporate spectators are starting to arrive, so I know I've got to be subtle. But as I hover at the entrance, hoping that, in the process of locating the offending article, I don't impale it on the heel of my Kurt Geigers, I can't help thinking that subtlety is a luxury I can't afford.

When the passers-by peter out, I scan the ground with the stealth of a Serengeti lioness, and as I pinpoint the item in question, my stomach turns over. I check for observers before stooping down, grimacing as I carefully attempt to negotiate it into the bag. I've seen Auntie Jill do this with her dog Dyson's offerings and the entire process takes milliseconds. She simply whips a blue bag from her pocket and deftly swipes the item away.

Deftness is not the term you'd use to describe my manoeuvre. I don't know if it's that Auntie Jill has more experience, or if it's the speed I attempt to employ – but I'm hit by a bout of cack-handedness that leaves me muttering expletives and so red in the face that it's clear my blood vessels are sizzling.

Eventually, I have the item in the bag in preparation for a sprint to the bins. But, as I spring triumphantly to my feet and attempt to zoom in on my destination, something blocks my view. A two-piece suit. A very nice two-piece suit, now you mention it.

'Hello. Are you one of the organizers?' The voice is deep and confident. I look up and hear myself gulp in the manner of a character from the *Beano*. He's about six foot two and broad-shouldered, with tanned skin, pre-Raphaelite lips and twinkling sable eyes that could get a woman into trouble with one look.

'Erm . . . that would be me,' I reply coolly.

'I'm on table three and wondered if we could order some more wine, please. I asked one of the staff members in the striped jackets – but that was twenty minutes ago.'

I smile with what I hope is warm professionalism. 'No problem at all, sir. I'll have some sent over right away.'

'Thanks,' he replies and goes to walk away. Then he turns back. 'Oh, and could you point me in the direction of the toilets?'

'Sure,' I say chirpily, pointing to the Portaloos.

I realize my mistake even before the bag of doggie detritus leaves my hand. He realizes my mistake as it takes flight in a spectacular arch I'm confident will be unmatched by any of the volleys on centre court this afternoon.

And we both watch, dumbfounded, as my fresh haul of bagged-up canine poo flies through the air . . . taking an age to land . . . directly on the top of my handcrafted table plan – where it perches, intact, on a decorative lily of the valley border.

I take a deep breath and turn to my guest as if this was completely intentional and meticulously planned, a see-through ziplock bag full of dog dirt being precisely what I'd envisaged as the finishing touch to my marquee design.

'Right,' I smile brightly, clapping my hands. 'That wine will be right over.'

Chapter 20

I'm finally relieved of tennis tournament duties at seven thirty on Saturday evening. Anything I haven't sorted now can be picked up on Monday morning. I know that what I should do is go home, run a relaxing bath and do nothing but chill. But, since I've been single, spending Saturday night alone has become inconceivable.

It's not that I used to spend every Saturday gallivanting with Jamie. If his band was playing, I'd be lucky to see him at all during the weekend. And there have been plenty of Saturday nights when I did nothing more exciting than devour a box of Maltesers in front of X *Factor*. But now the thought of staying in, listening to a series of tuneless renditions of Whitney Houston ballads is too much to bear.

Not that I have a choice. Jen's new love interest – the waiter from the Quarter – was only available for an afternoon-coffee date today as he's working tonight. And Ellie's about as likely to spend Saturday night at home with a Horlicks as she is to circumnavigate the globe in roller skates.

'Doesn't your man ever want you to spend Saturday night with him?' I ask as I meet her and Jen at the Shipping Forecast on Slater Street. More low-key than the other bars in this part of town, it's full of musos and thoughtful types who spend too much time twiddling with their guitar strings.

'I cooked a romantic dinner last night,' she says indignantly. 'Mind you, he had bought me flowers out of the blue last week, so he deserved it.'

'That's so sweet,' says Jen.

'I know,' shrugs Ellie. 'I don't take it for granted.'

'You shouldn't,' I point out. 'No man has ever bought me flowers.'

'Really?' they both say in unison.

'Oh come on – it's not Jamie's style. He's romantic, don't get me wrong . . . just, in other ways. So what did you cook?' I ask Ellie.

'Paella followed by home-made profiteroles. I can be a domestic goddess when I want. Turned into a late one, actually. You know when you eat too much, drink too much and end up dancing round the kitchen to your old CDs? Oh . . .' She suddenly realizes that this ode to being a couple might not be what I want to hear. 'Sorry, Sam.'

'Don't be silly,' I reply dismissively. 'I don't expect people to tiptoe around. It's not as if anyone's died. Besides, hopefully Jamie and I will do a bit of kitchen dancing again one day. Not that we ever liked the same music. He nearly put his head in the oven one day when I put on Michael Bublé.'

'You don't look like a woman who's spent the day nursing a hangover,' says Jen, giving Ellie the once-over. Ellie looks sensational in a short All Saints dress, sky-high heels and piled-up hair.

She almost outshines Jen. Only 'almost' because every man in the room has singularly failed to remove his eyes from our friend's legs. Unfortunately for them, she's smitten again. Despite having met the man in question only four days ago.

'How's the waiter shaping up?' I ask.

'Adam. And he's perfect. I never normally go for younger men, but maybe this is where I've been going wrong all these years. He's very intelligent. The waiter's job is only a stopgap.'

'Before what?'

'He's not sure yet. He's got such charisma. He's so funny and sweet and has . . .'

'Muscles, we know,' Ellie finishes for her. 'I knew the second I saw them that he didn't stand a chance with you around.'

'Am I that predictable?' she laughs. 'Anyway, what made you choose here, Sam?'

I shift in my seat and sip my Cuba Libre. 'I thought it'd make a change.'

The look on their faces tells me I'm fooling no one. The truth is that I'm here because this is one of Jamie's favourite places. Not that we ever came together; this was reserved for nights out with his band. At least, the start of nights out with his band. I never used to ask where they ended up on the basis that what I didn't know wouldn't hurt me.

It's never been my type of place, in all honesty – until now. Now it has my full attention and no mistake. My eyes have been glued to the door since we arrived, despite the fact that nobody interesting has walked in. By which I mean Jamie hasn't walked in.

'Well, Sam, you're looking exceptionally good at the moment,' Ellie tells me. 'Being single suits you.'

'Very funny. I've lost a bit of weight, that's all,' I tell her, but I know that my slimmed-down thighs and bum are but the start of my transformation.

I now spend my life imagining that there's a possibility of bumping into Jamie and – in contrast to my normal state of being – make sure I'm looking as good as physically possible at all times. Which is exhausting. But for the first time since I can remember, the effort I put into my appearance pays dividends. As we're shunted from bar to bar by Ellie, who can't bear to stay in one place for more than two martinis, I become aware that I'm attracting an above-average amount of attention, something that continues as I order drinks in the Hard Days Night Hotel.

I can sense somebody gazing at me from the other end of the bar. I don't look, at least not properly; I simply flash a half glance his way. But I can tell from just that that he's attractive. I can sense it. I can smell it. It's in his alpha-male swagger as he approaches, puts his elbow on the bar and leans in.

'Bloody hell you're looking hot, Sam.'

I spin round, startled, and come face to face with Luke –

Jamie's best friend. With the possible exception of bumping into the man himself, I couldn't be more excited. But for a very different reason than Luke is used to.

Chapter 21

I haven't seen Luke since the break-up, and the issue that's uppermost in my mind is how to quiz him about the emotional state of my ex-boyfriend. Which probably makes this the first time in Luke's life that a woman in a bar isn't fixated on him.

The term 'red-blooded male' was invented for him. No female fails to fall for his charms, the least of which are his muscular frame and killer smile. Did you spot the mention of muscles? Obviously, Jen's been there; she was swept up in a three-week whirlwind of his irrepressible magnetism and lust that left no room for argument.

If ever a relationship was doomed to failure, it was theirs. By the time she was musing about the colour of bridesmaids' dresses, he'd moved on to his neighbour's cousin, Heidi, a zoologist from Sweden, with whom he was more than happy to give his animal instincts a whirl.

The fact that Luke is so likeable is a source of constant inner turmoil for me and my sense of sisterhood. Frankly, I should disown him. But I can't – even if justifying my affection for him is increasingly challenging.

'What have you done to yourself?' he asks, looking me up and down with a grin.

I roll my eyes. 'Could you make that sound less like you think I looked like a compost heap beforehand?'

He tuts. 'Oh Sam, the only thing in my garden I'd compare you with is an English rose. Lovely, fragrant . . .' he shrugs, 'slightly thorny at times.'

I suppress a smile. 'Gee, thanks. I have a right to be thorny, anyway. I've been dumped.'

His expression changes and he looks serious all of a sudden. It's quite unnerving; the Luke I know is as shallow as a leaky paddling pool. 'If it means anything, I've tried to tell him he's making a mistake. And not just because you look fabulous,' he winks, pulling himself together.

I shake my head. 'I know I'm single, but it doesn't mean I'm available.'

'Paying you a compliment, that's all.'

'Fine. Thank you. So what's he said? And how is he? And is he still sleeping in your spare room? And—'

'Wooahh, slow down,' he replies. 'One question at a time, please. But let me buy you a drink, first.'

'I've already got them.' I go to give a note to the barman.

Luke pushes down my hand. 'No, you don't. Like you say, you've been dumped. You need to be looked after.'

'Oh purleease.' I tut while he grins and hands over a twenty. 'But thank you, anyway.'

'Who are the other two drinks for?'

'Jen and Ellie. They're over there.'

'Jen's here?' he says, raising his eyebrows. 'Bring her over. It's been a while.'

I narrow my eyes and glare at him. 'Do not go near my friend again. Or. I. Will. Kill. You. Is that clear?'

'I was only going to say a friendly hello.'

'I've seen where your friendly hellos lead and so has Jen. Besides, she's happy and has a new man.' Luke doesn't need to know that she first set eyes on him on Tuesday, when he served her cappuccino. 'Do me a favour and stay away, eh?'

'You have such a low opinion of me, Sam,' he tuts.

'Can't imagine why. Listen – wait here. I need to speak to you about some crucial matters.'

'There aren't many women I'd hang around waiting for at a bar, you know,' he calls after me.

I must be gone less than two minutes, but when I return, Luke's already chatting to another woman. She's ludicrously pretty, a no-less-than-five-hours-to-get-ready type, with smoky eyes and endless hair extensions that look as though they've been harvested from an Appaloosa pony.

I scold myself for such mean-spirited thoughts and almost hope that the conversation I'm walking in on is about the dissertation she's producing for her PhD.

'It's true,' she squeaks in an accent so thick you could spread it on your toast. 'Cheryl Cole used to be an HGV driver. She keeps it quiet these days but my dad's been on the lorries for years and he knew her when she was only twenty-three and would stop at the same Little Chef. She couldn't half put away a fry-up, apparently. You'd never guess, would you?'

'Lynne . . . that is fascinating,' Luke smiles in a way that would be totally convincing to her even if she wasn't so cerebrally challenged. 'Twenty-three? How old is she now?'

'My dad reckons early fifties,' she replies. 'Looks good for her age, doesn't she? It's the eyelashes. They take years off.'

I cough. 'Sorry to interrupt.'

'Oh hi,' says Luke, straightening his back. 'Where are your friends?'

'They'll be over shortly. I wanted to get you by yourself first.'

I look at Lynne-Nice-But-Dim, hoping she takes the hint. But she's no longer looking overly nice. In fact, she's throwing daggers. And is patently not in the mood to move.

'If I could discuss something with you privately . . .' I add.

Luke and I glance at Lynne but she couldn't be less likely to leave if her hem was pinned down with tent pegs.

'Well,' I begin, regardless. 'Jamie. Seriously, I need to know how he's been.'

Luke takes a deep breath. 'I don't know what to say, Sam. He's torn up about what happened. There's no mistaking that.'

'Has he mentioned me?' I ask.

'Of course,' he frowns. 'He mentions you all the time.'

'Do you think he misses me?'

Luke is about to answer when Lynne-Not-Very-Nice-But-Dim yawns pointedly.

'He does. Definitely. Look, let's have a proper chat at some point, shall we? Now,' he says, leaning into Lynne. 'Where were we?'

She looks as if someone's told her tomorrow is Christmas. I'm going to have to act.

'One more question, Luke,' I continue sweetly.

Lynne rolls her eyes so far back into her head it looks like she's about to have a fit.

'How did that chlamydia test go?'

I'd feel guilty about this course of action if it wasn't for two justifications: A, she was annoying, and B, I'm saving her from future heartache, so in fact I am doing her a favour. Luke doesn't quite see it like this.

'I was in there!' he says, exasperated, after Lynne has made her excuses and left.

'She was a bimbo,' I say dismissively.

'And . . .?'

'And I think you could do better,' I continue.

'Of course I could. But that's not the point. Anyway, there's nothing wrong with getting yourself checked out every so often. It was clear, by the way.'

'Glad to hear it.'

He shakes his head. 'You've got entirely the wrong impression of me, Samantha. Deep down, all I want is a nice girl who likes me for who I am. Someone to settle down with. Someone special.'

'But, in the meantime, you're going to get plenty of practice, eh?'

'Why the hell not?' he grins.

'How's it going, handsome?' says Ellie, kissing Luke on the cheek. There's a slight slur in her words that suggests she sneaked in an extra drink while I've been over here. 'Broken many hearts lately?'

Luke tuts. 'My reputation is in tatters, I see. It's a good job I think you're wonderful, Ellie Sanders.'

'What reputation?' asks Jen.

'Jennifer, lovely to see you,' he says, kissing her slowly on the cheek. 'It's been a long time.'

'Because you never phoned,' she points out.

'Didn't I?' he asks innocently. 'Phone trouble. Ah, we could have been so good together too.'

'I doubt that,' she replies.

'So where are we going after these drinks?' I ask, changing the subject.

'Let me come with you,' says Luke.

'Sorry, Luke,' Ellie replies, spinning round. 'There are some nights that just have to be girls only.'

Chapter 22

The rest of the evening is a riot – and a blur. What I can confirm is that we visit lots of bars, get tipsier than intended, run out of money (at least I do, until Ellie insists on thrusting twenty quid into my hand so I can keep going; she is a woman who has never known when to stop), and – despite a brief melancholy (Jamie-induced) moment – the whole thing is unrelentingly enjoyable.

Ellie, who has always been one of life's party animals, is on fire tonight. Although it never ceases to amaze me how much booze she can put away, and at a rate that makes Jen and me look like amateurs. It is insane o'clock when I get home – don't ask me for anything more specific.

When I wake the next morning, it's with a hangover that could justify a spell in intensive care. I stay in bed for as long as possible, then get up to shower and dress. Actually, that makes it sound like a perfunctory affair, whereas the reality is that it takes over an hour to perform the most basic ablutions. When I return to the living room, I glance at my phone and realize there's a missed call . . . from Jamie.

I phone back immediately.

'Sam. Erm. Thanks for returning my call.' His voice is slightly strangled, as if he's trying to come across as relaxed but isn't quite managing it.

'No problem.' My voice is so gravelly it sounds as though someone has taken a nail file to my tonsils. 'What's up?'

'Does something have to be up?' he asks awkwardly. 'I mean, we're still friends, aren't we? We'll always be friends. And . . . well, I just thought I'd phone to see how you are. In a friendly sort of way.'

'Well,' I reply, torn between delight and suspicion, 'I'm fine, Jamie. Had a great evening last night and am pottering round the house this morning. You know, the usual Sunday-morning stuff. There's a lot less to tidy up now you're not around.'

As soon as the words are out of my mouth I panic that this sounds like a dig about Jamie's lack of natural ability on the housework front. If you put a bottle of Cif in front of my ex-boyfriend, he'd think he was supposed to squeeze it on his chips. Nevertheless, the last thing I want is to bring that up and come across as a nag.

'Oh . . . by that I just mean, you know . . . that there aren't two of us any more. That's all,' I add hastily.

'Don't worry,' he laughs. 'I'm sure it's not just that. I know I'm not the tidiest of people. Luke keeps going mad about it. I don't treat his cushion covers with the respect they deserve, apparently.'

I join in with his laughter and it strikes me how good it feels to have a giggle with him again. To make the simplest human connection and remind ourselves of the bond we'd had for so many years.

'Speaking of whom,' he coughs, suddenly serious, 'I believe you bumped into Luke last night.'

'Yes. Did he mention it?'

He pauses. 'Hope he didn't come on to you,' he laughs, but it's a different kind of laugh from before; this one is laced with a distinct note of unease. It strikes me that he's seriously worried about this prospect. I'm about to leap in and reassure him, when something stops me.

'Well, you know Luke,' I say lightly.

There is a stutter of silence and for a second I wonder if I've gone too far. 'I'll take that as a yes, then, shall I?'

'Oh Jamie – Luke's a friend, you know that,' I say breezily, deliberately avoiding the question.

'Well, good. I mean, I know I have no right to tell you who you can and can't see . . . but, well, Luke would be difficult to cope with.'

'I understand,' I reply, though I can't help feeling a bit miffed that he's decided that I'm agreeing to not see Luke. He can't have it every way; the man has dumped me.

'But you're right about seeing people,' I continue pointedly. 'I've never been one of those girls who spend their life wallowing. I was never going to sit at home weeping into my wine glass. I know I need to get out there and rebuild my life – a different life. And, you know, have fun.'

He pauses. 'Fun?'

'Well, of course!' I reply enthusiastically. 'I'm not going to spend the rest of my life howling to 'I Will Survive', am I? I'm going to meet new people, do a bit of . . . living.' The word sounds wonderfully provocative.

'Living?' he croaks.

'Yep! I knew you'd understand.'

'Hmm,' he replies.

'Hmm,' I repeat.

Neither of us speaks for a moment and it strikes me that, for the first time in as long as I can remember, the break in conversation feels awkward. When you've been with someone for six years, you learn to live with their silences. They're not oppressive or difficult; they're part of life. But this is one silence I feel compelled to fill.

'I'd better run. I've got a million things to do.'

'Of course. Oh . . . Sam?'

'Yes?'

'I really miss you,' he says softly. 'I thought you ought to know.'

Chapter 23

So he really misses me. Great. Which does beg the question of why he's still intending to fly off to bloody South America.

Despite my niggling frustration, I nevertheless have a spring in my step by the time I reach Ellie's. Well, sort of. My physical state impedes anything approaching springiness – it's closer to a trudge. But a cheerful trudge, I'll give it that.

'You're more upbeat because you feel you're winning back some control,' says Alistair, filling up the kettle as Ellie chases Sophie round the living room in an attempt to win back the mascara she swiped.

'I love it when you psychoanalyse me, Alistair.'

'I bet you say that to all the guys,' he grins.

I'd only popped over to drop off the twenty pounds I borrowed from Ellie last night; but she'd forgotten about it, presumably because several billion brain cells were obliterated by the booze she put away. An hour later, Alistair has somehow been sucked into a therapy session.

'It makes sense, though. I hate that the decision to end the

133

relationship was made for me.' I lean forward to take a biscuit from the tin. It isn't my first. 'These hangover munchies are chronic,' I mutter.

He raises an eyebrow. 'My girlfriend claimed you hardly drank anything last night.'

'I can't speak for her, only myself,' I say diplomatically. 'And the only thing that would perk me up this morning is plunging my head in a vat of Red Bull.'

'I'll make you a PG Tips instead,' he says, splashing boiling water in the cups and leaning against the work surface as he folds his arms. 'When the end of a relationship is instigated by one party, it's natural for the other to experience contradictory feelings. Anger, frustration, desperation. Something's been snatched away from you, without you having any say. So as well as the loss of a person you love, you've also experienced a loss of power. The fact that Jamie's insecure about the idea of Luke being around you has made you feel as though you've regained some of that.'

'Should I be paying you by the hour for this?' I ask.

He smirks and finishes making the tea. 'Consider this a freebie.'

He hands me a cup of tea as Ellie and Sophie crash into the kitchen, giggling hysterically.

'Have you seen this?' Ellie laughs, scooping up Sophie and prizing away a mascara wand, which has already been smeared all over Sophie's face.

'She's done a better job than I was capable of this morning,' I grin.

Ellie kisses Sophie on the cheek before using a baby wipe to remove her efforts with the make-up.

'Atty Sam, Atty Sam, I going to be a bridemaid,' she announces.

'Wow! Are you?' I gasp.

'Alistair's sister, Cecilia, is getting married,' Ellie adds, showering Sophie with kisses. 'And she's going to have the most gorgeous bridesmaid in the whole wide world.'

'I going to have flowers,' Sophie tells me proudly. 'And posh shoes. And I go to walk down the owl.'

'Oooh,' I reply dutifully, assuming the ornithological reference was a mistake. 'So when's the big day?' I ask Ellie.

'In eighteen months. Which, given that she's asked every morning this week if the wedding's today, suddenly feels like a long way away.'

Sophie dives into the living room and Ellie runs after her.

'So, Alistair – one more question. What else can I do to make Jamie realize he shouldn't go?'

He frowns uncomfortably. 'I can't answer that, Sam. Only you and Jamie can work out between you whether you want to be together.'

'But it's not as simple as that,' I assure him.

He takes a deep breath. 'Can I ask one thing?'

I nod.

'It's perfectly natural for you to want him back, but it's also important to stand back and take a look at your relationship as it really was. Was it quite as perfect as you remember? And . . .

how can I put this? Are you one hundred per cent certain that getting back together with Jamie is the right thing for you both?'

I feel stung by the question, unable to believe he has to ask. 'Alistair, Jamie wasn't perfect. I've never said that he was. I know he had his flaws. God, he would drive me mad on occasions. But no one is perfect. I'm certainly not. And should we be together? Absolutely. Without a doubt.'

Chapter 24

I have a confession. One I'd never have made to Jamie; one I rarely discuss with even my best friends, because the last thing I want is anyone feeling sorry for me. I love weddings. No, I adore them. I'm intoxicated by their glorious romanticism and dizzying extravagance.

The reason this confession is tricky is that I'm in love with a man I know beyond a shadow of a doubt will never marry me. It's nothing personal; he'll never marry anyone.

Jamie is naturally suspicious of the institution of marriage, stating simply that he 'doesn't believe in it', as if he's referring to the tooth fairy. Given that his parents are still together after thirty-five years, it's unclear why he takes such a dim view of the concept, but he'll never change.

Which I'm relatively relaxed about. That's relatively. I buy the argument about it being only a bit of paper, and I am aware that almost half of marriages end in divorce. I'm equally aware that this absolute conviction is part of what makes Jamie the man he is. The man I love.

Yet if you asked whether a tiny bit of me ever hoped he might change his mind . . . well, that's a different matter.

Before I met him, I'd assumed it'd be something I'd do one day.

So when the subject first came up at his friend Bella's wedding, about a year after we met, it did give me a bit of a jolt. It was a beautiful day and the setting for the nuptials was Liverpool's most romantic venue: the Victorian Palm House in Sefton Park. It's a gorgeous domed conservatory in which sunlight glitters through the glass, illuminating your eyes and warming your skin.

The bride looked unbelievable. She'd lost three stones via a combination of Slimming World and pole-dancing lessons, a pastime she'd embraced so enthusiastically that she'd had a 'pole' installed in their soon-to-be marital home. It was slap bang in the middle of their living room so she could practise gyrating without moving from the telly. Curious elderly relatives were simply informed that it was a *Grand Designs*-style architectural feature, and no one seemed to question why it was the only semi in the street to boast one.

All was as it should be at a wedding. There was champagne, tipsy mothers-in-law, flirty bridesmaids, a nervous groom, one distant relative in a too-slutty dress, a pushy photographer and the optimum level of high jinks from the ushers.

'What a lovely day,' I sighed as Jamie and I went for a walk, taking a break from proceedings.

'Of course it is,' he smiled, gazing into my eyes as he pushed a strand of hair from my face. 'I'm with the woman I love.'

'Smooth talker,' I smirked.

'Ha! You do look amazing, though, Sam. Have I told you that?'

'Once or twice.' He hadn't stopped. He kissed me gently on the lips then pulled back.

'Unlike me. God, I hate this gear,' he laughed, shaking his head as he looked down despairingly at his suit.

'You look great,' I insisted, not entirely truthfully. He didn't look awful, but you know the way some people gain immediate stature when they put on a suit? I'm afraid Jamie wasn't one of them.

He acquired that awkward look of someone who'd picked up his first Primark two-piece in advance of an appearance at Youth Court. Not that the suit was cheap – far from it. Some men are simply sexier in jeans and T-shirts and my boyfriend was undoubtedly one of them.

'We'd better go back, hadn't we?' I asked.

'Yep. Back to the madness,' he grinned.

'Oh I've been to more riotous weddings,' I said. 'Besides, it's not yet nine. There's plenty of time for things to get out of hand.'

'I wasn't referring to that. I mean the whole thing's crazy.'

I frowned. 'What whole thing?'

'Weddings,' he replied matter-of-factly. 'What must this have cost Bella and Daniel? Five grand?' It was at least twice that. 'And for what? An excuse for a party. Insanity.'

I said nothing.

'Hope that doesn't disappoint you,' he grinned, throwing his arm around my waist casually. 'Because if you're after the puffy dress and big "do", you're with the wrong man.'

I rolled my eyes. 'Of course not! I mean, you're right. And I agree.'

I can't put my finger on why I gave that response. I suppose in that split second I realized something. That being together was what mattered.

That's the happy ending – not the other paraphernalia. Even *Four Weddings and a Funeral*, a film that revolves around the damn things, ended with the hero and heroine not getting hitched. So, actually, part of me thought this made Jamie more, not less, romantic.

'However,' he said, serious all of a sudden, 'there is one thing I do like about weddings.'

'Oh?'

'The fact that I get to strut my stuff,' he grinned. 'Come on, they're playing "I am the Resurrection".'

He grabbed my hand to lead me back into the Palm House, but I froze.

He spun round. 'What's up?'

'Erm, nothing,' I replied. 'I'm not a fan of dancing. You go, though. Luke'll dance with you.'

He screwed up his face. 'If I dance with Luke I'll risk the wrath of half the bridesmaids. Come on, I insist.'

Reluctantly, I approached the dance floor, feeling increasingly anxious. I don't do dancing in public. I don't know why, exactly, because I'm not catastrophically shy or anything – but this is my Achilles heel, even at a dad-dancing extravaganza such as a wedding, where the standard doesn't exactly match Anton du Beke's.

As we reached the dance floor, Luke was pogoing with his arms around one bride and two bridesmaids, which was good going even by his standards. Jamie took off his jacket and rolled up his shirt sleeves as we made our way to join them. He looked instantly more comfortable, instantly cooler.

The same could not be said for me. From the second I set foot on that dance floor, surrounded by guests giving it their all, I was overwhelmed with a realization of how uncool I was.

'I need the loo,' I muttered, leaving Luke, the bride and the bridesmaids to dive about enthusiastically with Jamie, who shook his head in mock despair. There's a part of my subconscious that now wishes I hadn't made my excuses; a part that knows I shouldn't have sought solace in another needless application of eyeliner, but put a bit more effort into being the sort of woman Jamie would've found impossible to leave.

Oh look, I know this isn't a big issue. In the scheme of things, it's minute. But it's another one for the list. The list of things that ultimately contributed to our downfall.

Chapter 25

I've seen my sister perform at the Royal Liverpool Philharmonic Hall more times than I can remember but I still feel like an impostor when I walk through its doors. It's so achingly sophisticated, despite the RLPO's valiant attempts to encourage plebs like me to give it a whirl in the hope that one bite of Rachmaninov's Piano Concerto No. 4 will convert them for life.

Of course, I don't need converting; they've got me for life already, courtesy of Julia. Which is a good job. Because, no matter how much I enjoy the experience, and it can be soul-stirring stuff, my knowledge of classical music wouldn't win me a Brownie badge in the subject.

It's not that I don't like how it sounds; I do, especially live and when my sister's playing. It's simply that most of the time I haven't the first clue what I'm listening to.

'Were you at Sibelius the other week?' asks the man from the row in front. He's a friendly sort in his late thirties, who never removes his *Dr Who* scarf, even if there's a heat wave. I've sat near him several times, though I've no idea if this is coincidence or because there's a season-ticket-type set-up, like at the football.

'I'm afraid I didn't,' I say earnestly, as if it was only because it clashed with Prokofiev at the Manchester Halle and not because I was probably at home waxing my bikini line.

'It was a real high point in the season,' he enthuses, in blissful ignorance of my blissful ignorance.

'Really?' I smile. 'Wish I'd been here.'

'You probably struggled to get a ticket?'

'Absolutely!'

He smiles. 'So what was the last concert you went to?'

'Er . . . the Killers,' I mutter, as the lights fall.

I'm soon listening to Mahler's Symphony No. 1, which I am determined to remember because it's electrifying. Of course, I know I won't. I'll do what I always do: recall the name of it for a week, at the end of which it will become the victim of my memory's indiscriminate delete button. I have this conversation with Julia when I meet her at the stage door at the end of the concert.

'How is it that I have no problem in remembering anything by Kasabian or Florence and the Machine, but this baffles me?'

'Because you're a simpleton?' she offers.

'Thank you, dear sister,' I smile sarcastically as we make our way down Hardman Street to grab a quick drink before we head home.

As I push open the door of the Magnet, my stomach rumbles and Julia glares at me. 'Haven't you eaten?'

'I meant to, but work was so crazy today I didn't get a chance. Remind me to get a bag of crisps in here.'

They don't have crisps; but they do have G&Ts, and that'll do for me at the moment, especially since I'm fond of this place. It's an intimate bar with eclectic music and lighting so dim you'd think there was an air raid.

'Have you done anything about your letter?' I ask, as we locate a booth and sink into its 1950s-style leather seats.

She shakes her head and gazes at her drink. 'No.'

'But you're obviously thinking of doing so?'

She nods and looks up. 'I wasn't prepared for how I'd feel if one of my parents sought me out. It's opened up all sorts of questions and, for the first time in my life, I've started to wonder what they're like. Curiosity's getting the better of me.'

'Has Mum said anything more?'

'We've had a brief chat, but she simply repeated the reassurances she made the other day.' Julia, who's usually unflappable, is clearly unsettled.

'So what are you worried about?'

'Oh come off it, Sam. You know why. There's a difference between the theory and the practice. Now that the prospect of me meeting him has become real, I think something's shifted in Mum. I can see it. It'd be impossible for this to be no big deal for her.'

I sip my drink. 'Do you think you'll end up meeting him?'

'Oh there are lots of steps before I have to decide that. I haven't even written back yet. I just need to put one foot in front of the other. I suppose, though, that once I think I've got my head round the idea, I may take the plunge.' She takes a deep breath. 'I'll be terrified.'

I lean over and clutch her hand. 'Anyone would be.'

'Well. We're a long way from that. So, come on,' she says, clearly wanting to change the subject. 'What's the latest on Jamie? Have you seen him recently? It must be a month since you split up, is it?'

I nod. Then I wonder where to start. Julia always liked Jamie. Well, almost always. There was one occasion when he turned up late to Sunday lunch following a marathon drinking session with the band, and she was more indignant on my behalf than I could bother myself to be. But mainly they got on well. Although she's a classical musician, she loves all types of music and was more than happy to chat to him about his band, his guitar and his own aspirations. Even if Split Atom were as likely to hit the dizzy heights of rock stardom as they were to win the Ryder Cup.

We're two drinks down and about to call it a night, when a shadow is cast over our table.

'You, lady, look gorgeous!' It's Lisa, Jamie's sister. She is dressed in leggings, jelly sandals and a cardigan so large it must've taken several decades to knit.

'Er . . . so do you.' That is the best I can do. I stand to give her a kiss on the cheek.

'I'm on a hen night,' she tells us, slurping her drink as she motions to a group of women in the corner. 'Denise at work is getting married. She's fifty-seven. Let that be a lesson to you,

Sam. Just because our Jamie – the idiot – has been daft enough to let you go, it doesn't mean you'll be left on the shelf.'

'Oh I never—'

'Speaking of Jamie,' she continues, barely pausing for breath, 'he's out tonight.'

I swallow. 'Really?' I reply, trying not to look too interested.

'The blokes from work have dragged him out. We bumped into them in Mathew Street. Don't think he's enjoying it much. You know what he's like . . . only usually goes to all those weird grungy places. Tonight, he's surrounded by people drinking alcopops and talking about *Top Gear*. Hey –' she nudges me conspiratorially – 'get down there and say hello.' She gives me a protracted wink that makes it seem as though something's flown into her eye.

'We were heading home, actually,' I tell her, glancing at Julia. 'It's a week night and I was already out on Saturday and . . .'

'Suit yourself,' Lisa shrugs. 'Well, I'd better run. Denise has been given a shop's worth of sex toys and the poor love hasn't a clue what to do with them. Looks like I'm in for a long night.'

As she scuttles away, I take a sip of my drink and glance furtively at Julia.

'You don't need to say anything,' she tells me.

'What do you mean?'

'Drink up. Mathew Street, here we come.'

Chapter 26

A strange transformation overcomes me as we head to Mathew Street in a taxi. Maybe it's due to the combination of alcohol, adrenalin and a particularly bumpy taxi ride.

'Why do you look so nervous?' Julia asks. 'You lived with the man for years.'

'It's ridiculous, I know,' I reply, shaking my head. 'But I want him back so badly I feel as though every time I see him, I've got to make the impression count.'

She frowns. 'You look gorgeous. It'll count without you doing anything. So relax.'

What Julia is forgetting is that Mathew Street is permanently populated by the most glamorous women in the north of England . . . and their sisters, cousins and badminton partners. And, while Jamie is undoubtedly attracted to understated beauty rather than full-on razzle-dazzle, he's also a red-blooded, one thousand per cent heterosexual man.

Julia seems to read my thoughts. 'Sam, you look gorgeous,' she repeats.

I take a deep breath and open my make-up bag, examining

myself in my compact mirror. Actually, I really don't look bad tonight. Losing half a stone helps, but it's more than that. My make-up is sultry, the black chiffon shirt sexy (at least now an extra button is undone), and I'm having my first good hair day since 2009. Or maybe, after only two G&Ts, I've got beer goggles about myself.

It's a good job too. It's only a Thursday night, but I step out of the taxi into a blingathon: flocks of short spangly dresses, sky-high heels and acres of flesh on show. This has the potential to intimidate me, but I'm determined that it won't. I'm a woman on a mission.

'Where do we start? It's years since I've been down here,' mutters Julia, striding to keep up as I march down the street. There are seven or eight bars and we've no idea where Jamie might be.

I look up and spot someone I recognize smoking in a doorway: Kevin, a young colleague of Jamie's with a Jim Royle paunch and a goatee so patchy it looks as though a family of field mice have been at it. I decide not to let on to him as we glide past the bouncers. That's not because I don't want to talk to Kevin eventually, but simply because my immediate priority is locating my target.

The bar is loud, hot and starting to get busy, but despite the number of revellers, I spot Jamie seconds after I walk through the door. The experience is like being winded.

Instead of weeping into a beer bottle, mourning our relationship, my ex-boyfriend is pinned against the bar by a brunette who is the definition of glamour.

My first instinct is to dive over and rescue him. But as I head in his direction I realize something that makes me feel queasy. It's not that he's exactly reciprocating. Not . . . exactly. But though her body language is so assertive it's one step short of unzipping his trousers with her central incisors, there's something undeniable about his reaction. The look in his eye. The way he's breathing.

He's not saying or doing anything wrong . . . not that I can see from this distance. And while I couldn't say for certain it's an experience he's actively enjoying, I can say for certain that it's an experience he isn't not enjoying. Which is enough to stop me in my tracks.

I flash a look at Julia.

'I'm sure he . . . wishes she wasn't doing that,' she says without conviction as the woman dips her finger in her drink and licks it slowly, as though she's appearing on a DVD with four Xs in the title.

'I'm sure,' I reply through gritted teeth as anger – and jealousy – bubble up inside me.

I could react in one of two ways. I could leave in tears, my short-lived burst of self-confidence shattered. Or I could do what any self-respecting woman would do. Have a large drink – and fight back.

I'm not going to let Jamie and this harlot make me feel envious. No bloody way. I'm going to beat them at their own game.

Chapter 27

I scan the bar like a heat-seeking missile programmed to locate the foxiest-looking male in the place.

It doesn't take long. Within minutes, I've bought myself a super-sized G&T and have zoomed in on someone at the other end of the bar who appears to be by himself. Which is baffling – and a miracle. This guy isn't just handsome: he's dynamite, with electric-blue eyes and features so chiselled they'd be at home on a Mills & Boon hero called Maximilian De Bigbollocks.

'Are you all right by yourself for a minute?' I ask Julia.

'Of course. I need to pop to the Ladies, anyway. Are you going to talk to Jamie?'

'Not yet,' I mutter, heading in the opposite direction.

I stride purposefully towards Mr Miracle, undoing another button and fluffing up my hair; behaviour that's totally alien to me. Even when I was single I never used to 'come on' to blokes. I couldn't do it. It was one of those things, a bit like an overarm serve in tennis, that I could never master, no matter how long and hard I tried.

Add to that the fact that my inner goddess hasn't had a proper outing for six years and I'm petrified. In the light of this, all I can do is employ the same tactic advocated for public speaking: tell myself that all that counts is to look and sound as though I know what I'm doing. Even if I'm falling to pieces inside.

'Um . . . hi,' I murmur, lowering my voice breathily as I lean on the bar. I'd be less intimidated if he wasn't so spectacular-looking, but that of course would defeat the object.

'Oh, er, hi,' he replies.

'I'm Sam. I couldn't resist coming over and saying hello . . .' I take a large mouthful of my drink to compose myself. 'I think you're . . . lovely.'

I'm cringing as I say this; it feels outrageously over the top. This is the sort of behaviour you'd expect from those women who engage in antics peddled to the tabloids by Max Clifford.

'Oh,' he says, looking surprised. 'Well . . . gosh.'

Then he does something I don't think I've ever seen a man do. He blushes. In fact, he's so flustered that he drops his twenty-pound note – into his pint of lager. 'Oh shoot! Oh . . . sugar! Oh Lordy, Lordy, Lord.'

He frantically dips his hand into the glass, sploshing beer onto the bar, which he then mops up with a napkin, apologizing profusely to an unmoved bar tender.

'Are you here by yourself?' I ask, attempting to reconnect.

'Er . . . no. I-I'm with my friend, Terry,' he stammers, looking simultaneously terrified and as if he's about to explode with excitement.

'So what's your name?' I ask, leaning in a little closer.

'Gordon.'

'Gordon,' I repeat, raising a seductive eyebrow. 'As in Ramsay? Are you as . . . fiery as he is?'

He gulps. 'I don't think so. Nobody's ever said that. Not so far, anyway. Definitely not. Well. Hmm.' He looks away awkwardly.

'Oh,' I giggle, flicking back my hair, 'maybe they just haven't seen that side of you. I wonder if I could . . . bring it out?'

He looks as though his brain is about to melt.

'So . . . are you from Liverpool?' I continue, deciding to tone things down a little.

He picks up his drink with trembling hands and takes a large mouthful. 'Runcorn.'

'That's not far,' I smile. His body is so broad and hard you'd think he'd been born in a gym and never left. 'So you've probably been to this place a few times before.'

'Not really,' he replies, gulping again. 'It's my mother, you see. She doesn't like me going far.'

'Oh. So you just go out in Runcorn?'

'No.'

'Oh.'

This isn't going as smoothly as I'd hoped.

'I rarely go out. Except Mother's in hospital having a hysterectomy so I came here with Terry straight from visiting. She'd needed quite a lot tonight – grapes, her *Reader's Digest* crossword books and some sanitary towels. The ones at the hospital weren't up to standard.'

This is all wrong.

The physical manifestation of this man simply does not correlate with his brain. He is without question the sexiest-looking bloke in the place, yet I cannot think of a less sexy conversation, short of him filling me in on further elaborate details of his mother's women's troubles.

But as I glance at Jamie on the other side of the room, I feel a rush of determination. I've got to stick to my guns.

Besides, Jamie never has to meet this guy and discover that he has all the charisma of a decomposing corpse. He only has to see me with him – and hopefully imagine I'm succumbing to a seduction technique that could teach James Bond a thing or two.

'What do you do for a living?' I ask, brushing dust off his shoulder. It's an old chestnut but it seems to work. He gulps again.

'I've just got a new job. As a salesman at Carpets R Us.'

'Fascinating,' I breathe, deliberately making my pupils dilate. He is momentarily fixated by my mouth and I take the opportunity to run my tongue slowly across my lips and flutter my eyelashes. He takes another gulp of beer. Then gulps once more. This man could gulp for his country.

'I don't know how long it'll last,' he says anxiously. 'Selling isn't my forte.'

'Really . . .?' I murmur, looking over to Jamie again. 'A gorgeous guy like you?'

At this, he splutters out his beer and launches into a coughing fit that makes me consider calling a paramedic.

'Are you okay?'

'Um . . . yes,' he replies, his eyes bloodshot and watery. 'Where was I? Oh yes, carpets. Well, Terry got me the job. But I've been doing it for two weeks and have sold only one. And that was . . . well, the management weren't very happy. I took down the measurements wrong. It was a foot too small. It was a lovely shagpile, as well. I felt awful.'

I glance up and realize that Jamie's looking in our direction. He's parted from the brunette slightly, as if something else has caught his attention. I sincerely hope it's me. Then a brilliant thought hits me.

'What do you think of my flower?' I say, deliberately forcing him to look at the rose at my neckline.

It makes his knees buckle.

'Ummmmm . . .' he says, averting his eyes, mortified.

'It's not wilting, is it?' I add, flashing a look at Jamie. It's a split-second look, not long at all. But long enough to notice that he has abandoned the brunette and is on his way over.

'Right!' I say, hastily grabbing my bag. 'Hold that thought – I'm going to the loo.'

I'm about to leave, when I feel compelled to spin round and add, 'Do you mind if I make an observation?'

'Of course not.'

'You are lovely – I meant what I said. You should have a bit more . . . belief in yourself.'

He straightens his back and looks as if this is the nicest thing anyone's said to him in a year. Which is a tragedy, but one I can't hang around thinking about.

I glide across the room – spotting Julia chatting to a woman I recognize as one of her old school friends – and weave through the crowds in the direction of the toilet, slowly enough to give Jamie a chance to catch up. Then I hear two words that send adrenalin rushing down my spine.

'Sam, wait!'

Chapter 28

I try to look shocked. I suspect Cate Blanchett won't be too concerned about her next Oscar bid, but it's the best I can do.

'Jamie! Fancy seeing you here.'

'Yeah, weird,' he says, shaking his head. 'I'd never normally dream of setting foot in a place like this, but the guys from work wanted to come. What are you doing here?'

'I went to see Julia at the Phil and she wanted a drink. We stumbled on this place. Coincidence, eh?' I laugh. 'So . . . the girl you were chatting to – is she new at work?' I can't help myself.

'Oh that's Lauren. She's the little sister of Michael, our new manager.' He says this dismissively, but I feel distinctly unreassured. 'What about you? Who were you with?' He looks over my shoulder.

'Oh . . .' My mind whirrs, not least with fears about my newfound competition. 'That's . . . Demitri.'

'Oh,' he says, raising an eyebrow.

'He's a friend,' I shrug, in a way that I hope looks distinctly suspicious. 'I know him through Julia.'

'So he's a musician?' he asks, not looking nearly jealous enough.

'Er . . . no. He lives near her. No, he's got a far more exciting career than that.'

'Oh?'

My brain spins with possibilities as I attempt to choose the most envy-inducing job on the planet. Underwear model? Cardiac surgeon? Owner of an upmarket boutique hotel? None seem nearly impressive enough. Then a flash of inspiration bursts into my head – and straight out of my mouth before I can gag myself.

'He's a spy.'

Jamie snorts and looks at me like I'm demented. 'A spy?'

We turn to look at Gordon as he enthusiastically blows his nose on a napkin, then examines the resulting contents.

'Obviously, he doesn't do it any more,' I splutter. 'I mean, that'd be ridiculous – because I'd have told you all about it and blown his cover.' I try to compose myself and look cool again. 'No . . . those days are over for Demitri. He, er, runs a property company these days. He's done very well for himself.' I decide that this is a far more manageable lie.

'Oh. He looks young,' replies Jamie.

'Yep. Early thirties and a millionaire . . . Can't be bad, eh? He drives, er . . . a Lambrini.'

Jamie blinks. 'You mean Lamborghini.'

Shit. 'That's the one!' I reply. 'He's not shallow at all, though. Very modest. Such a nice guy.'

Something catches Jamie's attention on the other side of the bar and I panic that I'm starting to lose him. That my crap about Gordon the carpet salesman hasn't had anything like the desired effect. I take another large gulp of my drink and hope I'm being paranoid just because I'm tipsy. And I really am tipsy. You know how, on some evenings, you can drink and drink and not feel drunk, then it hits you in a word-slurring, head-spinning, need-to-sit-down-before-I-fall-down sort of way?

I feel just like that. Although I haven't exactly drunk and drunk. I've only had three – the last one a double – but the effect appears to have been magnified by the fact that it's ten hours since I ate.

'Well . . . I think the guys want to move on shortly,' he says.

'What?' I blurt out. 'Oh . . . it feels like ages since we had a chat.'

He looks into my eyes and goes quiet. He looks glazed and serious and I get a surge of hope that I've made a connection with him again. But I know it's not enough. I've got to act. Having a twinge of regret isn't enough. I need Jamie to feel as desperate for me as I am for him. The problem is that I haven't a clue how to make that happen.

At that very moment, my guardian angel arrives.

He's an unlikely guardian angel, admittedly, but these things come in all shapes and sizes. Including carpet salesmen.

'I've been thinking about what you said,' says Gordon, looking significantly more nervous than 007 ever did in front of a woman. 'You know, the last thing you said to me. About—'

'Yes – I know,' I interrupt.

'Well,' he continues, taking a deep breath and apparently oblivious to Jamie's presence. 'Would you like to dance?'

If I was going on my instincts alone, there'd only be one answer and that would be a definite no: A, because of my chronic aversion to dancing, and B, because I'm standing here with the love of my life. Yet, when a flicker of disquiet appears on Jamie's face, I know that this is my chance. So I reply in the last way he'd ever expect. With an enthusiastic smile and a small but unprecedented sentence: 'I'd love to.'

Chapter 29

I can't decide whether the alcohol that's passed through my empty stomach and is now coursing through my bloodstream is a help or a hindrance. On the one hand, I know what booze does to my coordination. On the other, Dutch courage is an absolute necessity in this situation. Put simply, I couldn't do this unless I was on my way to being – to put it poetically – slightly lampshaded.

Under normal circumstances, my heart would be racing in panic as I step onto the dance floor. But this time, it's different. This time, it's personal.

I can feel Jamie's eyes burning into my back as Gordon takes my hand, and, knowing the role this is playing in my quest to win him back, I decide there's only one way to handle it: with bullish self-belief.

As the Black Eyed Peas song trails off and is replaced by another, I close my eyes, determined to submit to the music. To just go with it . . . whatever it is. The first beats begin and my eyes ping open. I can barely believe my luck: it's Shakira's 'Hips Don't Lie'.

The opening track on my *Belly Dance Abs Blast* DVD!

Every woman on the dance floor ups her game immediately – it's just one of those songs – and I know I've got serious competition.

But, for the first time in my life, I'm confident of stepping up to the mark. Gordon sways self-consciously as I get myself in position and launch into the only dance I've *ever* learned, courtesy of repeated instruction by Princess Karioca in my living room.

I know I'm capable of the wiggly hips and sashays but, under the circumstances, I also feel the need to . . . soup it up a little.

So I don't just shimmy . . . I shimmy like a Brazilian street dancer whose toes are on fire. This is no time to be shy and retiring: this is the time to give it everything I've got. And boy, do I. My hips go up and down, round and round; they swivel so madly you'd think they'd been given a squirt of WD40.

Princess Karioca's words are shrieking through my brain: 'Keep them loose! Keep them loose!'

My hips are as loose as a Weightwatcher's Gold Member's trousers. And together with my pouts, hair flicking and eyelid batting every time I glance at Gordon, he'd have to be in a coma to not be left with the (totally false) impression that I want to rip off his clothes.

Of course, I'm not following the *Belly Dance Abs Blast* DVD to the letter. Nothing like it. I'm going with the flow, frolicking so fast and energetically that I can see the reaction of no one – until I hone in on my partner. Whipping my shoulders back and forth while I simultaneously muster up the most seductive look I can,

I drape one hand on Gordon's shoulder and the other around his waist.

It's like the move Olivia Newton-John did on John Travolta at the end of *Grease*, only more overtly sexy: a soft-porn version of Sandra Dee. Gordon's eyes pop so far out of his head I'm convinced they're going to land in someone's drink.

'Enjoying yourself?' I murmur.

He nods, wide-eyed, as I let go and start twirling . . . and twirling . . . and twirling. It feels amazing . . . then not – as I stumble into a bloke behind me, nearly breaking several of his toes.

He pushes me back into position, while I hope I've managed to make it look like a perfectly choreographed move. I launch again into the routine that's technically brilliant for toning up your six-pack – but is doing a damn good job now too.

I deliberately don't catch Jamie's eye, despite him being at the front of my mind.

When the song reaches a crescendo, I fling out my arms and fall to my knees, significantly more enthusiastically than I ever do in front of my DVD. But it feels like the only fitting end to what I'm confident is a spectacular performance.

It's Julia's voice I hear first in the commotion.

'Honestly, I know what it looks like, but I promise you . . . my sister is not the type to do drugs.'

I stand up, feeling slightly more woozy than I expected.

'There's no way that exhibition was solely with the aid of a couple of Bacardis and Coke,' says the bouncer. 'Now, come on. Out. Both of you. And don't let me see you in here again.'

Within minutes I find myself outside the club, burning with a sense of injustice.

'What on earth washh all that about?' I ask.

'I might ask you the same question,' says Julia, shaking her head in disbelief. '*Are* you on drugs?'

'Don't be ridiculoush. I was dancing!'

'You weren't just dancing,' she says disapprovingly, holding her arm out to flag down a taxi. 'It looked like someone had booked a stripper.'

'I was belly dancing. That's how you do it,' I tut. 'I've got a DVD. Honestly, I've got a DVD.' I don't know why I thought saying it twice would convince her any more.

'I don't care what DVDs you've got . . . that did not look like belly dancing.'

I try to come up with a robust response. Only one thing springs to mind. 'I'm telling you . . . I've got a DVD.' Three times a charm. 'Was Jamie watching?'

We climb into a taxi and she gives the driver our addresses. 'Everyone was watching,' she answers.

I grin. 'Was he impressed?'

She stands up from her seat opposite and comes to sit next to me, putting her arm around my shoulders. 'Oh Sam.'

'What?' I ask.

She gives me a big squeeze. 'That hug is because I won't be there when you wake up tomorrow morning. When you are so going to need one.'

Chapter 30

I am never, ever drinking again. That's never. I am struggling to convey the level of mortification with which I wake the following morning but will simply say that it hangs heavily in my head, like a dark, festering blanket, poisoning my every thought.

This is not just 'the fear', when I worry that I've done or said something inappropriate. This is beyond fear; this is a certainty.

As I drag myself out of bed and start getting ready for work, a text from Julia lands.

How are we this morning?

U were right about that hug, I reply.

Aw . . . never mind, sis. You got Jamie's attention anyway! x

I let out a groan that sounds like the hounds of hell on the cusp of a full moon, before pressing the call button.

'What does that mean?' I rasp the second Julia answers.

'Good morning,' she replies. My sister is never hungover. Largely because my sister never gets drunk. In fact, she never acts with anything but total decorum. I wish it ran in the family. 'How's your head?'

'Come on. What does that mean? Was I that bad?'

'Actually,' she says thoughtfully, '"bad" isn't the word. There were a lot of people in that room who thought you were pretty damn good.'

'Really?' I straighten my back, feeling a vague swell of optimism.

'Mainly the men,' she clarifies. 'Particularly the sleazier ones. They loved you. The women generally weren't as keen.'

'What are you saying?' I ask defensively. 'I was trying to . . . let go a little, that's all. To really get into it.'

'If that was your objective I can say categorically that you achieved it.'

'You're trying to imply I looked like a slut,' I say, hoping she'll deny it.

'Was it only an implication . . .?'

'Ohhhwwww!'

'Oh come on, Sam. I'm only kidding. You're right: it wasn't that bad. Your technique itself was pretty accomplished. If you ever find yourself out of work, there are several lap-dancing bars that'd give you a job like a shot.'

'Do you have to?' I sob. 'Oh God . . . Jamie's going to hate me. He's going to think he was shacked up with a slapper for the last six years. He's never going to want to look at me again. He's going to—'

'Actually, Sam,' she interrupts.

'Yes?'

'I wouldn't worry. He looked as jealous as hell.'

I hear from Jamie that evening, when I'm lying in the bath. I'd cracked open the aromatherapy gift set that I got last Christmas, which has, until now, never seen the light of day. It consists of a satin eye masque that looks like the sort of thing that Margot from *The Good Life* would wear to bed, and several little bottles of oil.

I couldn't decide whether to go for the lavender, to try to relax me (as I've felt anything but all day), or the grapefruit, to energize me (ditto). So I went for broke and threw in both. The result is that I feel slightly schizophrenic and definitely no better.

When my phone lets out a little bleep I jolt out of my fitful snooze, splashing water over the edge of the bath as I grapple with my masque and fling it on the floor, then scramble to the sink. My hands are still wet when I read the text, which isn't ideal, but the second I see it's from Jamie I can't even think about bothering to dry them.

Hey . . . how's it going? Nice to see you last night x

'What the hell does that mean?' I say out loud. But I know what it means. At least I think so. It means my plan is really starting to work.

Chapter 31

Over the next week, Jamie becomes an almost constant presence in my life. It's as if he's never left. Whether he's round at the house to pick up more clothes, or popping into work to drop off some random household paperwork, I'm starting to see more of him than I did when we lived together.

Then, a week after the Mathew Street incident, he texts to ask if we could grab a coffee at lunchtime. I don't pick it up until three o'clock, when I phone him straight away.

'Is after work any good?' I ask.

'Umm . . . yeah, sure. I was supposed to have something on but . . . yeah.'

We meet at a pub near his work called the Fat Pheasant.

It's a tiny, dingy hovel of an establishment, the sort of place Jamie finds mysteriously appealing. He describes it as having 'character'. Which basically means it features a variety of grubby blokes looking as if they've developed cobwebs in their ears and the toilets are cleaned with a level of attention you'd expect in a Vietnamese prison.

He's at the bar when I arrive. I'm flustered and red-faced after my last meeting of the day overran. He kisses me on the cheek and I inhale his smell and close my eyes briefly. God, he smells so good. Particularly compared with the rest of the clientele.

'What are you drinking?' he asks.

'Diet Coke,' I say firmly. The never-drinking-again rule is sticking, believe me.

He has a pint of bitter and pays for the drinks as I look for a seat by the door. I like to have a visible escape route when in places like this. And, apart from the dubious patches on the seats and jammy rings of lager that have clearly adorned the table for several days, it's perfect.

'Great boozer this, isn't it?' he muses in all seriousness as he sits next to me.

'Hmm,' I reply.

Then there's a silence. Another of those awkward ones.

'I haven't really mentioned last week at Mathew Street,' I find myself announcing. 'I was sooo drunk.'

'I know,' he replies with a half-smile. 'You were a lot more . . . gregarious than I've seen before.'

I let out a little laugh. 'Well, there's a euphemism.'

'Whatever happened to the girl who didn't like dancing?' he asks softly.

I'm tempted to say, '*Belly Dance Abs Blast* is what happened', but manage not to. 'I suppose a few things have changed about me lately.'

'Really?' he asks with a flash of anxiety.

I shrug. 'I think I've worked out that life goes on, with or without you. That I'm determined to be the happy and positive person I always was.'

He suddenly looks sad. Unbelievably sad.

'I still wish you were in my life, though,' I reply. And when he responds with a smile I feel a swell of pure unadulterated love for him.

'Oh Sam,' he murmurs, and I notice his lip trembling. As our eyes meet it feels as though there's an electric current running between us and I'm overwhelmed with an absolute conviction that I can never be without this man. Not ever. 'Sam . . . I don't know where to begin.'

I reach over to take his hand and he squeezes it back so hard it hurts my fingers.

'Sam, I'm so confused,' he whispers.

'Still?' I say.

He nods, his face tortured. 'Some days I know exactly what I want, I know exactly what I've got to do . . . and that's South America.' He glances at me, then looks at his drink. 'Then other days, or nights . . . like last week in Mathew Street . . .'

'What did you want last Thursday?' I prompt, convinced that if I don't ask he'll say nothing.

He looks up. 'I wanted you. Unequivocally, I wanted you.'

I swallow, feeling tears well in my eyes. 'Then come back to me, Jamie. It's not too late.'

He nods. 'Can I ask you something, Sam?'

'Of course,' I say, breathless with anticipation.

He inhales deeply. 'I know you've got men chasing after you left, right and centre. You always had.'

This isn't remotely true, but I'm more than happy for Jamie to maintain the fantasy.

'And on Thursday night, when I saw how much attention you were attracting . . . well, it was a wake-up call.'

'I didn't mean it to be,' I say as convincingly as possible. 'I was a bit drunk and—'

'You don't need to explain,' he interrupts. 'It was nice to see you letting loose a little. And you looked . . . well, you looked amazing.'

Julia would disagree.

'The point I'm making is that . . . Oh look, things are far from settled in my mind. I've booked my flight and everything but . . . flights can be cancelled.'

'What date do you leave?' I ask.

'Tuesday the thirteenth of December.'

The timescale isn't news but I still feel as though I've been punched in the stomach.

'I know you could go out and get another boyfriend tomorrow if you wanted,' continues Jamie. 'And you're perfectly within your rights to do so. I suppose what I want . . . what I'm asking, Sam . . . Look, I need you to leave the door open for me. I need you to not shut me out. Just while I get my head together and work out what I want and need.'

Despite wanting Jamie more than anything, I feel a twinge of indignation at this request. I mean, he's dumped me. He's announced he's leaving me. Yet he still wants me to leave the door open?

Then another question explodes into my mind: if Jamie is essentially asking me to not go out with anyone else, what is his situation on this front? Is he allowed to see other women while we're in this state of limbo?

'It goes without saying that I haven't even thought about seeing anyone else,' he says softly, as if reading my thoughts.

I feel stupidly pleased about this, but make sure I don't let it show. And I think back to my original plan. I can't make this too easy for him. I can't let him think I'll just drop everything for him and be there whenever he decides to pull himself together.

'Jamie, I will leave the door open for you,' I tell him. 'But not unconditionally. If you're asking me to not go near another man while you try to make up your mind over the course of the next few months, then . . . I'm not sure that's reasonable.'

He looks as though someone's stabbed him in the chest. But I had to say this, even if the truth is that I couldn't even look at another man. I've got to give him some incentive to want to get back with me.

He nods. 'Is there someone else?'

'No! No, of course not. I'm talking about the principle,' I say. 'Plus, you know . . . while I'm willing to leave the door open, as you put it, that can't mean me sitting at home alone, praying that you're going to see the light of day.'

'O-of course,' he stammers. 'I'd never expect you to.'

'I need to get out there. In case you don't make the right decision.'

I glance up at him, desperate for him to leap in and say, 'But I will! I will make the right decision! Sod all this messing about. I already know what I want and I'm not prepared to risk letting you go.'

He catches my eye and smiles. 'I understand, Sam. And that's totally fair enough. Do you want another drink?'

Chapter 32

In the five days that follow, the contact Jamie makes with me starts to tail off. I'll admit I start to worry. It's not that he doesn't get in touch at all, because he does. However, it's definitely more intermittent.

But when I speak to Lisa on the phone on Tuesday, as I'm heading to the car park after work, she's convinced that I remain uppermost in Jamie's mind.

'Oh he's just been on a bit of a bender for a few days. The band were playing at the weekend,' she explains. 'But he had a day off today so he popped over to play with the kids. And I'll tell you this: I know he's bought the plane ticket but, seriously, there's hope. No doubt. He's thinking about you all the time. I can tell.'

'Why . . . what did he say?' I ask.

'It wasn't what he said so much as a feeling I got.'

'How can you get a feeling if it wasn't from what he said?'

'Intuition,' she replies knowingly.

'He didn't say anything about bumping into me in Mathew Street?'

'Er, no.'

'What about meeting me in the pub after work on Thursday?'

'Not that, no.'

'Did he ask about whether you'd seen me lately?'

'Well, no.'

I sigh. 'Did he say anything whatsoever about me, Lisa?'

She pauses. 'Strictly speaking, no. The idiot. This was despite my best efforts.'

'What did you say?'

'Well, I asked him if he wanted to share some thoughts with me because, if so, I'd be more than happy to give my honest and forthright opinion. And if anybody knows about holding a relationship together, it's me. Dave and I are solid as a rock and always will be. Admittedly, I've got *Hot Sex* volumes three, four, five and six partly to thank, but that's irrelevant.'

I'm about to change the subject before she gets on to Dave's toe-sucking techniques, but she does it for me.

'I mean, if the only person he's going to for advice is Luke, then God help him.'

When the call ends ten minutes later, it's that sentence that stays with me. Lisa's right about Luke. He isn't just Jamie's landlord at the moment; he's his best friend and, presumably, confidant as well.

Given that even a sniff of anything approaching commitment brings Luke out in a rash, I can't help worrying about his influence. The second I get Lisa off the phone, I dial Luke's number, hoping that, for once in his life, his diary is free tonight.

*

Luke and I meet at Pod, a smart low-key tapas bar five minutes from his house. We're there early but there's still a decent post-work crowd, the female contingent of which cannot prise their eyes away from my companion.

'What's it like, knowing you attract so much attention?' I ask, sipping a Diet Coke.

'Such a burden,' he sighs, smirking.

I suppress a smile. 'Yes, I can tell you hate it. Haven't you been at work today?'

Luke is freshly showered, wearing jeans and a simple, long sleeved T-shirt. It's nothing special, but he still manages to look as though his alternative career is modelling Y-fronts.

'Day off,' he replies. 'Now, come on . . . I know you've spent every day since I met you disapproving of my every move, so what prompted the change of heart?'

'What change of heart?' I screw up my nose.

'Well, you've asked me out for drinks, haven't you?' he grins.

'I did not ask you out for drinks,' I point out.

'What's this, then? I'm out. There are drinks. You asked me here. Therefore you asked me out for drinks. Oh look, don't worry. You're only human . . .'

I don't rise to the bait. 'I want a chat about Jamie.'

He tuts. 'Credit me with some insight, won't you? I was only kidding.'

I don't know what to say to that. I suspect everyone's sick of me talking about my failed relationship by now. He reaches across and squeezes my hand reassuringly. The female bar tender,

175

a pretty brunette wearing enough lip gloss to lubricate an internal combustion engine, looks consumed with envy.

'Hey. Talk about it all you want. What do you want to know? Or ask? I'm not sure I can shed any light but I'll do my best.'

He lets go of my hand and reaches for his beer as I take a deep breath. 'Well, does he talk about me?'

'You asked me that last time you saw me.'

'What's the answer?'

'Mmm . . . yes.'

'That means no.'

'It doesn't!'

'You hesitated too long,' I accuse him.

'Oh the logic of the female sex,' he mutters. 'Look, I'm not sure I'm any good at this stuff.'

'I thought you considered yourself a master at the art of manipulating women?'

'Manipulating?' he says, looking hurt. 'I don't manipulate anyone. I love women. And it's true what I said, that I am looking for the right person. I am just—'

'Yeah, so you say,' I interrupt, not believing him for a second.

He holds my eye. 'God, you're tough. I'm sure I don't deserve the scorn you pour on me.'

'Oh I'm sure you do.'

'Another drink?' purrs the brunette. I'm tempted to move the drip tray under her chin.

'Before you completely give up on me, Samantha, I have some news for you that may alter your horribly low opinion of me.'

'Do your best,' I reply.

He looks down at his drink. 'I've met someone.'

I frown, scrutinizing his expression. 'Someone?'

He looks at me seriously, before his face breaks into a smile. 'Someone . . . special.'

I blink. 'Liar!'

'I'm not lying!' he protests . . . and boy, do I come to believe him.

I spend three hours with Luke, and at least two and a half of those are devoted to discussing the new woman in his life, who is beautiful, smart . . . and, from what I can tell, giving him a serious run for his money.

'I have no idea where I stand with her,' he says, bewildered. 'I've never been keener on someone. I'm so keen I hardly know what to do with myself. Yet I have no idea whether the feeling's mutual. This has never happened before. It's a nightmare.'

'How many dates have you been on?' I ask.

'Three. And they're like no date I've been on before. We've only kissed – and I feel like a teenager again. I mean, what am I? Some sort of amateur?'

I grin. 'You're falling for her.'

He looks deeply worried. 'Christ . . . do you think so?'

'Who knows? Sounds promising, though.'

'Whatever it is, I need to pull myself together. I'm starting to be embarrassed for myself.'

We do get round to discussing Luke's take on his best friend's state of mind, although it isn't massively insightful. He simply says that Jamie still has feelings for me. It's also clear that those feelings are confused.

'Tell me something I don't know,' I mutter.

'Come on,' he says, finishing his drink and standing up. 'It's time I got you home.'

'Why, have you got another date?'

He rolls his eyes as we head to the door and he holds it open for me. When I get to my car, I click the key to unlock it then turn to him.

It's dark but the amber glow of the street light on his face makes him look . . . well, put it this way: I've known Luke so long that there are times I forget how breathtaking he is. This particular moment in time isn't one of them.

'Listen, thanks for tonight, Luke. It means a lot.'

'No problem,' he replies. 'What are friends for? Besides, I may be calling on you again for some advice. Assuming I get past date number four.'

'I'm sure you will,' I reassure him.

'I'm not,' he laughs, and as he heads in the other direction, I can't help wondering if the man who's broken a thousand hearts has finally met his match.

Chapter 33

The approach employed by Piers Smith – a.k.a. my boss – when managing the Liverpool office isn't what you'd call hands-on. I sometimes wonder if he's forgotten there is a Liverpool office until I turn up in Manchester at the fourteenth-floor penis extension that is his office, for our bi-monthly catch-up meeting. As ever, when I perch on a seat across from his ridiculously proportioned desk, clutching my A4 pad and pen, I get the impression that it takes a few seconds for him to register who I am. Which, I can't deny, has some benefits. As long as I keep my head down and hit our targets, Piers leaves me to get on with things. But there's a downside that's been gnawing at me for months.

'I wondered if you'd considered the issue of the reporting structure?' I ask tentatively. I've already talked him through next month's budget, explained our targets, and updated him on nine imminent events and several business leads I've generated. He was looking sleepy before I'd got to item two.

'Reporting structure?' he asks lazily, clicking on his mouse and failing to tear his eyes from the computer screen. He's playing Farmville, no doubt about it.

'We discussed it in my last appraisal,' I remind him, semi-apologetically. 'About how there are two staff members in the Liverpool office who report directly to you. And how that's not practical, given the distance . . . and the fact that you can't deal with them personally . . . and that the events they work on are ones I manage . . .'

I'm squirming through this waffle, though I don't know why. The set-up makes no sense at all, and only an unmitigated ego-maniac would construe my suggestion as an attempt to seize power.

'The upshot,' I say, straightening my back assertively, 'is that they'd be a lot easier to manage and motivate if they reported to me officially.'

Piers turns away from his computer, claps two suntanned hands together and inhales so deeply through both nostrils you'd think he was trying to hoover up dust on his desk. He's in his late forties and, to be fair, is looking well on it. Yet he's one of those men who, while technically good-looking – a chiselled-featured, sharp-suited version of Barbie's boyfriend, Ken – is simultaneously deeply unsexy. At least, I think so. Given that he seems to have bedded half the Manchester, Birmingham and Newcastle offices, unbeknown to his wife, Tracy, I'm apparently in a minority.

'Let me tell you something about leadership, Sal,' he purrs with a coffee-advert smile.

'Sam,' I correct him.

'Sam,' he repeats, nodding as if this was what he said in the first place. 'Leadership isn't something that comes from reporting structures. Leadership comes from here.' He taps a finger on his head. Twice. 'Allow me to lend you a book.'

He opens a vast drawer and roots around in it before flinging a paperback in my direction. It's bright red, with a retina-scorching pink title that reads: *Be a Winner Not a Wally!*

'Have a read of that,' he winks.

I shift in my seat. 'So . . . you wouldn't consider changing the reporting structure?'

He smiles. 'Tell you what. Why don't you email me with your ideas about the structure and I'll give it my consideration.'

'Erm, I did, Piers – a couple of times,' I mutter, finding it very difficult to conceal that I consider him a grade-A knobhead.

'Did you?' he replies, raising an eyebrow smoothly. 'Hmm. Which staff members are causing the issue?'

'It's not an issue, exactly . . . I don't want to overstate it. But Deana Arbinger and Natalie Maxwell.'

He looks at me blankly and shakes his head.

'Both blonde. Long legs. Tanned. Very, very tanned.'

Realization seeps across his face. 'Oh . . . those two! It's been a while since I had a one-to-one with those two,' he smiles.

I bite my lip.

He winks. 'Email me again and I'll see what I can do, eh?'

I'm still bubbling with indignation four hours later when I'm at Ellie's house, sitting on her patio watching the sun go down. The one thing that can be said for the issue is that, momentarily at least, it interrupts my constant thoughts about Jamie.

'Any more of that sparkly stuff going?' Ellie asks as Alistair emerges with a bottle of wine and some glasses.

'You've cleaned us out,' he says, pulling up a chair.

I wouldn't say Jamie, Ellie, Alistair and I were a regular four-some, but we certainly did the odd thing together. Sitting here like this prompts a vivid flashback of a barbeque at Ellie's mum's house last summer. I can't put my finger on anything specific that happened, but I do remember, as the smell of burnt sausages and British summertime infused the air, experiencing a real sense of contentment. Of everything being well and good with the world. It's not a feeling I have today.

'Don't be depressed about your crap boss,' says Ellie.

I snap out of my daze. 'Oh I'm not too worried about him.'

She nods. 'So what's eating you? Let me guess . . .'

'I'm fine,' I shrug, but, now she's mentioned it, my thoughts are dragged back to Jamie again.

She raises an eyebrow.

'Oh Ellie, it's not working,' I bluster. 'Our plan. My mission to win him back. Every time I think he's going to change his mind, he doesn't. He tells me he needs more time. Or that I should "leave the door open".' I roll my eyes.

Ellie shoots me a look, then glances at Alistair. He excuses himself to check that Sophie's still asleep.

'Is that what he said? That you should leave the door open?' She looks into the distance defiantly. 'I don't think that's a reasonable thing to ask you to do, Sam. I want to see you two back together more than anything. But part of me wonders whether this is just a prolonged period of purgatory for you while Jamie indulges his mini-midlife crisis.'

Now I start to get uncomfortable. 'It's not like that, Ellie. You know it isn't. He's confused, that's all.'

'How often are you in touch these days?'

'We text every day or two.'

'Well, he needs to start thinking of your feelings, not just his own.' She turns and clutches my hand before saying tentatively, 'You know, it really might be better for you to make a clean break.'

I pull my hand back in horror. 'Ellie! He's the love of my life. I couldn't make a break – clean or otherwise – even if I wanted to.' I take a deep breath and try to stay calm.

For the first time since the break-up I have a sense that she doesn't really understand. That she doesn't appreciate quite how much Jamie means to me.

'Ellie . . . he's simply asking me to give him some time, that's all. I'll admit it's killing me because all I want is for him to turn around and make the decision we all know is the right one. But I can't force the issue any more than anyone else.'

She bends down and picks up the wine bottle at her feet, topping up my glass before turning to her own.

'Okay,' she concedes. 'I'm frustrated with him, that's all.'

'You are?'

She bites her lip. 'I do think something, though. Don't bite my head off for suggesting this . . .'

'I've already eaten.'

'So far, the strategy has been for you to look like you're moving on. To stay cool, to not go to pieces, to make him a bit jealous by doing the odd bit of flirting. I don't think it's enough.'

'What do you mean?'

'So far, Sam, you've just pretended you're moving on. You haven't really been doing it. I think you need to stop pretending.'

'But I don't want to move on,' I protest. 'I want Jamie back and I'm not going to stop until either I succeed or he tells me he never wants to see me again.'

Ellie shakes her head. 'I think you're wrong to look at it like that. It's not healthy, Sam. You're obsessing over Jamie, when you need to remind yourself that you've got as much going for you without him as you did with him.'

'This is starting to sound like an edition of *Loose Women*.'

'At the moment, Jamie knows he could have you back in a second, so he has no incentive to get his act together. You need to disabuse him of that notion immediately.'

'How do I do that?'

'Easy,' she says, draining her glass. 'We need to get you a boyfriend.'

Chapter 34

'This is insane. Categorically, horrifically insane.'

Ellie throws me a look as if I'm exaggerating. I've never before questioned my best friend's mental state. But she has me closeted in her study, along with Jen and herself, to persuade me to do something I'd never have dreamed of doing. Even in the days when I was single and desperate. Join a dating website.

'We need a picture of you,' says Ellie, as if this is the most normal thing in the world to do on a Friday night.

'What about that one at Paul and Wendy's wedding last year? You looked gorgeous in that,' says Jen enthusiastically.

I glare at them, unable to remove my chin from the desk. 'Jennifer. Ellie. You. Cannot. Be. Serious. Not least because I had watercress stuck in my teeth in half those pictures.'

They smile at me demonically as if to say, 'Of course we're serious!'

'You honestly think I'm going to put my picture on this bloody thing and announce to the world that I'm shopping for another bloke?'

'Oh it's not like that,' Ellie says dismissively. 'Everyone does it this way these days.'

'Everyone? So why aren't you, Jen?' I ask defiantly.

'She's attached. She's got her waiter,' Ellie reminds me.

'I haven't any more,' Jen confesses.

'Oh. Sorry, Jen,' I say. 'When did this happen?'

'Yesterday,' she replies, looking surprisingly un-depressed. 'At least I know what went wrong with this one.'

'Too much texting?' suggests Ellie.

'Actually,' she says proudly, 'I dumped him.'

This is a first.

'He wanted to do webcam sex. And phone sex. And every type of sex except real sex,' Jen tells us. 'And while I've got nothing against it in principle . . . I mean, if I was married to a man who worked on an oil rig or something . . . well, I'd get that.'

'But?' asks Ellie.

'He lived five minutes away. Plus, I'd only known him three weeks, which begged the question of what he'd want to do after three months.' She takes a deep breath. 'Worse than that, though . . . I was no good at it, especially the phone stuff.'

'Really?' I frown.

'I couldn't stop giggling. And squirming. And –' she shrugs – 'I guess I'm not a throbbing-cocks and hungry-pussy sort of girl.'

There isn't a great deal you can say to that.

'You get seven times more interest if you put a picture on this,' Ellie announces, drawing us back to the website. 'So you're going to get nowhere without one.'

'You say that as if I want to get somewhere,' I point out.

Ellie tuts and closes down the site. 'Fine! I'm trying to help you, Sam. I'm starting to think you don't want to help yourself.'

A silence lingers.

'Look, I'm sorry,' I reply sheepishly. 'I know you're trying to help. And while I get the idea of finding a boyfriend, at least a pretend one, I feel uncomfortable doing it this way. On webuyanydate.com. It's so embarrassing.'

Ellie scrunches up her nose.

'I know loads of people do it these days,' I continue, pre-empting her response. 'I know that someone in your accounts department is getting married to someone they met online, and that my second cousin Sarah shagged a bloke who looked like Ashton Kutcher on a dating website.'

'Really? I wonder if he's still on there,' muses Jen.

'Then what's the problem?' adds Ellie. 'Besides, have you really got time to wait around for it to happen the old-fashioned way? It's only a few months until Jamie's going to be flying off into the sunset. You need to get your skates on.'

'I'll do it if you will,' Jen says, nudging me.

I look up. 'Really?'

'It's not as if I've got anything to lose. Neither, by the way, have you.'

We spend the next hour and a half perfecting our 'profiles', which isn't as easy as it sounds. I don't know why, but trying to sum myself up in less than seven paragraphs proves impossible because: A, it's cringe-worthy, and B (and this is really sad), I've spent so long defining myself as one half of a couple, I struggle to define just me.

So Ellie writes mine for me. But that involves fifteen rewrites and several major amendments by me – including the removal of any reference to my bra size – before we end up with a version close to acceptable.

'"I'm happy, sociable, ambitious, optimistic and easy to get along with",' Ellie reads out loud. '"I love my job but value my leisure time too. I am looking for a man who is loyal, well-travelled and with a good sense of humour."'

'Am I looking for those things?' I ask.

'Course,' she replies. 'Besides, everyone thinks they're loyal, well-travelled – even if the furthest they've been is Devon – and have a good sense of humour. You should get plenty of takers.'

She returns to the keyboard. '"I do a huge amount of charity work in my spare time" . . .'

I frown. 'But I don't. I don't have enough spare time. I'd like to do charity work—'

'Sam,' interrupts Ellie. 'You have taken it upon yourself to help more children in Africa than the United Nations has done. You've got so many good causes on your Facebook profile I'm surprised the thing hasn't crashed. You can't emerge from the supermarket unless you're plastered in collection-box stickers for everything from Macmillan nurses to the Cats' Rescue Society.'

'Actually, I don't do cats.'

'What's wrong with cats?' asks Jen indignantly. She has two.

'Nothing. But there's a whole world of people out there. I've got to prioritize.'

'You put some cash in an RSPCA collection box two weeks ago,' Ellie says accusingly.

'Look,' I huff. 'The point I'm making is that none of this is charity work. This is giving away my loose change. They aren't big donations.'

'They are when you add them up,' Ellie insists. 'Right, final sentence: "I also love sports and am the captain of my local volleyball team."'

'I haven't been near a volleyball since fifth year!' I snort.

'Everyone bends the truth a little,' Jen says dismissively. 'Besides, it will instantly conjure up an image of you in those teeny shorts the American girls wear on the beach.'

'Which is a hideous image,' I point out.

A long debate ensues during which Ellie and Jen repeatedly maintain that this is about creating an impression – not reality – and eventually I lose the will to live, so give up. A volleyball champion I apparently am.

I only hope nobody asks to see my dive and roll.

With my profile posted, the next stage in finding a boyfriend – or someone who can pose as my boyfriend until my rightful one comes back – involves searching the website.

'Now for the good bit,' says Ellie, bringing in a pack of crisps the size of a sleeping bag.

I am astonished to discover that on this website alone there are 427 eligible men within a twenty-mile radius of my postcode.

'That's unbelievable,' gasps Jen.

'I thought you'd been out with most of them,' quips Ellie, prompting Jen to throw the bag of Kettle Chips at her head.

It is fair to say, however, that while we have no complaints about the quantity, the quality is, well, variable. While you can happily filter out men for being too short, too heavy or living too far away, there is no filter that comes under the heading 'Loser'.

Some are so firmly in the 'not if he was the last man on earth' category I feel like crying for them. Such as the guy who fills up all eighteen available picture slots with photos of him and his parrot. Or the one who repeatedly emphasizes his enthusiasm for boiled eggs. Or the 'lusty older man (aged fifty-six)' looking for an 'attractive and energetic younger lady (max twenty-three) to share no-strings adventures'.

Then there're the usernames. Between 'Cunninglinguist' and 'Iwillgetyou', I'm convinced some must've been in the throes of a hallucinogenic trip when they signed up.

Having said that, I'm also pleasantly surprised. The majority are clearly normal, nice men who simply haven't found the right woman. And there are a few who are nothing less than devastatingly gorgeous.

As the night wears on, I reach several conclusions:

A. There are so many pictures of men snowboarding – presumably an attempt to give off a sporty image – that Britain should declare it a new national sport.

B. About ninety per cent list among their interests: cuddling up with a bottle of wine and a DVD. I can't help wondering why they wouldn't prefer cuddling up with a good woman.

C. This is actually quite good fun.

I'm not as enthusiastic as Jen, of course, who was sold in minute one.

'This is like being in a sweet shop,' she says breathlessly, clicking away on her laptop.

'This one looks good,' exclaims Ellie, who has taken on the role of my professional agent. She brings up the profile of a nice-looking thirty-year-old who lives in Frodsham.

'He says he's looking for a woman "aged max ninety-nine",' I tell her. 'I'm not saying I want someone fussy but a little more discernment is in order, surely?'

'How about this one, then?' she says.

I start reading. 'He can't spell.'

She throws me an exasperated look. 'Are you after someone beautiful and single or someone to write essays for you?'

'I could never be attracted to a man who couldn't spell,' I reply, sticking to my guns. 'There needs to be equality on an intellectual level, Ellie. I couldn't go out with a thicko—'

'Even if he looked like this?' Jen asks, gesturing to her screen.

I look over her shoulder at the profile.

His username is Iluvpotnoodles. He has smooth tanned skin, mesmerizing eyes and – as displayed in the fifteen shots of him on a beach – the most sumptuous biceps I've seen outside a professional swimmers' convention. I read his advert:

LOL! I never thort I wuld do this sort of thing – LOL! But thort I wuud try my look. LOL!

'Ooh,' I bite my lip. 'Moral dilemmas . . .'

'Let's give him a "wink",' Ellie suggests. And before I have a chance to argue, she has officially declared my interest in a man attempting to break the world record in the use of the term 'LOL'.

This is only the start. Jen and Ellie spend the rest of the evening winking so often you'd think they were touting for business ahead of a busy night in the bordello. Fortunately, these particular 'winks' are all virtual ones, because otherwise I'd be seriously worried for both their virtue and their optic muscles.

'What happens now?' I ask.

'We wait and see if anyone responds,' shrugs Ellie.

Within an hour, I've had four winks, two of whom (not, I should point out, the nineteen-year-old from Turkey called 'Ilovematureladies') are promising.

One wants to 'instant message' me. He's not one of my favourites. In all honesty, I suspect immediately that he won't be my type; he's too skinny and has too many ju-jitsu pictures.

But I remind myself of two things: first, that I'm not genuinely looking for a boyfriend (whatever Ellie thinks) – only a stand-in; and second, he can spell.

Ten minutes into our chat he has a question for me.

'So, how did you get so good at volleyball?'

Chapter 35

When I wake the next morning, my head is filled with a too-familiar subject: Jamie. Even now, nearly seven weeks after he left, I roll over in a half-sleep, expecting to drape my arm over his torso and press my body against his. The brutal reality hits me in seconds: I'm spooning my spare pillow.

As I open my eyes and let sunlight filter in, my thoughts turn to the men on the dating website. Scores of them, all over the country – the world, in fact – who are waking up on this Saturday morning, alone. Having still not found their soul mate. It was obvious last night that there was nothing wrong with most of them. There were solicitors, firemen, writers, doctors, entrepreneurs – all with one thing in common: they haven't found 'the one'.

The fact that I have found 'the one' only makes me more determined to keep hold of him. Even if I'm not one hundred per cent sold on Ellie's methods.

I drag myself out of bed, pull on my dressing gown and make a cup of tea to take through to the study, where I log on to my laptop with an unnerving thought: what if nobody asks me out?

Twenty-four hours ago I'd have thought that was an impossible scenario once you'd signed up to a dating website, but that was before I knew how they worked. I'd been under the impression that you simply posted your details, said 'hello' to whoever you liked the look of and instantly arranged to meet.

As I've now discovered, before there's a sniff of a get-together you have to endure a strangely old-fashioned courting ritual, involving declarations of interest, chats via instant messaging, and then – you hope – the elusive first date.

I'm indescribably chuffed to discover that I've had sixteen winks and five emails since last night. Admittedly, some aren't much to get excited about; three winks are from the guy with the parrot, and two consist of one line: 'hi hun how's u?'

But among the others are some genuine, bona fide prospects and I feel ridiculously excited. I reply briefly to them all. The brevity is for two reasons. First, I'm not sure what to say. Making small talk with blokes on the internet isn't something in which I've a great deal of experience. Secondly, although I'm doing this in order to win Jamie back, corresponding with other men feels like a betrayal.

Particularly given the text that arrives from the man himself at the exact moment that I'm scrutinizing the profile of a water-ski instructor from Cornwall.

Morning, Sam. Can't stop thinking about you at the moment x

I take a deep breath and return to the screen, reminding myself that this state we're in – of romantic limbo – is precisely the reason why I've got to take the dating website seriously, no matter how wrong it feels. Although perhaps the water-ski instructor might not be geographically practical.

I'm midway through an email when the doorbell rings, and I leap out of my chair.

I shut down the laptop and my first panicky thought as I scurry to the door is that this might be Jamie. Part of me would love it to be – except I'm not dressed, am wearing no make-up and my unbrushed hair looks capable of removing burnt food from a stainless-steel hob.

I tentatively open the door . . . and am confronted by Julia.

I use the word 'confronted' not because my sister announces herself aggressively, but because she is dressed in chic wide-legged trousers and a tailored stone-coloured leather jacket, and her hair is nothing less than immaculate.

'How can you possibly look like that first thing on a Saturday morning?' I ask, letting her in. She looks me up and down. 'I know I look like shit. I've only just got up,' I add, before she can answer.

She shakes her head. 'I simply wondered why you're so flushed. Have you been doing that belly-dancing DVD again?'

I briefly consider telling her about the website but dismiss the idea. Not because I think she won't understand, but because, no matter how many excellent specimens of manhood I'm discovering, I still find the whole thing embarrassing. Even in front of my sister. Especially in front of my sister.

'Not recently. Tea?' I offer, before the conversation can go any further.

'Please. I need to talk to you.' She suddenly looks cagey. 'Go and get yourself sorted, then we'll have a chat.'

I run upstairs and throw on some jeans and a T-shirt, before brushing my hair and applying a smudge of make-up. When I join Julia in the kitchen, she's already made the tea.

'So come on, Ms Mystery. Fill me in,' I say as she hands me a cup and I take a sip.

'You know my biological dad – Gary – wanted me to get in touch? Well . . . I got in touch.'

I nearly spit out my tea.

'Do you think I shouldn't have?' she asks anxiously.

'No, no,' I reassure her. 'I just hadn't expected you to have done it so soon. I thought you were still thinking about it.'

'I was. But I could've gone on thinking about it until my brain melted. So I thought I'd be decisive.'

'Hang on, when did you do this?'

She hesitates. 'A week ago. I emailed him. Just a short one – to say hello and thanks. Nothing more than that.'

'Wow,' I reply, taking a deep breath. 'What was the response?'

'He emailed me back. Then I emailed him. And, well, we got to emailing each other a few times a day.'

'You've been corresponding with him all week?'

She nods and bites her lip, then adds tentatively, 'And we've chatted on MSN.'

'Bloody hell,' is all I can say. A silence lingers as each of us wonders what to say next. 'So . . . what's he like?'

'Nice, as far as I can tell. He lives in Derbyshire, an hour and a half away. He's an engineer. Seems to have done well for himself. He's a widower; he was married to a woman for ten years but she passed away from cancer.'

'Any other children?'

She shakes her head. 'Maybe that's why he wanted to meet me.'

'He still wants to meet you, then?'

'Yes.'

'What have you said?'

She looks into her drink and responds quietly. 'I've said I'll do it.'

'Julia . . . I don't know what to say. I'm happy for you,' I tell her, even though I'm not sure what to think or feel. 'So when are you going to meet him?'

She shifts in her chair. 'That's the thing, Sam. I've arranged to meet him today. And I need you to come with me.'

Chapter 36

The first thing that strikes me when Julia's father opens the door is how alike they are.

Gary has the same almond eyes and handsome high cheekbones as she does. And, although his skin is a shade darker, it's totally clear that I'm in the presence of father and daughter; there is just no doubt about it. She is a smaller, paler and younger, but no less vivid, image of him.

Ironically, given that this is the first time I've seen him, it isn't Julia's father that I can't tear my eyes away from as we stand on the doorstep of his semi-detached cottage on the edge of a pretty, well-to-do village.

It's Julia. In all my twenty-eight years I don't think I've seen a look on her face like she's wearing now. It's a strange and wonderful combination of excitement, terror and anticipation; such a mixture of emotions that the result is impossible to define.

'Julia.' His voice is warm and strong and, if he's as nervous as she is, he doesn't show it.

'H-hello,' she whispers, pulling herself together. She holds out her hand to shake his but instead he steps forward decisively, taking her in his arms to hug her. They hold each other for no longer than a few seconds, but it's enough.

'Sorry,' he smiles, pulling back. 'I've just thought about doing that for a long time.'

Julia grins as a tiny tear swims down her cheek and she brushes it away, flustered.

'Hey,' smiles Gary, putting a hand on her arm. 'Are you okay?'

She sniffs self-consciously and shakes her head. 'Of course. Silly. I'm . . . sorry.'

'Not at all,' he insists. 'It's only natural. If there is such a thing in these circumstances. I've no idea how we're supposed to act . . . have you?'

'None at all,' she laughs. 'Um . . . this is Sam. My sister.'

Gary shakes my hand. 'Very pleased to meet you. I'm Gary. And thank you so much for coming all this way. I would have been happy to come to you.'

'Oh I know,' Julia replies. 'I thought . . . it was better this way.'

What she means is that she didn't want to take any chances that someone she knows might see her in Liverpool. Namely, Mum.

'Well, I'm very glad you're here,' he says, taking a deep breath. 'Please, come in. Let me get you both a cup of tea.'

He shows us into a bright living room that's comfortable and tidy without being overly fashionable. It's all beige sofas and cream carpets in a space that would be slightly bland if it weren't for the photographs of nieces and nephews and a few watercolour landscapes which, judging by the signatures, have all been painted by Gary himself.

'How long did it take you to get here?' he asks, returning with a teapot, a milk jug and three mugs on a tray.

I glance at Julia, who doesn't answer. She simply gazes at his face, as if she hasn't heard a word.

'Oh not long. An hour and a half,' I reply politely. 'So . . . Julia tells me you're an engineer.'

'That's right. I work on a hydrochloric acid plant at the moment.'

'Ooh,' I say approvingly, as if I have the first clue what a hydrochloric acid plant is.

'It's dull compared with what you do, Julia,' he says, glancing over.

She snaps out of her gaze. 'Oh. Not really.'

He perches on the edge of an armchair and leans in to pour the tea. 'You must have a lot of questions.'

My sister nods. Then nods again.

'Julia?' I squeeze her hand.

She shakes her head. 'God, I'm sorry. I don't know what to say. This is such a strange situation. The fact is . . .' She pauses, searching for something to call him. It's obvious she's not ready for 'Dad'. 'I never thought I wanted to meet you. No offence, but . . . well, I've explained the situation. So to be here is a little odd. I haven't had time to adjust to the idea.'

'Of course,' he replies. 'And I understand. I consider the fact that you've never felt the need to look for me to be a sign that you've been brought up very well.'

'I have,' she agrees firmly.

'So did you decide to track down Julia as soon as you saw her in that article?' I blurt out.

'I've thought about it for years,' he sighs. 'The law changed a while ago to allow biological parents to go through a licensed intermediary to contact their adopted children. I considered doing it then. But someone I work with did exactly that, and it took two years to track down his son, only for him to discover that his son wanted nothing to do with him. So I suppose I put off making a decision. Then I saw the article in the classical magazine . . . I saw your birthmark . . . read your story . . . and, well, I knew it was you. I just knew it. After that, I thought about going through the official channels to contact you, but I didn't see the point, so simply wrote to you at the Philharmonic. I just hope I didn't spook you by contacting you directly.'

'I must admit I did feel slightly spooked,' Julia smiles softly. 'But that would've been the case no matter how you'd got in touch. Under the circumstances, I think that's inevitable.'

'I wasn't certain I was doing the right thing,' he continues. 'I stood at the postbox for about two hours changing my mind about whether to put the letter in. But . . . well, my niece died recently.' He nods to one of the pictures on the mantelpiece. 'It made me realize how unpredictable life is, how many regrets I might have if I never even tried to make contact. I simply had to do so. Does that make sense?'

Julia nods and he smiles softly. 'Would you like me to tell you what happened?' he asks. 'When your mother and I met, I mean. That's the obvious place to start, isn't it?'

The next three hours pass in a flash. We miss lunch; Gary offers to make some, but I'm not hungry and eating is clearly the last thing on Julia's mind too. She goes from being barely able to string a sentence together, to firing questions like bullets from a machine gun.

The short version of the story is this.

Gary met Julia's mum in London in 1973 when she was young, beautiful and broken-hearted. The latter because she and the man she'd married four years earlier had separated and she'd taken a job in the capital to make a new start. However, she wasn't succeeding. She was grief-stricken, mourning the loss from her life of the only man she'd ever loved.

Though she'd never even thought about another man before, she and Gary quickly struck up a friendship . . . that one night, weeks later, turned into something more. Despite seeking comfort in each other, Gary was convinced that she was still in love with her husband.

He turned out to be right. Very soon afterwards, the couple were reconciled and she left London for good. Gary only discovered this after she'd fled the capital and wrote to him to explain. He forced himself to be happy for her. Then destiny threw them a curve ball.

She told Gary about the pregnancy months later, by

telephone. She hadn't even considered an abortion; it was against her beliefs. Yet how could she pretend that the child belonged to her husband? She and the husband were both Caucasian. Gary was not.

'So that's why I was put up for adoption,' says Julia flatly.

'Your mother did a very old-fashioned thing and went away for the latter stages of her pregnancy. She stayed with an elderly relative, I believe. Then when you were born . . . well, you know the rest. She felt she had no choice,' Gary says.

'Are you still in touch with her?' Julia asks.

'Not really,' he says apologetically. 'I know where she lives, but I haven't actually seen her for years.'

'May I ask her name?' she says quickly. 'And where she lives? And if she has any other children? I've got to know more about her.'

Gary closes his eyes and shakes his head. 'I'm sorry, Julia. But if your mother wants to get in touch with you, that will have to be her choice. It's not one I can make for her.'

Chapter 37

My first Saturday night alone in the house after the split with Jamie had to come at some point. And despite X *Factor*'s god-awful auditionees being as entertaining as ever, the house has never felt emptier. Tonight, I won't be lying in bed, fragrant and moisturized after an evening's pampering, to be woken at five o'clock by the acrid whiff of Jamie feeling amorous after a night out. Tonight, I'll stay fragrant. And lonely. It sucks.

I switch TV channels, vaguely considering giving myself a pedicure, before dismissing the idea. I should be out partying, not attacking my heels with a pumice stone.

My mind drifts to thoughts of what Jamie's doing now. I indulge in the fantasy that he might be lying on Luke's Laura Ashley sofa in his dressing gown, thinking of me in the same way I'm thinking of him. Admittedly, he probably isn't considering a pedicure. Jamie was never one for male grooming; the closest he got was accidentally shampooing his hair with my exfoliator, after which he spent days discovering apricot grit in his scalp.

If he is at home thinking of me, it will be with his guitar; he'll be strumming some profound acoustic melody by a band that must be good because nobody's heard of them.

I traipse upstairs to the study and grab my laptop to check the dating website. There are more winks and emails since this morning, which I can't deny gives me a surge of self-confidence.

It turns out to be momentary. The first email is from Tigerfeet79, who's five foot five, with a pointy nose and a grin halfway between those of Quentin Tarantino and Mr Potatohead. I am a firm believer that looks can be deceiving, however, so read his email with determined optimism. Which evaporates the second I begin reading . . . and feel as if I'm being shouted at.

HELLO!!!!!!!

I SEE YOU ARE NEW TO THIS SITE AND HAVE JOINED ALL THE SINGLE LADIES ON HERE. MAY I SAY YOU ARE A VERY ATTRACTIVE AND INTRIGUING LADY. I ALWAYS KNOW WHEN I SEE SOMETHING I LIKE, AND MAY I SAY THAT I LIKE WHAT I SEE.

I SEE FROM YOUR PROFILE THAT YOU DON'T LIKE SMOKING. MAY I SAY THAT I HAVE JUST GIVEN UP AND NOW USE AN ELECTRIC CIGARETTE.

I AM A HAIRDRESSER. WHAT DO YOU DO FOR A LIVING? MY SALON IS CALLED 'HAIRMAGGEDDON'. YOU MAY HAVE HEARD OF IT. WE WON AN AWARD ONCE. MAY I SAY YOU HAVE VERY NICE HAIR – THOUGH IF IT IS NOT TOO PRESUMPTUOUS I DO FEEL YOU WOULD BENEFIT FROM A ONCE-A-MONTH CONDITIONING TREATMENT.

FINALLY, MAY I SAY THAT IT WOULD BE GREAT TO GET
TOGETHER. I AM CERTAIN WE WOULD HAVE A CONNECTION. LET
ME KNOW WHEN YOU'RE FREE.

I scrunch up my nose and wonder whether or not you're meant to respond when you're totally uninterested. I decide to err on the side of politeness and send a reply.

Hi, thanks for getting in touch, but I'm coming off this site soon as I'm now engaged. Best of luck!

It seems the kindest way, like euthanizing a dying goldfish. I pause and look at my phone. I do this all the time these days, as if the more I look at it the more likely Jamie is to text. Stupidly, I forgot to ask last time we exchanged messages what he was up to this weekend. Once that thought is in my head, there's no getting it out. I know Ellie was determined that I should keep the texts to a minimum, but tonight I feel as if I'm in a padded cell: I have to know what he's doing.

How're things? What are u up to?

I try to keep it casual and friendly and am very glad he cannot see the vigour with which I text before pressing send. It's over an hour and a half before he responds. An hour and a half of hell during which I flit between sorting out a purely hypothetical list of online 'favourites' – blokes I'd consider dating – and imagining

Jamie in a Jacuzzi surrounded by melon-breasted women in bikinis the size of dolls' handkerchiefs.

Hey. On night out in Manchester. Spk soon x

'Hmmph,' I say out loud, and am glad, given the fishwifely overtones, that nobody is around to hear. If I'm in suffering alone on a Saturday night, so should he be. Isn't he supposed to be tortured?

I tell myself to be reasonable. It isn't as if I haven't been out on a bender every Saturday since he left. And the idea that Jamie would wallow in the break-up in quiet solitude was never likely as long as his musician chums were around – along with an endless supply of alcohol and God knows what else. But what the hell? He's undoubtedly suffering emotionally from this break-up so it's only natural for him to seek solace in a few nights out. I compose another text wishing him 'a great night', add a kiss and wait for a response. None is forthcoming.

So at 10.45 p.m., I turn off my phone, return to my laptop and open up the pages of each of the guys I'd listed as a 'favourite'. Then I start composing emails. To each and every one of them.

Chapter 38

'You've set up how many dates?' Jen asks, when I meet her and Ellie for a quick sandwich on Monday.

'Five,' I reply matter-of-factly.

'Five, Sam? Five?' Ellie splutters into her cappuccino. We're back at the Quarter. And I've passed again on the Lumpy Bumpy cake. Not because I've lost my appetite; it's more because my willpower has had an unexpected boost with the prospect of five blokes being lined up over the next week. 'What happened to the woman who was unconvinced by online dating?'

'I decided to open my mind,' I shrug.

Ellie sits back, smiles and crosses her arms. 'Well, good. This is the right thing to do. So tell us all about them.'

I fill them in on the five men I spent the rest of Saturday night and most of Sunday settling on. Let me tell you, it wasn't easy. Ohnosiree. It was unbelievably time consuming and I'm absolutely certain that if I didn't have the looming deadline of Jamie's flight into the sunset, there's no way I'd have put in the hours I did this weekend.

Despite there being 427 eligible men within a twenty-mile radius of Liverpool, after extensive research involving chatting, befriending, scrutinizing on Facebook, followed by a short telephone conversation with a couple, you might find it surprising that only these five were suitable. You might even come to the conclusion that I was being fussy.

Not so. In many cases – many more than my ego was ready for, actually – it was they who were being fussy.

I have had more knock-backs than I was ever prepared for, including several from men who emailed to say they were about to leave the site as they'd just got engaged. The cheek.

At least they had the decency to lie.

One came right out and said that at twenty-eight I was too old as he was looking for someone with whom to procreate. Apparently, once we'd got to know each other then perhaps moved in together, then got married, at least three years would have elapsed. That would make me thirty-one – six years older than the average woman at the peak of her fertility.

I responded with one line: 'No problem, you old romantic.'

So that leaves us with Phil, a thirty-three-year-old mechanic; Jonathan, a twenty-five-year-old accountant; Kyle, a thirty-one-year-old salesman specializing in video-conferencing solutions (whatever they are); Ben, a thirty-year-old vet; and Juan, a twenty-nine-year-old social worker originally from Barcelona.

'Nice work,' grins Ellie.

'Hang on a minute,' says Jen. 'Did you say Kyle? A video-something salesman? He asked me out yesterday.'

'The swine!' I gasp, outraged. 'Really? He told me when we got chatting that he hadn't had any luck on the website.'

'I cannot believe that,' says Jen, shaking her head.

'Before you both get too indignant, may I remind you, Sam, that you've lined up five of 'em, and Jen, you were talking about at least two when I spoke to you last night.'

'It's three, actually,' Jen sniffs. 'I didn't want to put all my eggs in one basket.'

'I'm sure Kyle feels the same way,' says Ellie.

'Well, I'm happy to let Kyle off if he proves suitable to requirements,' I tell them both.

Ellie narrows her eyes. 'Sam,' she says with a note of disapproval in her voice, 'when I suggested you went out and had yourself a fling – found yourself a boyfriend, or whatever – I did it because I genuinely thought it'd be good for you to realize that there's a whole world of men out there. I didn't just suggest it so you could go posing round the city with some good-looking bloke on the off-chance you might bump into Jamie.'

I throw her a cheeky smile. 'Heaven forbid.'

She tuts. 'Well, be careful. Where have you arranged to meet these people?'

'Different places. First one's after work tonight, in the Living Room. I know the bar staff there so will feel safe meeting a stranger. The rest I'm meeting at a variety of bars and restaurants. In three cases I'm meeting them at lunchtime, again so I can make my excuses and leave early if necessary.'

'Who is the best-looking?' Jen asks.

'Hmm . . . Juan, I think. Though Ben could be a surprise call.'

'Why?' asks Ellie.

'He's the only one I'm meeting who hasn't got a picture,' I tell them.

'WHAT?' they splutter, as if I'd just announced he hasn't got a head.

'What's the matter?' I ask.

'You are not serious. You're meeting someone with no picture?' asks Jen.

'He sounded lovely,' I tell them.

'Sam,' Ellie begins, exasperated. 'There's only one thing that will be guaranteed about this date: he'll be pig ugly.'

'Don't be so shallow,' I say, pretending I couldn't care less if he looked like Shrek's wartier cousin. 'Besides, I'm sure he won't be. He said he hadn't got round to putting up any pictures yet.'

Ellie and Jen both shake their heads in despair.

'Look, he was very nice and I'm certain it'll be a success. I have every confidence,' I insist, sipping my fizzy water while I try to think of a bloody good excuse to get out of the date.

Chapter 39

I'm torn between: A, my dog has died and I'm too grief-stricken to think about going on a date (he's a vet, so this one's bound to appeal); B, my boiler has broken down and the only time it can be fixed is the time I'm meant to be meeting him; and C, I have developed an unspecified fungal infection.

I opt for B. I mean, that's fair enough. It might be August but the nights are definitely getting chillier.

When I get back to my desk, I surreptitiously log on to the website, after checking carefully that Natalie and Deana are hard at work with their heads in their magazines. I compose a quick email to Ben-who's-undoubtedly-a-minger (as he's become known), asking if we could rearrange the date we'd made for the night after tomorrow – adding casually that it'd be lovely if he got round to adding some photos to the site in the meantime.

The rest of the afternoon is a whirlwind – not helped by one particular email. It's from the agent of Liverpool FC's hottest new striker, a twenty-four-year-old who's just signed from AC Milan and is featured in this month's Italian *Vogue*. This is a man who, under normal circumstances, I'd be very happy to hear from. The problem is that he's written to tell me I have competition for the night of Teen SOS's centenary party. On Wednesday 30 November, the MTV EMAs, the European Music Video Awards, are being held at the Echo Arena Liverpool. Which means I'm stuffed. Because it will be bursting at the seams with A-listers – none of whom are likely to want to forfeit their ticket to spend the evening on the other side of town with me, Lorelei and Kevin S. Chasen – no matter how good my canapés.

I have yet to break it to Lorelei, largely because I cannot get a word in edgeways.

'These canapés you've proposed,' she thunders, her South Wales lilt a long way from the dulcet tones of Catherine Zeta-Jones.

'Yes?'

'They're a frigging rip-off, my lovely. Twelve pounds ninety-five a head for a couple of vol-au-vents? Were the goats that made the goats-cheese tartlets reared in the penthouse suite at Claridge's or something?'

'Well,' I reply calmly, 'we use this catering firm all the time and the feedback we've had is that they're excellent value for money. Plus, I know from experience that the food is—'

'If you use them all the time I'll expect a discount. A good one too. We are a charity, after all. Now, where are we up to with Coleen?' she demands, so loudly I'm convinced those on the seventh floor of this office must be able to hear.

I take a deep breath. 'I spoke to Coleen's agent again yesterday and she's keen to come, but apparently one of the catalogues she models for may want her to fly to Dubai that week. But it's only a maybe. We won't know until a week beforehand.' This is all true. I omit to mention that, once Coleen finds out about the EMAs, no one could blame her for finding our event as enticing as a shindig at Pontins.

'A week?' she booms. 'A frigging week? In which case, my love, with all respect, you need to get someone bigger than Coleen. As a standby.'

'Actually, I need to talk to you about the issue of the celebrity guest list.'

Trying to keep my voice steady, I fill her in on the EMAs and the implications of the clash.

She pauses at the end. 'So, basically, your job just got a bit tougher. So what? Like I said, we need a standby.'

I grit my teeth. 'Did you have anyone in mind?'

'You're the expert. Oh soz, luvvie – I've got Tokyo on the other line. Sort it for me, babes, won't you? Otherwise your company's arse is on the line and your own personal bum cheeks will be held responsible.'

She slams down the phone.

I take a sip of tea. 'Anyone got a number for Nicole Kidman?' I mutter sarcastically. 'Because my client thinks I should be able to get her here with no budget, no staff and a mid-priced canapé menu that she still wants a discount on.'

'Ooh,' says Natalie, looking up from her *OK!* for the first time in an hour. 'I don't mind working that night if she's going.'

'Who?'

'Nicole Kidman. I've always thought me 'n' her would really hit it off.'

Despite the fact that I have arranged only an after-work drink with Jonathan, the accountant, I am outrageously nervous. Which is ridiculous, given that I'm not remotely interested in him as a real boyfriend – just as a decoy to make Jamie get his act together.

However, dating isn't something I've done a lot of. Not ever. I have stumbled from relationship to relationship, meeting people at university, or through friends, or – in the case of Jamie – on holiday. I've never been one of those people, like Jen or Samantha from *Sex and the City*, who go on dates for dates' sake. So I'm feeling a little green about the whole thing.

Although I've tarted myself up in the work lavatories for forty-five minutes before I left, I am still desperately early, so loiter around the corner from the Living Room in order to time my entrance to perfection. I plan to be four minutes late. Jen insisted that it should be at least seven, and Ellie ten, but I've gone with my instincts.

I'm about to head in when I feel a sharp tap on my shoulder and spin round to see . . . Jonathan the accountant. Except it isn't Jonathan the accountant.

This Jonathan is a mutant version of the god-like creature on the dating website; this is a shadow of the gorgeous hunk depicted in the single arty, black and white picture.

In that, his skin was baby's-bum smooth, his cheekbones were defined and masculine, and his eyes so sparkly they looked capable of blinding you with one look. On a slightly drizzly week night beside a bus stop in Victoria Street, the reality – the pimpled, gap-toothed, wonky-grinned reality – is somewhat different.

'It's Sam, isn't it?' he asks, in a voice so squeaky it makes David Beckham sound like James Earl Jones.

The date is not a success, despite my valiant attempts. We find a seat and I tell myself firmly that this could work. It really could. He's not that bad-looking in the darkest corner of the bar. And he's pleasant enough, if a little anxious.

'Have you been on many dates through the website?' I ask.

'A few,' he confesses, biting his thumbnail. 'But they've never worked out.'

'Oh that's a shame.'

'I say too much. Or give away too much. I have a tendency to put people off relatively early on.'

'Right.'

'I have this obsessive-compulsive disorder, you see, and I think that's part of it. Plus, my therapist says that I'm looking for someone to love me for who I am, warts and all, which is why I'm so quick to tell people about that. And my breakdowns. Both of them. Even though I'm totally over all that now and am feeling positive and upbeat. Though I don't think I'll ever be off the drugs, but as my other therapist says – she's the one based at the day clinic rather than the hospital itself – we think nothing of turning to chemical help when we've got a cough and a cold. This is just the same.'

'I see,' I say.

'You don't mind me mentioning this, do you? I do feel as if we made some sort of connection when we chatted online . . . don't you?'

'Erm . . . I suppose so.'

'That's the beauty of the internet, I think. You can really get to know someone before you meet them. You can decide if it's going to be a waste of time or not. I knew it wouldn't be with you,' he says, sucking the straw in his pina colada.

I forgot to mention that. He's onto his third already and we've been here only fifteen minutes. He's devoured the first two and eaten both chunks of pineapple and both morello cherries, though he did offer the latter to me. I declined and stuck to Diet Coke so I can drive home.

'Can I put your mind at rest about something?' he asks.

'Of course. What?'

'The age difference. You're three years older than me.'

'Oh I hadn't really thought about—'

'I always go for older women.'

'Really? Why is that?'

He frowns. 'Younger women are so . . . unbelievably . . . what's the word?'

'Inexperienced?' I offer.

'Fussy.'

He proceeds to tell me about a succession of dates he's been on. They haven't been just up and down the country; there have been three international ones too. If ever you needed proof of a man's desperation, the fact that three weeks ago he was prepared to fly to Rio de Janeiro to meet someone has to be it. This, despite her emailing the day before he left to warn him she had a bout of cystitis and wasn't feeling tip-top.

'It was worth it, though,' he says earnestly, ordering a fourth pina colada.

'Why . . . are you still seeing her?'

'No, no,' he says. 'The distance would have made it impossible. But I've made a pen pal for life.'

I don't ask how many times she's responded. I don't think I need to.

'So do you think we'll see each other again?' he asks boldly.

I glance at my drink and decide the only option is to be honest.

'Jonathan, I think you're a lovely person. But . . . probably not.'

He takes a violent bite of his pineapple chunk.

'I knew you were going to say that. It's my fault, I know.'

'It's nobody's fault,' I reassure him. 'But, when two people meet, either there is chemistry or there isn't. And there's nothing either of them can do about it. But you'll meet someone one day, I'm sure.'

'Really? You're such a good listener.'

Three hours, nine pina coladas and a full-blown counselling

session later, I've done so much listening that my ears are nearly bleeding. As I walk out of the Living Room towards the car park, I feel a combination of emotions. Disappointment. Pity. And a deep relief that at least my love life isn't as disastrous as some.

Chapter 40

Date number two is the following lunchtime and it's with Juan, the social worker originally from Barcelona.

Unlike Jonathan, he does look like his picture – better, in fact. He's six foot, with Bublé eyes. But, given the thick Lancashire accent, it's apparent that the 'originally from Barcelona' translates as 'hasn't lived in Barcelona since he was three weeks old'.

Still, this guy has potential.

'Do you mind if I sit next to you?' he smoulders, sinking into the seat and pressing his thigh against mine. We're only in Subway (his choice), so although it feels slightly strange that we're not opposite each other, it's not as if I need to worry about him getting too amorous. Or so I thought.

'Not at all,' I reply, feeling a rush of heat. I know my mind is firmly focused on Jamie but it's simply impossible not to feel some stirrings when an unbelievably gorgeous bloke makes overtures. 'Have you been on many dates?' I ask, attempting to negotiate an overstuffed chicken wrap.

He smiles and puts his arm around the back of my chair. 'I'm afraid so,' he smiles, gazing into my eyes. His manner is way too sexy for comfort – but I'm so stunned, flustered and hot, I can't think about moving away.

'Right,' I gulp. 'Any successes?'

He shrugs slowly. 'It depends how you define . . . success.' Despite having met this person less than eight minutes ago, his lips are within striking distance of mine. And I'm mesmerized by them. They're full and sumptuous and outrageously sensual. Plus, they keep getting closer. His pupils are dilated. And – at only eight and a half minutes – I'm totally convinced he's going to kiss me.

'Er . . . did any of them turn into girlfriends?' I ask, edging away.

He smiles and sits back. I don't know whether to be relieved or disappointed. 'One or two, no more than that.' He looks at me again and brushes a strand of hair from my face. 'I have high hopes for you, though.'

I take a bite of my wrap and a dollop of onion relish drops into my lap; I proceed to flip it onto the floor. It's the most unsophisticated movement imaginable, blowing any efforts to look elegant. Yet it doesn't seem to matter. His eyes are on me as I look up at him.

'I didn't mean to unsettle you,' he murmurs.

'You didn't,' I splutter, composing myself. He parts his lips.

Jamie and I didn't do a huge amount of getting down and dirty in the final months of our relationship. I didn't think much of it, only that everyone goes through periods in their life when their sex drive dips.

But, having been without any action for months, it's only now – as I sit before Dirk Diggler's digglier cousin – that I feel the sort of sensations it usually takes an episode of *True Blood* and half a bottle of wine to induce.

Which feels plain wrong: First, because I only met him in person less than ten minutes ago; second, because I'm still in love with Jamie; and third, because we're in Subway with 'Barbie Girl' being piped through the speakers, the pungent fragrance of meatballs in the air and tattooed staff members shouting colourfully at each other in the background.

I shift away and try to concentrate on my wrap. But I become aware of him focusing on my mouth as I take a bite, honing in on my parted lips like I'm starring in one of those old Flake adverts. It isn't quite the same with pieces of chicken teriyaki.

'So tell me about you,' Juan breathes.

I put down my wrap. He hasn't touched his.

'Um . . . like I said when we spoke, I'm an events coordinator and I live in Allerton.'

'You've just split from your boyfriend,' he says. I nod. 'Broken heart?'

'Oh I'm all right,' I shrug.

'You must miss . . . human touch, though. Am I right?' He's so close now I can feel his breath on my face – and realize the same must be true for him. I wish I'd passed on the onion relish.

'I suppose so. I hadn't really thought about it . . .'

'Until now?' he says and puts his hand on my leg, squeezing my flesh.

I freeze and glare at it as several facts whirr through my mind.

We are in Subway. It is lunchtime. We met – I glance at my watch – twelve minutes ago. Yet this stranger has his hand on my thigh. Who the hell do I think I am . . . Belle de flipping Jour?

Yet, ridiculously, I don't remove it. In fact, I don't move at all. Because – and I return to my original point – he is gorgeous. As sexy as hell. Or maybe I'm just in shock. I can't decide which.

'You know what?' he says, moving in closer. 'I wanted to kiss you the second you walked through the door.'

'Did you?' I squeak.

'In fact, I wanted to do a lot more.'

I'm swallowing, my mind and blood swirling, when I am distracted by a voice I recognize instantly.

'Look, babes, when I said I wanted salad, I didn't mean three poxy bits of cucumber. I want the works: lettuce, pickles, tomatoes, the lot. Oh soz, love – I've got Sydney on the line.' Lorelei Beer is at the front of the queue and I've never felt more relieved to see anyone in my life.

'There's someone over there I need to go and speak to,' I babble, grabbing my bag and abandoning my wrap.

'What?' asks Juan incredulously. 'You're leaving? What am I supposed to do with this?'

He points at his crotch to display a bulge that is admittedly magnificent but also – given it's now only thirteen minutes since we met – inappropriate to a frankly terrifying degree.

'I'm sure you'll think of something,' I smile, darting out of the door before Lorelei spots me.

Chapter 41

'Is that what they call one of those "intimate encounters"?' muses Ellie, when I phone her on the way home that night.

'Absolutely not!'

'Well, if I was single I'm not sure I'd complain about being propositioned by a tall Michael Bublé with a zip-straining bulge in his pants.'

'It was very sleazy,' I reply disapprovingly.

'But you stayed?'

'Only for thirteen minutes,' I clarify.

Actually, I've been thinking a lot about what went on today, and what's been happening to me lately. Since I've been single, I've started to experience a variety of, well, stirrings. Ones that never happened in the latter days of being a couple. My libido, twisted creature that it is, has decided to kick-start itself at the exact time when I can do nothing about it.

'Imagine what might have happened if you'd stuck around for twenty,' she sniggers. 'So who's next?'

'This is the problem. It was supposed to be the vet –

Ben-who's-undoubtedly-a-minger – but I cancelled. At least, I tried to cancel. I requested a read receipt on the email I sent him, asking if we could rearrange, but he hasn't even read it.'

'So you're going to stand him up?'

'Oh I can't, can I?' I sigh. 'He might be a minger but he doesn't deserve that. I'm going to have to go. I might need you to phone me twenty minutes into the date with a fake emergency, though.'

As it turns out, the issue with this date is not that Ben-who's-undoubtedly-a-minger is in fact a minger. The issue is that he stands me up. The bloody cheek. He's the one who's undoubtedly a minger, for God's sake!

I come to the realization that this is what's happened when – after fifteen minutes, a packet of pork scratchings and several tours of the pub – there is still nobody here that fits his description.

His description being that he'd be wearing jeans, carrying a copy of *The Times* (corny but effective) and wearing a dark blue T-shirt. Nobody here comes close. Not the two women in the corner still in their Tesco uniforms, not the large group of students next to the loos, and not the elderly gentleman who hasn't removed his hat or mac. I briefly wonder whether the dark blue T-shirt might be under the mac but decide not to investigate, and give the whole evening up as a bad job.

As I get home twenty minutes later and pop my M&S meal in the microwave, I can sense my hope about this strategy disintegrating. So far, I've had one OCD victim, one pervert (who, admittedly, I fancied), and one who stood me up. If I don't deserve a medal, I at least deserve a refund.

I finish my dinner and log on to the laptop to see if there are any other hot prospects – though it's with a very heavy heart.

As soon as I enter the website, however, I'm surprised to see that there is a response from Ben-who's-undoubtedly-a-minger.

Sam,

Very relieved to receive your email at the last minute. My neighbour Mildred's cat got run over and I had to step in and help. She's lived on her own for the last three years (Mildred, not the cat) and was in pieces – she adores the thing. Fortunately, we've managed to save her. The point is that I'd been planning to leave a message for you at the pub, but thankfully got this in time. So . . . result all round. Anyway, I enjoyed chatting the other night and would still really like to meet. (Though we need to exchange mobile numbers this time!) I'll get round to the pix tomorrow. Promise.

Ben x

Chapter 42

I'd love to say the dates with Kyle, the video-conferencing salesman, and Phil, the mechanic, are any better.

They're not. It's not that they're disastrous, only that neither Kyle nor Phil is my cup of tea. Kyle is a little too talkative (I said about three words during the whole date); Phil a little too opinionated (on everything from immigration to breast implants).

Still, my experiences so far have led me to one conclusion about online dating: despite me finding nobody I'd be able to realistically present as a gorgeous new boyfriend, I have no doubt about why it works for so many people.

There are definitely women out there who are future soul mates for Juan, Kyle, Phil – and even Jonathan, God love him, though I suspect he's more likely to meet her on his next stint in the Priory.

Having said all that, my optimism for other women – including Jen, who so far has been on two dates (with the same person), prompting Ellie to have another round of 'the talk' with her – hasn't materialized into anything for me.

So, on Friday night, as I log on to the website to check if I've had any winks lately, it's without much hope. I flick back and forth between the dating site and Jamie's Facebook page, on to which I've drifted so many times lately that even I recognize my behaviour as unhealthy. It's not as if I don't know what he looks like.

But, despite telling myself that moping over pictures of the two of us in New York and Ibiza is helping nobody, I can't stop myself. Particularly when there are updates on his page, such as the one I stumble across tonight:

Jamie Moyes is friends with Natasha Waterfield-Jones

'Who the hell is Natasha Waterfield-Jones?' I splutter, scrutinizing her picture. She's exceptionally pretty and exceptionally thin – two reasons to despise her immediately.

Moreover, she's got that look – that slightly grungy bohemian look – that I never quite mastered convincingly, but which I know Jamie adores. My mind swirls with possibilities before I eventually phone Ellie.

'So? She could be anyone.'

'But she's gorgeous!' I whimper.

'So are you!' she argues. 'Oh Sam . . . Seriously, you can't get your knickers in a twist over stuff like this. Chances are, she's absolutely nobody – she'll be someone who's recently started at work or someone he knows from way back. Whatever you do don't quiz him about it.'

'Don't be ridiculous,' I tell her. 'I might feel like a Facebook stalker, but I'm not going to act like one.'

'Put her out of your mind. I'm serious. This is a red herring.'

She's right, of course. I know she's right. And, given we're not even together, Jamie arguably wouldn't be doing anything wrong even if she wasn't. The thought kills me.

Sulkily, I drag myself away from Facebook and back to my email inbox, where a new one has landed from Ben-who's-undoubtedly-a-minger. It has the subject matter 'As promised x' and when I click on the link it takes me to his dating website profile, onto which he has tonight posted several photos.

I take them in with wide eyes and note that they represent two major surprises. First, Ben-who's-undoubtedly-a-minger is, in fact, no minger. Far from it. And secondly, we have met before. I only wish I hadn't been holding a bag full of dog poo at the time.

Chapter 43

After last Saturday night I can't even consider staying in, so I've arranged to head to Ellie's for a glass or two of wine, or, knowing her, bottles. But in the middle of the afternoon, I get a text from Julia.

What are you up to tonight?

It's rare for her to randomly enquire about my movements so I phone her.

'Why is sending you a text so suspicious?' she asks.

'I didn't say it was suspicious – I said it was unusual, for you.'

She doesn't reply.

'Well, come on . . . put me out of my misery,' I tell her.

'Okay. I invited Mum and Dad over for dinner tonight. I want to discuss Gary with them.'

'Let me guess. You've made enough beef casserole for me too?'

'The recipe serves four,' she says sheepishly. 'And it's lemon sole. Plus, I've made that raspberry cheesecake you love.'

'What makes you think that me being there will make the situation any better? Besides, I think you're making more of this than you need to.'

'Sam, I'd be really grateful if you could come, that's all. You could help diffuse the situation . . . if there is a situation.'

'Fine,' I sigh. 'But I need to be at Ellie's by nine thirty at the latest.'

Julia lives in an elegant apartment in a converted nineteenth-century villa in Cressington Park – and very lucky she is too.

The park, a leafy oasis overlooking the river, is set in a perfectly preserved conservation area that still features ornate street lamps and a *Brief Encounter*-style railway station. The first mansions were built in the 1840s, with fine iron balconies, beautifully proportioned windows and stucco details. And although Liverpool's fortunes have seen dramatic highs and lows since, these buildings have remained as pristine and robust as ever.

'Come in! You're the first here.' She holds open the huge oak door and takes my proffered wine, glancing at the label. 'Nice choice – it'll go brilliantly with the fish.'

I don't tell her that I only chose that bottle because it had a fiver off at Tesco.

The only possible criticism of Julia's apartment is that the kitchen is small. But it's an insignificant blemish as the rest of the place is as gorgeous inside as the setting outside; it's all stripped floors and leaded windows, with interesting paintings and knick-knacks she's picked up on her tours with the orchestra.

Music is at the heart of this home, from the cello, which sits next to the piano, to the floor-to-ceiling CDs. Julia puts on Alison Krauss, before we head through to the kitchen, where I eat olives and watch redundantly as she simmers sauces and chops vegetables.

My own cooking techniques are more fluid. If I'm rustling up anything more complicated than an omelette, I look like Animal from *Sesame Street*, with arms and ingredients everywhere. There are no spillages, conflagrations and strange burning smells when Julia's in charge. She works so effortlessly she'd make Nigella look like a school dinner lady on her first day, and has everything totally under control by the time Mum and Dad arrive.

Mum is understatedly glam in Levis and a purple chiffon shirt, her usually unruly hair done up in a loose chignon. Dad's in his favourite jumper, a maroon cashmere number offsetting the ubiquitous cotton shirt and plain blue tie. The jumper is V-neck. He thinks round-necks make him look like an anarchist.

'What's new in your life, daughter number two?' asks Mum. 'I haven't seen you in ages.'

I shift in my seat as thoughts of my four dates flick through my mind. 'It's been quiet really, Mum.'

'I saw you in the city centre the other day,' Dad pipes up while he's examining a dish of purple sprouting broccoli as if it's something that grew on Jupiter.

'Why didn't you say hello?' I ask.

'I was on my way to a meeting. Besides, you were with some-one.'

I stiffen. 'Where was I?' I ask casually, hoping he doesn't say Subway. It's one thing being almost seduced by a stranger, but quite another having your father witness it.

'That bar in Victoria Street. You were going in.'

'What's this?' asks Mum, her antennae as effective as anything NATO has. 'Have you got another man? Frank, you never told me.'

'Apologies, dear. I know you like to keep abreast of my every movement.'

She returns her attention to me. 'Tell all.'

'I do not have a new man,' I say, as my cheeks inflame to a vivid shade of ketchup.

She frowns. 'Well, why not? You should be moving on.'

'And you think another man is the answer? I thought they were all bastards?' I point out.

'That doesn't mean they're no good for anything. And a woman your age has some needs, doesn't she?' she says meaningfully.

'I don't want to continue this conversation,' I splutter, head-ing to the hob to stir a sauce.

Julia removes the spoon from my hand. 'Dinner's about to be served. Why don't you all go and sit down?'

This is the first family meal we've had in ages. Mum doesn't give up on the issue of Jamie, of course, although at least it's interwoven with other subjects, including her Remington Fuzz

Away, Colonel Gadaffi and *The Office* which, after watching her first-ever episode on UK Gold, she thinks is both highly entertaining . . . and real. Nobody bothers explaining, not least because we're quickly diverted by her next bombshell: one of her patients at the Women's Hospital yesterday had been Vagazzled.

'I'm all for celebrating the vagina, but in all my years as a midwife I've never seen anything like it,' Mum says. 'She was nine centimetres dilated and looked like a disco ball.'

Dad nearly chokes on a boiled potato. 'There's nothing I love more than a detailed gynaecological discussion when I'm midway through my main course.' Mum flashes him a look. 'Do carry on, dear,' he adds.

She turns to Julia and me. 'Imagine if Grandma Milly was still alive,' she continues.

I can't help but snigger. 'Given that Grandma Milly thought you were going to burn in hell for getting your ears pierced, it's probably not a bad thing she never lived to see the existence of the Vagazzle.'

Mum raises an eyebrow. 'Well, Samantha, you don't know how lucky you are to have grown up surrounded by tolerance.'

She jokes about it now, but as a slightly rebellious and bohemian teenager, my mum had a hard time being raised in such tyrannically old-fashioned conditions.

And when Mum and Dad turned up with an adopted baby who wasn't white, Grandma Milly, who died the year I was born, nearly had heart failure. Fortunately, nobody could resist Julia's charms even when she was a baby and Grandma ended up adoring her, a fact she underlined by leaving her all her jewellery when she passed away ten years later.

By nine o'clock, we've had the starter, the main course, and are tucking into the cheesecake, when it strikes me that not a word has yet been said about Gary. I glance at my watch then glare at Julia. She catches my eye – fully aware of the meaning behind my look – but drops her gaze.

'Well, this has been lovely,' I say, staring at my watch. 'It's a shame I'm going to have to dart off in fifteen minutes.'

Julia bites her lip.

'Have you got a date?' Mum asks excitedly.

'Only with Ellie, Jen and some Pringles.' I look at Julia again. She says nothing.

'That doesn't sound much good. On a Saturday night too.'

I sigh. 'How has my love life managed to dominate conversation – apart from the woman who had her lady bits done up like a Beaverbrooks display?'

Mum shrugs. 'You've had a lot going on in your life.'

I look at Julia again, my eyes drilling into her. Enough's enough. 'I'm not the only one. Am I, Julia?'

'Oh?' says Mum, turning to her. The second she looks at Julia, the penny drops. 'Oh.'

Julia swallows and goes to stand up. 'I'll clear away these dishes, then . . .'

'Julia's got something to tell you,' I announce. This might be unfair, but we'll be here until midnight otherwise. And she has to tell them.

Julia sits again, a dirty plate in either hand. 'I . . . I met my birth father.'

Mum says nothing. She doesn't even gasp.

It's my father who speaks first. 'And how is Gary?'

Chapter 44

Mum frowns at Dad, then turns back to Julia, before clearing her throat. 'Your biological father has been in touch with us too,' she confesses. 'He wanted to explain to us why he'd chosen to make contact with you. I think it's about more than just the article. You know about his niece dying?'

'But you never said,' Julia replies incredulously.

'I know, I know,' Mum replies hastily. 'I don't know why. I just preferred not to think about it, didn't I, Frank?'

Dad doesn't answer.

'So when did you meet? And where?' asks Mum.

Julia fills them in and it's impossible not to notice how agitated Mum is.

When she finishes, Dad coughs. 'So . . . what next? Are you going to stay in touch with him?'

'I think so,' Julia says tentatively. 'But –' she stands up and walks round the table, bending down to put her arms round Mum – 'I hope you both know that this does nothing to affect my relationship with you. Nothing at all. I just want to fill in some detail on my history, that's all.'

She squeezes Mum's hand. Mum nods and pushes through a smile. 'Thanks, sweetheart.'

'Your mother and I understand,' Dad says.

'Yes, we do,' echoes Mum as Julia returns to the other side of the table. 'And when you say you want detail, I take it that means . . . you want to know about your mother?'

Julia pauses. 'I suppose it might.'

Mum's face is blank. She simply looks at her wine glass, before picking it up and finishing the last drop.

For a moment no one speaks.

Then Mum stands up with a forced smile. 'Right, let's get these dishes cleared away. I'm dying for a cup of coffee.'

Chapter 45

I never make it to Ellie's place, though I glean from a phone call the next day that there was a lot to catch up on. Jen has been on three dates in one week with someone from the dating website. He's from west Lancashire – Ormskirk – and is not her first romantic venture in that neck of the woods. At the end of last year, she went out with a porter at her hospital who commuted from there. She hadn't given him a second look until he turned up to the Christmas fancy-dress party as Flash Gordon, revealing a hitherto invisible six-pack and biceps capable of bending the bars on his trolley. Their three dates went like a dream according to Jen (though the rest of us thought his tights were the best thing about him).

However, by the time she'd signed him up as her 'plus one' on the top table at her sister Linda's wedding, he'd moved on to a radiologist with a boob job capable of requiring Playtex to invent a new sizing policy.

So three dates is good news. What will happen next is anyone's guess, though Ellie's concerned. She spent last night pleading with Jen to stop texting the guy, but her pleas fell on deaf ears.

'She'll never learn,' Ellie sighs. 'I've done the only thing a good friend can do in this situation and bought her a self-help book.'

'About what?'

'Dating.'

'Jen has no problem with dates. She's been on so many she could write an encyclopaedia. It's relationships that are the problem.'

'She needs to learn some restraint,' Ellie continues. 'The latest one's as doomed as all the others. I've given up on it before it's even started.'

'Oh God,' I groan. 'I feel her pain already. So what's the book?'

'*How to Play Hard to Get – Treat Them Mean to Keep Them Keen and Other Tricks For Mad, Desperate Women*. Something along those lines anyway.'

'How did that go down? Is she receptive?'

'She was allegedly insulted. But only because she's already choosing the soft furnishings in their first marital home. I guarantee she'll have been disabused by this time next week, God love her. Urgh. I'll need more Pringles, no doubt about it. Anyway, what's new with you? Any more dates lined up?'

As I fill her in on Ben, I experience a flicker of excitement. On paper, this guy is perfect. Not least because Jamie would hate him.

He'd never admit it, of course.

Jamie likes to think of himself as totally laid back. But there is a distinct chip on his shoulder when he meets someone obviously more successful than him. This small personality flaw is totally outweighed by Jamie's good qualities. I've always overlooked the chip on the basis that nobody's perfect. Now I'm glad I did, because it could work in my favour.

Despite this, an undercurrent of pessimism about the date remains unshakeable. It's not as if my hit rate with the dating website has been anything to brag about. Plus, I'll confess to being disconcerted by his choice of venue.

Ben and I have arranged to meet on Tuesday night after work, not in a bar or a restaurant or cinema, or even Subway for that matter.

But in a church. It's not as odd as it sounds, for St Luke's – at the pinnacle of Bold Street in the city centre – isn't any old church. I'm not sure it even counts as one these days; as far as I'm aware, it hasn't been used for anything remotely holy since 1941, when it was bombed by the Luftwaffe.

While that fateful grenade all but destroyed the once resplendent Gothic building, its outer structure remains, and has stood in proud determination since. In fact, the shell of the 'Bombed-out Church' hasn't just survived, it's evolved; this is courtesy of a loving restoration of its gardens and, more recently, with some large-scale modern art installations finding a home in its open-air interior.

I arrive six minutes late – timed to perfection – and am momentarily distracted by the beauty of the place. Sunlight streams through the windows of the church and casts filigree patterns onto the lush rose gardens below. Lovers sit enraptured on the cast-iron benches, unable to appreciate the gorgeousness of anything but each other. And groups of office workers laze on the grass, their top buttons undone, as they laugh and gossip.

I cross the lawn, scanning faces, and it strikes me how nervous I am.

I know I shouldn't be. After four dates, I should be an old hand – even if every one of those was totally uninspiring (with the exception of Juan, who was too inspiring for comfort).

I spot Ben sitting on a bench. He is in jeans and a striped cotton shirt with the sleeves rolled up. My insides flip so violently I am almost queasy, but the reflex action feels strangely good.

He's far more attractive than in his pictures – and more good-looking than I remember from the tennis event. But, beyond that, he's sexy too, with that strange and wonderful quality that's about so much more than the way someone looks.

My stomach clenches into a knot as I approach him. While the last thing on my mind is actually starting a relationship, the simple fact of being here with someone so gorgeous – on a date – arouses a rush of exhilaration. Part of me loves it. The other part wants to go and hide behind a bush.

He stands up as I approach and greets me with a slow, confident smile and a kiss on the cheek.

'Sam. Lovely to meet you.' He pulls back and doesn't remove his eyes from mine.

'You too,' I reply, shrivelling up with self-consciousness.

'I hope you don't mind the unusual choice of venue.'

'Not at all.' I can hear my voice wobbling. This didn't happen on any of the other dates. 'It's a great choice, actually. I've certainly never been on a first date here before.'

He pauses. 'You've been on many, then?'

'Oh . . . only one or two,' I clarify hastily. 'Three, maybe. Or four.'

'Not that it matters,' he laughs softly. 'None of us would be doing this if we weren't looking for the right person. And the chances of the first person you stumble across being the right one are slim, don't you think?'

'Absolutely,' I reply, feeling my throat dry up. I suddenly wish I could think of something witty to say, but anything vaguely amusing, entertaining or intelligent escapes me.

I take a seat on the bench and Ben disappears briefly to buy ice creams. As he returns, his powerful thighs striding across the lawn and his handsome face breaking into a smile, I wonder about something.

What's someone like him doing on a dating website?

There must be something wrong with him. And my top bet is that – exactly like Juan – he's a player. He oozes it, and it's more than just his good looks that make me say that. It's his confident swagger. The overt eye contact. The unashamedly flirtatious smile.

He's in the same category as Luke, I just know it. They could've been separated at birth. This guy probably has a matching Laura Ashley toilet-roll holder in his downstairs loo. Not that that matters, of course. His motivation is irrelevant; the only issue is the reaction he's capable of provoking in Jamie.

When Ben is six feet away, with two cups of ice cream, I notice that his pace slows slightly.

'Is something the matter?' I ask.

'I . . . No,' he says, shaking his head, before peering at me again. 'Have we met somewhere before?'

Chapter 46

'So do you mind me asking your surname?' Ben says. 'That's the thing about this online dating – you don't get to find out some fairly rudimentary details.'

'Brooks,' I reply.

'Samantha Brooks,' he muses. 'That's a lovely name. And it suits you.'

I smile. 'Good job, really. How's Mildred's cat?'

He grins and rolls his eyes. 'Fighting fit again. I think Mildred may just want to marry me as a result.'

I laugh and his eyes glint in the sunshine. We've moved from the bench to a prime location on the lawn in a bid to stay in the sun. He insisted I sat on his sweatshirt, despite my protestations, which weren't just motivated by the potential grass stains, but also by the idea of those stains being in the shape (and size) of my bum cheeks. It doesn't matter that I've lost weight. I could be the size of a hamster and still worry about my bum cheeks.

'How long have you been single, Sam?' he asks.

'Oh . . . not long really. I split up with someone a couple of months ago.'

He takes this in. 'Had you been together long?'

I nod, trying to look as if this fact is as inconsequential as the colour of my ex's favourite socks.

'Your decision or his?'

The temptation to fib is suddenly overwhelming. While I know that everybody's been dumped at some point in their life – and if you haven't there's probably something wrong with you – I still feel as if admitting it puts me in a category where I'd rather not be. Loser. Victim.

However, I'm such a pathetic liar that I'm aware that if I attempt to say I ditched Jamie in the same manner Alexis Carrington might dump her sixth toy boy of the year, he'd realize instantly. And given that I've already had to confess to being the woman who catapulted a pile of dog poo through the air, I'd be expecting way too much for him to overlook that as well.

'It was his, I'm afraid.'

'I see. Then . . . isn't it a little early to be on a dating website if you've just had your heart broken?' he asks gently.

'Oh he didn't break my heart,' I insist, with an annoyingly unconvincing twang. 'My heart's fine. Everything about me's fine. Fine, fine, fine.' I sound like I'm yodelling.

'Glad to hear it,' he replies, clearly not believing a word. 'So what made you take the plunge and sign up to the site?'

'I was roped into it by my two best friends.'

He suppresses a smile. 'Ah. Another one who was coerced.'

'You had a similar experience?'

He nods. 'My sister, Kate, insisted I signed up. Though "insisted" might not be the word. She's very bossy. In fact, she'd have been at home in Stalinist Russia.'

I laugh. 'Have you been single for a while?' I ask.

When he returns my gaze, our eyes lock momentarily and time stands still, for no reason I can put my finger on. One thought runs through my head as fast as the blood pumping in my veins: I *so* want this man to find me attractive. I am more bothered about his opinion than I was about that of any of the others.

'About six months,' he replies. 'And, since I haven't lived in the UK for a while, I was largely starting from scratch.'

'You haven't been living in the UK?' It's only then that I become aware of how much my situation has dominated the conversation. I rectify that by grilling Ben-who's-far-from-a-minger for the next hour and a half.

It turns out he's spent the last five years living in Australia. He moved back to the UK – to Aigburth, about a mile from me – to be close to his parents; his father is being treated for cancer.

'Not quite as glamorous as Sydney,' I say.

'Maybe not,' he concedes. 'But, despite the circumstances, I'm enjoying being back in the UK. My dad's getting better and his prognosis is pretty good. Plus, the practice where I'm working is great; there's a really nice crowd of people there.'

Ben goes on to tell me that he'd always wanted to be a vet,

despite never having pets of his own as a child (his mum is allergic to anything with fur).

'Do you have lots of friends still in Liverpool?' I ask.

'Not as many as I'd like. There's hardly anyone I went to school with still around. Certainly nobody I'd consider eligible. Lisa Smith, who I used to sit next to in geography when we were thirteen, did get in touch and offer to show me a good time. She's a lap dancer these days,' he grins.

'And you turned her down? That sets the bar high for what you expect from a woman.'

'Ha! Well, I don't want to scare you off so soon,' he grins. 'No lap dancing is required – until at least the third date.'

When he kisses me on the cheek at the end of the date, the tingle of his lips lingers on my skin. I drive home smiling from ear to ear and with the radio turned up so high my indicators are vibrating.

I pull up at some traffic lights and find my mind drifting to his sparkling eyes and luscious mouth, the gentle and oh-so-sexy contours of his face. A certainty rushes through me: this is him. I've found the man who's going to help me win Jamie back.

I just pray he wants a second date.

I put the car in gear and am pulling away, when a familiar spluttering noise is emitted from the engine and my beloved car judders to an excruciating halt.

An almighty beep from behind jolts me further and I glance in my mirror to witness a middle-aged man, with teeth shaped like toe separators, shaking his fist. I frantically put on my hazard lights and grab my phone to contact the AA yet again.

I'm about to type in the number, when a text beeps and I open it with a thrashing heart. It's from Ben.

Samantha Brooks, you're lovely. Would you like to get together again?

Chapter 47

'You need a new car, Sam,' Ellie tells me the following night. 'I'm glad there's a possible new man on the horizon too, of course – but I can't help thinking your automotive needs are becoming more pressing.'

'I love that car,' I say, squirming because I know she's probably right. 'It's perfect for me.'

'Apart from the fact that it doesn't go?' she points out, glancing up from her compact mirror as she puts the finishing touches to her eyeliner. She perches on the edge of the sofa in the stunning Merlot-coloured gown she bought for Alistair's awards ceremony in Manchester tonight. He's in line for some psychotherapy award, so she wants to look the part.

'You're exaggerating. It's temperamental, that's all.'

She sniggers and takes a slug of wine. Ellie always has a drink, or several, when she's getting ready, claiming she can't put her eyeliner on straight without doing so. 'So, Ben sounds like a hot prospect.'

'He's nice,' I shrug. 'Though I'm clearly not the only one who thinks so. We made friends on Facebook today and you should see his wall. It's covered in messages from fawning females thanking him for saving their pet poodles.'

'You've got competition, then?'

'Looks that way. So, young Sophie,' I say, as Ellie's little girl scuttles into the living room in cute pink pyjamas, the effect of which is marred slightly by a trail of snot on her top lip that resembles an exotic mollusc. 'It's you and me tonight. Would you like some milk?'

'No,' she replies, while Ellie wipes her nose with a tissue. 'I like a lollipop.'

'I'm afraid I haven't got lollipops. Wouldn't milk do?'

'Only lollipops.'

I frown. 'Well, how about we get you some milk, and if you don't want it you can leave it?'

'Only want lollipops.'

I take a deep breath. 'Pretty certain about this lollipop business, aren't you?'

Ellie snorts with laughter.

'Are you nearly ready for bed?' I attempt instead.

'NO BED, Auntie Sam!' she says, as if I suggested she becomes a practising Satanist. 'It not bedtime.'

'I think you'll find it is bedtime,' Ellie interjects, scooping her up and kissing her soft curls.

'No not!' replies Sophie determinedly, trying not to giggle.

'Well, if it's not bedtime, what time is it?' I say, deciding there's no way she can get out of that argument.

She thinks for a second. 'Party time.'

Ellie laughs and, after another kiss, hands her over. 'Good luck,' she winks, as she and Alistair slip into the night, leaving me to deal with an insomniac two-year-old who'd rather have a rave than a good night's sleep.

In the event, she goes down quietly. At least, I think so for a couple of minutes, until I realize that I've forgotten to turn on the baby monitor. She is in fact pumping out a medley of nursery rhymes from her cot bed, accompanied by a dance routine that's part cancan, part JLS.

When she finally drifts off, it's into such a deep sleep that I feel slightly anxious every time I look in to check she's still breathing . . . about every four minutes. I've got no reason to think she won't be breathing; she's never decided to stop in her entire two and a half years, so I don't know why I'm worried that she'll change that policy on my watch.

As I close the door to her very pink bedroom, I have a flashback of the first time Jamie and I met her. It was at Liverpool Women's Hospital, fourteen hours after she'd entered the world.

'Jamie, you're insane,' I told him, as he stumbled to the hospital carrying an enormous teddy that we'd squeezed onto the back seat of the car – where I'm still not sure it sat legally without a seatbelt.

The bear wasn't Jamie's only gift. There was an enormous box of chocolates for Ellie, a crocheted cardigan for Sophie from his mum (Jamie's mother is always crocheting baby cardigans, even if nobody she knows is having a baby), and the promise of a well-earned pint for Alistair. I'd got used to Jamie's preposterous level of gift-buying over the years, but even by his standards this was something else.

I'd love to say that Ellie looked radiantly maternal. But she looked like she'd survived a natural disaster and was waiting for the Red Cross. After I'd given her a kiss and gently hugged her squashy midriff, tiny cries came from the cot at the end of the bed.

Jamie was looking down at Sophie. 'She's beautiful.'

'She's not bad, my girl, is she?' beamed Ellie, happier than I'd ever seen her.

'Does she need feeding?' he asked, as her cries became more insistent.

'I've just done that. And changed her nappy,' Ellie frowned.

'Shall I give her a cuddle?' said Jamie.

'Why not?' she shrugged.

He reached into the cot and picked up her tiny frame with the confidence that only an uncle with enough nieces and nephews to cast the stage version of *Annie* could possess. Sophie settled immediately, soothed by his assured rocking, while he gazed into her cloudy newborn eyes.

An hour later, as Jamie turned the key in the car's ignition, I kissed him on the cheek. 'What was that for?' he laughed. 'Not that I'm complaining.'

'Nothing. Sure you weren't getting a little broody in there?'

'Me? Nah,' he grinned, pulling out of the car park. 'Kids are great and I love them. But, fundamentally, I'm just like you, Sam: happy to give them back.'

I smiled and gazed out of the window, wondering how he'd come to the conclusion that was just like me.

Chapter 48

The choice of venue for my second date with Ben is critical. As is the day. And the timing. So, while he'd actually asked me out on Saturday, it had to be twenty-four hours earlier. And, rather than the eight o'clock start he'd suggested, it had to be five-fifteen. Fortunately, he was very understanding about the non-existent great-aunt's non-existent birthday party that I can't miss in Solihull tomorrow.

'You believe in starting early, then, Samantha Brooks?' he smiles as we sit in the least offensive corner of the Fat Pheasant. Ben is sipping lager, and has been polite enough not to mention that his drink looks like the sort of industrial waste that causes birth defects.

I stick with a bottle of Budweiser on the basis that I personally watched as it was opened (so know that it isn't contaminated with whatever's festered in the beer pumps for seventy years). Plus, the last time I ordered wine here I received a liquid that would only have tasted right sprinkled on fish and chips.

'I just thought it might be easier, given it's a Friday night, to come straight from work, rather than rush home and go through the palaver of getting a taxi back,' I tell him.

'I'd hate you to go to any effort on my account,' he teases.

I give him a playful nudge, then the door opens and my heart nearly stops. A man enters who could be anything between the ages of twenty-five and seventy-five and is sporting trousers that look a century older. I relax momentarily.

Ben and I are, without question, the two best-groomed individuals here, despite both wearing jeans. Admittedly, mine are my posh Ted Baker ones that I squeezed into in the loos at work, before commencing a beautification regime that involved a full makeover, underarm shave and manicure. I bunked off at four o'clock to do it, though obviously my attire is low-key enough to give the impression that I just threw it on.

My date looks every inch as gorgeous as I'd hoped, if not more so. He is in uber-cool casual gear, the sort Jamie would covet almost as much as his six-pack. At least, that's the plan. Because a lot's riding on my ex-boyfriend's reaction when he arrives in – by my calculations – half an hour.

The time goes surprisingly fast. If you'd told me an hour ago that I'd be able to think of anything except Jamie, I wouldn't have believed you.

What I hadn't counted on was Ben being so entertaining. My theory about him being a player must be bang on: he has confidence and charisma in spades and you can see a mile off that he's trouble. If I really was looking for a snog from this guy – rather than what I am looking for – I'd be concerned. He's flirtatious, funny to the point of occasional hilarity and self-deprecating enough to come across as a genuinely nice guy. In other words, he has those killer factors that obviously leave women falling at his feet (and I don't just mean elderly cat-owning neighbours such as Mildred).

Fortunately, the only feet I'm interested in are Jamie's and, as I look at my watch and realize it's ten to six, I wonder where the hell they are.

'Is everything okay?' Ben asks, sensing my unease.

'Yeah. Sure. So tell me a bit more about your job.'

Ben tells me all about his life as a vet and some of the time he spent abroad . . . et cetera, et cetera. It's interesting, but there comes a point at about 6.03 p.m. when all I can think about is whether Jamie's ever going to turn up.

Maybe I presumed too much. There is a possibility that he won't come, slight as that seems, given that there hasn't been a Friday night since he started at the phone shop when he hasn't stopped by for an after-work drink.

With Ben in full flow, I glance at the door again as it creaks open and a group of young, besuited men files in. The first is vaguely familiar, the second I definitely know. But it's the third I'm most interested in. He hasn't seen me – but he's going to, any second now. And I wonder what on earth Jamie will think when he does.

Chapter 49

My ex-boyfriend is quickly engrossed in a conversation with the barman, who, incidentally, looks like he's walked out of a haunted house. My heart is pounding through my ears and I'm not listening to a word Ben says, even though I'm looking steadfastly at him. Actually, that's not true. Every few seconds I glance at Jamie. He still hasn't seen me, and after a while I realize I've got to act.

So I take a deep breath and a giant slug of Budweiser, and gaze with loving infatuation into Ben's eyes. He doesn't instantly notice my shift in demeanour. But gradually, as I nod, feigning interest with dreamy eyes, his expression softens.

'So,' I say, putting an elbow on the chair behind him and flicking back my hair. 'The dates you've had since joining the website . . . has nobody fitted the bill?'

I hold his gaze brazenly, despite being so firmly outside my comfort zone that my bones are almost creaking. Ben looks entirely unfazed. He doesn't attempt to remove his eyes from mine. In fact, the corners of his mouth turn up. 'They hadn't . . . but I guess I'll have to let you know.'

I'm the first to look away, and can't decide whether it's due to the heat spreading up my neck, or my unstoppable urge to check on Jamie. Infuriatingly, he remains engrossed.

'Um . . . Ben, excuse me a minute. I'm going to pop to the Ladies.'

Under normal circumstances, I wouldn't go near the facilities here for fear of catching something that'd require a course of strong antibiotics. I wouldn't even hover over these toilet seats in case the germs on them pole-vault in my direction in a bid to escape.

However, the toilets have one thing going for them: location. While I don't get to walk directly past Jamie to reach them, they are in his general vicinity. I head across the room maintaining the illusion that I haven't seen him and doing my best to look sophisticated – which is a word probably last used here when they got their first delivery of Blue Nun.

To my utter frustration, I reach the Ladies without a second glance from my ex-boyfriend.

Inside, I top up my lipstick and fluff up my hair, satisfying myself that I look as hot as physically possible for the big walk back. However, as I push open the door and my eyes flash to where Jamie was . . . he's gone! I don't believe it. I really don't believe it. I've brought a perfectly nice man to this noxious hole of a place – and all for nothing.

I head back to Ben and he catches my eye and smiles. I smile back, simply because it's impossible not to.

He's still grinning when I reach our table. 'Interesting choice of venue.'

I hold my hands up. 'It's hideous, isn't it?'

'I'll be diplomatic. It looks like the sort of place where they'd lock up hostages. How come we're here?'

I laugh. 'Shall we go somewhere else?'

'Most definitely.'

With Ben's hand on the small of my back as I stand, something propels me to glance to my right. It's for a split second, but that's all it takes. Jamie hasn't left the building at all. He and his colleagues have simply moved to the other side of the bar . . . and he's glaring at me.

My legs wobble as we approach the door and I feel Jamie's eyes burning into my back. Then Ben does something that under any circumstances would make my heart do somersaults – but, in full view of Jamie, it almost sends it cartwheeling around the pub.

He holds my hand. As if it's the most normal, natural thing in the world.

I look up, momentarily startled, and he responds with a squeeze as two contradictory thoughts race through my head: doing this in front of Jamie is horrendous, and it couldn't be more perfect.

Chapter 50

The rest of the date is a slightly strange affair. Ben seems to enjoy himself, and I put on a semblance of doing so too. But my mind is elsewhere. Namely, trying to work out why Jamie didn't follow us into the Bar and Grill on Fenwick Street when we headed there for cocktails.

At first, I think it's not his sort of place, being way too clean for a start. But, after a while, the question starts to gnaw at me.

I'm torn between, on the one hand, thinking that tonight was a great idea in my quest to make Jamie realize what he's lost, and, on the other, wondering if I've vastly overstepped the mark. Maybe he thinks I'm a floozy. Maybe he thinks I don't love him any more. But, and this is worse than both of those scenarios: maybe he thinks . . . so what?

The thought that my little trick has left Jamie underwhelmed tortures me for the entire evening. Which is a shame because I'm vaguely conscious that I might be enjoying it otherwise. Ben is funny, warm, good company and, yes, okay, spectacular eye candy. He'd be irresistible if I really was in the market for this.

But I'm not. So at the end of the night, when he goes to kiss me, I don't respond as he expects. Instead, I pull away and smile, kissing him briefly on the cheek. It's obvious this isn't a situation he's used to.

'A coffee's out of the question, then?' he laughs.

'I only drink tea at this time of night,' I smile, semi-apologetically.

'I'm sure I could make do with PG Tips.'

'I'm sure you could,' I laugh. 'Hey . . . it's been lovely. Thank you.'

'No, thank you.' He adds cautiously, 'I'd like to do it again . . . if you would?'

I pause, thinking hard about my plan and whether this is really the right strategy.

He rolls his eyes and laughs at my slowness to answer. 'If it's that unappealing a prospect . . .'

'It's not unappealing at all. Send me a text and we'll sort something.'

He nods and backs away with a big, unabashed smile, blowing me a kiss with his hand. 'Sleep tight, then . . . and I'll catch you soon. If you didn't catch anything from that pub.'

Over the next two days – in the absence of any contact from him – I'm consumed with what Jamie must be thinking.

Then I bump into Lisa in Liverpool One on Monday lunchtime as she's coming out of Hollister. Yes, Hollister. Even I feel intimidated in there, such is its colossal degree of coolness.

Not that that bothers Lisa, who today is sporting Uggs, a nursing-home-chic cardi and a voluminous floral skirt that could accommodate half a boy-scout camp.

She's laden with bags and surrounded by children – her own and another couple she appears to have accumulated – and panting so heavily I half expect a lung to pop out of her mouth as she thrusts the buggy down a step.

'Hey, Lisa!' I call, while two buff male shop assistants rush to her aid.

'Oooh – hiya!' she waves, as three bags plummet to the floor. An assistant picks them up. 'Ta for that,' she winks, surging towards me. 'Just the woman I've been meaning to phone.'

'Oh . . . why?'

She plonks the bags on the ground and pauses to catch her breath. It takes several minutes – at least it feels like it. 'What's this I hear about you having a new man?'

I stiffen. 'What makes you say that?'

'Jamie told me yesterday.' She says this with a distinct undercurrent of indignation. 'You're a quick worker, I'll give you that. I thought you were still in love with my brother. Idiot that he is.'

I think carefully about how to handle this. 'It's nothing serious, Lisa. Honestly.'

'So he's just a friend?'

I bite my lip and try to work out a diplomatic answer. My instinct is to reassure her that he's nobody and Jamie has nothing to worry about. But that would destroy the object of the exercise, so I hedge my bets. 'He's nice – but it's nothing compared with what Jamie and I had.'

She narrows her eyes. 'So you do still want our Jamie back?'

'Lisa, you know I do.'

'Hmm,' she says, as one of the children pulls her skirt and starts a conversation about whether they can go to McDonald's for lunch. Then another pipes up to ask for some M&Ms. And another about what time his mum's picking him up. Eventually, there are so many voices fighting to be heard, it's like the trading floor of an investment bank.

'Had I better leave you to it?' I scrunch up my nose.

'Yes . . . no . . . ohhh,' she says distractedly as she momentarily steps forward and lets the kids chirrup among themselves. 'I tell you something, though. He's as jealous as hell. The idiot.'

My ears prick up. 'Really? What did he say?'

'One or two things.'

'Such as?'

'It wasn't what he said, but the way he said it.'

I sigh. 'But what did he say?'

'Hmm. Strictly speaking . . . nothing. Except that you have a new man. But that's not the point.'

I frown.

'All I'm saying is – and it's a feeling so you'll have to go with me on this one,' she says, tapping her nose knowingly. 'When he first told me you'd met someone else, I admit I felt a bit annoyed, what with me doing all I can to persuade him to see reason.'

'I still want him back, Lisa, I promise. And your efforts are appreciated.'

She flashes me a beaming smile. 'Are they? Aw . . . well, you can buy me some chocs when he moves back in. That's when – not if. I'm that confident.'

'Really?' I ask hopefully.

'Really. I'd bet my house on it. Not that that's saying much, given the state the kids left it in this morning.'

I laugh. 'Did you buy anything nice?'

'Flip-flops,' she says, producing them from a bag. They're the same as the pair I've seen on the Hollister promo posters, worn with denim hot pants and a barely there bikini top. 'What do you think? I thought they'd be smashing with a nice comfy tracksuit.'

As I look up, I spot someone and am saved from having to answer. 'Oh look, there's Dorrie.'

'I haven't seen her for ages,' Lisa hoots. 'Dorrie! Dorrie!' she calls, and Jamie's childhood friend turns and waves. As she walks over, she slows slightly.

'Oh . . . hi, Lisa. Sam,' she says with an uncomfortable smile. Despite wearing torn jeans and a casual vest top, she looks as gorgeous as ever.

'What have you been up to?' Lisa asks, nudging her.

'Oh me? Not a lot. How are you, Sam?'

Dorrie has been Jamie's friend since they were three foot tall and she knows me only as his girlfriend – so this moment is clearly awkward for her. It's the first time she's seen me since the split. I want to reassure her that there's no need to feel uncomfortable, and that her loyalties needn't feel torn because, no matter what happens, I'll have nothing but goodwill towards Jamie. But now is neither the time nor the place.

'I'm good. Thanks for asking,' I reply. 'How are you?'

'I'm great. Listen, lovely to see you both and, sorry, but I've got to dash. Take care, won't you?' she adds as she focuses on me and squeezes my arm.

And as she heads into a shop, I realize that the emotion her eyes betrayed as she looked at me just now was unmistakable: it was pity. Oh God, help me.

Chapter 51

As Lisa is the High Priestess of Speculation, I know better than to read too much into her words, determined as she was. Until, that is, I bump into Luke in the newsagent's the following morning on the way to work.

'Have you really got another bloke?' he asks, screwing up his nose. 'Jamie said he saw you with someone on Friday.'

I swallow. 'I . . . he's . . . I was on a date, that's all.'

Luke raises his eyebrows. 'Well, Jamie's been a pain in the arse ever since. He's in such a bad mood.'

'Really?' I reply, feeling my heart surge.

'Really. I made a nice dinner last night to cheer him up, but he turned up about five hours late from work,' he says, clearly torn between indignation and sympathy. 'He's obviously upset, but really.'

'Well,' I shrug. 'Jamie would do that sometimes if something was getting to him.'

He tuts. 'It's not a trait I'd put up with. Anyway, Sam, I need to talk to you.'

I feel my heartbeat double in speed, but it turns out that the impending revelation is absolutely nothing to do with me, Jamie or indeed anyone else but Luke.

'I'm in love,' he declares, like a bewildered puppy.

'You are joking.'

'I'm not,' he says, grabbing a pack of gum. 'It's bloody terrifying.'

I scrunch up my nose. 'Why the fear? I thought all you wanted was – and I quote – "to settle down and find someone special".'

'I do,' he protests. 'But I have no idea if she feels the same way.'

'Have you told her you love her?'

'Yes.'

'When?'

'I texted her at half past two on Saturday night, after I'd had a skin full.'

I roll my eyes. 'How romantic. What did she say?'

'That I was a knobhead.'

I snigger. 'Sounds like my sort of woman.'

'I thought you were supposed to be a good listener. The thing is, she's friends with a woman I once went out with. Well, two, actually. So she knows about my . . . you know . . .'

'Sordid past?'

He frowns. 'The point is that she's wary. Even though she has no reason to be. I'm interested in nobody but her. I haven't looked at another woman. In all honesty, I'm worried about myself.'

269

'Luke, you'll just have to play it by ear and see how things develop. If it's meant to be, it's meant to be,' I tell him sagely, feeling like Yoda addressing Luke Skywalker.

I'm heading back to my car when a text arrives from Jamie.

Hey – what's up? You doing anything nice this week? xx

I smile and take a deep breath. This is his fourth since last night. Which – along with Lisa and Luke's feedback – brings me to one conclusion about the prospect of more dates with Ben: they can only be a good thing.

So when one of his emails ends with him asking me out again, I don't hesitate to say yes.

Date number three is at the Taverna, a romantic shabby-chic place in south Liverpool. It's perfect – except for a small point: we don't bump into Jamie.

Date four is lunch at Tabac, an arty coffee-shop-cum-bar filled with people putting the world to rights. It's also perfect – except we don't bump into Jamie.

Date five is at 3345 next to the Parr Street studios, a second home to musicians and, again, perfect – except we don't bump into Jamie.

This is despite the fact that these venues are Jamie's favourite spots, places he's virtually lived in for the last few years. I'm not saying I expected to see him every time, but I didn't think once was asking too much.

Even on date six, when I casually suggest a stroll in the park and we detour past Luke's house (whoops-a-daisy, how did that happen?), he's nowhere to be seen.

Short of suggesting that the next date takes place in the entrance of Phones-A-Go-Go, I'm at a loss.

Still, I persevere. Although 'persevere' is the wrong word because seeing Ben is about as far from the definition of a chore as you could get. He is lovely. This is a conclusion I came to early on and it is reinforced every time I see him. I find it hard to stop myself from telling him this and yet I must. However, I'm conscious that keeping my thoughts a secret is not only a terrible travesty, but it must also raise questions in Ben's mind.

Not least, why we haven't kissed yet. On the couple of occasions he's attempted it, I've pretended not to notice; instead, I peck him on the cheek and hastily move on to something else. Giving into it would be a step too far, given how badly I still want Jamie back. But it's an odd situation, I can't deny it, and I'm aware that it's ultimately not sustainable.

Date seven is at a bar in the Albert Dock because I heard from Luke, who is now emailing regularly for romantic advice, that Jamie has gone to a gig tonight at the arena next door. He's only there for the support act, who've apparently kept it more real than the band everyone else is there to see.

I have positioned us at an area of the bar with a panoramic view of the entrance. The prime location means I am quite prepared to live with a defective stool boasting one leg shorter than the others; it's a fault that's left me rocking from side to side as if I'm on a playground ride.

But Jamie has singularly failed to turn up for a pre-concert drink.

'So what's the deal between you and me, Samantha Brooks?' asks Ben.

The door pushes open and someone wearing a jacket that looks like Jamie's makes his way in. My heart loops the loop . . . until I realize he's thirty-five years older and sporting a toupee that looks as if it crawled into place.

'Hmm?' I say, snapping out of it.

'The deal. Between you and me.' His eyes are glinting mischievously.

'What do you mean?' I ask, sipping my drink. 'What deal?'

He grins and crosses his arms. 'Well, both of us presumably went on that website to find someone with whom we had . . . chemistry.'

'Er . . . yes.'

'So have we got chemistry?'

I ponder the question. 'I think we have. That's a funny thing to ask, though,' I smile, raising an eyebrow.

'Why?'

'Well, it's been a while since I dated, but that sort of analysis is meant to be a woman's domain, isn't it?' I tease, rocking back on my stool.

'I'll admit it's a new one for me. Then may I ask another question . . . if it's not too personal?' It might sound as though he's going to quiz me about something deep, but it's said so lightheartedly that I'm convinced he's about to tell a joke.

'Ask away!' I whisper, grinning as I rock forward.

'I will!' he responds with a laugh. Then he stops laughing. The light gives Ben's skin a warm glow and as his eyes gaze into mine it strikes me how badly I wish Jamie was here. To see a man like this looking into my eyes . . . it would've sealed the deal.

'Is there a reason we haven't kissed?'

I rock backwards on my chair leg, but so violently this time that the stool decides it's going with me. Momentum gathers as I plunge back with Bugs Bunny eyes, squawking like a strangled flamingo.

As Ben dives forward in slow motion and grabs me by the hand, the stool clatters to the ground. Were karma on my side, I would no doubt bounce up daintily into the safety of his arms, completely retaining my dignity.

Instead, I drag him on top of me until we're scrambling in a heap on the floor as though we're taking part in a hideous, bastardized version of *Total Wipeout*. My skirt has bunched round my thighs and Ben attempts to avert his eyes. Unlike the barman. He gazes lazily at us while polishing a wine glass as if contemplating some sort of modern art installation.

'Yet another beautiful response,' mutters Ben, getting to his feet and helping me up. 'I'd better give up on you, hadn't I?' he adds.

'No!' I leap in.

'Oh Sam, I know when to throw in the towel.' He swaps stools to give me his, clearly considering me not sufficiently responsible to be left in charge of the wobbly one.

'Don't throw in the towel,' I add, panicking. 'I mean it. The towel should stay where it is. Very much so.'

He looks serious. 'But . . . where is the towel?'

I swallow, desperately thinking of something to say – or do.

I know there's only one option. With adrenalin racing through my veins, I stand up slowly, brush down my skirt and tentatively move towards him until I'm so close I can feel the warmth of his breath on my face.

This man, who could probably have his pick of women, shows a rare flicker of vulnerability. He doesn't move, not even an inch, while, exhilarated and terrified, my face draws towards his.

'The towel,' I whisper, 'is here.'

Before our lips touch, all I can think of is the fact that this will be the first time I've kissed a man other than Jamie in six years – and I've forgotten how. I'm suddenly a teenager in a woman's body. I'm consumed with insecurities about what to do with my tongue . . . where to put my hands . . . whether to close my eyes.

As his mouth presses against my trembling lips, those thoughts melt away. I'm instantly lost in the kiss, the sublime sensation of his tongue brushing mine, the strength in his hand as it presses against the small of my back, pulling me into him. I'm completely oblivious to onlookers. My heartbeat fills the room as his mouth explores mine. Blood rushes through my veins, leaving me tingling with feelings I'd forgotten existed.

When I eventually pull away, I am elated, reeling, a little bit overwhelmed.

'Hey . . . okay?' he smiles, his warm fingers wrapping around my hand.

I can only manage to nod and breathe: 'Okay.'

And it strikes me that my quest to win back Jamie isn't all hard work, after all.

Chapter 52

Kissing is all I'm ever going to do with Ben, but I still feel guilty. Even though I'm technically doing nothing wrong, I can't shake the feeling of betrayal. Because, while I'm fully aware that kissing is not sex, I'd forgotten how intimate it can be. It can blow your mind if you let it, and cause sensations that I'm finding all the more intense because it has been so long since I did it with anyone but Jamie.

It's with these thoughts uppermost in my mind that I prepare lunch at my house for Ben and myself on Saturday, although I'm still tingling from the glorious, mind-blowing kiss he gave me the second he walked in the door.

It isn't the first time Ben's been to the house. We ended up back here after our last date, and on that occasion, between the drinks and conversation, he methodically worked his way round the house, fixing all those bits and bobs I've never got round to fixing. I was torn between disbelief, gratitude and amusement.

The cabinet door is now perfect. The wonky shelf in the living room is now straight. The curtain rail I've been meaning to put up is secured with screws, rather than Blu-Tack. I never asked him to do this; but, since he offered, I felt as if only a masochist would say, 'Oh don't worry. I love the wobbly headboard that gives me concussion every time I lie down.'

Today, he's sorting out the spotlights in the kitchen as I put together a salad.

'Are you sure you don't mind doing that?' I ask, frowning, when he steps down from the ladder.

He brushes his hands and moves towards me, taking me in his arms and gently kissing my lips, sending ripples of pleasure down my spine.

'Of course not. Why would I?'

His lips sink onto mine again, making my breath quicken and my body melt into his. While I know Ben isn't pressurizing me to go further, desire seeps from his every pore. I have an undercurrent of concern that this can only go on so long. So I decide to introduce one or two excuses.

'Where did you go to school, Ben? I don't think I've ever asked,' I say idly, as I prise myself away from him and toss tomatoes into the salad bowl.

'Oh just the local comp.'

'I went to a church school,' I announce meaningfully. 'A super-strict one. Strictness is a good thing in my book. It's certainly played a big part in shaping my values.'

'Right,' he says casually. He's wearing a checked shirt and jeans that make his bum look like it should be framed and hung in the National Gallery. 'Good for you.'

I add some dressing to the salad. 'I'm not a religious nut or anything – just old-fashioned about certain things. Very old-fashioned.'

'I see. What sort of things?'

'Well,' I swallow, turning back to concentrate on the rocket leaves. 'Mainly . . . sex.'

He coughs. 'Sex?'

'Mmm. Yep,' I reply brightly.

'I see.' Without even looking, I can tell he's smirking. 'So what are you saying? You think sex is evil?'

I straighten my back and turn around, still unable to meet his eyes. 'Not between a loving and committed couple, obviously. But I think it's important to wait a while.'

Despite the enthusiasm with which I slip into the role of Ms Pro-Chastity, it's not an image that those who knew me at university would recognize. I'm not saying I've slept with loads of people. Fewer than Ellie and Jen by a long way – though, admittedly, Jen would have the sex life of a Trappist monk if she always waited until the fifth date.

But I can't claim that before Jamie was on the scene I had a will of iron on this front. When I met someone for whom I had the almighty hots, all it might take was four bottles of Budweiser before my determination to keep it zipped up would disappear quicker than an ice cube in a cup of Ovaltine. To listen to me now, you'd think I'd never been near a set of man bits in my life. Not that Ben needs to know the truth. He can't.

'Well . . . I think waiting a while's fine too,' Ben says, taking a sip of tea. 'But I don't think it makes anyone who doesn't a bad person. As long as they're doing it safely.'

'Agreed. I'd never judge anyone. These are just personal choices. My personal choices.' I turn my back on him and open a drawer to take out some cutlery.

'So . . . how do you feel about me kissing you?' He's suddenly behind me with his arms round my waist, his still-hot lips tenderly making their way up the back of my neck as he presses his body against mine.

What I feel couldn't be clearer. What I feel is this: outrageously horny.

But given that I've just delivered a speech that gives the impression I have a wardrobe full of chastity belts upstairs, I can hardly let him know. I turn round and let him melt into me. 'Um . . . absolutely fine with that,' I manage, as his mouth devours mine and I fight a growing desire for him to lift up my skirt and continue this kissing session on my inner thighs.

Fortunately, I'm saved by the bell. Well, not quite the bell – but my mobile phone, whose ringtone makes me leap out of Ben's arms.

I pick it up and see Jamie's number.

'Give me a minute,' I mumble, scurrying to the next room as I answer it. I shut the door behind me and try to sound natural. 'Jamie, how are you?'

'Hi! Great, thanks,' he replies. 'Listen, I'll be driving past in five minutes and wanted to stop by and get some sheet music for my guitar. You haven't thrown it away, have you?'

'Of course not,' I reply in a hushed tone. 'Does it have to be now?'

I know I'd wanted Jamie to think I had a new man on the scene, but seeing him at our house is a step too far, surely? The only conclusion he'll come to is that I'm sleeping with Ben – and given that I've gone to the trouble of abstaining, that's not an impression I want to give.

'I'm on the way to a practice session with the band and need to get some, that's all. Why? Are you . . . busy?' He emphasizes the word 'busy' to make it clear that we both know what he's implying.

'I am slightly . . . busy,' I reply, deliberately vague. 'But if you just want me to have it ready for you . . .'

'I won't stay.' His voice is tinged with sulkiness and suspicion. 'I'm only round the corner, so if you could have it ready I'd appreciate it.'

When I put down the phone, I haven't even got time to politely keep Ben abreast of developments. I simply race upstairs to get the music – and to check my make-up is in tact.

The doorbell rings as I'm racing down and, before I can pause to think, I fling the door wide open.

Jamie's expression is thunderous as he takes the music from my hand. 'I won't stop,' he says, glancing over my shoulder. The wine Ben brought is on the table with two glasses and a bowl of olives sitting significantly next to it.

'Probably best not,' I tell him, biting my lip.

Tension hovers in the air before he backs away, looking distraught. For a split second, I'm not even thinking about the fact that I have another man in my kitchen, a man who's about to demolish my salade niçoise before smooching with me for the rest of the afternoon. I only want to run after Jamie and say, 'It's not what you think. This is all for you! It's you I want, for God's sake!'

Then I remind myself that he knows where I am if he wants me. He knows all he has to do is say the word – and I'll drop everything and be his again.

He knows all that and yet he still backs away down the path, albeit looking like a man with the weight of the world on his shoulders.

Chapter 53

'So did Jamie not see Ben at all?' asks Ellie, swiping a glass of champagne from a passing waiter's tray.

We're at a corporate networking event the following Monday at the Tate Gallery in the Albert Dock. The room is a vast white space housing modern art that's being idly gazed upon by the top team at DLB Harrow law firm – my clients – and their clients.

The evening is going smoothly, especially since no one heard Deana complaining that my request for her to remove her Hubba Bubba amounted to a breach of her human rights.

'No, but he knew he was there,' I reply. 'Ben's car was parked outside and Jamie could see the wine and olives on the living-room table.'

'Olives? Ooh. Dead giveaway. That must've hurt.'

'Hey, go easy on that champers, will you?' I tell her. Ellie only stopped in on her way home from a course in the city centre; I hadn't counted on her helping herself to half the drinks list. 'It's not me paying.'

'Oh don't be such a spoilsport,' she tuts, taking a large

mouthful. 'Anyway, I need a drink. The new class of GCSE students I've been assigned are an absolute nightmare. They'd drive anyone to alcoholism. Besides, I'm a valid person for DLV Barrow lawyers to network with, aren't I? If I need a lawyer in the future they'll be my first port of call.'

'DLB Harrow,' I correct her. 'And as for you being a potential customer . . . they only deal with big multinational companies or private individuals with more spare cash than the average Russian oligarch.'

'I'll buy a lottery ticket this weekend, then,' she winks. 'So isn't Ben beginning to suspect anything?'

I'm about to say no, but pause and think back to the date. He did seem a little on edge afterwards, though not for any reason I can put my finger on. 'Hmm. I don't know.'

'And what about you?'

'What about me?'

'Are you not getting attached to Ben?'

'God, no,' I splutter. 'He's a lovely guy and one hell of a kisser. But, no. I know who the love of my life is and that isn't going to change, even if it remains unrequited for the rest of my days.'

Ellie screws up her face. 'There's nothing big and clever about unrequited love, Sam. It only makes a woman feel shit about herself. There comes a time when you've just got to get over it.'

I tut. 'Well, we're far from there yet in Jamie's case.'

She touches my arm. 'I know, sweetheart. And from what you say, he's coming closer to realizing what a terrible mistake he's made. But . . .'

'What?'

'When I suggested this thing in the first place, I rather thought he'd have his grand realization a bit sooner. The fact that he hasn't . . . I've got to be honest, Sam. I'm starting to think that maybe you ought to cut your losses.'

'Ellie,' I hiss, disbelievingly. 'This is not some bloke I've been dating for a few weeks. This is Jamie. The man I want to spend the rest of my life with. He's not that disposable, I'm afraid. Besides, lots of couples have periods apart and get back together. It makes them stronger. Look at Prince William and Kate. He dumped her for a few months and now look at them. It made him realize what he'd lost. I'm only looking to bag Jamie, not the future heir to the throne.'

'You're right,' she nods. 'It does happen. I'm sorry, gorgeous, but I've only got your best interests at heart.'

I know this is true, of course. Ellie is the best friend anyone could ask for, which is probably why I say nothing when she proceeds to get comprehensively sloshed and falls down the stairs in full view of DLB Harrow's managing partner.

Nevertheless, the following day, when I'm at the dentist waiting to have a filling, I can't help pondering my friend's words about Jamie – and wishing she hadn't uttered them. My grim mood isn't helped by my location, of course. I'm not good with dentists. I can tell myself till I'm purple in the face that it isn't going to hurt (and it never actually has, unless you count the near-shattering of my knuckles from gripping the chair). But the musty whiff of freshly drilled enamel is enough to set my heart flapping so hard I'm convinced I'll hover ten inches off the chair one day.

I pick up a three-year-old glossy magazine and marvel at its longevity, despite being thumbed by hundreds of anxious patients trying to take their mind off the tasty injection of local anaesthetic they're about to be served.

The magazine features a health special, with a 'well-being' quiz designed to ascertain what shape you're in. Judging by my results, it's amazing that I'm still alive.

My trans-fat levels from all the ready meals I've consumed – even in these post-Jamie days – should by rights have left me as one giant walking blob of cellulite, unable to make my way through revolving doors or into the seats of budget aircraft.

My brain-boosting Omega 3 is so low it's a wonder I scraped a single GCSE, and – tsk! – I've never even had a colonic irrigation. How my bum's still functioning I'll never know.

Fortunately, I'm not classed as an alcoholic; although what Ellie's results would be don't bear thinking about. The woman is unstoppable. She always has been unstoppable, but these days she can't go near a glass of wine without instigating a full-scale party.

'Miss Brooks.' The dental nurse is in her mid-forties with an air of Norman Bates, which has done nothing to put me at ease. I'm about to stand to meet my fate, when my mobile rings.

'Hey, Sam. It's Ben.'

'Hi, there! I can't really talk at the moment.'

'I'll be quick. I know this is short notice, but I wondered if I could return the favour and invite you for lunch today. I've taken a day off and you said you were planning to go home after the dentist because you're owed so much lieu time.'

Mrs Bates taps her foot impatiently. 'If you come over when you're done,' he continues, 'we could go out to get some supplies, then I'll impress you with my culinary skills.'

'Oh Ben, it's lovely of you to offer—'

I'm about to refuse because I've got a lot on today; even though I had planned to go home, it was to catch up on a mountain of paperwork.

Then something strikes me. Jamie does his shopping at the supermarket on Allerton Road every Tuesday. It's his day off for working at the weekend and this is literally the one and only element of routine in his otherwise unpredictable leisure time. I haven't had a text from him since the other day, and I realize this could be my big opportunity because, ultimately, having Ben around is pointless unless Jamie sees a little more of me with him.

The only time he laid eyes on him was in the pub – and he could have come to the conclusion that it was a meaningless fling. The fact that it *is* a meaningless fling is irrelevant. Jamie needs to be reminded that he has competition.

'Ben, that'd be great,' I say firmly. 'I'll be over in an hour.'

When I arrive at Ben's apartment, I'm slightly late, having made a brief detour home to grab some make-up and sort out my hair, which was in danger of having a flock of baby eagles setting up home in it.

I'm looking as I always try to appear these days: hot and happy. I read that that's the look Victoria Beckham advises any woman to master when times get tough. I'm fully aware that, technically, Posh Spice isn't really up there with the world's great philosophical gurus, but on this particular issue I think she's one hundred per cent right.

The only problem, however, is that, following my anaesthetic, my face is temporarily as wonky as a three-wheeled shopping trolley. When I attempt to smile, or talk or do anything involving my mouth, one side stays put.

Which means that, despite the carefully applied foundation, skinny jeans and on-trend boots, I'm not looking nearly as hot or as happy as I'd like.

'I'll come down to you and we'll go straight off,' says Ben into his intercom, while I stand in the foyer of the apartment block he calls home. He arrives thirty seconds later looking gorgeous – in jeans, a long-sleeved black T-shirt and a Berghaus gilet that makes him look fantastically outdoorsy.

'Hello, there,' he says when he appears, kissing me on the lips. This would undoubtedly be pleasurable if I could feel them. He pulls back and looks at me, registering. 'Oh. You okay?'

I hold up my hand to my mouth self-consciously. 'Had a filling. I'll be back to normal in the next hour or two.'

'Okay,' he smiles, taking me by the hand as we head to the car. 'Let's go and get this food.'

When we pull into the supermarket car park, I scan my surroundings. While Jamie always comes to this place on a Tuesday morning, narrowing it down any further isn't easy. There is a window of several hours and, despite my world-class talent for shopping, even I'd struggle to stretch out a trip to Tesco that long. So I'm hoping and praying that, for once, luck might be on my side.

As we push the trolley round the store, Ben picks up a variety of foodstuffs: bits and bobs from the deli, a walnut loaf, olive oil. But I can't concentrate on the food. All I can concentrate on is scanning the aisles for Jamie. Except, by the time Ben's finished his shopping, he still isn't here.

'Do you mind if we look at the books? I've finished the one I'm reading and need a new one.'

In fact, the collection of unread books on my bedside table is vast. I have good intentions with my reading material. I see a book, read the blurb and know I'll love it . . . then never quite get round to opening more than about forty per cent of the ones I buy.

I promised myself recently that I'd stop purchasing so many new ones until I'd read those I already own – but that resolution is irrelevant in this context. The only issue is that the books section is at the front of the store, with a grandstand view of the entrance.

I flick through the new Jackie Collins, or pretend to, while Ben looks at the new Lee Child. Then I move on to a Paige Toon novel, glancing anxiously at the door. After ten minutes, Ben appears at my side.

'Anything take your fancy?'

'Oooh. Spoiled for choice. Can I have a couple more minutes?'

'Sure – take your time.'

But, as I return the paperback to the shelf and pick up another, something catches my eye and I glance up, drawing a breath.

It's Jamie, pushing a trolley. And heading directly towards us.

Chapter 54

I'm frozen to the spot as Jamie sails past us, heading towards the toiletries. I can't make it obvious that I'm following him; this must be done with the subtlety and stealth of a preying jaguar.

'I need a pumice stone!' I announce, flinging the paperback onto the shelf.

Ben looks at me as if I have Tourette's.

'This way!' I hoot, grabbing the end of his trolley and thundering up the aisle, past the DVDs, vases and mops.

My heart is break-dancing around my ribcage as I approach the toiletries aisle. I take a deep breath and head round the corner. Except – Jamie isn't there!

Slowing my steps, I continue to guide the trolley and Ben along the aisle.

'Is this what you were after?' Ben asks, holding up a Scholl packet.

'Er . . . possibly. Let me just have a look over here,' I say, spinning us round as if in a dodgem car and heading back to see if Jamie's in the next aisle.

As I hurtle past bread makers and slow cookers, breaking into a sweat, I panic that he's given us the slip. That he's *never* going to see me with Ben. Another wasted opportunity!

A dozen imaginary scenarios burst into my mind . . . visions of what I could be doing if only Jamie could see us. Ben could be pecking me gently on the cheek beside the broccoli. Smooching at the eggs. Kissing my hand as I choose a baguette.

Hang on a minute . . .

The second those thoughts hit my frontal cortex, another engulfs me. What if kissing isn't enough? I mean, what's a kiss? A kiss is nothing. A kiss is meaningless! Ben and I have been kissing non-stop for the past few weeks and what I feel for him cannot be compared with what I feel for Jamie.

What the hell can I do if he spots us together? What can I do that's going to make a real impression? With fire in my chest, I grab Ben by the hand and thrust the trolley forward, whizzing past other shoppers and darting up aisles like I'm on *Top Gear*.

'Sam . . . what's the rush? You've just spent fifteen minutes totally immobile in the books section,' Ben points out, bewildered.

'I'm really hungry all of a sudden,' I reply cheerily, heading back to the toiletries to make a last check. But, as I whisk my trolley round the corner, my plan goes awry. Significantly.

I can't work out whether it's the sound or the impact that registers first. As my trolley rams violently into Jamie's gut, we come to a catastrophic halt, our food is involved in a multi-item pile-up, and my ex-boyfriend emits the sort of noise that a vomiting shire horse would make.

'Jamie!' I gasp. 'Are you all right?' I fling the trolley away – sending it flying across the aisle – and dive towards him. 'I'm so sorry,' I say, putting my arm around his back.

He straightens up. 'It's fine. I'm fine. I'm . . . I'm . . . Who's this?'

He looks Ben up and down. Ben smiles, unfazed.

'I'm Ben. Pleased to meet you,' he replies, holding out his hand for Jamie to shake.

Jamie stares at it for an uncomfortable second, clearly considering not taking up his offer. Eventually, he relents and grabs Ben's fingers, shaking them with a conspicuous lack of enthusiasm before he turns to me.

'How're things?' he asks flatly.

'Fine. I . . .' Then I look back at Ben and remember my concern only a few seconds ago. Not only am I not even kissing – the act I was worried wouldn't make enough impression – I'm huddled next to my *ex*-boyfriend instead of my current one. I untangle myself from Jamie and edge back to Ben.

'I'm . . . fine,' I smile and, locking my eyes with Jamie, I defiantly lift up my arm and place it around Ben's shoulder.

But I'd forgotten how tall he is and I am immediately aware of how stiff and odd it looks – like a young child attempting to befriend a big kid in the playground. Not that that matters. All that matters is Jamie's reaction. And Jamie's reaction is . . . utterly underwhelming.

I grit my teeth, unable to believe how unmoved he is. I remove my arm and return it to my side, feeling ridiculous.

'Right, well, I'm in a rush. Catch you soon, Sam,' Jamie says.

'Yep,' I croak as he heads up the aisle to examine the back of some Lemsips.

I'm ready to explode with frustration. My mind is filled with the thought that I've blown it. I've singularly failed to provoke any emotional reaction whatsoever by anything I did with Ben. Not that I did much.

Cursing under my breath, I'm about to scuttle away and take Ben with me, when Jamie glances over again. Then I spot something on the shelf in front of me – and I'm hit by a moment of pure inspiration.

'Hmm,' I murmur, picking up a bumper pack of Durex and giving it the once-over, then demonstratively flinging it in the trolley. I glance up . . . and realize Jamie wasn't looking. Bugger.

With my eyes firmly on my ex-boyfriend, I grab the next thing I see on the shelf: a bottle of lubricant called Play. Jamie looks over. I slowly hold it over the trolley, making absolutely sure it's in full view, and chuck it in. Then I realize they have them in three other flavours. So I pick up a strawberry one and throw that in.

I don't even need to look up at Jamie now to realize I have his attention. His jaw is trailing so far on the floor it's virtually gathering dust, and my sense of empowerment is intoxicating. Addictive.

So addictive that I pick up a banana-flavoured lube, a kiwi-flavoured one, a few more condoms and then – the pièce de résistance – something called a Durex Play Vibrations, which is without question the raunchiest item I have ever seen stocked in Tesco.

'That's all, darling,' I say sweetly, standing on my tiptoes to kiss Ben briefly on the mouth. 'For now,' I wink.

Then I push the trolley past Jamie, slowly enough for him to get a full view of my mammoth stash of exotic contraceptive devices and rainbow-coloured bottles of lubrication. As I sail past, his cheeks are green.

But I pretend not to notice; instead, I march straight to the checkout – where Ben's hand appears on my arm.

'What is it?' I ask, glancing up.

He looks almost stunned. I say almost because . . . there's something else there too.

'What was all that about?'

It is anger.

I open my mouth, but don't know what to say.

'Sam?' he says, furious.

'I . . . I just . . . thought I'd stock up,' I reply weakly.

He crosses his arms. 'So . . . a woman who doesn't believe in sex unless it's in a "loving and committed relationship" suddenly thinks it's a good idea to fill her shopping trolley full of –' he picks up the vibrating ring between two fingers – 'these?'

'They're for my . . . cousin,' I say, flustered. 'She does a lot of . . . um . . . shagging. In her spare time.'

He looks at me blankly. 'Your cousin,' he repeats.

I swallow.

'Sam,' he says calmly. 'What complete rubbish.'

'I can explain,' I say, blood rushing to my cheeks. 'I can definitely explain. I'm sure I can.'

He pauses and waits for me to come up with something brilliant. Except I can't come up with something brilliant. I can't come up with anything.

So he turns and marches away. I've never seen someone more determined to get away from me in my life.

Chapter 55

The next few days are a strange time, and not in a good way. Having spent for ever brooding over Jamie, I now find myself with an additional worry – one that actually makes me feel worse.

At least with Jamie I could take the moral high ground. I could tell myself that I'd been rejected through no fault of my own. The hollow feeling in my stomach now isn't caused by rejection, but by all-encompassing guilt.

I might never have envisaged Ben as a real boyfriend, but that doesn't mean I didn't end up liking him. A lot. It's taken until now to make me realize something I'd become blind to because of my obsession with getting Jamie back: I've used Ben – with a total disregard for his feelings.

Hurting him was the last thing I'd wanted. Yet I can't deny how deliberate and calculated I've been. And in being so, I didn't stop for a second to think about the implications.

'I take it you've tried to contact him?' Jen asks as she sits on my sofa sipping tea, her long legs propped up on the arm. She's stopped by after work on Sunday to drop off the *Inbetweeners* DVD she borrowed months ago.

'Several times,' I reply. 'I've had only one text back, saying "Don't worry about it".'

'That's worrying,' she frowns. 'What about Jamie?'

'Jamie's done nothing but text and email. He wrote me a massive one yesterday telling me how tortured he is, how it crippled him to see me with "that man", how he doesn't know what to do, how he still loves me. Basically, he's driving me insane. He might say all this . . . but has he come back? No.'

'So are you going back on the dating website?'

'I signed up for three months,' I reply grimly. 'But I've had it with the making-him-jealous strategy. I won't be logging on again in the near future.'

'Oh but you should! You never know what might happen,' she insists.

'I haven't been very inspired by the others,' I tell her.

'Maybe you're not looking hard enough. Come on, let's log on again.'

It turns out my inbox is straining under the weight of unread emails and 'winks', most of which come either from Saudi Arabia or from people who look like they spend their spare time organizing hamster-baiting rings.

Reluctantly, I open the first email. It's from somebody called CaringGent4U. He's five foot five, fifty-one and has no picture, which, frankly, is the best thing about his profile.

Hello there! I was struck by such an attractive woman as you undoubtedly and undeniably are. I imagine you have been deluged with mail off of admirers on this website! You sound quite an intriueging lady, a very intriueging lady in fact – with a 'playful' and 'light' attitude to life if I may be so bold! As for me, if you give me your email address I will send you some photographs, though they don't do me justice as I am constantly being told what a handsome and charming gentleman I am in the flesh! I am also very, very intelligent and have refurbished my home to a high standard! In summary, I am an impressive man and we would be a very good match. I am currently in waiting for my boiler to be serviced so it would be a pleasure to hear from you!

I groan and open the next one, from someone called MrLoveRocket.

Hey bbe – wanna chat?

'That is the most depressing thing I've ever read,' I mutter.

Jen sniggers.

'Why are you so upbeat?' I ask suspiciously. 'I didn't think you were seeing anybody.'

She takes a deep breath. 'I wasn't. I'm not. But I . . . I fancy somebody. It's almost as enjoyable.'

My eyes widen. 'And?'

'He's a doctor who's just started in our paediatrics department. He's thirty-seven and has eyes to die for and a bum to die for and—'

'Muscles?' I venture.

She pauses and looks into the middle distance. 'Actually –' she frowns – 'I'm not sure he has got muscles.' She shakes her head. 'The point is that he's lovely. And we've been for coffee. And he's asked for my number.'

'And?'

'And it's absolutely bloody well killing me not texting him to ask him out!' she screams.

I sit back in shock. 'Why haven't you?'

'I've been reading Ellie's book,' she says earnestly.

'Ah . . . the dating book.'

'It's called *Make Him Fall for You*.' Not quite the title Ellie had remembered. 'It says that asking a guy out, or even texting, or in any way coming on strong, is against the rules. Which I hate. I can't even tell you how much I hate it. But . . . well, he does seem interested.'

Under normal circumstances I'd argue that that was outdated nonsense, but this is Jen we're talking about. She needs all the encouragement I can give to follow this strategy.

'Well, good girl,' I reply, standing up. 'Do you want another cup of tea? Stay for dinner, if you like.'

'No . . . I'd better be off. I swore I'd go to the gym tonight. Thanks, anyway.'

As I see her out and shut the front door, I notice Ben's scarf hanging next to my coat. I hadn't realized he'd even left it. I pick it up and hold it to my nose as my mind floods with an image of him kissing me that sends heat rushing through my body. I think of his face in the supermarket and how angry and hurt he looked. When I think of how hurt he looked it makes me feel sick. He showed me nothing but kindness and affection and how did I repay him? Urgh!

I take a deep breath and snuggle my cheek next to his scarf, breathing in his smell. Then I close my eyes, noticing as I do how hot and sore they suddenly feel.

Chapter 56

Julia phones a few days later to invite me to lunch with her and Gary at the weekend. I tell her I'd have loved to, but I have to work so can't make it.

'Anyway, wouldn't you like to spend time with him on your own?' I ask.

'Well . . . I sort of . . . have,' she confesses. 'He's been over a few times. It's been fascinating. Lovely, actually.'

'Things are obviously going well, then?'

'They are,' she says, almost surprising herself. 'He's a fantastic person. And I was totally right about the fact that knowing him doesn't change how I feel towards Mum and Dad.'

'I never thought it would. Though I'm not sure Mum's convinced yet. Not that she's mentioned it lately.'

'No,' she says solemnly. 'She's said nothing to me either. And I must admit I'm avoiding the issue.'

I sigh. 'I don't think you can, Julia.'

'I know. The thing is, the more I see Gary, the more intrigued I am about my birth mother.'

'What's he told you about her?'

'Not much. He's mysterious. The only thing I have worked out is that she lives in Wales. Or has some sort of Welsh connection – I'm not sure which. Anyway, knowing so little is difficult to deal with because he's been so open about himself. God knows what he's hiding,' she laughs.

'Do you think he's hiding something?' I ask.

'He's respecting the wishes of my mother, that's all,' she says. 'As he said, meeting me has to be her decision, not his – or even mine. It's bloody frustrating, though, like an unsolved mystery. The idea that I may never know who my own flesh and blood is . . . Well, it's suddenly become difficult to deal with.'

'It never bothered you before,' I point out.

'I know!' she replies, then hesitates. 'Which is why I'm not sure I've done the right thing.'

I frown. 'What have you done?'

'Written to her – via Gary,' she says quietly. 'He knows where she lives and has agreed to forward my letter to her. I've told her I'd like to meet her.'

'Oh Julia,' is all I can say.

'Do you think I've done the wrong thing?'

'I just worry that you'll be hurt if she doesn't write back.' She doesn't answer. 'You will, won't you? Be hurt, I mean.'

'I don't know, Sam,' she replies. 'I really don't know.'

Jamie's flight remains booked. Our bed is inhabited by me and me alone. We're not back together – nothing like it. Yet his texts and emails since the supermarket incident mean that giving up on him isn't an option. Not when there are still weeks in which to change his mind. But I'm running out of ideas about how to do it.

It doesn't help that Ellie – my mentor at the beginning – hasn't been encouraging of late. She keeps saying that Jamie should have acted by now. As if I didn't want him to!

I know she has my best interests at heart and is trying to prepare me for the worst. But I don't want to prepare myself for the worst. Plus, she hasn't seen at first hand how torn he is about this. She hasn't read his emails. She didn't see the envy in his eyes in Tesco. With time and encouragement, there's still hope. There has to be. And I think Ellie's distracted by work a lot lately. She's finding both the workload, and some of her students, difficult to deal with this year. At least, that's what she says whenever I phone shortly after home time and she's already cracked into what I know is the first of way too many glasses of wine.

One person who hasn't lost her enthusiasm for a reconciliation is Lisa. She texts me on Wednesday to ask me to pop over for a cup of tea and, as I'm passing on the way back from a meeting, I decide to stop off.

When I arrive at the house, it's quieter than usual, as three-fifths of the children are at school and the baby is asleep upstairs. Nevertheless, I enter the living room and Elvis hurtles towards me.

'Auntie Sam! Come and look at Timberlake!' he says, tugging my jeans.

'Your guinea pig?' I reply, a chill running down my spine. I'm terrified of rodents. I know that technically this isn't one, but it's got four legs, fur, and is small enough to crawl up a trouser leg, all of which makes it close enough in my book.

'Cuppa?' shouts Lisa from the kitchen.

'Please! Right. Timberlake. Where is he?' I say, putting on a brave face.

'Here!' Elvis declares, opening up a box that once contained a pair of size eleven Reeboks and removing the creature. I instinctively sit back, trying to look unfazed.

Despite the distance I put between me and Timberlake, however, I notice immediately that something isn't right.

'Is he . . . okay?' I ask tentatively.

'Oh yes,' he grins, stroking the animal. 'He doesn't mind.'

'Mind what?'

'Being dead.'

I draw a breath but feign calmness. 'Timberlake is dead?'

'Yes. Do you want to give him a cuddle?' He thrusts the decomposing corpse of his beloved pet in front of my nose and I jerk back so fast I bang my head on the wall.

'I'll pass, sweetheart. Are you sure you're meant to be holding him?'

'I'm just giving him a hug.' He rubs his cheek against the fur and looks up, sensing my unease. 'He was more fun when he wasn't dead,' he tells me.

Lisa walks through the door. 'Oh yes . . . poor Timberlake. He went this morning. I thought we'd let him lie in state in the

shoebox under the telly till Dave gets home. He's nipping out in
his lunch hour to give him a proper funeral. Oh put him back
now, Elvis, won't you, love? He's as stiff as a board. And wash
your hands before you have any more of them Wotsits. Now,' she
says, turning to me. 'How are things with Jamie?'

I take a deep breath and glance at Elvis. He is filling the
guinea pig's coffin with a variety of items to see him through to
the afterlife – namely, three pieces of Lego and a Dairylea cheese
string.

'Oh . . . I don't know, Lisa,' I say wearily.

She narrows her eyes as the front door slams and Dave walks
in. He's three years older than Lisa but, despite the thinning hair,
he looks younger. He's got one of those baby faces you suspect
will remain unmarked by time, even when he's collecting his
pension.

'What's all this about a dead guinea pig? What have you been
feeding it? Curry and chips?'

Elvis rushes over and leaps into his father's arms. 'Have you
got any Polos, Dad?'

'There – just for you,' he replies, and Elvis gratefully takes a
small handful and places them lovingly in Timberlake's tiny
paws.

'Hi, Sam,' says Dave. 'How're things?'

'Fine, thanks,' I smile.

'Apart from my idiot brother, obviously,' Lisa interjects. 'He'll
see the light soon – don't worry.'

I take a sip of tea. 'I'm starting to worry that nothing can be done about this situation,' I tell her. As the words spill from my mouth, I suddenly don't know whether I'm saying this for reassurance or because I believe it. 'I mean, why am I bothering with this? Jamie can't love me that much, otherwise it'd be a no-brainer. Why should I have to do all the chasing?' I look at Lisa. 'It isn't supposed to be like this.'

Dave and Lisa exchange looks.

'You're not chasing anything other than your heart,' insists Lisa, and I wonder what TV show she picked that up from.

'I don't think he's interested,' I add flatly, overcome with negativity.

'But he is, Sam!' Lisa blurts out obligingly. 'Dave, we need to manufacture an excuse to get these two lovebirds together. Why don't we do a big roast dinner for everyone? Or you could come to Suzuki's birthday party the week after next.'

She babbles away, concocting all manner of potential scenarios in which to reconcile Jamie and me. But as I glance at Timberlake – lying rigidly amid a heap of Lego bricks and mints – one question leaps out at me.

Is it sometimes better to just let something go?

Chapter 57

The next day at work is so hectic there's barely time to go for a wee. I have these days sometimes. You attempt to break for a rudimentary biological necessity – but someone phones, or calls you into a meeting, or thrusts an invoice at you that absolutely-must-be-signed-there-and-then-or-the-sky-will-cave-in.

I hadn't predicted it was going to be quite so chaotic today, though I knew I had a bit to finish on the tender for a bridal show. I hadn't counted on Lorelei Beer demanding an impromptu meeting before she had to race to her mother's in Cardiff for a family funeral, or on 'urgent' business with three other clients (their definition of which was a long way from mine), or on the drinks machine electrocuting the work-experience girl.

Why I ever signed up as the nominated first aider I'll never know.

'We're going to have to get you to A&E,' I tell her. She looks fine, but the first thing I learned on my course was to defer responsibility whenever possible.

The 'fine', by the way, refers to her immediate medical requirements, rather than anything else about her appearance. She's twenty-one, with disastrous hair, an explosion of acne and an apparent inability to say anything. When she first arrived, clutching a CV boasting twenty-seven A-star GCSEs, nine A-star A levels, and a double first, along with her Tupperware sandwich box, I genuinely wondered if she had a vocal-cord malfunction.

'Would that be okay?' I ask her softly.

She nods shakily but says nothing. I'm constantly torn between feeling so sorry for her I want to hug her till her sides hurt – and shaking her by the shoulders and declaring: 'Speak, woman!'

'I don't think you should drive,' I tell her. 'We'll get you a taxi. Mind you, we need someone to sit with you.' I look up and hone in on the corner.

Deana, who has been filling Natalie in all morning on what a useless reprobate her sister's friend's second cousin's current boyfriend is, has paused momentarily – to dye her eyelashes. She is surrounded by pots and Petri dishes – as if she is on the brink of discovering a cure for cancer – and is smearing Vaseline under her eye area with a cotton bud.

'Deana!' I stand up decisively and clap my hands. She raises her head briefly and looks at me along her nose, like a Roman empress. 'I've got a job for you.'

Natalie drops her magazine and screws up her face.

'I'd like you to take Anna to hospital.'

Anna flinches. I feel for her, I really do. But there's no other way. Being in a car with Deana will be character-building, at least.

'You wha—?' says Deana.

'Hospital. Please. She's injured. Or possibly isn't, actually. But she needs checking out.'

'My car's in the car park and the ticket only lets you in once,' she protests. 'Wharrama gonna do when I get back?'

'Either get another ticket and put it on expenses, or get a taxi. Come on, please.'

Deana's urgency is some way removed from anything you see on *Casualty*.

I go back to my desk and fend off a further series of phone calls, including one from the organizers of the Santa Dash – a charity race I've taken part in for the last three years. They want me to sign up the whole office for the event this December, obviously unaware of the total lack of influence I have on Deana and Natalie during work hours, let alone during their own time.

Still, I register the office for the run – deciding to worry about practicalities later – and return to my tender. I've been doing it for only five minutes, when I realize that I can't focus. My mind is elsewhere. Namely, on the men in my life.

I log on to Facebook and hold my breath when I see Ben online. I open up a chat box and compose a message before I can even think.

'Hi there. Hope you're well.'

I know it's bland, but it's the only way to go. I sit glaring at the screen, as if waiting for a boiling kettle . . . but there is no response for an age. Then a message flashes. Not any old message. This is the message every single woman dreads when they've just started a chat conversation with a man.

'Ben is offline.'

'Great,' I blurt out, noting that another three women – one of whom looks like Pamela Anderson's poutier sister – have posted more gushing messages of thanks about the miracles he's worked on their pets.

Natalie looks up.

'Unpaid invoice,' I lie.

She pulls a face as if to say: 'Why would I care?'

I flick back to my tender document and start attempting to add figures, unable to concentrate. Suddenly, I hear a muffled ping – and flick back to Facebook.

'Sorry about that – just got your message. I'd gone into the other room. I'm good. You?'

I take a deep breath. I could use this moment to make chit-chat, to sweep things under the carpet – or I could get straight to the point. Thinking fast, I reply:

'I'm fine, thanks. Listen – I feel awful about what happened. I need to explain.'

I hit return and watch impatiently as words flash up to tell me that Ben is writing a reply. Eventually, a new message appears.

'Think I worked out what was going on . . . it was obvious I'm afraid!'

I swallow.

'Erm . . . was it?'

There's an interminable silence as he composes his response.

'You're still in love with your ex.'

I close my eyes and feel tears gathering. How do I respond to that? I start writing something, then delete it. Then I write something else, and delete that too. Eventually I take a deep breath and type in one word, before hitting enter.

'Yes.'

My heart is thudding, filled with dread as I await his response. He'd be perfectly entitled to call me every name under the sun.

'I guessed something was going on the day I came for lunch. But, hey – neither of us can help it if you didn't find me irresistible enough to fall for me instead. I won't hold it against you!'

I can't help but smile.

'You're wonderful, Ben.'

'Ah – you recognize a good man when you see one. You're not all bad, then, Samantha Brooks.'

I laugh.

'Listen – I've got to run. Stay in touch, won't you? Despite all this, I happen to think you're a pretty special woman. If it doesn't make things too tricky, maybe we could be friendly. Deal?'

'Deal.'

As I send my reply, I'm feeling better than I have for days. I'm about to close down Facebook and return to some legitimate work, when another message flashes up.

'One more thing that struck me during your little performance with the sex toys . . . '

I groan.

'Yes?'

'It's about what I thought about your ex.'

'Oh?'

'I don't know if this offers any comfort . . .'

'Go on – what is it?'

'It's obvious he still has feelings for you too.'

Chapter 58

Part of me wishes I could let Jamie go quietly, but I don't have it in me. Occasionally, I have a vague sense that it could be for the best, until I remind myself of everything about him that I loved and still love.

There's never been anyone like Jamie in my life.

I know that if I was reading my own story on a problem page, I'd be screaming at the magazine that it's time to move on and find someone else. But the reality is different when you're living it.

Besides, don't passion and all-consuming love count for anything these days? Are they concepts that are now too old-fashioned? They weren't once. Shakespeare might have had less of an impact if Romeo had reacted to Juliet's apparent tragic death by keeping a stiff upper lip and joining a dating website.

These days, when someone's left you, people are frustrated if you can't 'move on' quickly. You're allowed to wallow for only a certain amount of time before you're expected to give it a rest and get on with life. But I believe this: sometimes love is dysfunctional and damaging and dangerous. Moreover, we can't help who we love. And I still love Jamie.

'Have you ever got back together with someone after splitting up?'

I type the question into my laptop early on Saturday evening before Jen and Ellie arrive for a girls' night in.

Ben and I have been chatting online most nights since we made friends again last week. I've confessed everything to him about my strategy to win Jamie back. It was the only way. And he's been totally understanding. Instead of getting annoyed at me for the part I forced him to play in it, he's accepted my – truthful – reassurances that there was more to it than that. I told him that I genuinely enjoyed his company and I genuinely saw him as my friend. And that's something I'd love him to still be.

'Once. A girl I went out with in Sydney.'

'Did it work out?'

'Er . . . well, I'm single.'

'Oh. Good point.'

I pop to the kitchen briefly, and when I return there's a new reply from Ben.

'Something occurred to me recently, Sam. Do you mind if I am blunt . . . ?'

There's a pause.

'I'll assume from the fact that you haven't leaped in like you usually do that you DON'T mind. Either that or you've gone for a wee . . .'

I roll my eyes and continue reading.

'Maybe you're trying too hard to get Jamie back.'

I bite my lip and start typing.

'So, what do I do? Nothing?'

'I'm not saying that. But can I give you a man's perspective?'

I sit up and take a sip of wine.

'Please do.'

'I think you need to be straight with him. Meet him on neutral ground and tell him you love him and you want him back – but say that you won't wait around for ever. Then leave him to it. Give him some space. Let him think.'

'That's it?'

'That's it. Sorry. Is that not complicated enough?'

'Okay, Denise Robertson . . . Any more advice?'

'There is one more thing.'

'Yes . . .?'

'Look hot.'

I burst out laughing.

'Look hot. Gotcha. I'd been thinking of turning up in my old sweatpants and hoodie.'

'I'm sure you'd look delightful. Though you know that little white top with the flowers? That'd work for me.'

I grin.

'Really? You liked that?'

'I did. Plus, the way you did your hair that time we met

in the Taverna . . . very sexy. Not that I am thinking sexy thoughts about you any more, obviously. My friend ;-)'

I smile to myself.

'Anyway, catch you soon. Have a nice night in with the girls.'

'Goodnight, my friend,' I say out loud as I close down the chat box. It's at the exact second that his picture disappears that I am assaulted by a vivid flashback of Ben's kisses as we sat in that noisy bar. His mouth is pressed against mine, his tongue brushing my lips and gently pushing into my mouth. It sends a rush of butterflies through my insides and I groan, momentarily giving in to the pleasure.

I shake my head and take a deep breath.

'This is what celibacy does to a girl,' I scold myself. 'Get a grip, Sam.'

Ellie and Jen arrive together twenty minutes later, having shared a taxi. Ellie enters first, in stripy tights, a tiny miniskirt – and with two bottles of wine.

'Good God, Ellie! This is meant to be just a quiet night in,' I laugh.

'It's been a tough week,' she grins. 'Believe me, I'll have finished both of those single-handedly by about nine o'clock.'

I pop to the kitchen for nibbles and wine glasses, and when I return she's enquiring about Jen's paediatrician – the one without the muscles. The absence of Jen's usual physiological requirement does nothing to dampen our friend's enthusiasm. 'He. Is. Gorgeous. Nothing less. You'd so approve.'

'So what's happening?' asks Ellie, munching on a Kettle Chip. 'Fill us in.'

'What's happening is . . . bugger all!' she replies, exasperated. 'We go for coffee, we sit next to each other in the cafeteria, we chat in the staff room. That's it! And the reason is that, having read *Make Him Fall for You*, I daren't text him, contact him, or do anything that could be construed as neediness. I can't bloody move without thinking I've broken the rules.'

'I'm not sure I'd go along with this book,' I say sceptically.

Ellie throws me a look. 'It's working, isn't it?'

'It's *not* working! He hasn't asked me out!' cries Jen.

'He will,' says Ellie confidently. 'In the meantime, he's buying you coffee, going for lunch, seeking you out. Normally after – what? – three weeks of knowing someone, by now you'd have asked them out, slept with them and they'd have moved on to someone else.'

'Well, that's a bit harsh,' tuts Jen. 'Completely true, but harsh.'

Ellie leans over and hugs her. 'Sorry, gorgeous. You know I think they're crazy to let you go.'

'No, you're right,' Jen sighs. 'Actually, I can't believe what I was like before. I'm embarrassed for myself. But, no more. I've seen the light.'

'You're doing the right thing,' says Ellie. 'Give him some space.'

'I had the same advice today, funnily enough,' I tell her.

'Oh,' she replies. 'Who from?'

I fill them in on some of my conversation with Ben – specifically, his advice about what my next move should be.

'Your lover knows what he's talking about,' says Ellie.

'Not my lover,' I wince. 'We never . . . you know. Now he's my friend.'

'Whatever,' she shrugs. 'I think he might be on to something.'

With those words ringing in my brain, a thought engulfs me, and it's difficult to continue with the rest of our evening until it's been addressed.

So, with my two best friends tucking into snacks, and, in Ellie's case, so much wine I'll be surprised if she remembers her own name by the time the night's out, I decide I *am* going to address it. I pick up my phone, excuse myself and wander through to the hall. And I dial Jamie's number.

Chapter 59

I arrange to meet Jamie the next morning at a cafe on Allerton Road, but he phones to say he'll come to the house instead. He's rehearsing in the afternoon and doesn't want to traipse round with his guitar, which to him is the equivalent of a Ming vase.

He arrives twenty minutes late, but that doesn't faze me. Not this time.

There's been a subtle but distinct shift in my attitude since Ben gave me his advice. My head is clear and unclouded. And for the first time since I embarked on this process I feel a tiny sense of . . . que sera sera. I need to let fate take its course.

All I can do is state my case and leave him to it. It's his turn now to grapple with this issue and come to a decision. I can only pray that it's the right one.

When he arrives on the doorstep and I let him in, it strikes me how it feels wrong for him to be ringing the bell of a house that was his for so long. We never owned it together, but it was still as much his home as mine.

He steps through the door uncertainly and kisses me on the

319

cheek. We say our hellos and he makes his way into the living room while I go to the kitchen to make us a cup of tea.

As I'm about to return, music stops me in my tracks. Jamie is playing his guitar. I close my eyes and momentarily lose myself in the music. It's a track by one of his favourite bands: the Vomiting Giraffes. They're an ensemble that have never been famous and are never likely to be, unless pretentious crap ever becomes fashionable.

Jamie's version is even more off-key than the original, if I'm entirely honest. But that's not the point. The point is that it's not perfect, but it's Jamie. And it's a sound that belongs in this house.

He stops when I walk in. 'You wanted to have a chat?'

'Yes,' I say, taking a seat.

'It's about the guy you've been seeing, isn't it?' I realize his lip is trembling.

'Sort of.'

'It's too late for me, isn't it? That's what you want to tell me. I knew it the second I saw you in the supermarket. I could see the way he was looking at you.'

'We're not together any more,' I reply calmly, thinking how good it feels to be telling the truth for once.

He looks at me as if he is holding his breath. 'Really?'

'Really. Jamie . . . there are just over two months until you're supposed to fly out. I'll be straight with you. I want you back. No more games. I want you back for all the reasons I told you in the first place.'

I put down my tea and walk over to where he sits on the sofa, on the other side of the coffee table. But I don't kiss him. I simply hold his hand and look at him directly.

'You told me once that you and I would be together for ever. You told me that because you believed it. I believed it too. In fact, Jamie, I still do. But I can't wait around for ever. I'm a survivor, Jamie, and if you're going to do this, if you're going to leave, then so be it. But I need to know one way or the other.'

'The thing is—'

'Wait,' I say gently. 'Don't answer now, Jamie. Just think. Give it a couple of days . . . a week. But you need to come to a decision.'

He pauses and nods.

'As long as you come to the right one, obviously,' I tease gently.

He looks into my eyes. 'That's all I've ever tried to do.'

Chapter 60

Dr Dan has asked Jen out to dinner. You would think he'd asked her to shack up in a spacious home in Cheshire complete with babies, swimming pool and view of the Welsh hills.

'God, I'm so nervous!' she shrieks down the phone as I arrive home from work on Friday.

'I thought you'd been on so many dates you didn't get nervous any more?'

'That's before I read *Make Him Fall for You*. The rules are different now. I can't sleep with him, for a start. Which is a total bloody drag, let me tell you. I'm nearly climbing the walls.'

'It hasn't been that long since you last . . . you know.'

'Long enough. I also can't talk about certain things. Like "the future". Or my previous break-ups. Or his. Or whether I want kids. Or whether he wants kids. Or—'

'What are you going to talk about? You'll have exhausted the weather in the first ten seconds.'

'I've made a list. So far, I've got the political situation in

Pakistan, NHS funding cuts, the new Kings of Leon album, football—'

'You hate football,' I tell her.

'So?'

'So you know nothing about it. And knowing something about it tends to be a prerequisite of making it central to your conversation.'

'Oh I'll just ask him what he thinks about the top of the Premiership at the moment and let him go. In my experience men can waffle on for hours about that.'

'That's hardly going to be much fun for you. Plus, what if he asks you what you think about it?'

'I'll nod and tell him I agree wholeheartedly with whatever he said. Anyway, I'm not too worried because it isn't really a first date: I've been for coffee with him dozens of times . . .'

Jen is midway through her sentence when my lights start flickering like I'm in a scene from *Poltergeist*. Then they go out entirely.

'Are you still there?' she asks.

'Yeah. But there's a power cut.'

'Oh I heard on the news tonight that some of south Liverpool is affected by that. It should only be temporary.' The lights flicker back on. 'What are you up to tonight?' she asks.

'Ben's coming over. I'm cooking dinner. At least, I am if the electricity stays on.'

She pauses. 'I thought it was all over with him?'

'It is. But he's become a friend.'

'Well, good for you. Right, have a lovely evening. Not as lovely as mine – hopefully! – but lovely all the same.'

The reason I'm particularly glad of some company is that, since Jamie left the house last Sunday morning, I've been consumed by the question of what he's going to do. Of what he's thinking and feeling. Of how much I wish he'd get a move on. I keep telling myself I need to stop obsessing about this, but it's easier said than done.

When Ben arrives at seven thirty, I feel strangely nervous. We're both totally clear that our relationship is nothing but platonic now. But although we've chatted loads online, we haven't seen each other in the flesh or spoken on the phone since the day in the supermarket. The day I'd rather forget.

The second I open the door, however, I'm instantly at ease, thanks to his familiar, generous smile – and the bouquet of flowers he produces from behind his back.

'What are these for?' I laugh incredulously, taking them as he kisses me on the cheek. They're gorgeous and a million per cent nicer than my normal supermarket bunches, without being remotely flashy. Just a tasteful, generous and utterly lovely arrangement of gerberas.

'Well, you're cooking – and it was technically my turn.'

I roll my eyes and squirm. 'Given that it was my fault that "your turn" never took place, I'll let you off. Thank you, anyway.'

'I wonder what happened to our trolley of food?' he muses as he enters the living room and sits on the sofa.

'It was still there weeks later. I went to pick it up today. That's what you're having for dinner: mouldy olives and walnut bread you could break a window with.'

As he laughs, I find myself momentarily rooted to the spot.

I'd forgotten how handsome Ben is. But it's more than that. His features are a blaze of contradictions: strong, masculine bone structure; gentle, kind eyes.

'Nice picture,' he says, nodding at the wall. 'Is it new?'

I put the New York picture back up yesterday. The wall looked empty without it – a fact that's been nagging at me since the day I slid it under my spare bed. Plus, there's a part of me that thought: if Jamie doesn't like this, I can have that debate with him if he moves back in. Until then, he relinquishes all say over my home furnishings.

'Not new, no. I rediscovered it. Right. I'll get you a . . . er, bottle of wine.'

'A glass will be fine for now,' he says. 'Unless you're intending to get me drunk and seduce me.'

'I'll try to control myself,' I joke and head for the kitchen before he notices that I'm blushing.

Chapter 61

Given the fact that, since my tête-à-tête with Jamie last Sunday, I've done nothing but eat, sleep and breathe the subject, it might seem strange that it doesn't enter my conversation with Ben.

Raising the subject again doesn't feel right. I'm conscious that the amount I've been banging on about my ex must be getting tedious for all my friends. Besides, our conversation is no less interesting for its omission.

So we talk about work, *Mad Men*, losing our virginity, cooking and Halloween.

When Ben does finally bring it up, after I've cracked open our second bottle of wine, I feel almost uncomfortable.

'So, Sam, any word from Jamie since your big talk?'

My chicken suddenly becomes difficult to swallow – and not because I inadvertently cooked it for twenty minutes too long when the virginity topic came up.

I take a deep breath. 'Just a few texts but no firm decision yet. He knows the ball's in his court, though. You were right. If he doesn't want me, I need to move on. I've been in limbo for too long.'

'I'm not surprised you feel like that. I know what you feel for Jamie but, as insensitive as this sounds, it might have been easier if he'd made his decision and stuck with it.'

I'm about to protest, when I stop myself, because I'm not sure I can argue with that. I've had a growing sense in the last few weeks that Jamie's indecision hasn't been good for either of us. But I'm also clear that I can't put the blame for that solely on his shoulders. I hardly let him go quietly.

'You're right. But it was me that embarked on this intensive strategy to win him back.'

'Don't be hard on yourself, Sam. We all do funny things where love is concerned.'

It strikes me that the bitter twist in my stomach is no longer so acute. I've set out to behave like a woman who is happy and self-assured – and tonight it's a self-fulfilling prophecy. Tonight, I feel more at peace with myself than I have since the day Jamie left.

The crux of the matter is this: I still want Jamie back and I'm still certain we should be together. But if he makes the wrong choice, it won't be the end of my world. The difference between now and nearly four months ago is that I don't need him; I just want him.

'Fabulous dinner, anyway, Samantha Brooks,' says Ben, standing up to clear the dishes.

'Ben, leave those,' I tell him. 'I'll do them after you've gone.'

'What sort of guest would I be if I let you cook without offering to wash up?' he tuts, grinning as he goes to the kitchen.

As the last song on my Rumer album fades away, I head to the iPod and scroll to the first playlist I come across. It's only as I sit down again that the opening bars reveal what it is: the compilation I put together to seduce Jamie. It's far too sexy to play in Ben's presence; he'll think I've been popping Viagra between courses.

But, before I flick to something else, the house is plunged into darkness, stopping me in my tracks. The iPod continues, backed up with batteries, but the pulsating beat of Goldfrapp's 'Ooh La La' is violently interrupted by an almighty crash from the kitchen.

'Ben, are you okay?' I yell, edging to the door and trying to remember where everything is. I've lived in this house for four years, but still manage to bang my knee on the table before I reach the kitchen.

'Sorry. I've dropped your casserole dish,' he confesses. 'What happened? I can't see a thing.'

'There was a power cut earlier, but the electricity returned within a minute, so hopefully it'll be back soon. Let me guide you to the sofa.'

I reach for his hand and inadvertently find my fingers on his stomach. They're there for an instant, but the feel of his taut body underneath my fingertips sends a rush of heat to my cheeks.

'Sorry. I wasn't trying to feel you up,' I joke.

He lets out a gentle laugh and threads his fingers through mine. The blanket of darkness intensifies his touch, sending shockwaves up my arm. My breath quickens, and I swallow as I turn back to the door.

'This way,' I whisper, while the sliding bars of the next song, 'Wicked Game' by Chris Isaac, fill the house.

Slowly and silently, I lead him from the kitchen and across the living-room floor. Guiding Ben is a strange and lovely sensation; I don't know why but it is. And with a wine buzz tingling round my body, we reach the sofa and fall into the cushions.

Except, Ben doesn't just fall back; he catches his shin on the edge of the coffee table and we simultaneously burst out laughing. Which is a relief, because it momentarily diffuses an atmosphere that was starting to feel . . . too strange and lovely.

When the laughter dies down, I realize that the diversion was temporary.

Electricity throbs in the air between us and my heartbeat gallops through my ears. I realize we are both still. The room's pitch black and my eyes haven't adjusted. Technically, there is no evidence that he's looking directly at me, nor me at him.

Except . . . we know.

I pull up my knee onto the sofa and it brushes his leg, making us freeze. My head is swirling, but I have a moment of total clarity: I know what I want and I know it's not right. But I've never cared less.

This is a moment in time, a snapshot in the dark, when two people sit before each other and instinctively know – without speaking or even seeing – that desire scorches their veins.

My chest rises and falls, and just as I am starting to wonder if

I should do something or say something – anything – I get my answer. Ben's hand sweeps up my leg and round the back of my waist. He pulls me towards him, so fast and decisively, that it takes my breath away. Our bodies press together, my breasts against his chest, and I'm tingling with hunger for him.

I have an unstoppable urge to be even closer to him and instinctively swirl my hips in his direction. He responds by pulling my entire body onto his in a smooth, powerful movement. And before I can think, I'm sitting on top of him, my thighs gripping his hips and his hands on my backside. He buries his head in my hair and presses the crotch of his jeans into mine, while my body floods with desire.

He kisses me softly at first, but it's soon not enough for either of us. Suddenly, I don't just want his lips on mine. I want his lips everywhere. And as he lifts my T-shirt over my head, I know that's exactly where they're about to be.

Waking up with a new lover is a strange sensation, not least because it's something I haven't done for more than six years.

I remember it as an awkward experience. It would start with an under-eye swipe to de-crust your mascara, and would be followed by a clandestine bathroom dash to brush your teeth (it being essential to create the impression that you always wake up fragrant and minty, no matter what quantities of curry and lager were consumed the previous night). Then there would be that other moment: when you debate whether a cuddle is in order – because the last thing you want is to look clingy.

However, this morning, I don't have time to think about the teeth brushing or the mascara or anything else before I feel a strong arm across my body and Ben's cheek against my neck.

It's an extension of my dreams, for he's filled my subconscious all night. I failed utterly to fall into a deep sleep, but it didn't matter. Not one bit. It was an exquisite insomnia during which I bubbled with euphoria and had to work hard to stop myself from continually kissing the soft skin on his arm.

I don't even open my eyes before we melt into each other's naked body and make tender morning love in a way that's totally different from the first time the night before, or the three-thirty time, or the five-fifteen time. Afterwards, I lie in Ben's arms and he presses his lips to my forehead and squeezes me into him.

'You're quite a hostess, Samantha Brooks,' he smirks.

I grab a pillow and gently swipe him with it. 'Not all my dinner guests get those extras, you know.'

'I should hope not. I dread to think what those nuns who taught you would think.'

I can't help laughing. 'Are you going to keep reminding me of that?'

'As often as possible,' he grins.

'Fine,' I say. 'Well, I'll try not to hold it against you. I'll go and make you some tea and toast, shall I?'

'That'd be wonderful. Make sure you don't tread on the casserole dish.'

'Well remembered.' I go to stand up but he grabs me by the arm and pulls me back, kissing me on the mouth.

'Last night . . . this morning . . . It was wonderful, Sam,' he whispers.

A smile creeps onto my lips as I return the kiss. 'It was, wasn't it?'

To say downstairs is a scene of devastation doesn't give you the complete picture.

I tiptoe into the kitchen to discover shards of Pyrex and chicken jambalaya on every available surface. It looks like someone has taken a machine gun to my crockery.

Once I've cleaned it up as best I can, I fill the kettle, put some bread in the toaster and enter the living room. Which isn't a great deal better. The lights came on at half-past three, which I know because, having thus far successfully prevented Ben from seeing my wobbly bits, he got an uncompromising eyeful of the lot at exactly that point. Still, they can't have been all bad, given subsequent events.

The curtains are drawn and every lamp still glows. Clothes are everywhere: hastily removed jeans with one leg inside out, a bra with curled-up straps hanging comically from the door handle, Calvin Klein trunks peeping from underneath the sofa.

While the kettle is boiling, I spend five minutes piecing the room together so that at least it looks less like the scene of a TA assault course.

I return to the kitchen, place the folded-up clothes on the work surface, fix the toast and tea, and then take a sip from one of the mugs. God, tea tastes good after sex, doesn't it? I know that'll never be a slogan for a Typhoo advert, but it's so true.

Smiling to myself, I put down my drink and pick up Ben's to take it up to him with his toast. I'm almost at the stairs when the doorbell rings. Lazily, I pad to the front door, still feeling barely awake, despite it being after ten.

It's not a sensation that lasts. As I open the door and stare wide-eyed and dumbstruck at my visitor, I've suddenly never felt more awake in my life.

'Jamie,' I splutter, as my legs almost give way. 'What a surprise!'

Chapter 62

Yes, I know, 'surprise' is an understatement. And being confronted by Jamie is not the only thing that unsettles me. This
time yesterday, no man had ever bought me flowers. Now it's
happened twice in just over twelve hours.

If I was being a total pedant, I'd say Jamie's aren't quite as
tasteful as Ben's, but it's the thought that counts. And the
thought terrifies me. I know the second I set eyes on him as he
stands on the doorstep – gazing at me in my dressing gown while
I clutch the tea and toast of my new lover – what they represent.

I know what he's about to say before he opens his mouth.
These flowers might be swathed in plastic, with a supermarket
sticker revealing that they had £3 off. But they're flowers – and
there's only one reason why a man who's never bought flowers
makes a sudden and drastic policy change.

To show he means business.

So when Jamie asks if he can come in and talk, because he's
come to a decision and he thinks I'm going to be happy about it,
frankly, I can barely hear what he's saying.

As I show him into the living room, my eyes dart about, surveying the environment for stray pants in a similar technique to that used by Kiefer Sutherland in *24* when he's looking for unexploded bombs. My breathing is shallow and I can think of nothing except my muted prayers that Ben does not move. An inch.

The room swims in and out of focus as Jamie sits opposite me, smiling. He looks confident and happy – two qualities totally alien to him lately.

'I've been a fool,' he says, shaking his head. 'You, on the other hand . . . Sam, you're a revelation. You've stayed strong, you've stayed beautiful. You haven't got angry, you haven't wallowed. You're amazing. I don't know how it took me so long.'

'Aren't you supposed to be at work?' I blurt out.

'I took the day off. I had to. I couldn't wait a moment longer to tell you this.'

'What is it you're telling me, Jamie?' I manage, but I don't even care about his response. It's a response for which I've yearned for months; yet, while I'm conscious that what happened last night hasn't changed that, the immediate, horrific circumstances – and getting my arse out of them – is my only priority.

All Ben needs to do is go to the loo and step on a creaky floorboard for me to be busted. It's a fact of which I'm excruciatingly aware.

'I'm coming home, Sam,' Jamie tells me with glazed eyes. He stands up and approaches me, first taking me by the hands, then throwing his arms around me. All I can think of – as I struggle to breathe with anxiety – is that I smell of Ben.

'That's . . . amazing, Jamie,' I reply, pulling away.

He smiles.

'Do you mind if I ask . . . when?'

He looks puzzled. 'When what?'

'When are you moving back?'

He grins widely. 'Now's as good a time as any.'

Only one response pops into my mind – and straight out of my mouth: 'I'm not sure now's a good time.'

He looks stunned. 'What?'

'I just mean . . . I . . . I don't know what I mean.' My head is spinning.

'Have you changed your mind?' he blusters.

'No!' I leap in, squeezing his hand. 'Of course not. Not at all.'

He narrows his eyes. 'Look . . . this is obviously a shock for you. I don't know why I expected anything different. Why don't you get dressed while I get my first load of gear from Luke's house? We can go out for breakfast together and talk.'

'That'd be nice,' I nod. 'I'd like that.'

He smiles and turns towards the door.

'How long will you be?' I ask, hearing my voice wobble. 'Just . . . an estimate, I mean.'

'Oh I don't know. Fifteen, twenty minutes. That long enough for you?' he jokes.

'Of course!' I shriek.

He enters the hall and at the exact moment he stoops to pick up something, I can hear the creak of Ben's footsteps.

'What on earth . . .'

My pulse skyrockets. I know I've been caught. He's heard Ben and the whole gaff is blown. Everything I've fought for, my entire future happiness, is up in smoke.

'What are these doing here?' Jamie grins, holding up a curled pair of lacy knickers.

I grab them so fast I nearly karate-chop his fingers. 'I've just put a load of washing on. Must've dropped them. Right – see you soon!' I say, shuffling him out of the house. I slam the door louder than intended and take a colossal breath as I hear Jamie's foot-steps walking down the path.

Then I glance at my watch. I have to get rid of someone – fast.

I abandon Ben's tea and toast downstairs. Given that my ex-boyfriend – sorry, boyfriend – will be back in fifteen minutes, a leisurely breakfast is no longer an option. I gallop upstairs three at a time and burst into the bedroom as if it's the O.K. Corral. Ben is sitting on the edge of the bed with a towel round his waist.

'Ben . . .' I begin the sentence without knowing how to end it. In the event, I don't have to.

'Don't worry, I'm on my way. Are my clothes still downstairs?'

'They are,' I mumble.

He stands up, clutching his towel, as I follow him downstairs silently.

When we reach the living room, I scurry to the kitchen to retrieve his clothes and hand them to him. He sits on the sofa and pulls his T-shirt over his muscular chest. I look away, awkwardly pulling my dressing gown tighter. When he's dressed and tugging on his boots, something strikes me.

'Were you . . . leaving anyway?' I ask, my mind whirring with the events that got us here. He looks at me and softens his intense expression.

'Actually, I was looking forward to having tea and toast then possibly making love to a beautiful woman all morning. Looks like I'll be going for a run instead.'

I bite my lip.

'I wasn't listening to your conversation with Jamie . . . but I couldn't not hear.' He pulls on his jacket. 'And . . . obviously, there's no choice for you. I know that. Of course I do.'

I instinctively reach out to touch him, but think better of it at the last second. 'I'm sorry, Ben. I . . . I don't know what to say.'

He grabs his wallet, pushing it into the back pocket of his jeans. 'You don't need to say anything,' he says, forcing a smile. 'I understand.'

I glance at the clock and realize that more than five minutes have elapsed since Jamie left. Panic must register on my face.

'It's all right, I'm going,' he says.

Then he touches my arm and kisses me slowly on the top of my head, breathing in my hair. He lingers a little too long and a rush of something with which I became very familiar last night makes my heart race.

'Bye, Sam. And good luck.'

Chapter 63

I don't know what I'd expected from Jamie moving back in, but the experience is beyond expectations. Perhaps I'd become so pessimistic about it happening that I hadn't ever pictured the scenario. If I had, I'm enough of a realist to have never imagined it being this good.

'Is it weird? It must be,' asks Ellie on the phone. I'm in the car on the hands-free four days after his return.

'It is weird . . . but amazing. I haven't just got Jamie back. I've got a new and improved Jamie.'

'Wow,' she laughs. 'Well, I must admit I'm surprised. Pleased, obviously, but surprised. I've been worried that if it ever happened, it'd be a let-down. Sounds as if that's far from the case.'

It definitely isn't a let-down. Though I'd be lying if I said I didn't feel hideous about the circumstances in which it came about. If ever there was a man who didn't deserve to suffer the indignity of sleeping with a woman then being booted out before his toast is cold, it's Ben.

It's not just that, though. While I was perfectly within my

rights to sleep with Ben, the postman or half the GB shot-putting team, there's no way I can compromise Jamie's feelings by letting him know about it. And carrying the secret – as though what happened was dirty and shameful, as opposed to lovely and mind-blowing – feels horrible.

'Have you spoken to Jen much since her date?' I ask, changing the subject.

'You're joking, aren't you? She hasn't been off the phone.'

'It went well, by the sound of it.'

'Er . . . yes. Except he hasn't been in touch.'

'Are you serious?' I say incredulously. 'I haven't spoken to her since the day after the date; she left a voice message earlier today but by the time I phoned back she was busy with patients.'

'Well, it's been five days since the date and not a peep. And she won't contact him, clearly, after reading that book. I fear the worst.'

'Oh God . . . poor Jen,' I groan. 'She did everything right this time. No shagging or anything. She can't win.'

I finish the call as I enter the house, and I am engulfed in such a delicious smell, I'm momentarily convinced I've walked into Sylvia's, next door.

'Hi!' I call, bewildered. 'I'm home!'

The bewilderment, incidentally, is because Jamie and cooking simply do not mix. The last time he was put in charge of catering for the household it almost resulted in a 999 call. Nevertheless, he appears at the door of the kitchen wearing his combat shorts, vintage Billabong T-shirt (now so vintage that it boasts an effective air-conditioning system in the form of several holes under each armpit) . . . and my pinny. It's the strangest sight I've ever seen. I don't know what I was thinking when I bought it. I was going through a Cath Kidston phase and, in all honesty, that's not really me. And the delphiniums-on-acid look definitely isn't Jamie either.

'What are you wearing?' I laugh.

'Sexy, eh?'

'Do you want the truth?' I grin, dropping my keys on the sofa and walking towards him.

'Come on, you love it really,' he says, sliding his arms around my waist and kissing my neck.

I close my eyes and try to relax. But I can't shake the strange sensation that if I get too close, Jamie will somehow work out what happened between Ben and me. I know it's stupid, but I can't help it.

I kiss him on the cheek and head into the kitchen. 'So, what's going on? Has the real Jamie been abducted by aliens?'

He follows me and puts his hands on his hips. 'I've been cooking.'

'Well, it looks inspired . . .' I reply, spotting a jar of ready-made sauce, 'by Crosse and Blackwell.'

'Aww! I'm busted! '

I laugh. 'Look, I'm not complaining. This is a whole new you.'

He throws a tea towel over his shoulder and shrugs, serious all of a sudden. 'I just want to do everything I can to make this work, Sam. That's all. I did everything wrong. Now I'm determined to do everything right. And I'm going to prove to you – in case there is any doubt – that you were right all along. You and I, Sam, are for ever.'

My phone beeps and my first thought is that it's Ben texting. I've heard nothing from him since the horrific events of the weekend.

'Have I got five minutes before dinner to get changed?'

'Take all the time you want.'

My heart is pounding as I pick up the phone – and find a text from Jen.

Going on another date tonight! On cloud nine!

Chapter 64

I'm lying in bed that night, drinking cocoa made by my boyfriend and reading a book – looking a lot like Sybil Fawlty, minus the rollers and Silk Cut.

Jamie's brushing his teeth in the bathroom, using his old-fashioned toothbrush, which he insists is more effective than electric ones, despite overwhelming expert opinion to the contrary. When he enters the room, the handle on the bathroom door comes off in his hand. 'Bugger,' he shrugs, throwing it onto the floor before climbing into bed.

It strikes me how much better he looks now he's happy.

'Our break-up could be the best thing that ever happened to us,' I say, kissing him on the cheek. 'Perhaps it'll make us appreciate how much we mean to one another. I mean, look at you – cooking, buying me flowers. If I didn't know any better I'd be suspicious.'

He laughs. 'It's as simple and unexciting as this: I recognized what I'd lost.'

I must admit, there's a part of me that's taking some getting used to another change in circumstances. Or maybe it's the hint of scepticism I retain about how long this perfect version of Jamie will last. Will Stepford Jamie disappear as fast as he appeared?

Don't get me wrong: I wish I wasn't thinking this. It'd be far easier to simply enjoy it. But I can't help it. It'd be naive to not even think about our imperfections as a couple – imperfections that I can't pretend never existed. Even though I've done a good job of trying over the last few months.

If I'm entirely honest, our relationship was never this perfect. And maybe it's the contrast between now and before that makes me realize how long I spent rose-tinting our years together, air-brushing the bumpy bits.

But bumpy bits exist for all couples, don't they? To pretend they don't won't do any of us any good. It's with this thought that, as I turn off the light and close my eyes, I am assaulted by a vivid flashback of a time when Jamie was . . . less than nice. And he wasn't the only one.

It was a year ago, after he'd recently joined a band called the Bad Scientists. It was an ensemble he stayed with for only four months, until the bass player, a bin man called Ronny, ran off with the lead singer's girlfriend, a nail technician named Charlene, who gave him significantly more than a manicure and buff.

Before the Ronny/Charlene debacle, Jamie was convinced that the Bad Scientists were his one-way ticket to success. The fact that he's thought that about every one of the scores of bands he's joined over the years – and that it's happened precisely never – was irrelevant. This time was different, and as a result he devoted as much time as possible to them.

Don't get the impression that this enthusiasm manifested itself in intense rehearsals, or endless creative sessions in which their self-proclaimed 'urban lullabies' were honed. This manifested itself in going out and getting off their faces as often and as comprehensively as possible.

There wasn't a single member of the band who let their modest day-job incomes get in the way of a thoroughly rock 'n' roll lifestyle. And Jamie, as ever when he'd joined a new band, was in it for the ride.

I say 'as ever' because, over time, I'd got used to his hedonistic binges. They started off as a few drinks after a gig. Then turned into a load of drinks after a gig. Then, over the course of the six years I was with him, his nights of total wipe-out became days of total wipe-out.

Before I knew it, we'd got into a situation whereby Jamie could switch off his phone and disappear for two days, without me even contemplating phoning the police. I didn't have a clue where he was, yet he hadn't gone missing. I'd got used to this enough to be certain that he was in a locked-up pub or someone's basement or apartment, where he was living the lifestyle of a member of Babyshambles, without the record deal or fan base.

When he returned to the house, whenever that finally was, he would look as if he needed hosing down and I'd be bubbling with bad emotions. Then I had to remind myself: we're not married; we have no kids; he's a grown man and can do what he wants; I have no claims over him at all, so how can I disapprove? The most challenging I ever got was making the odd barbed comment that leaped off my tongue before I could stop it.

But last June – the day before Grandma's eightieth birthday – I said more than the odd comment. A lot more.

Now, Grandma Laura – my dad's mum – loved Jamie. She died of a heart attack in November, an event as sudden and as unexpected as you can ever say it is for someone her age. She'd seemed in good health and was living a full and enjoyable life right up until the day she died. And one thing's for sure: she'd have been devastated to know that Jamie and I hadn't lasted.

You only had to see him in her presence to understand why she loved him so much. He flirted outrageously with her (to her utter delight, especially when it was around her nursing-home buddies) and would listen patiently to her as if she was the only woman on earth.

The big family party Mum and Dad had organized at a hotel for her was the day after an average Bad Scientists' gig. I could see trouble brewing when he refused to get a taxi home with me, instead saying he was having one or two beers with the band. Only he swore – under intense questioning – that he wouldn't miss Grandma's party for the world.

I woke the next morning to an empty bed and a grinding knot in my stomach. After a frantic few hours of failing to reach him on his phone, I came to the conclusion that, yet again, his friends, his band and he himself had all come first. I turned up at Grandma's party alone and overflowing with excuses.

'Where's that lovely boyfriend of yours?' she said as I handed over her gift. 'He asked you to marry him yet?'

'Not everyone gets married these days, Grandma,' I told her. 'And he's had to go away for the weekend to visit a sick relative. He was devastated not to be here.'

When he turned up on Monday evening – having been gone since Saturday night – we had the sort of row that shatters glass.

I'd had enough. So I screamed at him. And not just a little. I'm talking a full-blown slanging match in which I dredged the murkiest parts of my brain to produce the most cutting accusations possible, and flung every one in his direction.

Urgh. The thought of that night makes me feel ill. Not only because of what Jamie had done, but because of how bitter I'd let myself become as a result.

'I'll make it up to her,' he croaked, trudging up the stairs, reeking of booze and two-day-old clothes. To be fair, he did take her a box of chocolates the following week. And it wasn't his fault that the toffee ones dislodged one of her false teeth.

'Can't you sleep, Sam?' says Jamie suddenly, pulling my thoughts back to the present day.

'Oh I'm okay,' I tell him. 'A lot going on at work, that's all.'

He leans over and kisses me softly on my cheek. 'Just as long as you're not having second thoughts.'

'Hey . . . we've had our ups and downs, haven't we? But I'm optimistic,' I say truthfully.

He smiles and clutches my hand. 'Me too, sweetheart. Me too.'

Chapter 65

It takes me a further two days to identify another reason why it's not entirely easy to slip back into things with Jamie. It isn't the fact that he's now bought more flowers, cooked again and cleaned the toilet (even if it was with an Egyptian-cotton hand towel). It's also not only because I'm waiting for the first crack to appear, as it surely will, sooner or later.

It's Ben.

The rancid feeling that I've treated like him crap gets more unpleasant by the day, not least because he hasn't responded to any texts, Facebook messages or emails. And I've sent a few.

'I'm over the bloody moon for you,' Lisa shrieks down the phone as I drive back to the office after a client meeting on Friday. 'I knew he'd come good.'

I resist the temptation to point out that she's called him an idiot every time I've spoken to her for the last four months.

'We're all made up. Oh, and Dave said that if you decide to get married, his mate has just got a job as head chef of that swish hotel Marco Pierre White's opened a restaurant in. He'll knock a few quid off the vol-au-vents I'm sure.'

'Lisa, Jamie and I aren't going to get married,' I frown. 'He doesn't want to. He's always been clear on that.'

'He'll bow to pressure eventually,' she giggles. 'We ground him down on this one, didn't we?'

Great. Yet another thing to feel uneasy about: the idea that I've been the ringleader in a grand conspiracy to domesticate Jamie, a man who, three weeks ago, thought the only worthwhile use for a duster was cleaning his guitar strings.

When I get to the office, my thoughts are back where they started, and I check my inbox to see if Ben has been in touch. A few days ago, I'd have done this with a flutter in my throat, eagerly awaiting his message. Now I'm resigned to the fact that there's unlikely to be one.

Except, as I log on this time, I gasp.

Hey – sorry I haven't been in touch. Mad busy at work.
How are you?

I respond to Ben's email immediately.

Good, thanks. What about you? How's your dad's
treatment going? . . . Fancy coffee at some point? xxx

The last part I added spontaneously – not because I thought it was a good idea, but because not doing so was suddenly not an option.

He doesn't respond all day. When he does, with a message I pick up in the evening on my laptop, it's polite – and clear.

Hi, again. Dad's doing really well, thanks for asking (although Mum's driving him round the twist!). Hope you're well too. Coffee would be nice at some point, but I've got lots on at the moment and so perhaps we should leave it for now.
Take care.
B x

I swallow and start flicking through his Facebook profile. His adoring female fan base has been on fine form in the last twenty-four hours. And while I'm sure the ball python owned by Tabitha Byron (whoever she is) is relieved to be free of scale rot, I can't help thinking that sending nine virtual 'gifts' and asking Ben to slink in her direction might be over the top.

I close down my laptop.

'Everything okay?' asks Jamie, entering the living room.

'Fine – you?'

'Yeah, good. What's for dinner?'

'Oh . . . you said you were going to do something out of that recipe book you've discovered.'

'Did I?' he frowns. 'Don't remember.'

'Let's get a takeaway,' I say, and I'm checking I've got some cash in my purse, when the phone rings. It's Jen.

'Hello, you – how're things with Dr Dan?' I might as well

get straight to the point as I know this is what she's phoning for.

'Oh . . . I don't know,' she sighs.

'Really? I thought things were going well?'

'They were. They are. But . . .'

'But what?'

'He seems to want to see me only once or twice a week, and no more. Do you think that's an issue?'

I think about this for a second. 'Well, it depends if you're happy about it.'

'Of course I'm not. But I'm not going to tell him that.'

'Oh of course – your book. Well, why don't you suggest going out a little sooner and see what he says?'

'Oh Sam,' she tuts. 'I couldn't do that. I'd be breaking the rules. I might as well get a tattoo saying "bunny boiler" on my forehead.'

'O-kay,' I say sceptically. 'Well, what's your concern?'

I can almost hear her rolling her eyes. 'My concern is that he hasn't asked me out on a Saturday-night date yet, so he could be seeing someone else in between the dates with me. Which, technically, isn't against the rules because, until you're engaged, seeing other people is allowed. Except, I don't want him to. And if he is seeing someone else, it begs the question: why aren't I his Saturday-night girl?'

I bite my lip. 'Do you think you might be thinking about this too much?'

'Obviously. I'm me.'

'How are things when you're together?'

'Amazing! Nothing less. But that's when we're together. I have no idea what he's getting up to in the meantime. The thing is that I've got no claims over him. But no matter how cool and hard to get I am, I'm starting to like this guy. So now I want claims. Do you know what I'm saying?'

'I do, Jen, I do.'

I grab my car keys and go to leave the house, realizing my head is starting to hurt.

One thing's clear: love never used to be this complicated.

Chapter 66

'Back on the Lumpy Bumpy cake, I see,' Julia smiles, sipping herbal tea as we sit at a window table in the Quarter the following Monday.

It's mid-afternoon; I'm between meetings and so, it appears, is everybody else. The place is busier than ever, with a bustle of coffee drinkers valiantly attempting to resist the cakes.

'It's a rare treat,' I insist, negotiating a dollop of cream.

'Don't get me wrong: I'm glad to see you eating again. Skinny didn't suit you, Sam.'

'Good, because it's not a look I have the willpower to maintain,' I tell her.

She laughs. 'Well, I'm thrilled you and Jamie are back together, I really am. You deserve to be happy.'

I take a bite of cake and glance at my watch. 'What time have you got to be back?'

The Quarter is round the corner from the Philharmonic Hall, where Julia is currently rehearsing for the orchestra's forthcoming tour of China. It's a hard life.

'I'm okay for twenty minutes,' she replies.

'Did you want to tell me something?' I ask, wondering whether I'll need to be hospitalized if I attempt another cappuccino on top of this cake. 'I got the impression on the phone that you did.'

She takes a deep breath and nods, gazing into her tea. 'Gary phoned yesterday. He got an email from my birth mother.'

'Really? And?'

'She's apparently decided, after much careful deliberation . . . that it's best if we leave things as they are.' She looks up at me with flat eyes. 'She doesn't want to meet me.'

Suddenly, my Lumpy Bumpy cake isn't as delicious as it was.

'You're joking,' I reply, although I don't know whether I'm surprised or not. I suppose I shouldn't be; this is exactly what I feared. After all, we're talking about a woman who gave up her baby and hasn't made any attempt to contact her in thirty-eight years. But the approach from Gary made it feel as though there was a possibility. If he was compelled to get in touch with Julia after so long, surely her mother could be tempted too? 'I'm really sorry, Julia,' I say, scrutinizing her expression.

She scrunches up her nose and shrugs. 'Yes. Me too, actually. Ah well, nothing's lost, I suppose.'

'You must be so disappointed, though. Did she say why?'

She shakes her head. 'Gary was very vague . . . and clearly a bit worried about how I'd take the news.'

I frown. 'Are you okay?'

'Of course. It's fine, honestly.'

However, as she sips her drink, I notice her eyes are glazed and red. And I can't help thinking that it probably isn't fine at all.

My next client meeting is in Chester, where I'm coordinating a big new restaurant opening.

I've left plenty of time to get there, simply because they're a new client and there's no faster way to make a bad impression than by turning up scarlet-faced and gasping for breath.

The journey is going swimmingly: a rare absence of road-works, no breakdowns in the Wallasey tunnel, a blissfully clear M53 stretching in front. Mika is on the radio, the sky's cobalt blue, and I'm contemplating how pleasant it is to know you're in plenty of time for a meeting . . . when something odd happens.

Except, by now, it's not odd. It's frustratingly familiar. The clang, the long, slow squeak and, to complete the medley, a sym-phony of jangling that sounds like a demented primate playing the triangle.

'You are joking,' I splutter, as if attempting to reason with this vehicle has ever got me anywhere.

As my steering wheel judders, I slow down, flick on the hazard lights and drive my spluttering car up the next slip road. There, I find a spot to park and resign myself to another wait for my knight in shining yellow van. The nice lady at the call centre promises me someone will be here within the hour, but it's still too long for me to stick with my meeting and I'm forced to phone and make my excuses. Then I sit and wait as cars whizz past, presumably commandeered by drivers who aren't going to be late for their appointments.

Despite the plethora of zippy disco tunes on the radio, sitting at the side of the road waiting to be rescued has become one of my least favourite pastimes. I pull my phone from my handbag and log on to Facebook for distraction.

There's a status update from Lisa, saying she has 'just had an amazing bath' – one of her more scintillating ones – and a succession of bewildering and increasingly irate exchanges about football between various male friends.

I flick to Ben's page and start looking through his photos.

There's one of him at a pavement cafe in Sydney, tanned and smiling, biceps resplendent as he drinks espresso, followed by a succession of others from a holiday in Greece, and one with his mum and sister, Kate, at a barbeque.

I'm about to switch radio stations, when the opening bars of a song start . . . and stop me in my tracks. It's Goldfrapp.

A flashback of Ben kissing the naked skin on the small of my back floods into my head and I close my eyes, submitting to the pleasure of the memory. Half of my brain is telling me to stop thinking sweet-dirty thoughts about a man I'm no longer supposed to fancy.

The other half is recalling that convenient advice I read in *Cosmopolitan* when I was fifteen: fantasy and reality are two separate things, so you should never worry about who you fantasize over, be it Johnny Depp, your old geography teacher . . . Or Ben.

Except . . . it does matter, doesn't it?

It matters that I'm reclining on my car seat, as I sit in a road just off the M53, feeling distinctly fruity about the memory of my former lover doing a variety of unmentionable things to me at three-thirty in the morning.

My eyes ping open. Come on now – I've got to get a grip. Not least because I don't want the AA man wondering if the cause of my flush is something to do with his high-vis trousers.

I drum my fingers on the window ledge, wondering how much longer I'm going to have to spend here. Then I flick on to Facebook again, this time determined to keep away from Ben's page. My good intentions last just seconds: I'd never logged off and a wall post I hadn't noticed leaps off the screen and virtually hits me on the nose. The message is written by a woman in her early twenties with a cleavage that takes up half her profile picture.

Hey . . . enjoyed getting to know you the other night. Stay in touch xxx

I am gasping for air when I phone Ellie and she answers.

'Bloody Facebook,' she mutters when I've filled her in. 'I had Jen on the phone last night complaining that Dr Dan has been adding as friends a mass of women whose status describes them as "single and interested in men".'

'That doesn't sound good,' I say.

She tuts. 'The point I'm making is that digital spying is not a good thing.'

357

'I wasn't spying; it was all there in front of me. Look, I wasn't after a philosophical debate . . . I was just phoning to ask what you thought. Does that message sound as if they're romantically attached or not?'

'Sam,' she says, sounding slightly exasperated. 'What does it matter? You're back with Jamie. Which, as you've been telling me and everybody else since July, is exactly where you want to be.'

'I know – and it is. I'm interested, that's all.'

She pauses for a second. 'Why, Sam? Are your feelings for Ben more than you've been letting on?'

I open my mouth to protest, but something stops me answering. 'I've got to go,' I say, as a yellow van pulls up behind me. Not for the first time, it's a sight I'm very glad to see.

Chapter 67

Despite six hours having passed, my little fantasy in the car plagues me for the rest of the day. Which is a worry.

'You're going to have to bite the bullet and get rid of that car, Sam,' Jamie tells me as I stir the pasta.

Jamie's foray into the culinary world turned out to be temporary, as predicted. I'm not entirely upset about this because, frankly, we've exhausted every flavour of Chicken Tonight and – although he declared it his own special twist on a classic – I'm afraid it just doesn't go all that well with mince. Even less well than it went with tinned crab.

'I know. It's beyond a joke now,' I mutter, forcing non-sexy thoughts into my mind. It's surprisingly difficult, given that we're talking about the condition of my vehicle.

I take the pasta off the boil and am tipping it into a colander when I feel Jamie come up behind me. He kisses the nape of my neck and I pause, my eyes glazing over. I spin round and, seeing he's about to walk away to get a beer from the fridge, I grab his T-shirt and pull him back to me.

'Wha—' he says, as I close my mouth over his, taken over by an overwhelming urge to find an outlet for the funny feelings I've been having all day.

We kiss passionately as Jamie puts his hand up my top and runs his tongue down my neck. I'm in a whirlwind of lust, focusing on none of my surroundings, only the feel of hungry lips on my skin. Encouraged – and clearly a bit surprised – by my enthusiasm, Jamie lifts me up so my legs are wrapped around him. It's incredibly sexy, yet I must admit I'm slightly worried he's going to drop me.

But I can't think about that for too long. Instead, I think about kisses, lust, strange fluttery feelings. Jamie staggers across the kitchen as our kissing intensifies, then lifts my behind onto the work surface in a move reminiscent of *Nine and a Half Weeks*.

At least, he attempts to. In the event, he misjudges our position and plants both bum cheeks on the still-hot ring on which I've recently boiled 500 grams of tagliatelle.

'Arrrghhh!'

A flicker of self-satisfaction crosses his face and it's evident he thinks I'm in the throes of the world's most spectacular orgasm.

'My bum!' I squawk, making it clear that my outburst is not due to sexual ecstasy, but the fact that my buttocks may have been branded.

'Oh God . . . Are you okay?' he gasps as I scramble to the floor.

'Yes,' I say, breathless, checking the damage and realizing my yell was more from shock. 'I think so. Thank God it was off, though. I'm not sure how I'd have explained the burn in A&E otherwise.'

'Shit. Sorry.'

'Hey, it's okay. Where were we?'

I kiss him again and am soon back in the zone. We end up on the sofa, my skin tingling as we undress. Yet my need is suddenly so urgent that kisses aren't enough, even when he's looking at me as if I'm a woman possessed. I grab him and pull him into me, submitting to the pleasure totally.

'Oh . . . Ben,' I murmur.

He freezes and glares at me. 'WHAT?'

I attempt to pull him back. 'What do you mean, what?' I smile. 'I want you. Simple as that.'

His face is thunderous. 'You called me Ben.'

The blood in my veins turns to ash as I stare at him, replaying the last ten seconds.

'I don't think I did,' I laugh, feeling my cheeks inflame to a colour that matches my buttocks.

'You did, Sam,' he says, standing up. I can almost see steam tickling his ear hair. 'You bloody did.'

He grabs his clothes, and puts them back on, piece by piece.

'I d-didn't say "Ben",' I stammer, standing in the doorway, never having felt more naked in my life. 'It was "when" . . . as in when are you going to come? That's what I meant. I thought I'd ask for an update as to how close you were to . . . you know. That's all. Honestly.'

He glares at me as I pick up my clothes and clutch them to my chest.

He eats dinner in silence; I pick at my pasta, and, with a hammering heart, curse myself, my libido and my horribly vivid imagination.

Chapter 68

When Jen walks through the doors at Palm Sugar, every head in the place turns. Which is quite an achievement, given that the bar is wall-to-wall glitz and packed with women who are glamorous, beautiful and have an approach to fashion that's about as understated as Lady GaGa's.

Jen's wearing a short, sexy, Kirsty Doyle dress that makes her legs appear so long and toned you'd have to look closely to check they're real. And plenty of men are looking closely, believe me.

'Shall we do cocktails?' says Ellie, already at the bar. She looks fabulous tonight too, in a green satin dress and high-heeled lace-ups. 'I fancy a French martini; what about you two?'

As the bar tender sets about mixing our drinks, we sit on stools at the bar and Jen fills us in on the latest with Dr Dan, in advance of his arrival.

Yes, you heard that right. After enough hype to fill an edition of *Heat* magazine, we're going to meet the man himself, before he and Jen head off for dinner.

She still hasn't had a Saturday night out with him, of course, but this is Friday, which amounts to the same thing. Plus, the fact that he's agreed to meet her friends – however briefly – is a big step forward, without doubt.

'I'm falling for him. It's as simple as that,' Jen says, sipping her drink. 'I know I've said that before but it's never been like this. I mean it.'

The worrying thing is that I think she does.

'And the feeling definitely isn't mutual?' asks Ellie, with some trepidation because we're both aware of Jen's tendency to err on the side of blind optimism.

She sighs. 'He talks about wanting to meet "the one" – someone he feels passionately enough about to want to settle down and get married to and have dozens of babies with. When he says it, it's with an "oh if only she'd walk through the door right now" sigh. And I'm thinking: "Why the hell can't I be her? Where do I fit into all of this?"'

I frown and put my hand on hers. Ellie and I are seriously starting to have our doubts about Dr Dan.

'The fact is,' she continues, 'that I know exactly where I fit in: I'm just someone to have sex with. He doesn't love me, or show any prospect of falling in love with me. It's so depressing.'

'Hello, Jen.'

The voice is smooth and deep and when we turn round we are confronted by a well-dressed, conventionally attractive but by no means stunning man in his mid-thirties. With no muscles.

'Oh hi, there,' Jen says, suddenly flustered simply to be in Dr Dan's presence. 'Lovely to see you.'

He kisses her on the cheek and smiles widely. 'You look stunning.'

'Thanks,' she says self-consciously. 'Let me introduce you to my friends. This is Ellie and this is Sam.'

He shakes our hands. 'Lovely to meet you. Jen's told me lots about you both.'

'I dread to think,' says Ellie. 'What can I get you to drink?'

'No, let me – I insist,' he says.

Two hours later – an hour and a half after they were due to go off on their own – I must admit I'm finding it difficult not to like Dan. He's totally affable, unassuming and completely relaxed in our company. There's something else too.

He clearly does like Jen. A lot. And it's about more than sex, whatever she thinks. When she's speaking, there's a sparkle in his eyes that is unmistakable.

'Jen's an amazing doctor, you know,' he tells Ellie and me. 'Seriously. She's one of the most talented people I've ever met.'

'Oh stop it – you'll make me blush,' Jen laughs.

He grins and pinches her playfully on the waist. 'Do you really want me to stop?'

'Well, obviously not!'

'No, I didn't think so,' he laughs.

This is the other thing: these two are good together. They bounce off each other, bantering like old friends.

When they finally head to dinner, Ellie turns to me and hiccups. 'Are you thinking what I'm thinking?'

'What – that you're drunk already?'

She rolls her eyes and slumps against the bar, tutting. 'I hope you're not about to lecture me. If there's one thing I can't stand it's—'

'Up?' I grin.

'Don't be silly,' she laughs.

'You mean that he's lovely?' I ask seriously.

'Yes! How frustrating. You and I are really meant to disapprove of this guy because, from the way things have been going, Jen says he can't like her as much as she likes him. Except . . . well, tonight I got the impression that he did.'

'I agree,' I reply. 'I can definitely see what she sees in him.'

'Absolutely,' she shrugs. 'Still, no matter how charming, funny and all-round nice he seems, I'm afraid if he messes our Jen around, he's had it.'

'I'll drink to that,' I say, clinking her glass.

'You know what I hope, though?' says Ellie, putting her elbow on the bar. 'I hope he does like her as much as she likes him. He just doesn't realize it yet.'

Chapter 69

It's when we're at our fourth bar that Ellie tells me she'd been planning to go on a detox this week. Only it didn't really happen. She didn't need to tell me that last bit, given that I've already witnessed her bleeding dry the alcoholic reserves of the city.

'I'm going to do it next week instead,' she tells me, hiccuping. 'Or maybe the week after. Sometime in the very near future, anyway.'

'Well, I think that's a good idea. If a little . . . out of character,' I say, as we head out of the bar and onto the floodlit terrace of Chavasse Park.

'Don't sound so surprised,' she says, hiccuping again and linking my arm. 'Besides, if I'm going all Gillian McKeith I at least want to go out with a bang.'

'I'm sure you'll manage it,' I tell her.

When we reach the Albert Dock, Ellie proceeds to drink like there is no tomorrow, ordering cocktail after cocktail, chasers and then – at this, I glare at her incredulously – a bottle of champagne, which she splashes into glasses, looking like the demon child of Patsy from *Absolutely Fabulous*.

'Ellie . . . you must have spent a fortune,' I say, watching her swaying from side to side. I'm feeling distinctly woozy myself, though I haven't put away even a fraction of the booze she has.

'It's only money!' she grins. She winks at a bar man then perches flirtatiously on a stool. He smiles back. 'Hello, gorgeous!' she slurs.

'For God's sake, what are you doing?!' I frown, grabbing her by the arm.

She wrestles away from me. 'I know! Can't I have a bit of fun? Anyway, I'd never do anything. I love my Ali more than life itself.'

At that, she goes from being high on life to being close to tears.

'I really do love my Ali, Sam,' she says, her lip trembling as she throws her arm around me. 'And I love you too.' All of sudden she loses her balance and almost slips off the stool, while her head wobbles so violently I'm convinced it's going to drop off.

I rush round and take her weight, lifting her up and helping her to stagger in the direction of the sofas, where she'll be able to sit down less perilously. But it's like a doctors' waiting room during a flu epidemic: there isn't a seat to be had.

'Can I . . . er, really sorry, but can we sit down for a minute? My friend isn't well.' A group of guys step out of the way and help me plonk her down on the sofa. Her head flops to the side . . . and she starts snoring.

'Ellie! Ellie – come on, wake up.' I begin to feel as if I'm starring in one of those ITV2 documentaries about binge drinking and am wondering when the paramedic is going to turn up and someone's going to show me their boobs.

'Ellie – seriously,' I add urgently. But she's out cold. At least, I think she is. Until she hiccups again and a large blob of vomit spews from her mouth and dribbles down her chin onto her dress. I grab a tissue from my bag and wipe it away before anyone can see it. I'm about to try to dispose of the tissue, when something makes me pause and look at her. Really look at her.

It's a sight that makes my stomach twist.

What I see is a woman who's gone beyond being the life and soul of the party. Someone I've seen in this sort of state way too often. Someone who, without me even noticing it, has crossed a line.

I don't know when she did it, but there's suddenly no doubt at all that she has. My best friend is in trouble. It's a fact that, if I'm honest with myself, I've probably known for a long time. And I have no idea what the hell I'm going to do to help her.

Chapter 70

Jamie is in a sulk when I wake the next morning. I can tell without even looking at him. Not that he's been in a good mood at all since Sofagate, when I allegedly called out Ben's name during sex. I can't blame him, of course, and I'm cursing myself, even if the story I'm sticking to is that I didn't actually do it.

I genuinely don't know if I did or not, but it doesn't matter: Jamie is not a happy man. I've spent every moment in his presence panicking about this, although I hope he'll snap out of it sooner or later. He roots around on the dressing table for his keys and I pull the duvet over me, pretending to be asleep.

'You woke me up when you came in last night,' he announces. 'I've got work this morning.'

'Sorry,' I mumble.

'It was nearly three o'clock,' he adds, and I hear the clatter of keys as he finally locates them. 'And you used to complain about me coming in late.'

'Yes. I'm sorry,' I repeat but he's already out of the room, galloping down the stairs.

I get up slowly, feeling as though my head is in a vice. After I've showered and dressed I pad downstairs to make a doorstep of toast. Then another two. It's one of those hangovers that make me feel simultaneously nauseous and as if I could eat my body weight in carbohydrates. God knows what Ellie must feel like.

I take a deep breath, grab my keys and head out of the house to have a conversation that fills my stomach with a hot, hard dread.

When I arrive at my best friend's house, Alistair is on his way out with Sophie. She looks adorable: all curls, bunny-rabbit tights and a toothy grin.

'Daddy, I want a snack,' she announces.

'Er . . . okay, sweetheart. Don't forget to say please.'

'Peez!'

'Good girl. What would you like – an apple, carrot sticks or a banana?'

'A sausage.'

'Glad the healthy-eating messages are getting through, then,' he mutters. 'Hi, Sam. How're things?'

'Good, thanks, Alistair. Is Ellie inside?'

'She's just getting up,' he smiles. 'Late night for you ladies, then?'

'Er . . . yes.'

'I was asleep when Ellie came to bed, but she's been out cold for most of the morning,' he laughs.

I gaze at Alistair, wondering how such an intelligent man can live with Ellie and be so apparently unconcerned at how bad her drinking has become. He's been in denial; he must have been. Yet, isn't the same true of me? Ellie and I have known each other for years and her increasingly damaging attitude to drink has crept up in front of me.

There are dozens of occasions – that have become worse and worse – when I could and should have realized. Such as when she broke her arm on holiday in Turkey . . . or the time she plummeted into the gutter outside a pub at New Year . . . or when she violently threw up after a quiet Sunday afternoon pint became a major session . . . and the slurring in her words when I've phoned at four thirty on a Monday afternoon.

Individually, they'd be no big deal. Together, they represent a bulky and growing scrapbook of incidents that paint a picture of someone who's lost control.

'Go straight in. She'll be out of the shower soon,' Alistair adds, standing aside for me.

The house is silent when I shut the door, and after the crunch of gravel as Alistair drives away.

'Hi, Ellie!' There's no answer.

I creep upstairs, passing dozens of family portraits on the wall, in which Ellie looks every inch the devoted mother she undoubtedly is. There's a photo of her and Sophie aged only weeks old; another of her leading her daughter along on a pony at Center Parcs.

'Ellie?' I knock when I reach her bedroom door. As I prise it open and enter, the sheets are a crumpled mass and there's no sign of her. Then an ugly sound from the en-suite bathroom breaks the silence.

Retching.

I creep to the door and find Ellie in her dressing gown, fresh from the shower. Although 'fresh' isn't the word. She's kneeling on the floor, holding back her hair and throwing up her guts into the toilet.

'Ellie,' I whisper as an acidic smell fills the air.

She turns and looks at me, her eyes bloodshot and lifeless. It's a sight with which I've been confronted so many times. Suddenly, it's one of the saddest things I've ever seen.

Chapter 71

As Ellie stands up her legs almost give way, but she reaches out and steadies herself against the sink.

'Shit,' she croaks with dead eyes. 'You bad too, this morning?'

'Er . . . yes.' Though nothing like as bad as she is.

'Put the kettle on, would you? I'll brush my teeth and be down in a sec.'

I turn to go downstairs when her voice stops me. 'Sam?'

'Yes, Ellie?'

'You won't mention to Alistair that I . . . you know, puked, will you?' she smiles languidly. 'He can be a bit of an old woman about this sort of stuff.'

I gaze at her, unsure of how to answer. Does this mean Alistair's noticed too? When I think back, I've detected unease from him about Ellie's drinking – but nothing more. Which means he's probably taken the same approach as me and pretended it wasn't happening. 'Shall I make you some toast?'

'Oh yeah. Lots of butter, please.'

She joins me in the kitchen a few minutes later, looking

cleaner – though it wouldn't take much – and dressed in slouchy jeans and a sweatshirt.

'Phew . . .' she wheezes, sounding as if there's an elastic band around her tonsils. She starts massaging her temples. 'Great night, from what I remember.' She pauses when a wave of nausea hits her, her face turning the colour of a dirty puddle. 'Eugh . . . I don't mean to be rude –' she can barely get her words out – 'but I might have to go back to bed.'

I put the toast in front of her and sit as she picks it up with shaking hands and takes a bite.

She instantly looks as though she's about to throw up again. 'Oh . . . God,' she groans, then glances up at me. 'What's up?'

I swallow, wondering how I'm going to tackle this.

'Ellie, listen. I'm worried about you.'

She knows I'm serious the second I say it and puts down her apparently inedible toast. 'Me?' she says huskily.

I nod. 'Look, I'm only saying this because you're my best friend and I love you and I don't want anything to happen to you.'

She appears bewildered. 'What's going to happen to me?'

'Ellie . . .' I reach over and clasp her hand. It's clammy and cold. 'I'm worried about your drinking.'

She hesitates, taking in my expression. Then she explodes in a throaty laugh, coughing uncontrollably as she lets go of my hand. 'Bloody hell, you had me going for a second. Hilarious. Right – I'm going to see if some jam will make this toast go down any easier.' She stands up.

I touch her arm and she freezes, swaying slightly. She sits down slowly, holding my gaze as her expression darkens with a prickly awareness.

'You're not serious?'

'I am, Ellie.' My heart is hammering.

She laughs coldly. 'Sam . . . really? Oh my God, I don't believe this. I go on a night out and get a bit drunk and suddenly I'm an alcoholic? You're mad!'

I bite my lip, dreading her response to what I'm about to say. 'It's not been suddenly, though, has it?' I say softly. 'Ellie, I'm saying this because I love you. But you drink too much. Way too much. When's the last time you went a day without a drink?'

'Oh come off it,' she splutters, her neck flushing. 'Everyone has a couple of glasses of wine to wind down at night.'

'Yeah, but it's not just a glass or two any more. I mean . . . is it?'

Fury bubbles up inside her, right in front of me. 'What I drink, Sam, is perfectly average. I drink alcohol because I enjoy it and not because I'm addicted to it. Just because I get tipsy every so often does not mean I've got a problem.'

'Ellie, the last thing I want is to upset you. But I think you need to slow down . . . try to cut back . . . and possibly –' my eyes flash up at her – 'possibly get some help.'

She slams down her tea, blinking back tears. 'You are joking, Sam! Aren't you?'

'I'm not, Ellie. I'm not,' I plead, reaching out for her hand. She pulls it away, her face etched with anger.

'You know what, Sam? You and I have been mates for ever.

But I'm finding it very hard not to be insulted here. This is laughable. Just because you, Ms Goody Two Shoes, don't happen to have a couple of glasses every night like I do, doesn't mean it isn't normal. I've got a stressful job. I've got a baby who's beautiful but hard work. A little something to help me relax at the end of the day is no big deal. End of story.'

'But Ellie, it's more than that, isn't it?' I say, desperately trying to find the balance between sympathy and strength. If Ellie can't even face up to the fact that she has a problem, we're never going to get anywhere.

'What it is, Sam, is none of your sodding business.'

'But I—'

'And I'd like you to leave,' she says flatly, refusing to meet my gaze.

'Oh Ellie, come on . . .'

'Get out, Sam,' she snaps. 'I'm serious. Get out of here right now. I don't even want to look at you.'

Chapter 72

The next five days probably count as the worst in my life. I don't think I'd appreciated at the time how catastrophic my blunder on the sofa was . . . but it's been nothing less. Jamie has stopped sulking. To his credit, I can see he's trying to forget the issue. He buys me flowers again on Tuesday and even has another whirl with Chicken Tonight – though it tastes even worse with squid than it did with mince.

Not that I can blame the hideous food. The fact is that, no matter how hard we try to get things back on track, something's not quite right. I can't put my finger on what it is, but it's there.

It doesn't help that we haven't had sex since the incident.

You might not think this is a big deal; long-term couples often go through stretches of abstinence. But I'm scared that it's representative of something bigger. So much so that I made an attempt to get it on with him the other night – in the Figleaves undies, no less – but his lack of enthusiasm was beyond dispiriting.

Then there's Ben, who I mustn't think about. Except I am

thinking about him. I find myself peeping at his Facebook page way too often, to check for further evidence of activity with attractive females. And, while there isn't any, he's still entering my thoughts more than he should.

While all this is going on, I've also got Ellie to worry about. Ellie, who refuses to speak to me.

I've phoned, texted and tried turning up on the doorstep twice. And although I think she was genuinely out once, I'm certain I could hear movement inside the second time.

It is not an exaggeration to say that it feels like a bereavement. Ellie is more than a friend to me: she's been my rock; she got me through the hard times with Jamie and countless others before. We share a history together and I love every bit of her. So it's killing me to think that she feels so strongly about what I said that she doesn't even want to see me, let alone talk about it.

Which brings me to the subject itself. I've started to question whether I was right. I sometimes think that maybe what she said was true. Maybe her drinking is average – there's no doubt people consume more alcohol than they used to – so it could be that it's not that big a deal after all.

As soon as that thought infiltrates my head, however, I get a flashback of Ellie collapsed on the toilet of her en-suite bathroom, with zombie eyes and sick on her chin. And the scores of other times I've seen her like that or worse.

In the light of this, not saying something wasn't an option. Not saying something would've made me an even worse friend than she clearly thinks I am. Yet, what good has it done? Not only am I not helping Ellie, it's also looking increasingly likely that our friendship is over.

The only person I feel I can confide in about this is Jen – but she's away on a conference. Discussing it with Luke when I meet him for coffee on Tuesday lunchtime is out of the question – not least because there's only one topic of conversation he wants to talk about. His love life.

'I feel like she won't commit,' he tells me earnestly. I can barely believe the irony. Casanova has turned into Bridget Jones. 'She's holding back, no matter how close I try to get. God, she's wonderful, Sam. Funny, intelligent, gorgeous . . . but totally convinced that, when I say I love her, she's just another notch on my bedpost.'

'Wow.'

'Every moment I spend with her is pure magic,' he continues. 'It doesn't matter whether we're out at dinner or sitting at home in front of a film . . . though I must admit that's becoming a ball ache.'

'Why?'

'I've watched *An Officer and a Gentleman* seven times; it's her favourite film. I see Richard Gere more often than my own brother these days.'

I shake my head and, as we head out of the coffee shop, I feel a sudden urge to give Luke a hug. He squeezes me into his chest, then laughs, pulls back and kisses me on the head. 'What was that for?'

'I just never thought I'd see the day when you – of all people – felt like this about someone.'

'Well . . . don't get too carried away. It might all end in tears.'

'I hope not,' I reply.

'Me too. And I'm so glad you and Jamie have made it up again, you know.' I force a smile. 'Because if he hadn't moved out, I'd have kicked him out. The state that man leaves a tea towel . . .'

Jen returns home on Thursday, and I call at her flat after work.

'What happened?' she asks, flicking on her Alessi kettle in the open-plan kitchen.

Jen's apartment is magazine-shoot stylish, with a white sofa that's remained so pristine you'd think it had never been touched by human hand (though there was an incident with Sophie and a jam tart that Jen was surprisingly cool about, given she's been forced to strategically position her cushions since then).

After I've filled her in – on my conversation with Ellie, on why I felt I needed to have it, on the issue that's been staring us all in the face for so long – she pauses, her expression one of shock. Sort of.

'Ellie's an alcoholic,' she says numbly. It's not a question, but a statement of fact. She recognized the problem instantly.

'I think she is,' I reply quietly.

Jen shakes her head, struggling for words.

'You know,' she sighs, 'I've seen Ellie falling over, throwing up, doing the sort of stuff she does, for years and years. And . . . it's become so commonplace, I never even questioned it.' She walks to the living area and sits opposite me on an armchair. 'You know . . . I once caught her drinking when I went round there at eleven in the morning. God, I feel awful. I've pretended it wasn't happening.'

'You're not the only one, Jen. I thought of Ellie as one of life's party animals, someone whose love for a glass of wine – or ten – was just part of her. But I looked at her the other night and thought: I'm sorry, this isn't right. This isn't normal.'

Jen looks down at her tea. 'You were incredibly brave to broach the subject head-on.'

I roll my eyes. 'Urh! I haven't done anything except upset her. And make her hate me.'

'Don't be silly. She loves you.'

'Not at the moment. She doesn't want to speak to me.'

She takes a deep breath. 'So what do we do?'

'If you go round there and tell her we've had this conversation and that you agree with me, she'll think it's a conspiracy. Which is exactly why I haven't told Alistair about this; she'd consider it a betrayal.'

'So how about I don't mention the booze, pretend I don't know what the cause of your row is, but try to get her to talk to you again?'

I shrug. 'I guess that's the first step. Though, judging by her reaction, I don't fancy your chances.'

Chapter 73

Twenty minutes later, Jen's in the car on the way to Ellie's house . . . and I am a fireball of nerves. I don't hear from her for hours, except for a text, clearly sent surreptitiously, saying she'd arrived but couldn't talk to Ellie until Alistair had gone out and Sophie was in bed. I can neither eat nor relax and my state of agitation isn't helped by Jamie randomly failing to return from work and refusing to answer his phone.

I run a bath to try to take my mind off things. But as I sink into it, it's at least two degrees too cold for comfort, then when I turn on the hot tap, with a carefully mastered technique using only two toes, the water's so hot it almost strips off my nail polish.

Afterwards, I head downstairs and flick on the television, checking my phone every ten seconds as I fire up my laptop. The magnetic qualities of Facebook draw me to my profile page, though I'm determined to stay away from Ben's. I succeed too, despite extreme temptation, particularly when the only distraction Lisa's update offers is to tell the world that she has just spread Philadelphia on Elvis's toast. How she can manage to plumb such depths of tedium and still get twelve 'likes' I have no idea.

I'm about to navigate away from the site when the familiar ping of a chat box sends my heartbeat racing.

'Hey there xx'

Ben's picture makes me catch my breath.

It's been three weeks since I heard from him and the fact that he's actively contacting me sends me into meltdown, particularly in the light of how popular I appear to be with arguably the two most important people in my life: Jamie and Ellie.

I hold my breath and compose a response.

'Hey to you too. How's tricks?'

His response seems to take an age to pop up, but when it does, I feel a swell of elation. Pathetic, I know.

'Good, thanks . . . keeping busy. Lots on at work. Trying to book a holiday. Where shall I go?'

I smile and type back.

'Only one choice for me . . . New York. Greatest city on earth.'

'But you can't scuba dive there.'

'Why would you want to do that, when you can shop?'

'Ha! I suspect you and I might have different priorities . . .'

It's the start of an hour and a half of unadulterated, frivolous chat in which we discuss everything from the most gorgeous woman on earth (Natalie Portman, apparently) to techniques for unblocking drains. I don't move from my laptop and spurn the television – unadulterated frivolousness is far more entertaining. I almost get lost in it, until I hear Jamie's key in the lock and rapidly but politely tell Ben that I've got to go.

'How're things?' I ask, my heart racing as I log off.

'Great,' he replies, throwing down his work bag as he comes to sit beside me on the sofa with his arm behind my neck.

I pull back and take a look at him.

His suit's so crumpled you'd think he'd had it rolled up in his glove compartment for the last three weeks, and the faint whiff of eau de Stella Artois does little to enhance the effect. That said, I'm so grateful that he's actually approached me for something vaguely romantic that I don't care.

'What about you?' he asks.

I haven't told Jamie about Ellie and her problems. I don't know why; except that getting off your face as often as possible is probably not something of which he'd disapprove.

'Yeah – not bad. Busy day at work but—' And before I get a chance to finish my sentence, he has his lips on mine and is kissing me with the wanton hunger – and lack of coordination – of a man who's clearly had at least six pints.

He's soon on top of me, removing his suit jacket and ripping off his tie. It's all happening so quickly that I barely know what to do with myself, so I close my eyes and attempt to think sexy thoughts. Jamie's running his tongue behind my ear, when the ring of my mobile interrupts us.

'Leave it,' he whispers furiously as he fumbles with my dressing gown.

I swallow, and glance at the phone, which is dancing as it vibrates on the coffee table. But, after three rings, temptation gets the better of me. I've got to know the score with Ellie. 'I'll only be a minute.'

'Hi, Sam,' says Jen in a tone I can't quite decipher.

'How did it go?' I ask urgently as I refasten my dressing gown and Jamie stands up, distinctly unimpressed.

Jen pauses, clearly struggling for her words. 'Oh Sam,' she sighs eventually. 'I don't know what to say. I'm sure this is temporary. Honestly . . . I really am. I—'

'Jen, be straight with me. What did she say?'

'Sam . . . she doesn't want anything to do with you.'

Chapter 74

The more that certain parts of my world are falling apart, the more I take solace in chatting with Ben. However, after a while it seems ridiculous to make contact solely via the internet when we live so close to each other. So a week and a bit after Jen's first attempt to get Ellie to see sense, I meet him for coffee. Then I meet him several times more in the days that follow. He's a breath of fresh air.

As ever, we talk about everything and nothing and, although I'm regularly assaulted by flashbacks of the night of the power cut, my overwhelming feeling is this: I'm so happy that he's my friend.

Everything seems easy when he's around, and that is a very good, if increasingly rare, feeling. He occupies a corner of my life that's constantly bright and sunny. It's not that I couldn't live without him; I'm simply glad I don't have to.

I never ask about his love life, of course, though my curiosity is all-encompassing, particularly because his female Facebook fans still seem to swoon at his every move.

Ellie is a far less controversial issue, at least between Ben and me. I've sounded him out repeatedly about what's going on and he's certain that I should be quietly persistent. And try not to get frustrated about her behaviour, because she's clearly not thinking straight and is on the defensive. Jen, meanwhile, attempts to chip away, gently raising the issue of her relationship with me every time she sees Ellie. She wants to raise the issue of her drinking too, but I've urged her not to just yet as I know it'd be counter-productive; Ellie would only fly off the handle at Jen too.

There's a part of me that feels annoyed about how Ellie's behaving. But mainly I feel desperately sorry for her. I only hope that she'll come round: to the idea of speaking to me and to addressing her problem.

About a week and a half after we started meeting again, Ben and I are walking along Allerton Road, having stopped for a quick drink after work.

'Sam,' he says, glancing at me awkwardly. 'How are things at home? I haven't asked you for a while.'

I look at him, more shocked at the question than I should be. 'Er . . . pretty good, actually.'

He smiles broadly. 'Good. Only you haven't spoken about things with Jamie and I hoped that didn't mean anything was wrong.'

'God, no,' I say quickly. 'Everything's good. It'll never be perfect, but no relationship is. We're the same people we were, with all our faults. We're both more conscious of them now; both keen to be considerate, I suppose.'

'Hey, I'm pleased for you.' He briefly puts his arm round me and squeezes. It's a friendly gesture – nothing more – but it turns my legs to custard.

Yet I know that the goosebumps Ben gives me are nothing more than that. A quick, if pleasurable, thrill. And I'm not joking about life with Jamie. Frankly, the cooking, cleaning and flower-purchasing frenzy he went into on his return didn't suit him. Now we've settled into the routine we were in before he left and, while it isn't exactly knee-quivering, it's good. Really.

'Well, I'd better leave you to it,' says Ben, clicking open his car.

'Catch you soon, trouble,' I say, smiling, as I go to leave. But he grabs me gently by the arm and pulls me towards him in a move that feels dangerously close to being more than friendly.

'Can I at least have a kiss on the cheek?' he whispers. He's trying to look as though this is a teasing, flippant comment, but his expression wavers.

'O-of course,' I stammer, pausing, then I stand on my tiptoes and press my hot cheek against his.

The hand he has on my arm tenses, as if he doesn't want me to move. And I don't move. For at least three seconds. I stand and drink in the smell of his skin and feel the heat pulsing between us.

When I pull away, I can't look at him. So I mutter my good-byes and walk away. And as I turn the corner and break into a run, it's with elation and despair running like quicksilver through my veins.

*

I open the door to the house and the first thing that hits me is what a tip it is. I'd love to meet someone who disproves the apparently universal truth that men don't see mess like women do. Someone except Luke, that is, whose other imperfections cancel out that quality.

Jamie's presence in the house has had a similar effect to that of a recently detonated hand grenade. He leaves later than me each morning (his isn't the sort of job for which you need to get in at seven to put in extra hours), and in that short period he manages to leave the place like it's been ravaged by a teething Labrador puppy.

A sports bag has materialized in the hallway – not that Jamie plays any sport – and a mug lies on its side on the dining table, swimming in a circle of cold coffee that's seeped onto my direct-debit confirmation for a homeless charity. Presumably, it's the housework fairy's job to clean it up.

I take a deep breath. I used to nag him about this stuff. Which was something that never made me feel good, but it was an unstoppable urge that only a partial lobotomy could have prevented. However, I'm not going to fall into that trap again, because I know where it got me last time.

So I suppress ripples of indignation as I put away the butter that's been left out all day and wipe away the pebbledash of toast crumbs on the work surface, before traipsing upstairs with a pile of clean laundry.

I'm putting his clothes away in his drawers when, among a tangle of underpants, I come across some travel documents and realize that they're the ones from his flight to South America.

Only Jamie would keep these in his underwear drawer. I shake my head and can't help smiling as I pick them up to examine them. They're another reminder of how close I came to losing him . . . Suddenly, having to put away the butter seems like an infinitesimal price to pay.

I briefly flick through the documents, wondering if I should put them away – or bin them, for that matter – when I realize there are a couple of email printouts underneath. They're exchanges between him and Dorrie, who's been strangely absent from our lives recently. Given that she and Jamie have known each other since they were toddlers – and both lived in south Liverpool – they would often get together for a drink or two. That hasn't happened for ages.

It's only as I'm about to put them back that I read something in one of Dorrie's emails that stops me in my tracks.

Stupidly excited about this trip xxxxxxxxx

I frown and scan the page, spotting sentence after sentence that makes me prickle with unease, confusion . . . then ugly clarity.

One fact becomes clear: Jamie wasn't going to South America by himself. He was going with Dorrie. My mind races with possible explanations, but returns to one urgent question. Why wouldn't he have told me that?

He and Dorrie are friends who've known each other for ever and whose feelings are nothing but platonic.

As I continue to read the practical details of flight times and visa requirements, I'm confronted by too many kisses, too much affection . . . and too much suggestion. While there's nothing that proves something untoward, there's enough to make my skin tingle with suspicion.

I walk downstairs, clutching the emails with trembling hands, my heart hammering, and I am halfway down when I hear the shuffle of Jamie's key in the door. I sink onto a stair and freeze, glaring at him and feeling as if I'm having an out-of-body experience.

'What is it?' he asks as he walks towards me, his expression contorted with anxiety.

'You and Dorrie.'

His face blanches.

'You cheated on me. Didn't you?'

Time stands still as I gaze at his face and at the bead of sweat that appears on his forehead and travels slowly down his skin. He doesn't need to respond for me to know, without question, what the answer is.

Chapter 75

When Jamie and I split up, my strategy in the aftermath was to appear calm. Not to shout, scream or cry, but tell him rationally that I loved him and he was making a mistake. I look at him now, bumbling through excuses as he attempts to explain the unexplainable, and, frankly, rationality isn't something to which I feel particularly inclined.

Rage rises inside me while his words swirl above us, as flimsy and vacuous as bubbles bursting in the wind. I know without even hearing what he's saying that it's meaningless. That doesn't stop him trying, though.

'Sam, it was a mistake. I know that,' he pleads, reaching out, but I slap away his hands and storm into the living room. He follows me. 'It hadn't been going on for long before I left. A few weeks. It wasn't years or anything.'

I throw myself onto the sofa. 'As if that matters!' I scream, giving him everything my tonsils have got. 'You were sleeping with her while you were living with me! That's all that fucking matters!'

He takes a step back as if I've punched him in the stomach.

I'm not a big swearer, but there are times when nothing but a proper, gold-plated expletive will do.

'Can you let me explain?' he whimpers, perching on the edge of the sofa opposite me. 'Please, Sam.'

I throw him such a dirty look it almost needs flushing down the toilet.

I attempt to compose my thoughts. 'You can start by telling me if it's still going on.'

'Of course not,' he leaps in. 'Do you think I'd have come back to you if it had been?'

I throw him another filthy look. 'Being with me didn't stop you getting it on with her in the first place.'

He sighs and rubs his temples. 'I know, Sam, and I'm sorry.' He puts his head in his hands. After I don't know how long, he looks up again and a tear drips off his chin. 'Please let me tell you what happened. Let me explain.'

As I sit back on the sofa and cross my arms, violent outrage swims through me. 'Try me,' I growl.

'Okay,' he replies, taking a deep breath. 'First, let me put it in context.'

'Context?'

He hesitates. 'Sam . . . you and I hadn't been right for ages.'

'What do you mean by "right"?'

'I mean we'd been arguing, going in separate directions . . . we wanted different things. More than that, though, Sam, we'd stopped being nice to each other. Don't you think? We'd stopped behaving like two people in love.'

I swallow, unable to speak.

He continues. 'Everything I did was wrong, from staying out too late with the band, to not keeping up with your impossible standards of housekeeping.'

I catch my breath. 'Jamie, my standards of housekeeping are normal. I don't ask for much, for God's sake. Are you trying to say I brought this on myself?'

'No! God, no . . . Look,' he says, holding up his hands and clearly not wanting to go down this route. 'I know I was at fault for an awful lot. I know that. But . . . let's not apportion blame. Please. I'm simply saying that things weren't as great after six years as they were in the beginning.'

I gaze into the middle distance. He's right, of course. Things weren't like they were at the start. But that doesn't mean we didn't love each other. We had a few rows. But the odd disagreement doesn't change how good a couple are together. Rowing is normal.

'Jamie, we had our ups and downs. But I never even looked at another man. Never. Unlike you.' I realize what I've said. 'Not another man, obviously. I meant another woman.'

'I know what you meant.'

He looks at me as if this is the most difficult confession of his life. 'Dorrie and I were always close, but until a few weeks before you and I split up, it'd never been anything but platonic. I promise you.'

'So what changed?'

He swallows. 'When things got difficult between us, I suppose I confided in her.'

'So instead of talking to me about our problems, you went running to another woman.'

'It wasn't like that.'

'Oh?'

He closes his eyes and, despite a trembling lip, tries to compose himself. 'Not at the beginning. It was just that . . . being able to talk about it was a release. And she became . . . easy to be with.'

The word makes me blanch – not only because of the implication that I was the opposite, but also because it hurls my thoughts briefly to Ben. To how I feel about him. 'Go on,' I insist.

'Somewhere along the way, my feelings for her became confused and . . . we did stuff we shouldn't have. Not just – you know,' he flashes me a glance.

'Yes, I know, Jamie,' I reply with a steely glare.

'I mean,' he continues, pretending he hasn't seen me, 'I mean, planning to go away together. She'd wanted to go to South America for ages, anyway. We weren't eloping or anything. She just kind of invited herself.' He closes his eyes. 'Look, I'm not blaming Dorrie; I know this was my fault. I was the one in a relationship. But I need you to believe me when I tell you, Sam, that I knew it was never going to work out with her. I knew I still loved you.'

'What?'

'I knew that even before you tried to persuade me to come back.'

I can feel myself trembling, afraid to admit how good this is to hear.

'Sam . . . you were right. You are the love of my life. Not Dorrie, not anybody else. And while I want more than anything not to be stuck in this shit job, I'm prepared to do it to be with you.'

He falls to his knees and crawls towards me, reaching for my hand and clasping it so hard my knuckles go white. 'Sam, I am sorry. I am so, so sorry.' He says each word so firmly it hurts my ears. 'I was an idiot. But I went full circle, Sam,' he adds, his face contorted with emotion. 'Before I came back to you, I told Dorrie I didn't want to see her again. That was my decision. I love you, Sam. You.'

I snatch my hand away from him, unable to take everything in. 'Are you seriously suggesting that my reaction to the discovery that you dumped me for another woman – that you were sleeping with someone else and were planning to take her on your grand trip abroad . . . are you really suggesting my reaction should be: "No hard feelings"?'

He shakes his head and stands up, walking to the window and glaring out. I sit in silence. Eventually, he turns to me.

'You're right,' he says flatly. 'You're absolutely right. There's only one way to deal with this, isn't there?'

I tense my jaw.

'The only way is for me to leave again. For good, this time.' Another tear spills down his cheek. 'I'm sorry, Sam. I'm so ashamed. You don't deserve this.'

I stare at him, totally numb.

'I'll pack my bags,' he whispers and leaves the room.

I cannot move and I cannot say anything. I can do nothing but listen to the sound of him thudding up the stairs. Gathering his belongings. Pausing in the hall for a few brief moments. Opening and shutting the front door. His footsteps on the garden path fading to silence.

I can do nothing.

I can only sit, alone again, as hot tears spill down my face and pure pain seeps into my heart.

Chapter 76

There's only one person I need right now. Not want, but need.

'Is Ellie there, Alistair?' I'm trying not to let him hear how croaky my voice is, despite feeling as if I have a handful of grit in my mouth.

'Hi, Sam. She's getting out of the bath. Let me give her a shout.'

He's gone for more than a minute before he comes back to say, 'Um . . . Sam. Sorry about this, but she's tied up. She asked if she could phone you back.'

The urge to cry is overwhelming. I hold the receiver a foot away and am absolutely incapable of stopping the tears. Then I remember I need to finish this call.

'No problem, Alistair. Thanks.'

I'm about to put down the phone, when Alistair's voice stops me. 'Sam?'

The television that was on in the background is no longer audible; he's moved into a different room.

'Yes?'

'Is everything all right between you and Ellie?'

I swallow, not knowing what to say. My mind is swirling with possible responses, the most prominent of which is: No, Alistair, everything is not all right. And by the way, have you noticed that the mother of your child is an alcoholic?

Instead, I manage a weak: 'What makes you ask that?'

He hesitates. 'I don't know . . . It struck me you hadn't been round much lately. And Ellie's been acting a little . . .'

'What?'

'Oh it's nothing. Forget it. Sorry – I'm going to have to go, Sam. I think Sophie's awake.'

I phone Jen next.

'Oh God . . . I'm so glad you phoned,' she says breathlessly before I can start to tell her what's happened. 'I can't stay on for long because I'm at work and we've got a staffing crisis.'

'What's up, Jen?' I ask, almost on autopilot.

'I've got to split up with Dan. It's the only way.' I say nothing. 'Sam . . . are you there?'

'Yes,' I reply.

'We went out for dinner last night and he started banging on about how frustrating it was for him to have still not found "the one". So I came out with it and said, "Where do I fit into all this?"'

'Right.'

'He started squirming and said, "Well, I really like getting together with you and . . . I think you're wonderful, just wonderful . . . but, well, I like what we've got. You don't want a big full-on relationship, do you?"'

Jen continues for the next two minutes and she's clearly upset, but I'm of no comfort. I don't even get round to interrupting her frantic conversation to tell her what happened with Jamie.

'Look, I really do need to go. Is everything all right with you, Sam?'

I'm about to answer, but she interrupts again. 'Oh God – sorry, honey. There's an emergency here. And I'm due to see Ellie again tonight. I'm determined to get her to see sense. I'll text you if there's news.'

For the rest of the evening, I feel as if my house is not my own. Nothing is going to mend today. Not a million-pound lottery win. Not a lifetime's supply of Jimmy Choos. Not God deciding I can eat as much cake as I want for the rest of my life and never put on weight.

I wander round the house aimlessly, considering possible ways of cheering myself up. But the music on my iPod just hurts my insides and the Galaxy bar in the fridge has never been less appetizing. I pour a glass of wine, but can't touch it. I just look at it and think of what it and its kind have done to my best friend.

So I follow an urge that grabbed hold of me the second Jamie walked out of the door and hasn't left since. I race upstairs to my laptop and, sitting on my bed as I wipe away tears, I frantically log on. I go straight to Facebook to see if Ben is online – and my heart sinks when he isn't. I pick up my phone and stare at it, wondering if I should confide in him about this. This man for whom my feelings remain so complicated.

I am about to press call, when a new status update appears. It says he's at Panoramic – one of the city's best restaurants – with Mildred Muldoon.

I frown. Mildred. That's his elderly cat-owning neighbour, is it not?

As I click on to her profile picture my heart is thrashing. And what I see manages to make me feel even worse than I felt already. Which, frankly, I hadn't thought possible.

Mildred – who, Ben jokingly said on our first date, 'might want to marry' him – is not a seventy-four-year-old, blue-rinsed, varicose-veined pensioner as I had assumed. Mildred is a twenty-four-year-old pseudo-supermodel, whose public profile boasts no fewer than 372 pictures, not one of which makes her look less than jaw-droppingly gorgeous.

Frantically, I flick to Ben's page, and am confronted by a sentence that hits me like a freight train.

Ben Moran is in a relationship.

Chapter 77

By the time I get to my mum's, it's gone ten o'clock, and she opens the door with something in her hand which, on closer inspection, turns out to be a novelty shoe horn fashioned in the shape of a piece of broccoli.

'It's Aunt Jill's birthday next week and she's so tricky to buy for. So I got something that I thought would have universal appeal,' she says, apparently seriously.

She sits on the sofa and starts wrapping the gift as I plunge into the chair opposite. I close my eyes briefly and wonder if I can actually confide in Mum. It's not something I've ever done before.

'Jamie and I have split up again.' The words tumble out surprisingly easily. 'I haven't told anyone yet.'

I wait for her to respond with the 'all men are bastards except your father' speech. Except it isn't forthcoming. Instead, she stands up silently and walks towards me, perching on the arm of the chair and pulling my head to her chest.

'I'm sorry, sweetheart,' she whispers, rubbing my back. 'I really am.'

I pull back and take in the look on her face. The concern, empathy, unconditional love. I feel suddenly and significantly better.

'What happened?'

I fill her in on the details and she listens calmly, offering the occasional word of support and advice. After everything else tonight, it feels low-key, undramatic – and exactly what I need.

'Stay here tonight, if you like,' she tells me.

I smile. 'I might take you up on that.'

'Good, because—'

She's interrupted by the sound of a key in the door, and I compose myself, expecting it to be Dad back from the pub. It isn't Dad, though; it's Julia.

In every other way but one she looks her usual self: stylishly dressed, beautifully made-up. But when she enters the room this evening she almost skulks. It's so unlike her usual elegance that it changes her entire demeanour, and reminds me of how miserable she's looked since the news that her birth mum wants nothing to do with her.

Mum straightens up. 'Is everything all right, Julia?'

'Just thought I'd stop and say hello on my way home from tonight's concert,' she replies. 'What are you doing here, Sam?'

'Do you really want to know?' I ask.

I don't know what it is about the way I repeat the story, but Julia's reaction is unbelievably emotional. She wipes away a tear and throws her arms around me, then beckons Mum to join in. It's like a rugby scrum, but with less mud and more oestrogen.

'Look,' says Julia, her lip trembling. 'No matter what happens, we've got each other.'

'That's the corniest thing you've ever said,' I reply. 'But totally true.'

'If Jamie doesn't want you, Sam, that's his loss. That's what I've told myself about my birth mother,' she adds. Now I realize what's eating her. 'The more I think about the outright "no" I got from her, the more I fail to comprehend what sort of woman she must be. I'm better off without her.'

Mum pulls away and goes to sit on the sofa. Julia follows and sits next to her, squeezing her hand.

'Mum,' she continues. 'I'm so sorry for everything I put you through. The rejection – from my own mother – has totally reinforced what I've got with you. I can't imagine why any woman would want nothing to do with her daughter, can you?'

I am struck by a sensation that this animosity towards a woman she's never met isn't doing Julia any good at all.

'Maybe she has her reasons,' I say weakly.

'Like what?' she replies, agitated. 'There's no good reason.' A tear comes from nowhere and slides down her cheek. 'I swing between telling myself it doesn't matter . . . and feeling, I'll be honest, awful. About my mum. About me. About what I could possibly have done to her. About why after, all these years, she can't bring herself to even say hello.'

She turns to me again, and I've never seen her so upset.

'Does she hate me or something? I'm coming to the conclusion that she must.'

The silence is suddenly so oppressive that, when Mum breaks it, her words almost echo off the walls. 'She doesn't hate you.'

Julia whips round her head to glare at her. 'What?'

Mum's jaw tightens. 'She doesn't hate you.'

Julia's eyes are blazing. 'You know who she is, don't you? You know.'

Mum looks away and stares into the middle distance, shaking her head. But she isn't denying Julia's question. She simply has no idea what to do or say – and, clearly, neither does my sister.

'Mum,' I say insistently. 'Do you know who Julia's mother is?'

She swallows hard and, with glazed eyes, turns to look directly at Julia. 'I do.'

For a moment my sister seems to stop breathing. 'Then who the hell is she?' she erupts.

Mum closes her eyes, filling her lungs with air, attempting to find strength.

'She's me, sweetheart,' she replies. 'She's me.'

Chapter 78

Julia and I sit numbly, trying to work out what we've missed. Dissecting Mum's words and trying to make sense of them. We reach the same conclusion.

'Mum,' she says, 'you know you mean as much to me as any biological mother. But I'm talking in literal terms. I'm talking about the woman who physically gave birth to me.'

Mum's face is devoid of colour, but it has a veil of calm as she stares at the clock on the mantelpiece. 'I know. So am I.'

Julia shakes her head, looking as if every breath has been sucked from her.

'You're my birth mother?'

My heart is hammering so fast I can barely concentrate on anything else.

Mum puts her head in her hands briefly, then looks up and composes herself. 'I am, sweetheart. And I know I've got a lot of explaining to do.'

Julia is clearly failing to comprehend any of this. She's not alone. Mum needs to start talking.

'Gary already told you the outline of the events, and that, essentially, is it. He told the truth. Your dad and I had met a few years earlier and fell totally in love. But we had . . . a rough patch. At the time, I thought we'd never recover from it.'

'What happened?' I splutter.

She takes a deep breath. 'Our first years as a married couple were no honeymoon period. So much went wrong, particularly in that third year. Your dad's father died. He lost his job. In the event, he was out of work for only a short period, but at the time it was horrendous. Plus, as you already know, I had five miscarriages.'

'Which was why you adopted Julia,' I mutter. 'Or we thought you'd adopted Julia.'

Mum swallows. 'I can't tell you what that was like – with the babies, I mean. Every time we got our hopes up that this was it . . . this was the child we desperately wanted . . . I lost it. My job meant I was always delivering other people's babies so, every time we experienced it again, the pressure, the pain – it was unbearable. I was six months pregnant with the last baby. The grief was indescribable . . .' She shudders and her voice trails off before she continues. 'We'd been together for four years and the pressure got to us. Badly. And, well, we decided we needed to be apart for some time. Your dad was convinced that the worry about him losing his job had contributed to me losing the last baby. Six months was the furthest along I'd ever got.' She shakes her head. 'That was ridiculous, of course. But the point is that neither of us was in a good place.'

'So Dad left you?'

'We both agreed that splitting up was the best thing to do. The thing is that sometimes, when difficult things happen, relationships get stronger. But we were young and . . . we didn't know how to handle it.'

Julia and I can't speak as we take all this in.

'He was – and always has been – the love of my life,' Mum tells us. 'And although I thought having some time apart was the right thing to do, equally I couldn't cope with the idea of not spending the rest of my life with him. It was a mess. I decided to make a clean break.'

'You went to London, like Gary said,' Julia offers.

Mum nods. 'My parents were, obviously, completely against the whole thing. Well, you know what they were like, Grandma Milly in particular. I was a married woman, for goodness' sake. It was a difficult time. I got a job in a maternity hospital, which some people thought I was mad to do, given what I'd been going through with the miscarriages, but that was my vocation. I'd always been a midwife; I didn't know anything else. Not that I can deny I was as miserable as sin. I was lonely. And I desperately missed your father. That's when I met Gary.'

Julia swallows. 'I see.'

Mum squirms. 'He was living in the same street where I was renting a room and we became friends. That was all. But, one night, we got talking about what had gone on between Frank and me. I got upset and . . . I don't know, I felt in need of human contact, I suppose. That night it turned out to be more than that.

You don't need me to spell it out. I . . . I made a mistake.' She looks at her hands. 'It happened only once and we agreed to put the whole thing behind us. My feelings for him were nothing like those I had for your father. I couldn't have started a relationship with him; I was still in love with someone else. With Frank.'

'So when did you get back together with Dad?' I ask.

'Four days later, I got home from work to find your dad waiting on the doorstep. He'd got another job. He'd wanted me back all along but had been determined to get work before he approached me. There was simply no other man for me.'

'So you moved back up north straight away?' I ask.

'Yes. Gary and I promised to stay in touch, but things were awkward. Then . . . well, life threw us a googly.'

'You found out you were pregnant?' Julia asks.

Mum nods. 'I didn't start showing until I was about seven months gone. It was the same ten years later with you, Sam.'

'But how did you know it wasn't Dad's child?'

'I didn't,' shrugs Mum. 'I hoped it was. But the timing was such that it could as easily be Gary's. And given Gary's beautiful, chocolate-brown skin, it was going to be immediately apparent if the baby turned out to be his. I couldn't risk your dad discovering everything in the labour room like that. I had to tell him.'

Neither Julia nor I can move; we're stunned.

'And he never doubted he wanted to stay with you – even though you were possibly carrying another man's child?' I ask.

Mum looks at me with glassy eyes. 'Never. That didn't stop us both being shell-shocked, of course. We didn't know what to do. The thought of how this would go down with my family . . . Well, can you imagine? It would have been impossible. So I went to stay with Great-Aunt Maggie – Grandma Milly's sister – until I gave birth. She lived in Colwyn Bay. What is it, Julia?'

'Nothing,' she says, shaking her head dismissively. 'Gary mentioned some sort of Welsh connection, that's all.'

'Well, Maggie kept the secret for me,' Mum says. 'I told everyone I was working in London again. My hope, of course, was that I'd give birth to the baby and it'd turn out to be your dad's. We didn't have a plan about what to say to people; we were making it up as we went along.'

'But it didn't turn out to be his,' Julia says numbly. 'It turned out to be Gary's. You must have had to make a plan, then?'

'We decided . . .' Mum swallows and a tear streams down her cheek. 'We decided that all we could do was to have you adopted. To do with you exactly as you thought did happen.'

'Why didn't you?' Julia whispers.

Mum shakes her head. 'Because when I held your tiny body in my arms in that labour ward, everything changed.' Her expression is a strange combination of elation and pain. 'You were beautiful. I see babies every day, but I'd never seen one as beautiful as you. You were a gorgeous, tiny, healthy baby with a rosebud mouth and fingers that curled around mine as if you were saying to me: "Mummy, I'm yours. You can't let me go." And you know what, Julia? I couldn't. I absolutely couldn't. Frank couldn't either. I promise you, Julia, that even if keeping you had meant my own mother and father would never have spoken to me again, then that's what I would have done. Without question. However . . .'

'Yes?' says Julia.

Mum takes a deep breath. 'Grandma Milly was in frail health. She'd had a bout of pneumonia and I was worried sick that she wasn't going to survive it. In the event, she recovered and lived another ten years, but at the time that looked very unlikely. The last thing I wanted was to inflict more drama on her. As unreasonable as her prejudices were. So I came up with an idea that I knew could solve everything.'

'To tell everyone that Julia was adopted,' I say.

Mum nods. 'My story was that a woman at the adoption agency – who I knew through work – had told me about you and, when I saw you, I had an overwhelming urge to look after you. Particularly since your dad and I had had trouble conceiving, which Grandma Milly knew all about.'

'And everyone believed it?' I ask.

'Why wouldn't they? I simply told them Julia had faced an uncertain future otherwise and, having worked with babies all my life, I couldn't let that happen. Everyone accepted it.' She turns to Julia. 'I was desperate to keep you. It seemed like the only option.'

Julia frowns, shaking her head. 'But that was then. That was thirty-eight years ago. Why wouldn't you have told the truth since? I don't understand.'

Mum swallows. 'The more time that passed, the more I

thought that announcing to everyone the reality of the situation would either kill my mother with shock, or make everyone think I needed carting away by men in white coats.' She scrunches up her forehead. 'It was more than that, though. It just . . . ceased to become an issue, all by itself somehow. None of us ever really thought about it. I mean, you don't, do you? You just get on with life.'

She swallows and bites the nail on her thumb. 'Plus, whenever we did talk about it, Julia, you were so fixed in your view that biology was irrelevant. That you didn't give two hoots about finding your birth mother. That I was your mum, no matter what happened. So I convinced myself it wasn't an issue. I convinced myself – and Frank – that knowing the truth wasn't that important to you.'

She pauses and looks at her hands. 'I was kidding myself. Of course, I was. I was taking the easy option. Plus, I was ashamed of what I'd done. I felt, very early on, that I should have stood up to my mother and said, "I don't care what you think. This is my daughter and I'm proud of her." Because –' she looks at Julia – 'I am, you know. I'm so very proud of you.'

Julia kneels down on the floor and rests her head in Mum's lap. Mum strokes Julia's skin, wiping away her tears.

'I know you are, Mum,' Julia says. 'I know.'

Chapter 79

I am experiencing what I can only describe as emotion overload. And information overload. And . . . just overload.

There are only so many revelations I can cope with in twenty-four hours, and the facts that my Jamie cheated on me, and that Ben is 'in a relationship', are now the least of them. The idea that Mum and Dad have experienced more melodrama than in an *EastEnders* special . . . I don't know how to begin taking that in.

It must be even harder for Julia. She's at the heart of this matter; she's the one who's lived with this bizarre lie, albeit obliviously. Mum says she's got a right to be angry, and I think there's a small part of Julia, and indeed of me too, that is.

But, most of all, it feels like a missing piece of the jigsaw has been found – and effortlessly slotted in. Part of me thinks: Wow . . . Julia's my sister! Another part thinks: And? . . . She always has been, shared gene pool or not.

When I wake the next morning, it's to the beep of a text message from Jen.

I've done it – dumped Dan. Am distraught xx

I hit call, but she must be on an early shift because it goes straight to voicemail, so I leave a message: 'Hey, Jen – got your text. Hope everything's okay. There's been a bit of drama round here too, actually. Come round tonight and we'll have a good chat. Keep your chin up, sweetheart.'

It's advice I feel totally incapable of following myself. My feelings about my family are one thing; those about Jamie – and Ben, for that matter – are entirely another. I consider throwing a sickie for the first time in my life, but decide against it: I've got a hell of a lot to think about, but I don't really want to think any more. I've done nothing but think since Jamie left.

'Right, my luvs. Give it to me straight,' Lorelei demands. 'Have we got Coleen or not?'

There are five days until the Teen SOS centenary event and I'm counting the minutes until it's all over.

I take a deep breath. 'Coleen unfortunately isn't able to come, but we have a number of celebrities.'

This is not just stretching the truth; it's coating the truth in Lycra and pulling it until it's barely visible to the naked eye. The best I've managed to do are four members of the *Hollyoaks* cast, a handful of minor WAGs and Fern Britton's make-up artist.

As I break this to Lorelei, I'm convinced I can hear steam whistling out of her ears.

'There are plenty of others who will add value.' I decide

against telling her about Rusty Lee. 'Such as local DJ Sullivan Price – oh, and Dr Darren Bosco.'

'Doctor . . . who?'

'Dr Darren Bosco,' I repeat, wishing I hadn't mentioned him. He's the medical expert on a local radio station and is about as A-list as my dad.

'Ooh,' she says, sounding surprisingly upbeat. 'Ooooh.'

'Ooh?' I repeat.

'Ooooh, yesss. I like him.'

'Really?'

'Always been a fan. Can you get me an introduction?'

'Of course!' I reply, wishing I'd known it would be this straightforward.

The rest of the day is a blur. Deana and Natalie are as helpful as ever and, frankly, nothing at all would get done if Anna, the work-experience girl (who's more productive than the two of them together), wasn't back. Still, emails are pinging into my inbox so rapidly my computer sounds like a Chemical Brothers remix and I can't focus on work at all. I am instead compelled to log on to Facebook and flick between Jamie's page and Ben's, looking for clues about what they're both up to.

'Hey, there xx'

When the chat box appears, my heart thuds against my chest . . . until I realize it's Luke.

'Hey, how are you? Not at work? x'

I open my inbox and note that six emails have arrived in the last one and a half minutes. I flick back to Luke's response.

'Day off. I heard about what happened with Jamie.'

'Yep. Not good.'

I hit enter and wait for a response, wondering how much Jamie's told him. And whether or not he knew about Dorrie.

'So sorry, Sam. If it means anything, you're not alone. Gemma's dumped me.'

'Oh no! What happened?'

'Long story. You feeling okay?'

I start composing a reply, saying I'm fine. But something makes me stop and stare at it. I delete the word 'fine' and replace it with 'shit'. Then I delete that and reinstate 'fine'. Then I delete everything and simply gaze at the screen, not having a clue how to respond.

'I'll take that as a no. What time are you back from work? I'm coming over.'

I feel numb at the prospect. I'd prefer to be able to splurge to Jen instead, because if there's one thing I've learned women can do in a crisis, it's talk. At the exact moment I think that, she sends me a text.

Hey, can't come over tonight . . . it's Mum's bday. What's your drama? Hope everything's okay. x

I postpone replying and return to my screen. Luke does have one benefit, and that's his ability to fill me in on what Jamie's been saying.

*

He arrives at seven in a checked shirt and black jeans, looking every inch the Adonis that turns women's brains to mush. He kisses me briefly on the cheek, then throws his arms around me and gives me a bear hug. 'How you doing, kiddo?'

I shrug as we head into the living room. 'I'm okay. So what happened with Gemma?'

'Her best friend, Sadie, told her she saw you and me coming out of that coffee shop with, and I quote, "their arms around each other",' he says, sitting down. 'Gemma's been on holiday and only got back this week – the first thing Sadie did was tell her this. She got completely the wrong end of the stick.'

'Oh no,' I say, catching my breath and unable to believe I've been dragged into this. 'All we did was hug!'

'Given what Gemma knows about my . . . colourful past, she won't believe that we're just friends.'

In the six years I've known him, I don't think I've ever seen Luke so upset. I spend the next half-hour offering to phone her, speak to her, do anything I can to reassure her that there's nothing to it; but he's unsure about whether that'll help or make things worse. Eventually, the conversation is steered to the subject of Jamie and me.

'Did you know about him and Dorrie?'

'No,' he insists. 'I swear I didn't, Sam.'

'And you'd have told me if you had?'

'Interesting question,' he shrugs. 'Jamie is my best friend. I'm one hundred per cent certain I'd have told him he's an idiot, though.'

'So what has he said?'

'Oh he's all over the place, Sam,' he replies. 'He clearly loves you. And he knows how badly he's messed things up by getting involved with Dorrie. But he also knows that, once you've cheated on a woman, well . . . there's no going back, is there? Has he told you about South America?'

The words send a jolt of electricity through my chest and I look up. 'We haven't been in touch. What about it?'

Luke frowns. 'He's decided to look into going on his trip again. There's nothing left for him here any more.'

I stare at him numbly. 'I see. So the job he was offered is still there for him?'

'He thinks so,' says Luke.

I'd suspected that reinstating his grand trip abroad would be on the cards, but hearing it confirmed makes me feel ill. Part of me wonders if he ever cancelled the flight.

'I'm sorry, Sam,' Luke adds.

I take a huge gulp of wine and let it slip down my throat. It's miraculously medicinal tonight. Partly, I'm sure, because I haven't touched any alcohol since my argument with Ellie, despite recent events. After a couple of glasses, the world seems an easier place than before, of that there's no doubt. It's an illustration of how even someone like me – who can normally take or leave a drink – can see the lure of it all too clearly.

However, by glasses four and five, I'm not seeing a great deal clearly. By the time Luke and I have put the world to rights, and he's moved over to my sofa and cuddled up, I can't help thinking that tucking my head into his chest would be a nice thing to do.

When I'm *not* concentrating on this, the other two men in my life keep springing into my head. Jamie, who rejected me for another woman and has now left me for a second time. And Ben, who is 'in a relationship'.

'Do you fancy me, Luke?' I slur, gazing up at him.

He looks down at me and grins. 'Course I do, Sam. You're a top bird.'

I roll my eyes drunkenly. 'What a pity that's the most romantic thing anyone's likely to say to me these days.'

'Oh listen,' he says, squeezing me to him. 'You're going to be okay, you know. It's all just raw at the moment. Maybe you need another man.'

'I had another man who should have been perfectly up to the job of taking my mind off it, but I managed to bugger things up with him too. He's got a girlfriend now. And I . . . I feel shit about that. Which I've got absolutely no right to, after what I've done to him.'

'What's he like?'

'Lovely and good-looking and intelligent and nice and . . . oh just gorgeous. Perfect, actually.'

'What? There's someone else out there just like me?'

I ignore him. 'Then we've got the situation with Jamie, a situation I can't work out.'

'In what way? It's all straightforward, isn't it? You found out he cheated. Surely it's a no-brainer.'

'It should be,' I croak. 'I should hate him.'

'But you don't?'

'I can't switch off my feelings for him, no matter how badly he's behaved.'

He pulls back and looks at me, frowning. 'Look, he's my mate and even I thought you were made for each other. But I assumed that you wouldn't even consider taking him back now.'

'I assumed that too.'

'But . . .?'

'But . . .' It's at this point that a realization hits me. One I hate, one I know is pathetic, but one that's unequivocally, unarguably true. 'I feel jealous,' I confess.

'Of Dorrie?'

I nod. 'And I think I still love him. Even though I hate him.' I pause. 'Except . . . how can I when I'm also torn apart by the fact that Ben has now got another girlfriend?'

He takes a deep breath. 'You know that book *Women Who Think Too Much*?'

'Yes?'

'I'm buying it for you for Christmas.'

I laugh and suddenly feel a rush of a nausea so powerful I suspect there's more neat Pinot Grigio than haemoglobin being pumped round my body right now.

I steady my head and bury it into Luke's neck, casting my thoughts back to that night with Ben. On this sofa. I remain still for a few seconds, then clear my mind of anything, concentrating only on the feel of a man's skin against mine.

I look up at his lips and – although horribly drunk – I am flooded with the same sensation I experienced with Ben sitting next to me. Slowly, I inch up and kiss him. I don't know what I'm thinking about, except the flock of butterflies in my stomach. Which sure as hell beats everything else in my life at the moment. He closes his eyes and his shoulders relax as I kiss him again, just as gently.

Then he opens his eyes and shakes his head.

'What is it?' I slur.

'I'd better go,' he says, kissing me on the head and moving away. 'Are you going to be all right?'

I nod, blinking away tears as he puts on his coat to leave. Then he pauses and bends down, so his face is a foot away from mine.

'Sam. You're gorgeous. You're fantastic. Basically, you rock. But you'd regret this instantly, I promise you. Goodbye, sweetheart.' He straightens up and walks to the door, leaving me alone. Yet again.

And with the thought that I've now been turned down by a man who would have an erotic encounter with anything if it kept still long enough. Marvellous.

Chapter 80

I don't know why the day of the Teen SOS event, at the very end of November, counts among the most stressful of the year. I've organized hundreds of functions like this – bigger, in fact – and always retained my cool. But someone on high is throwing every possible challenge at me, whether it's a shortage of champagne glasses or the food poisoning contracted by Kevin S. Chasen's chauffeur or the fact that the flowers Lorelei chose have made me sneeze every ten seconds since they arrived.

As a result, I am now as swollen with mucus as a hamster with swine flu and, with ten minutes left before the guests are due to arrive at the sumptuous hotel, I am still struggling with transporting the corporate gift bags between my car and the entrance. The box is three times my weight-lifting capabilities, a fact not helped by my choice of three-inch heels, shoes that are already responsible for blisters the size of ping-pong balls.

'Would you like a hand?'

I'm sweating, flushed and seconds from the climax of another sneeze, when this voice makes my knees buckle. Ben rescues the box and marches into the lobby, the tendons in his arms undulating against the weight.

'We're in the function room,' I say, following him breathlessly. 'What are you doing here?'

He puts down the box and looks at me, prompting a wave of insecurity about my appearance. Knowing I'd be surrounded by WAGs and soap stars – albeit catastrophically minor-league ones – I opted for an outfit that's a tad more chichi than usual. I can't say it's entirely me. The short spangly dress is okay, the heels are passable (if painful) . . . but my hair is closer to the definition of absurd than a French existentialist painting.

The seven-inch hairpiece I'm currently sporting had been lying in my dressing-table drawer like a cryogenically frozen rodent for the last year, but, as the result of a snap decision this afternoon, it is now attached to my bonce with a mass of hairpins.

'Um . . . I had a meeting over the road,' he replies, frowning at my head, clearly wondering what they put in the water round here for my hair to have experienced such a tremendous growth spurt. 'I was heading to catch the train when I saw your car. How are you? Busy, by the look of it.'

I blow my fringe off my face. 'You could say that.'

This is the first time I've seen Ben since Jamie and I split up again – and since Facebook announced that he was in a relationship. Both issues are at the forefront of my mind, but it feels neither the time nor the place to raise them.

'Do you need a hand with anything?' he asks.

I'm about to say no, but change my mind. 'You could help me finish packing the goody bags.'

He mock-salutes and smiles. 'No problem at all, Ms Brooks.'

'How I wish all my staff members were so deferential.'

Despite the chaotic afternoon, by the time the two hundred and fifty VIP guests are in situ, the motto by which I've lived today – it'll be all right on the night – has come good. I've even managed to pick up a couple of half-decent celebrities at the last minute, courtesy of one agent cocking up their appearance on the guest list at the arena.

'This is absolutely brilliant!' gushes Natalie in a rare fit of enthusiasm – and she's right.

It isn't only that the atmosphere is electric. Or that the caterers have pulled out all the stops on the canapés, cocktails and service. Or even that we've managed all this despite Lorelei getting a discount that would have done Robin Hood proud.

The event has that indefinable quality that means everyone is simply enjoying themselves. More importantly, given that this is doubling up as a fundraiser, people seem to be putting megabucks in the raffle envelopes, and several wealthy local entrepreneurs have already committed to providing substantial ongoing financial support.

As have I. Despite vowing to myself that I was going to ration my charitable giving and stop getting sucked into donating to . . . well, everything, this one's been added to the list. I don't begrudge a penny of it, though. The more I've found out about this charity since I started working with it, the more in awe I am.

Thousands of vulnerable teenagers have had their lives transformed in the last year as a direct result of the money this organization has raised. And although Lorelei isn't always the easiest to deal with, behind her are swathes of dedicated and passionate people making a real difference to those who need it most.

Of course, as far as Lorelei's concerned, the only criterion against which tonight's event will be judged is what Kevin S. Chasen thinks of it. I haven't even seen him yet, although he is here, as a hyperventilating Lorelei tells me every ten seconds.

'Ooh, I love these cocktails,' grins Deana, grabbing two martinis from a passing tray. I can't help noticing that Deana and Natalie are enjoying themselves a little too much.

'Deana,' I hiss.

'Wha—?'

'Oh you are a spoilsport, Sal,' says Piers, appearing from nowhere and winking at Deana. She giggles and bats her eyelids so enthusiastically it makes her cleavage wobble.

'Um . . . Piers? I think Lorelei wanted a chat with you at some point,' I tell him.

'Who? Oh her,' he says, failing to remove his eyes from Deana's jiggling décolletage. 'I've already spoken to the main man – her boss. Nice chap. He was thoroughly impressed with the event management tonight. I told him he should be; we've worked bloody hard on it.'

I let the 'we' go without comment even though until four thirty this afternoon – when Piers phoned after a meeting in

Liverpool to ask me to recommend a pub – he was entirely unaware of the event's existence.

I head to the bar to check everything is in order and spot Ben a few feet away. He is being chatted up by an impossibly glamorous redhead with up-to-the-armpit legs and a hemline to match. He excuses himself and heads over.

'Your party's amazing,' he tells me, the lights from the bar glistening in his eyes. 'I'm so impressed.'

'You're too easily impressed, then,' I reply, sneezing and taking another tissue from my bag.

'Don't be so modest,' he replies. 'I was talking to an American guy earlier who said the same.'

I stiffen. 'An American? Who was he?'

'I think he said he was the boss.'

'Kevin S. Chasen? Has everyone seen this guy except me? What did he say?'

Ben frowns. 'Well, he mainly wanted to talk about . . .'

'Yes?' I ask anxiously.

'His cat.'

I scrunch up my nose. 'His cat?'

'Suffers with hairballs, apparently. He wanted my advice.'

'Are you kidding me?' I huff. 'What did he say about the event? Did he look like he was enjoying himself? And how long were you with him, exactly?'

'About twenty minutes. I told him about a new type of cat food they've developed that can help and—'

'Ben!'

He pauses and smiles. 'The answer is yes, he was enjoying himself, and he seemed impressed. Obviously, I left him under no illusions that you were the genius behind this extravaganza.'

'Oh stop – I'm serious.'

'I'm serious too,' he grins. 'He was having a whale of a time – apart from being hounded by a woman about a speech.'

Suddenly, I am grabbed by the arm with a grip that could rival that of a shot-putter.

'Right, my loves, Kevin S. Chasen wants me to say a few words before him,' Lorelei declares. 'So it's time to do my stuff. And you need to introduce me.'

I respond with a sneeze. 'Er, okay, Lorelei,' I reply, trying to look unmoved. I hate public speaking and normally I'd employ a formal announcer to do this, but Lorelei's budget put paid to that. 'Have you prepared a speech?'

'You're kidding, aren't you, babe?' she laughs. 'I can talk to Olympic standard. I don't need to write something in advance.'

I suppress another sneeze and feel my eyes swelling up. 'Would you like me to say anything in particular?'

'Describe me as one of the leading female figures in the north west.' She pauses and thinks. 'If not the north.' She thinks again. 'If not *the* leading female figure.' I try to work out if she's joking. It appears not. 'Then I think you should explain how I was brought up on a council estate in south Wales and – although I've become the mega-success I am today – I've never forgotten my roots.'

I sneeze, and hold my tissue to my nose. 'O-kay.'

'And you should also mention that I'm an inspiration to everyone who meets me.' She pauses and glares at me. 'Obviously, it needs to be clear that this is your description, not mine. I don't want to look like a bighead.'

'Of course— Aitchoo! Though I'll keep the intro relatively short, don't you think? We're on a tight timescale and I don't want to encroach on what you have to say.'

She turns up her nose and thinks. 'Good point. Off you go.'

I take a deep breath and make my way to the stage, feeling my blood turn to molten lava. Although my speech is going to be significantly shorter than Lorelei's requested eulogy, I'm as nervous as hell. I stumble up the steps and take the mike.

'Excuse me, ladies and gentlemen,' I begin, and precisely nobody turns to look. 'Hi. . . Could I have everyone's attention, please?' Despite the tinge of desperation in my voice, the only soul paying attention is Ben, who already looks mortified on my behalf.

'Right,' I begin again, determined to say something to get everyone to shut up. However, I don't need to say anything – because nature takes over. My chest rises, my eyes close . . . and I explode with such a devastating sneeze it nearly melts the speakers.

The room falls silent. 'Bloody hell,' says Deana helpfully.

'Sorry about that,' I mumble, flushing. 'Erm, I'd like to introduce a woman who needs no introduction. She's one of the leading female figures in the north, if not the north west. I mean— Aitchoo!'

When I look up, Lorelei is glaring at me. 'She's never forgotten her roots, despite living on a council estate.' Her eyes widen. 'She doesn't live on a council estate now, of course. God, no!' I laugh. Then sneeze. 'At least, I don't think so. Without further ado, please let me introduce the Director of International Marketing for Teen SOS, Ms Lorelei Beer.'

There is a smattering of applause as Lorelei storms onto the stage. I meet her on the second step, and she snatches the mike from my hand then whirls past me as I prepare to make my getaway.

Except that I'm going nowhere. Instead of slipping anonymously into the crowd, a sharp yank to my head forces me to stumble back onto the stage. It feels exactly like a move undertaken on various first-formers by Alison Hardface, my old school's resident bully. Although Lorelei Beer is a lot scarier. And it's her diamanté brooch in which my hairpiece is caught up.

'Hiya, ladies and gentlemen, my loves!' she booms, momentarily unaware that I'm bent double and attached to her right shoulder.

I grab my hairpiece with both hands and, to the delight of the audience, who appear to think this is a comedy prelude to the main act, wrestle with its strands, as if I'm being held ransom.

Lorelei turns and looks at me. Then, taking matters into her own hands, she attempts to disentangle my headwear from her jewellery. To the increasing hysteria of the crowd she tugs and pulls, I twist and turn. I'm writhing in agony and shame when I finally manage to disengage. My head is throbbing as I dust myself off, straighten my back and, with as much dignity as possible, step casually down the stairs.

Lorelei's speech begins, but I barely hear it. Instead, I stride to the other side of the room, where I catch a glimpse of my hairpiece in the mirror. It is standing a foot above my head, like a small-scale re-creation of the *The Wicker Man*.

I never get to subtly quiz Ben about being 'in a relationship'. I don't even get to say goodbye properly. I manage only a perfunctory wave as he heads to the exit while Lorelei launches into a diatribe about the disaster with my hairpiece.

Not that I can blame her. And, although I'm aware that her unrelenting nit-picking – about everything from the Wasabi on one of the canapés to the choice of air freshener in the ladies' loos – isn't reasonable, it hardly matters.

My client isn't happy and that's all that counts. Plus, I have no idea if she witnessed Deana and Natalie disappearing early on the arms of two Premiership footballers – presumably for a strenuous session of something that had little to do with soccer.

None of this alleviates my mood when I meet Jen for a late drink after the event.

It's gone one o'clock and I'm as tired as hell, but she's just finished a late shift and I feel a need to catch up, even if it's only for half an hour before we both collapse into bed.

'I cannot believe what's been happening in your life lately,' she sighs. 'I feel so stupid now, texting you about my daft romantic problems. My troubles are nothing compared with yours. Ellie needs to know this and stop being so silly,' she frowns.

'Has she been in touch?' I ask.

'Hardly at all. She's avoiding me too, I'm certain of it. Mind you, I've hardly been good company lately.'

'Don't be silly, sweetheart. We're all here for each other, aren't we? Come on, fill me in on what's been happening.'

She swallows. 'I split up with Dan on Friday and it's the hardest thing I've ever done. It was the last thing I wanted to do, but I came to the conclusion that, while he's a lovely, caring, fantastic person, he's bad for me.'

I bite my lip. 'In what sense?'

'In the sense that he likes me but doesn't love me. I, on the other hand, think I love him. The real deal. And you simply can't have that imbalance in a relationship. Even someone as feckless as me knows that. So I dumped him.'

'What was his reaction?'

She takes a deep breath. 'He tried to persuade me to change my mind. He couldn't work out what was going on because he thought I was as relaxed about the situation as he was. I don't want to be his bed-buddy, Sam. I want to be his girlfriend.'

'You've got every right to want that.'

'I know. But it's killing me. Having been so aloof for so many weeks, now that I've dumped him he's texting me all the time, calling me. Every time he bumps into me in the corridor at work, he asks me for coffee. And I've resisted, even though I just want to dive into his arms and smother him with kisses.'

'If he's that keen, isn't he worth a second chance?'

She shrugs. 'If he was that keen, the idea of committing wouldn't make him recoil in horror. He'd do or say something that showed me how much I meant to him. But, unfortunately, I'm one hundred per cent certain of what I mean to him: a good shag. That's what he misses. He's made that perfectly clear.'

Chapter 81

I wake the next morning and look up at the ceiling as thoughts occur like light bulbs being switched on, one by one. Jamie. Ben. Last night's event. Jen. And Ellie. Oh Ellie.

She knows nothing about what's going on in my life. And I know nothing about hers. Plus, what Jen said last night – about Ellie avoiding her too – troubles me deeply. All Jen and I want is to help her; yet to accept our help would mean admitting she has an issue. The fact that Ellie's clearly so far from doing that is even more worrying than the disintegration of our friendship.

I decide to drive to her house after work, though I'm certain it's a futile exercise. When I get there and ring the bell, it's like a scene from *Groundhog Day*. Despite the shuffling inside, nobody answers.

Dejected, I turn and head down the drive, then the door opens. I spin round to see Alistair looking clean but crumpled.

'Sorry, Sam. You caught me as I was getting out of the shower. Come in. Ellie won't be long; she's at the supermarket with

Sophie.' I hesitate. 'Come on. I'll stick the kettle on. Or do you want a glass of wine? It's never too early in this house,' he grins.

'Tea's fine,' I reply, entering the house.

'Before I forget, I'm off to a conference for a few days at the end of next week,' he says. 'Why don't you pop over one night to keep Ellie company?'

I smile. 'That'd be great.'

'Oh, and don't leave without me finally lending you *The Wire* on DVD. The dialogue takes some getting used to, but persevere and you'll get into it. It's brilliant.'

'Er, sure. Thanks.' Enough is enough: I have to confront Alistair. 'Listen, I need to talk to you about Ellie.'

'Oh?' he says idly, pouring water from the kettle into two mugs.

'I've been in two minds about whether to raise this.'

'It's not like you to be backward in coming forward, Sam,' he laughs, straining out a tea bag.

I swallow, taking a seat. 'Okay. Well, it's about her—'

'We're home!'

Ellie's voice echoes through the house, followed by the slam of the door.

A few seconds later, Sophie runs into the room. 'Auntie Sam! Santa Claus is going to bring me a golf set.'

I scoop her up in my arms as Ellie walks in after her. 'You don't want a Barbie any more, then?'

'Nope,' she replies firmly. 'A golf set. Or telescope. Or Transformers.'

'Hi, Sam!' Ellie says it as brightly as possible, glancing nervously at Alistair. The forced joviality is obviously for his benefit.

'How're things, Ellie? I thought I'd pop over after work to say hi.'

'I'll get you that DVD,' Alistair says, disappearing briefly into the living room and returning with *The Wire*, before starting on tonight's dinner. It's clear that he's failed to notice the strain between Ellie and me. The falseness. The fact that we're pretending everything's okay, when everything's far from it.

The time it takes to drink my tea is the longest twenty minutes I've ever lived through. Under normal circumstances I'd be frothing over to fill her in about what's happened in my life. But it doesn't seem right, particularly with Sophie running about and Alistair hovering.

'I'd better get Sophie into the bath,' says Ellie eventually.

'Of course,' I reply, taking the hint. I stand up and heave my bag over my shoulder.

'I'll see you out,' she adds, picking up Sophie as we head into the hall.

My heart is hammering. 'Some stuff's been going on between Jamie and me,' I blurt out.

'Oh . . . what? Jen mentioned something but I assumed it was just teething troubles after he'd moved in again. It's not something serious, is it?' She looks concerned, with the same expression she had when I turned up here on the night he first left and stood hugging her in this very spot in the hall. It brings back a flood of memories – and a million more emotions.

'We've split up again. He cheated on me, with Dorrie. His South America trip is back on.'

Her jaw almost hits the floor. 'Go and see Daddy, will you, sweetheart?' she says, putting Sophie down. The little girl scurries away.

'Oh God, Sam, I'm so sorry. Come here,' she says, putting her arms around me. As she squeezes me, I wonder if this is it – if everything's going to be okay between us from now on.

'About . . . the other thing,' I begin, but she shakes her head and backs away.

'I've got to go. I'm sorry about Jamie. Give me a ring and we'll talk about that, shall we?' she smiles anxiously.

As I head down the drive to my car, I feel a wave of relief that my friend is talking to me. About some things, at least. But the overwhelming feeling I get from her parting words is that her drinking is still firmly off the agenda.

Chapter 82

Over the next few days, the countdown to Jamie's South America trip feels like it's happening at the speed with which Clark Kent gets into his undies and tights. He's leaving me now, for good. I know that not even a tiny part of me should want him back. But a part of me does, and it isn't tiny.

At the same time, I'm bombarded with thoughts about Ben. About how, despite the fact that it was me who drove him into the arms of another woman, part of me wants him back too. Working out who I want more is as impossible as it is futile. Since neither man is interested in having me.

That hurts like hell.

I'm also dreading the official feedback from Lorelei after the Teen SOS event. If the abuse she gave me after the party itself was anything to go by, it's going to be catastrophic. And, given that I was counting on her booking us for several other events during the next year, this is not going to be good for my attempt to hit my targets. But she's in New York until the end of next week so hopefully will have time to calm down about the whole thing.

As ever, I've got a million things to do. But craving a diversion like never before, I arrange to meet Jen for lunch at the Quarter.

'My main discovery in the last ten days or so has been that men have a sixth sense,' Jen declares, as a new waiter bats his eyelids before serving her salad.

'What makes you say that?'

'Every time I convince myself I'm happy without Dan and would be better off if he never got in touch . . . he gets in touch. I swear, all it takes is for me to play the opening bars of "Fighter" by Christina Aguilera and the phone rings.'

'But he hasn't changed his standpoint?'

She sighs. 'Dan wants to be friends . . . with benefits.' She raises her eyebrow meaningfully. 'And it's not enough for me.'

'He actually said that?'

'Not in so many words.'

'I don't think that'd be enough for anyone, Jen,' I agree. 'At least, not long term.'

'I've told him that. And I'm not playing hardball. I'm not playing any games, in fact. I really don't want to see him any more if this is all he wants. And for the first time in my life, I mean it. I'm prepared to take things slowly, but I'm not settling for a man who feels lukewarm about me. And this is a *He's Just Not That into You* situation if ever there was one.'

I look up. 'You've read that book too?'

'I've read them all,' she says dismissively. 'These days there is nothing I do not know about keeping a man on his toes. Sadly, the theory and the practice are two different things. The point is that Dan doesn't like me enough to commit to anything more than a casual shag. He can't even say the word "girlfriend" without looking like he's got a chicken bone stuck in his throat. So I'm moving on. It's that simple.'

I can't help but be impressed. 'How do you feel about that?' I ask tentatively.

She takes a sip of water. 'I feel empowered, obviously. And I feel like crap, obviously. What I really want is the one thing that isn't going to happen.'

'Which is?'

'Oh for him to walk in here and— Hit me with a kipper!' Her fork falls to her lap, sending a cascade of Caesar dressing across the table, while she stares at the door.

'What is it?'

'He's just walked in here,' she hisses.

I spin round to see Dan marching towards us carrying such a massive bouquet of flowers it almost qualifies as an RHS show garden.

'Dan,' she mutters.

'A-a-aitchoo!' I say.

'Bless you,' he says, failing to take his eyes off Jen as he plunges into the seat next to her.

'Jen, I've been . . .' He looks at his flowers as if he's forgotten about their existence, though how that's possible I'm not sure, given that some of them are the size of a triffid. 'These are for you.'

She takes them from him in silent astonishment. 'What are they for?'

He closes his eyes and draws breath. 'They're my way of saying that I've been thinking. I've been thinking . . . how much I don't want to lose you.'

'I see,' she says coolly. I suppress a smile. 'And what does that mean?'

He swallows. 'It means I think I'd better start acting a little more . . . like you deserve.'

He holds her hand and looks into her eyes. 'It's taken the thought of not being with you to make me realize how much you mean to me. I don't want to lose you, Jen. And I asked myself a question: why is the idea of being in a proper, committed relationship so difficult? The answer is . . . it isn't,' he shrugs, almost surprising himself. 'Not one bit. It is the concept I couldn't cope with, not the reality. And, okay, I don't know where this is going or could go . . . all I know is how I feel.'

'Wh-what do you feel?'

'That I don't want to be without you. I can't be without you. And I want you to meet my parents and I want to take you away for weekends and I want you to be my . . . my girlfriend. I want us to be together, Jen. Just together. Is that good enough?'

She looks up at him and whispers, 'As long as you mean it.'

'Jen, I do,' he says, reaching over and pulling her into his arms.

For the next few moments they're so absorbed in one another

that the rest of the world might as well not exist. All I can do is sip my coffee and ponder the fact that there's a week to go until Jamie travels nearly five thousand miles out of my life. And I wonder whether I'll share a similar moment with someone I love, ever again.

Chapter 83

The thing I'm discovering about moments is that they appear to come all at once.

After a busy and torturous few days, I'm up early on Sunday to take part in a charity event to which I signed up the Liverpool office of BJD Productions ages ago. I rarely do this, taking the view that my obsession with doing my bit is mine and mine alone. But I (naively) thought the Santa Dash could be fun for the others too. Personally, I'm relishing the distraction.

It involves donning a Father Christmas suit that's four times too large and running five kilometres in the company of thousands of other preposterously attired competitors. My enthusiasm for the event has somehow survived despite the sleet, snow, rain, or all three, that consistently plagues it. And despite managing last year to appear in the local paper – in the background of a shot of some page-three girls in mini-Miss Christmas outfits low-cut enough to make Santa's hat stand on end. You can imagine how gorgeous I looked by comparison: as if I'd fallen off the back of a Rotary Club float.

The event is overflowing with camaraderie and cheer. We're all doing it for charity, so it doesn't matter if you sprint home or, as in my case, limp.

Today, though, I feel deflated. I'm happy for Jen, of course. But it's made me think even more, if that's possible, about my own situation. I wish I felt as certain about the man I want in my life as Jen does. And – whoever he is – I want him to want me back.

It's this precise thought that is going through my mind as I head down Dale Street, red pantaloons flapping in the wind, with Deana and Natalie plodding alongside.

To say they're unhappy doesn't quite cover it. It's not only the outfit they find offensive, although after Deana's attempts to customize hers, she still looks like the result of a breeding experiment between an elf and a cosmetic-counter girl, complete with trowelled-on panstick and lip gloss. It's everything from the weather to the simple fact that this is encroaching on their precious weekend.

'I can't run in these,' Deana complains, dragging her Uggs through the slush.

'I hope we're getting overtime,' grumbles Natalie for the fourth time.

'It's for charity, Natalie,' I point out breathlessly.

'I don't give a shit!' she hoots. 'It's Sunday. I shouldn't be awake for another four hours.'

'Spoken with the true spirit of Christmas in your heart,' I mutter.

As we approach the flyover, I hear something that almost stops me in my tracks. At least I think I do.

'Sam!'

I think little of it at first. It's not as if it's an uncommon name. But then I hear it again.

I grind to a halt and try to work out where it's coming from.

Then I see arms waving at the side of the road. I stand, mesmerized, as Deana and Natalie run ahead, and a blur of red whizzes past. Among the crowds is a solitary figure, walking against the flow of runners. He's calling my name, but he hasn't seen me.

Then he does.

I'm rooted to the spot as Jamie attempts to dodge the Santas but is knocked about like a Subbuteo ball. Before I know it, he's in front of me, holding my hands while a stream of runners keep coming.

'Sam,' he says, as the cold whips my cheeks. 'I'm due to leave in forty-eight hours. I'm all ready. I've got my ticket. I've worked my last day at the phone shop. I've sold my car. Basically . . . I'm all set.'

'I know,' I reply.

'I. Don't. Want. To. Leave,' he says, his face ablaze with emotion. I sniff. 'Why?'

'I don't want to leave because I want you. I want to turn back the clock and pretend the last six months didn't happen. I've been –' he looks up at the heavens as if searching for inspiration – 'I've been a total and utter prick. I took everything for granted. But I want you back with every single bit of my heart. I'm desperate, Sam.'

'But what about your trip? Wasn't that everything you wanted? Haven't you maintained the whole time that you'd be unhappy staying here, settling down with me?'

He shakes his head, his blue eyes watery and red. 'Like I said, I was a prick.'

'No,' I insist, then temper my statement. 'I mean, you were a prick for cheating on me. But the trip . . . you had your reasons. You hate your job. You've got a host of unfulfilled dreams and—'

'Sam,' he interrupts firmly, reaching into his pocket. 'My flight's booked and my bags are packed. If you don't want me then there's no longer anything here for me. And I'd understand if you didn't. You've got every right to hate me. But I couldn't go without proving how much I love you. I couldn't.'

'Proving?'

I look down and register that he has slipped something in my hand: a box. I swallow, and my fingers are creaky from the cold as I open it up with total disbelief. It's a diamond ring, a beautiful one too. I can tell the second I set eyes on it that this is no cheap knock-off. It's the real deal.

'Will you marry me, Sam?'

He says the words with total certainty, as if all the doubts he's ever had have evaporated like snowflakes in the sun. But I can't look at him. All I can do is stare at the ring for seconds or minutes, until a single hot tear lands on its tiny pillow.

'But you don't want to get married, Jamie,' I mumble.

'I do, Sam. I want to do everything I can to keep you,' he insists.

'Even if it means not following your dreams? Even if it means doing the thing you said you never wanted to do?'

'Absolutely. Absolutely.'

I shut my eyes momentarily and breathe deeply.

'Come on, love, don't give up now!' shouts a passing Santa, slapping me playfully on the back.

'What's your answer, Sam? This is make or break time. I need to know.'

'My answer . . .' I begin, my head spinning. 'My answer is . . . I just don't know.'

He closes his eyes as if the tumbling clouds above us are about to fall down. Then he nods and squeezes my hand. 'The plane takes off at eleven forty-five on Tuesday morning. You know where I am in the meantime. And you know what I want. I'd do anything for you, Sam – anything to put this situation right.'

'I need to think,' I mutter, shaking my head and handing back his ring. 'I really just need to think.'

He swallows, his eyes heavy with tears. 'I understand. But make the right decision, Sam, won't you?'

I watch as he turns away. 'That's all I've ever tried to do.'

Chapter 84

For the rest of the day, time passes excruciatingly slowly and terrifyingly fast. Every time I look at the clock in the kitchen I'm another hour closer to having to make the most important decision of my life.

Yet, make a decision I cannot. On the one hand, Jamie has offered everything that I wanted, and more. All I ever wanted was him, so the idea that he's now prepared to put a ring on my finger is, or at least should be, the icing on the cake.

Except it's not that simple, is it? The goalposts have moved since July. The Jamie who stood before me while ten thousand Santas ran past wasn't quite the same man I loved for six years.

He was similar, yes; but with some fundamental differences – ones I'd been entirely unaware of until this year. I fell in love with my most optimistic version of Jamie, and the reality falls a long way short. Yet, that sparkling version of Jamie still exists on many levels. He's still kind, generous and funny. I recognize now that he's other things too, not all of them particularly palatable.

But is anybody perfect? It's hardly an attribute I could claim for myself.

Which brings me to the reason I don't feel overly high and mighty about Jamie's catastrophic mistakes: Ben. I've spent increasing amounts of my time thinking about a man I'd thought was a decoy, a means to an end, a gorgeous pretender. Now, as I picture his eyes gazing into mine, I can't help slipping into a fantasy that life with him could be a better option.

Except . . . it's not an option, is it?

The man is now 'in a relationship' – something that no doubt accounts for the fact that I've hardly heard from him, apart for the odd text, since the Teen SOS event. In a relationship. How I despise that phrase. Particularly since, by the time I'd even thought about reinstating it on my own Facebook page, Jamie had buggered off again.

I'm considering heading for the gym for want of a distraction, when I receive a text from Julia telling me she and Mum are on their way over for a cup of tea.

'Mum and I have been Christmas shopping,' Julia tells me as they enter the house laden with so many bags I'm surprised they haven't dislocated their shoulders.

'At least, we've tried to. Your father is a nightmare to buy for,' Mum mutters, plonking down herself and her bags.

'What did you get him?' I ask.

'A jumper and some egg cups,' she frowns, clearly not satisfied with her choices.

'I thought you'd vowed never to buy him clothes again on the basis that everything ends up in a drawer, never to be worn?' I point out.

'Well, I know. But I was totally stuck,' she huffs. 'I had to buy this, even though I know he'll decide it's one of my attempts to make him more "with it".'

'Even Dad can't object to that,' smirks Julia, as Mum produces the plainest of grey cashmere jumpers. 'Besides, at some point he's got to come to terms with C&A having ceased trading.'

Despite the massive, dramatic revelations that unfolded, things feel decidedly normal between Julia and our parents. The theory she always had – about her past being irrelevant to her feelings for Mum and Dad – has proved to be totally accurate.

Very little has changed. There's an added sense of her own history, maybe. Oh, and one more guest for our annual Boxing Day party: Gary. Although whether he'll ever return in the future when he sees how competitive Pictionary can get is another matter.

They leave after an hour and I log on to my laptop in an attempt to concentrate on my work emails, not least because I have a stack of tasks to catch up on before the world closes down for Christmas. There's little in my inbox that offers a surprise or a distraction, though.

Until, that is, a message appears from Lorelei, with the subject matter 'Feedback on Teen SOS event'. My stomach plunges. I cannot overstate my sense of dread about this.

Luvvie . . . Soz to only just get back to you now – it's been all go! Now, my thoughts: first of all, the wasabi on those canapés. Jesus H. Christ. I nearly needed skin grafts on my tongue it was so bloody hot. And those gold curtains . . . what were you thinking? They looked like Aunt Mary's old nets.

I gotta tell you, though, luvs, overall the night was an absolute sensation. Loved every bit of it. The atmosphere was great, the guests had a whale of a time. We raised a packet and have signed up several big new supporters. Oh and thanks for your donation too, gorgeous girl – very kind! Most importantly, Kevin S. Chasen was DEAD impressed. Did you get talking to him or something? He knew who you were. Anyway, all in all, it was brilliant! So well done, cos I know full well it was you who made this happen and not the other useless shower of bastards.

Right . . . gotta run, luvs. I've got Paris on the other line. Ooh, are you around tomorrow? There's something I want to have a chat with you about. And I know you'll love me for it.

Ciao, honey,

L x

P.S. Have you got Dr Darren Bosco's email address? I think I was in there!

Just as I'm thinking the world has finally lost its grip on reality, I'm jolted by the faint ping of a chat box.

'Hey, there xx'

Ben's name prompts a sharp intake of breath. I swallow and set about responding in a manner that I hope is pleasant but cool.

'Hey to you too. We haven't had a coffee for ages, have we?'

'Aha. Well, guilty as charged. It's been a bit of a strange time.'

'Oh? Nothing's wrong, I hope? Is your dad okay?'

'Oh he's doing great. The doctors think he'll be ready to go back to work in a month or two. No – I just meant . . .'

I pause, waiting for him to continue writing. I'm about to give up and write something myself when another line appears.

'Er . . . women trouble!'

My heart does a backflip.

'Oh dear . . . Well, I don't know what to suggest!'

'Nope, neither do I. How are things with you?'

'Er . . . good.'

With my fingers hovering over the keyboard, I wonder if I should just leave it at that. But something compels me not to. Something compels me to expand.

'Although . . . tricky.'

'Tricky?'

I hesitate, considering whether to tell him. For a reason I can't put my finger on, I feel the need to spill my heart. Exactly as I did so many other times, before I screwed things up between the two of us.

'Jamie wants to marry me. I think I'm going to say yes.'

Even as I write the sentence, it surprises me. However, the second it's on the screen, the second it's out there, the more comfortable I feel about the idea. There's a silence. A long one.

'You there?'

'Just had to answer a phone call. Wow . . . a wedding! Well, congratulations.'

'I haven't said yes yet . . .'

There's another silence.

'. . . but I think I'm going to.'

I hit return and bite my nail. Am I really telling Ben this because I want a friendly heart to heart? Or is it because I want him to leap in and tell me he's the man for me instead?

'So what's tricky? You okay?'

'Of course. Nothing's tricky, really. Just been a funny year, if you know what I mean.'

'Well, yes. Though it sounds like things are back on track. Listen, I need to run. Just wanted to say hi. Take care, won't you?'

'I will. And let's not leave it so long next time, eh?'

As I type the response, I can't help dwelling on how much I mean that. On how much I'd love to see him. Next week. Tomorrow. Now.

But, as I hit return and glance at the picture of Jamie and me on the mantelpiece, I know that never seeing Ben again would be the best thing for all of us.

Perhaps it's that thought that makes me flick to his profile page before I can reason with myself not to. The first entry leaps out and almost bites me on the nose.

Ben Moran is single.

Chapter 85

Deana has been promoted. And her best pal, Natalie, couldn't be happier for her.

'I can't believe you're leaving me in this shit-hole,' she sulks, sticking out her lip as if it requires medical attention.

'It was an offer I couldn't refuse,' Deana says smugly.

The offer, incidentally, is to be Piers's new right-hand woman. As well as a move to Manchester, it involves a healthy pay rise, something she's failed to stop gloating about all morning.

While her promotion is thoroughly undeserved, the idea of Piers experiencing Deana in action – or inaction – fills me with a sense that all is right with the world again. I'll give him half a day before her jiggling cleavage loses its novelty value and he has to address the subject of her waxing her legs at her desk.

In the meantime, I'm tasked with finding her replacement. I have already had a brief conversation with Anna, the work-experience girl – who was so shocked and pleased to hear from me she actually managed to talk.

If she can keep that up – and combine it with her extreme

conscientiousness – she'll be running the company by next September.

The rest of the morning is relatively quiet until, just before lunchtime, a massive bouquet of flowers arrives and Deana leaps up.

'Oooh! I don't believe it!' she hoots. 'Well, they took their time, but bloody hell, it was worth the wait! I thought they were going to be the sort of blokes who shagged and ran, didn't you, Natalie?'

'Is it for you or me?' says Natalie breathlessly, acrylic nails clashing as they fumble with the tag.

They read the label and turn to each other in disgust. 'Bloody hell,' exclaims Deana. 'Sam, they're for you.'

I glance up and it strikes me that Jamie has surpassed himself today. Except, as I open the envelope, I realize they're not from Jamie.

A small token of my appreciation, luv . . . and don't forget to give me a ring when you get a min! Lorelei xxx

Obviously, I forget to give Lorelei a ring. The only ring I can focus on all day as the clock inches closer to 11.45 a.m. tomorrow is Jamie's ring.

All I've got to do is leap up from this desk, jump in my car and drive to Luke's house for that ring – and the man I've spent most of my adult life adoring – to be mine.

Yet a weird force of gravity keeps my backside firmly on my seat. I can't move. I can't do anything. As the office buzzes with Christmas cheer and discussions about the most effective form of nail glue, all I can do is sit here tinkering with paperclips, opening emails and not reading them . . . and logging on to Ben's Facebook page to read those words over and over again: Ben Moran is single.

I tell myself that they change nothing. That I can't let a status update alter the course of my entire future happiness.

The clock ticks on, hour by hour, and I consider phoning people for advice. Even if Mum and Dad hadn't left this morning for a Warner Leisure break, this isn't something I feel able to discuss with them. Julia is in London and while Jen would have some views, I'm sure, I don't really want them, for some reason. The only person I could even consider talking to about this is Ellie and when I phone her mobile it goes straight to her voicemail.

At three o'clock my phone rings and I examine the number flashing on the screen. It's Jamie. But as my finger hovers over the keypad, I can't bring myself to answer it. The phone rings off and he leaves a message, his voice sounding urgent and wobbly.

'It's me. Sam . . . can you phone me? Sam, I don't know what else to say. I'm all ready to go but I'm torn in two here because all I want is to come home and be with you. I want you to walk through this door and tell me you want to get married to me and that you'll forgive me. I know I don't deserve it, but for all the reasons you tried to persuade me to change my mind . . . think about changing yours too. Please.'

It's not the only voicemail I get. About an hour later, Luke phones and leaves a message.

'Two things, Sam. First, Jamie really loves you. Really. I know he's been a prat but the guy's paying for it, I swear. The other thing I wanted to tell you is that I'm back with Gemma. I dressed up as Richard Gere in *An Officer and a Gentleman* this morning and marched into her office. I shoved my hat on her head and picked her up in my arms. Then I told her – in front of every-one – that I was in love with her. She told me I was a knobhead. Then she told me that she loves me too,' he laughs. 'I can't believe it, Sam. She gave me a second chance. I honestly, truly think you should consider doing that with Jamie too.'

My mobile rings repeatedly over the course of the next couple of hours – all calls from Jamie. But I can't bring myself to answer. I can't bring myself to do anything but work, or at least pretend to.

By six o'clock I find myself in the centre of an open-plan room, with only the cleaners for company.

'Working late again, love?' asks one, as I stand and move my chair for her to vacuum underneath it – a task she approaches with such vigour she must have biceps like Mr Incredible under that apron.

'Afraid so,' I reply.

She has candyfloss hair in a strange shade of peach and when she smiles she reveals two missing teeth on the bottom row. 'You work as late as it takes, sweetheart. Take my advice: keep your head buried in that t'internet.'

'I shouldn't be long,' I tell her.

She pauses and switches off her vacuum cleaner. 'Me, I put getting married and having kids before trying to get a career.'

'That's not such a bad thing,' I offer.

She rolls her eyes and snorts. 'Look where it's got me, girly. Oh don't get me wrong: I love my kids. But if I had my time again, I'd do things differently.'

I smile. 'How?'

'Put myself before any bloke,' she laughs. 'What a cynic, eh!'

As she heads off to vacuum up half the contents of Deana's desk – including two packs of eyelashes – my phone rings again. This time I know I've got to face Jamie. I want to face Jamie. Not least because I've got one hell of a lot to say.

'Is that Miss Brooks?'

I'm jolted by a clipped voice that I don't recognize. 'Yes?'

'This is Margaret Finnegan from Little Stars Nursery.'

I frown. That's where Sophie goes when Ellie's at work.

'I'm sorry to bother you but . . . well, nobody has come to pick up Sophie.'

'What?'

'The nursery closes at five forty-five and we've tried over and over again to get in touch with her parents but we can't reach either of them.'

'Alistair's in Germany,' I reply.

'It was Ms Sanders who dropped her off this morning. We've phoned repeatedly but there's no answer. There is only one other person with authorization to pick her up, and that's you.'

A chill runs down my spine. 'I'll be there in fifteen minutes,' I reply, instantly free of the inaction that's gripped me all day.

Chapter 86

Margaret Finnegan politely told me to take my time. By that, she presumably meant twenty minutes would be reasonable. What she probably didn't count on was the chain of events that subsequently unfolds; I sure as hell didn't.

I race out of the building, across to the car park on the other side of the road and into my driver's seat, where I proceed to start up the car and rocket to the exit. I turn onto the road that will take me across the city centre, repeatedly trying to reach Ellie on my hands-free while my mind whirrs with macabre visions of Sophie, destitute and alone on the steps of the nursery, like a Dickensian orphan.

I can tell there's something wrong with the car before I even get to Smithdown Road, but purposefully ignore the judders and cranks and the fact that – even though my accelerator foot is on the floor – my vehicle is no longer inclined to go faster than twenty miles an hour.

By the time I've turned down Ullet Road and am crawling past Princes Park, it becomes all too apparent that my automotive problems are haunting me again. With the beeps of rankled drivers ringing in my ears, the car moves in a stop-start fashion, until the stop-start becomes . . . a stop.

'Oh shit! Oh buggery flipping hell,' I cry, slamming my hands on the steering wheel.

I leap out of the car and attempt to push it to the kerb, managing to move it about an inch. Then I pick up my mobile . . . but who the hell do I phone? My immediate family are all miles away. Jamie's sold his car and Jen's at work – although, admittedly, she occasionally has her phone on. I ring her and it goes straight to voicemail. So does Luke's. Could I phone Ben? Should I? I decide that Sophie's needs are greater than my romantic torment, and dial his number. It goes to messages.

'Oh GODDDDDD!' Then I realize it's recording. 'Sorry. Ben, I need your help. I'm on Princes Road and I've broken down and I need to pick up Sophie, quickly. If you happen to get this can you give me a ring? I might manage to get a taxi, of course, but . . . oh . . . it's just – it'd be great if you could phone.'

I frantically ring the nursery and leave an apologetic message on their answer machine then, with traffic whizzing past, I step into the road and stick out my hand for what I think is a taxi; but it turns out to be a road gritter.

'Oh God . . . what am I going to do?' I whine, trudging along the road and turning back to look for taxis. After five minutes I realize that drastic measures are required. I take a deep breath and stick out my thumb, thinking of how Sophie is relying on me.

About ten seconds later, a white van with one flickering head-light slows to a crawl. I lean in and am poised to ask the driver if he can take me to Woolton, when I get a good look at his face. It takes me a second to recognize him; when I do, both our eyes widen. It's 'Cunninglinguist' from the dating website. He grins and winks at me.

'Oh . . . it's okay,' I insist, stumbling backwards as I shake my head. He shrugs and speeds off, leaving my wool-blend trousers caked in more mud than the Dead Sea. I break into a run; the nursery is miles away but by now I'm convinced running is the only option. Every so often, I look back but the thumb I've got stuck out is resulting in no offers whatsoever.

My veins flood with panic when I realize another car has slowed down.

I'm already regretting this whole idea: anyone who stops to pick up a lone female in the dark has got to be dodgy in the very best case – and an axe murderer in the worst. And I'm not going to be much good to Sophie if I've been chopped up into little pieces and hidden in bin bags across the city.

'Er . . . it's okay,' I mumble, shaking my hands at the driver, before shoving them in my pockets and walking away as fast as possible.

'Sam! It's me.'

I don't need to turn around to know who it is. My knight in shining armour. Except in this case it's a knight in an Audi A4. And I've never felt as happy to see another human being as I am to see Ben right now.

Chapter 87

I've no idea what Margaret Finnegan thinks when I turn up at the nursery looking as if I've been through an assault course, although it can't be any worse than what she thinks of the fact that Sophie's mother has failed to pick her up.

'Ellie finally got hold of me from a land line,' I lie. 'She'd got stuck in traffic on the motorway on the way home from a conference in Cheshire, and her phone ran out of juice. She asked me to apologize sincerely. She's mortified.'

'These things happen,' smiles Margaret Finnegan, though I get the distinct impression from the look on her face that they don't happen often.

Sophie is pleased to see me, at least. Although when she asks, 'Where's Mummy?' I'm at a bit of a loss about what to say, except to reassure her that she'll see her mother soon.

I strap her into the car seat the nursery let us borrow. This is a procedure that takes twenty minutes, and I'm convinced a NASA scientist would struggle to master it.

'Thanks again for this, Ben,' I say, as we head to my place.

He turns to look at me, and when he smiles I feel a rush of longing.

'Not a problem. I was on my way home from work. In fact, I wasn't far away.'

I turn back to Sophie, and look at her playing contentedly with a teddy bear. 'I don't think I've got much for you to eat at home, Sophie. We'll have to rustle something up, won't we?'

'I want a lollipop,' she grins.

'Er . . . I haven't even got one of those.'

'Do you need me to stop somewhere?' Ben offers.

'Hmm . . . I guess so. Do you like beans on toast, Sophie?'

'No. Lollipops.'

'Well, okay . . . maybe after dinner. Do you like cheese on toast?'

'Only lollipops.'

I'm starting to get the feeling that we might be having lollipops on toast. I frown. 'How about . . . carrots?'

'Lollipops.'

'Chips?'

'No – lollipops.'

'Oh Lord!' I'm about to suggest pasta – which I've seen her mother cook for her countless times – when my phone rings. It's Ellie.

With a racing heart I press answer. Ellie's voice is muffled and strange-sounding, and I can barely hear her over the background noise.

'I got your message,' she says, her voice awash with emotion. 'Have you got her? Have you got my Sophie?'

'Yes, I've got her. We're on our way back to my place. She's fine. But where the hell are you?'

'Take her . . . home – my home, I mean. I'm coming now . . . I'll meetsh you there.'

She rings off and I look anxiously at Ben.

'Everything all right?' he asks.

I bite my lip. 'Not really.'

Chapter 88

We sit in the car outside Ellie's with the engine running so that the heaters keep us warm. Sophie is giggling in the back as Ben pulls funny faces, and I'm smiling almost as much as she is. Part of me doesn't know how I can smile, except that, if I dwell on it, the hideousness of the situation is overwhelming.

My head is swollen with thoughts – of Ellie, of Jamie, of me – yet I find myself watching Ben, as his playful eyes and impossibly handsome face make this little girl happy. He turns to look at me at one point and I glance away, embarrassed. If he catches me looking at him too long he'll guess some of the thoughts behind the mist in my eyes.

'Can I ask you something, Ben?'

He pauses from playing with Sophie and looks up. 'Of course.'

'Your Facebook page – it said you were in a relationship.'

He takes a deep breath. 'A brief one,' he laughs. 'It was with my neighbour, Mildred.'

I grin. 'I'd assumed she was in her seventies and the recipient of Meals on Wheels.'

'Oh . . . Mildred?' he smiles. 'No, she's a bit younger than that.'

'And a lot more attractive,' I point out.

'She's pretty,' he concedes. 'But my heart wasn't in it. I don't know why I even changed my status on Facebook. I think I was trying to convince myself about the whole thing.'

'Why?'

He looks at me awkwardly, then holds my gaze. 'Diversionary tactics.'

A taxi door slams, accompanied by a crunch of gravel, and I look up to witness Ellie taking unsteady steps towards us, trying desperately to look sober. Ben and I glance at each other, before I open the car door and get out.

'Where is she?' Ellie asks frantically, stumbling to the door at the back.

'Hey, it's okay, I'll get her out,' I tell her, concerned about her capability.

She looks at me and frowns. 'I'm f-fine,' she replies, moving to edge me out of the way.

'Ellie . . . let me,' I say firmly, putting my hand on the handle. She throws me a tired-eyed look and realizes I'm not going to back down.

I open the car door and Sophie's face lights up with happiness. 'Mummy!'

'Hi, shweeetheart,' Ellie slurs, her eyes filling with tears.

I lift Sophie out of the car, but it's clear that it isn't my arms she wants: it's her mother's. And before I can do anything to stop her, she dives at Ellie, who staggers back, trying to steady herself.

'Hello, gorgeous,' Ellie whispers, stroking Sophie's hair and kissing her. 'I'm here now. Mummy's here.'

Ellie puts Sophie down and I follow them as the little girl runs to the front door. Ellie takes an age trying to get the key in the door; the more she fumbles drunkenly, the more impossible the task seems. Eventually, I take it from her and open the door myself.

Ellie and Sophie enter the house, and as Ben appears at my side, the warmth from inside hits us. In the opaque glow from the hall light I notice that flakes of snow have begun to float from the sky and are falling on to his face.

Ben touches me on the arm. 'What are you going to do?' he whispers. 'I'm not sure Ellie should be left alone . . . if you know what I mean.'

I nod and hold his gaze. 'I'm going to stay with her. I'll get Sophie to bed and see if I can sober Ellie up.'

He doesn't take his eyes from me. 'Would you like me to stay? How are you going to get home?'

'Taxi. It'll be fine. Honestly,' I smile. 'Thank you for this. I don't know what I'd have done if you hadn't appeared.'

He shrugs. 'I never usually take that route, but there are roadworks on the way I usually go. Must've been fate.'

The snow is suddenly heavier. I watch as whispers of it land on Ben's skin and turn instantly into droplets. I can see his breath in the cold night air and I find myself drawn to the mouth from which it comes, to his soft, parted lips.

'I haven't said congratulations,' he says.

'About what?' I ask, hyper-aware of my heartbeat.

'Your engagement.'

I look up, almost surprised. 'Oh . . . I'll be honest, Ben. I don't know what to do about that.'

He hesitates. 'Really?'

I swallow. 'I'm a bit confused.'

'What's the issue?'

'The issue is that . . . I think I have feelings . . . for someone else.'

I don't know what I expect his reaction to be. He closes his eyes and shakes his head.

'What?' I say, touching his arm. It's through about four layers, but I can still feel its muscular curve.

'You've met someone else? Another man?'

Then I realize that I shouldn't be confessing what I'm about to confess. I realize I could be about make a fool of myself. I also realize that he hasn't clicked that I'm talking about him. So I still have my get-out-of-jail-free card.

'Yes.'

He gulps. And when he looks away his face is so confused and hurt it makes my heart twist.

'Sam. Let me tell you something.' He swallows. 'I've got a job that involves meeting dozens, hundreds of people, all the time. I meet clever people, funny people, entertaining people, good people. But, sometimes . . . a person comes into your life who blows everyone else out of the water.'

The intensity on his face makes my pulse quicken. 'I'm talking about a person who makes you laugh, who makes you cry, a person who infuriates and delights you . . . but, above all, someone who brings out the best in you.'

He swallows, and takes my hand. 'Of all the people I've ever met, Sam, you're quite simply the best.' I close my eyes and tears drip from my chin. 'You're the best person I know – nothing less. And I know it makes me a bloody idiot to be standing here confessing that I'm in love with you when you've just told me you have feelings for not just one but two other men, but . . .' He looks, consumed with emotion. 'What an arse I am!'

I open my mouth to say something, but he beats me to it. 'There are some things you just need to get off your chest, I suppose.'

I finally feel able to speak. 'There's no other man. I mean . . . there's just Jamie – and you. Plus a whole lot of complicated stuff going on in my head.'

'What?' He blinks. 'You mean I'm the person that's making you think twice about marrying Jamie?'

I nod.

'I don't know what to say,' he mumbles. 'I mean . . . I want you, Sam. But you've got to do the right thing by yourself. You've got to follow your heart.'

I nod again. 'But I need you to know this, Ben . . .'

There's so much I want to tell him that I barely know where to start. And yet it all seems so contradictory. The fact is that I think he's the kindest, funniest, most admirable and gorgeous person I know. And he brings out the best in me too. He's amazing.

Except, while I can think all of these things in my head, I don't know how to say them without sounding insincere, or shallow, or I don't know what . . . because of one other crucial matter: Jamie, and my feelings for him.

'I need you to know . . .'

'Sam!' Little Sophie comes running along the hall and grabs me round the legs. I look down at her. 'I want a lollipop. And Mummy's too tired.'

My eyes return to Ben and I see him backing away.

'I'll leave you to it,' he murmurs.

I nod once more, taking Sophie's hand as she pulls me into the house.

Chapter 89

I don't know who's more difficult to get to bed, Sophie or her mother.

Sophie is determined that the pasta dish I've whipped up is a poor substitute for a lollipop. Then she becomes hell-bent on rereading *The Gruffalo* so many times, I'll be chanting 'A mouse took a stroll through the deep dark wood' in my sleep tonight.

In Ellie's case, the issue is that sometime after entering the house with Sophie following her, she fell asleep on the sofa and hasn't moved since.

I don't want to leave her in charge of a two-year-old, even after Sophie does get to sleep. Not because I think Ellie would do anything actively wrong, but because I'm worried about what she wouldn't do. If Sophie woke in the middle of the night shouting for her mum, I doubt anything short of a sharp slap around the cheeks would rouse my friend.

I gaze at her on the sofa and wonder how I'm going to pick her up. They do it on the movies all the time: a quasi-fireman's lift manoeuvre that involves an effortless sweep of the hand round someone's back and a quick hoist up.

I take a deep breath, grip her round the waist and – grunting like a walrus in the latter stages of a difficult labour – try again to heave her up. Ellie might look petite, but all I achieve is a red face and possible hernia.

In the end, I decide to simply take off her shoes and cover her with a quilt I bring down from the spare room. I spend the next few hours sitting in front of the television – flicking through everything from *Ocean's Eleven* to *Famous and Fearless* – and then my mobile rings. It's Lorelei's number.

I take the call and go through to the other room, where I gaze out of the window and watch the floodlit snow dance across the sky and fall onto the grass, creating a perfect blanket.

I barely have anything to say to Lorelei, but as ever she talks and talks. And this time she has something seriously interesting to say. So I listen. And I think. And I wonder . . .

It's nearly midnight before I switch off the living-room lamp, my head heavy with thoughts as I curl up on the sofa opposite my friend.

I can't sleep, obviously. I have only hours until Jamie's plane leaves in the morning and all I can do is let my mind flash with images and words: Jamie's ring, Ben's eyes. And another idea, coming from the left field, that there shouldn't even be room for in my head.

I manage a fitful sleep, one that's broken when Ellie's home phone rings at seven o'clock. I let it go to answer phone, but it wakes Ellie.

'Hi, honey, I'm home!' says Alistair. 'At least, I've landed at Manchester, so by the time I've collected my baggage I should be back in an hour or so. Can't wait to see you both. Bye for now.'

Ellie takes in her surroundings, puzzling over why she's on the sofa in the living room with me, instead of tucked up in bed. She looks like the worst version of Ellie in the world: she has flaky grey skin, crusty mascara and lips that are dry and peeling. You can tell it hurts to keep her eyes open; her hangover's going to be so bad today I can almost hear her head banging from the other side of the room. Still, at least she's in one piece.

'I need to check on Sophie,' she croaks, getting shakily to her feet. She stands dizzily and makes her way to the door, then creeps up the stairs. She's gone for five minutes, reappearing in clean clothes and in the process of removing last night's make-up with a wipe.

'She okay?' I ask.

'She's fine – just having a little lie-in. I'm sure she'll be awake in the next half-hour or so.'

Then her hand drops and she looks at me, her shoulders slumping as her face crumples. She closes her eyes as if the weight of her own self-hatred won't let her keep them open. I watch silently as she slides onto the sofa and puts her head in her hands.

I don't say anything.

Honestly, I'm lost for words.

I'm furious with Ellie. Sophie is the most important person in her world and what she did last night was utterly unforgivable. Yet . . . she's ill. My best friend is ill. Of that I have no doubt.

'I'm so, so sorry.' She looks at me with red, waxy eyes, and her puffy skin is wet and salty with tears. 'I know that's not enough. I just don't know what else to say. Shit. I hate myself, Sam. I can't tell you how much I hate myself.'

The tragic thing about this statement is that I don't doubt it. Ellie has everything going for her – a great job, an amazing family, a fantastic and warm personality that makes everyone love her – yet she despises herself. And it's little wonder, this morning. I race over to sit next to her and throw my arms around her, letting her sob into my chest while I kiss her hair.

'Ellie,' I whisper, lifting up her chin. 'You know what you've got to do, don't you? What happened last night . . . that can never happen again. Never.'

She shakes her head. 'I don't deserve Sophie. I don't even know how it happened. It was meant to be only a quick drink after work, then I had another . . . and I, I lost track of time. I'm the worst mother in the world.'

'No you're not. Of course you're not. You adore her and you'd do anything for her. But you don't need me to tell you that life can't go on like this. Not when you're a mother. It's not a job that's compatible with being . . . an alcoholic.'

Her gaze drops to her hands. 'That's what I am, isn't it?'

I nod. 'But you're not going to deal with this by yourself, Ellie. You're going to do it with me, with Alistair . . . and with some people who know what they're doing. Some professionals.'

'I can't carry on like this,' she murmurs, her face soaked with tears. 'I won't carry on like this.'

'No, honey, you won't.'

I look up as Sophie's call drifts down the stairs. 'Mu-mmy!'

'I'll go and get her,' says Ellie, standing up. Then she turns to me. 'I'm so sorry, Sam. For everything. I know I wasn't there for you when you and Jamie split up again. I've got so much to apologize for.'

'All I want is for you to sort yourself out.'

Ellie's face crumples with emotion again. 'I'm going to. I swear I'm going to.'

I stay for another hour at the house, playing with Sophie and filling Ellie in properly on what's been happening in my life. When Alistair arrives home and flings his arms around his little girl, he can tell something's not right immediately. But he says nothing while I'm there.

'When are you going to tell him?' I ask, as Ellie shows me out.

'Right now,' she says, attempting to straighten her back. 'So, Sam. What are you going to do?' She kisses me on the cheek and looks at her watch. 'If you're going to make it to the airport to tell Jamie you want to spend the rest of your life with him, you've got precisely two hours in which to do it. Or are you going to track Ben down instead?'

I take a deep breath. 'Oh . . . what the hell should I do, Ellie?'

'I can't decide who you're in love with, Sam. Only you can do that.'

476

Chapter 90

As I stride through virgin snow towards Cressington Station it's as if I'm having an out-of-body experience. The street is ethereally bright, with sunlight bouncing off the blanket of whiteness that swathes everything in sight.

It's the quietest of streets and all I can hear is the crunch of my footsteps and the thunder of my heart as I break into a run, passing the Victorian mansions, cast-iron street lamps and chocolate-box church. There are minutes to go before the next train arrives, minutes before my decision is cemented. But it's a decision I could still alter, even now.

I can always change my mind.

The words are ringing through my head as my legs get faster, my thighs burn, the sun beats on my face and I arrive, breathless, at the station entrance. I pay for a ticket and head across the iron bridge, running my fingers along its filigree patterns as if it's a xylophone. I'm halfway when I stop.

I can always change my mind.

I put my arms on the thick iron railings and, with blurred eyes, gaze at the tracks below, my brain loaded with choices.

It's as simple as this: I can take the train in one direction to Manchester Airport – to Jamie. Or I can take the train in the other direction to Aigburth – to Ben.

Two destinations. Two men.

Which one is it going to be, Sam?

I can always change my mind.

My breathing slows as I step back from the railings and gaze at the perfect winter blue above the horizon. At the world beyond the station, beyond the decision. I look up and think of all the people, all over the world, looking at this sky with a million tiny and monumental decisions to make, just like mine.

I lean over again and I watch silently as something falls from my hand, fluttering like an oak leaf in the wind. My ticket floats towards the tracks in slow motion, so unrushed and leisurely that it's an age before I lose focus, and only then do I register the shuddering of the bridge. The train below me slows to a stop, and commuters file in and out before the crank of metal sets it moving again.

It's the train to Manchester Airport. The train to Jamie. Gone.

I fill my lungs with cold air as a tiny candyfloss cloud, so perfect it barely looks real, glides across the sky and my mind rushes with possibilities.

Possibilities that, over the next ten minutes, envelop me in hope. Optimism. And something else. Freedom.

Another series of cranks passes below me, shaking the bridge and making my spine tingle. When the train stops, two people get off. Three get on. I, on the other hand, don't move. I simply watch as it glides along the tracks, taking with it another possible destiny.

It's the train to Aigburth. The train to Ben. Gone.

I pull up my collar as warmth spreads through me. Then I walk out of the station, smiling as light blisters through the trees.

I've made my choice.

It isn't Jamie or Ben.

It's me.

Chapter 91

Dear Facebook friends,

I am going into cyber retirement. Temporarily, at least.

I thought I ought to let you know, in case you were wondering if my profile was suspended as a result of any dubious online activity on my part. It's all above board, I promise you.

As some of you already know, I'm starting a new job in New York next week, one to which I need to devote every last drop of my attention. And I'm afraid you're all far too entertaining . . . and distracting. So, for the time being, *adios amigos*. I'll miss you!

Sam xxx

A comment appears two minutes later from my second cousin Paige in Perth, Australia.

Sammy – mate! I'll give ya two days!

Exactly four weeks after the day I stood at Cressington Station, I am on a plane, gazing out of the window. I've had twenty-eight days and a manic family Christmas since my decision. With every second that's passed I've become clearer that what I'm doing is right. Even if it's ripping me in two.

So . . . where do I start?

I put up my house for rent and, although it's a tricky time of year, an agency found me some tenants who'll be moving in the week after next. I sold my car, even if the money I got for that wouldn't have paid for a couple of nice handbags. I handed in my notice and work agreed to let me go a week early. Not that they had much choice, given that Lorelei is one of their biggest clients. And if Lorelei hadn't got me when she wanted me, there'd have been hell to pay.

It was Lorelei – or rather Kevin S. Chasen – who gave me my get-out clause. It's the opportunity of a lifetime, and one I can't wait to experience . . . in every way but one. That one being the absence of Ben.

Despite my fear that I'm gambling with the love of a man whom I've come to adore and admire, a man my instincts pull me towards with an almost interstellar force, this really is the only thing to do.

And these are my reasons.

I've been in a relationship for over six years. But I've spent the last few months with my emotions being tugged in every direction – torn between one person and another.

And somewhere along the way it struck me that, before I leap into the arms of a man, as incomparably wonderful as he is, I need to get some things straight.

I need to prove what I already believe: that I don't need another person to make me content. That being on my own isn't that bad. That happiness – that vague and powerful notion – comes from myself, not someone else.

When I left the station that day, I phoned Lorelei and accepted the job offer as an events manager for Teen SOS's head office in New York. Their operation is so big that they don't out-source their events; they have people in-house. And a six-month contract covering maternity leave has recently arisen. Apparently, I'm the only woman for the job: Kevin S. Chasen is insistent.

Which means that, finally, I get to do something for charity that goes above filling out endless direct-debit forms. And I get to do it in the city I consider the best place on earth.

I take out my in-flight magazine and lean back in my seat, flicking through the pages, but not reading. Because all I can think of is Ben. Ben, who became the only contender for me in the end. The only man I wanted.

So while I'm completely sure I have to do this, it isn't without risk or sadness. This isn't easy. It isn't straightforward. It definitely isn't the happy ending I expected.

He cried as we embraced at the airport gate, but not as much as me. I'll miss him more than I can possibly express. Even after minutes apart I can feel his absence so acutely it makes my chest ache.

I realize that we're about to take off and remember I've forgotten to switch off my mobile. I retrieve it from my bag and discover four messages – from Ellie, from Jen, from Julia . . . all wishing me luck.

The fourth is from Ben.

I open it with a knot in my stomach and read the saddest and happiest words in the English language.

Samantha Brooks, I love you x

Epilogue

I'd forgotten how beautiful summer in the UK can be. How clean the air and crisp the sunshine. People thought I'd come back from America with a tan, but I'm paler than before I left, courtesy of a whirlwind six months working – largely indoors – in the heart of Manhattan.

Liverpool, the big city in which I grew up, looks quiet and small by comparison. Yet returning is about as far from an anticlimax as possible. I take the bus into the city and disembark near Hope Street, passing Georgian houses on Rodney Street and heading down the hill.

I'm still dizzy with jet lag, in that strange twilight state where my bed is the first and last place I want to be. My heart is racing so fast I can barely control my breathing, but I'm trying to keep my cool, just like the last time I was on my way to a date here. I'm two minutes away when my phone beeps. It's a text from Ellie.

Good luck, gorgeous. Give him a great big sloppy kiss from Jen and me. xx

I grin and put the phone back into my bag. A kiss. Now there's a thought. One that makes my heartbeat triple in speed.

Ellie and Jen met me off the plane when I landed this morning. What struck me when I saw them was how fantastic they both looked, Ellie in particular.

She's been sober for six months. She's still dying for a drink, of course, and assured me on the way home that she could happily stop off for a couple of tequila slammers, despite it being ten past ten in the morning. But she's determined to beat this problem, taking her membership of AA (not the yellow-van kind) as seriously as her pledge to take one day at a time.

Jen is still in love with Dr Dan and, I'm delighted to report, the feeling is, without question, mutual. He's asked her to move in with him. Her reaction to this was to take three deep breaths and – brainwashed by her dating manuals – suggest that they wait a while, not rush things. So he asked her again. Five minutes later, she started choosing the curtains.

The girls drove me back to Mum and Dad's place, where I'll be staying until next week, when my tenants move out. It's going to be strange moving back to the house I shared with Jamie for so many years, though if I'm honest by the end of our relationship it felt like my place, rather than ours. Even earlier, in fact – although I never admitted that. Everything from the decor to the food in the fridge was chosen by me and, months after he'd left, it didn't feel empty without him there. It felt right. As I know it will this time. My place, my space – to do with as I want.

There are some things, however, that are going to be different now. I was offered my old job back with BJD Productions, but am in the rather lovely position of having another option. One I'm really excited about. I was approached a few months ago by the boss of a rival events company in Manchester, who recently decided to go it alone and set up her own business. I've worked with her on five or six events in the last three years and she is wonderful. She wants me to be her partner. We've exchanged endless emails and I've got a meeting lined up with her tomorrow to discuss how we're going to get started.

I don't feel too guilty about not going back to BJD. Especially as, from what I hear, the place is ticking over nicely. That's thanks to Anna, who has proved to be an absolute star, and no thanks – you'll be unsurprised to hear – to either Natalie (now retraining as an eyelash technician) or Deana, who was sacked after three weeks with Piers and is working in a bar on Hanover Street.

Jamie has been in touch once in the last six months; he emailed me to say hi and to let me know he's returning to the UK. He spent four months in South America but the trip wasn't all he'd hoped for. He didn't explain why exactly, although Lisa – who Skyped me so often it was like having my own personal Sky News correspondent – says he simply didn't enjoy the travelling as much as he had when he was younger.

If I had any romantic feelings left for him, I might feel a bit frustrated by this. All that turmoil to end up back at Phones-A-Go-Go.

But I don't. I feel nothing for him except a vague fondness and the recognition that, while we had some great times together, those times came to an end. Times I shouldn't have clung on to for dear life when the relationship was on its last legs. Still, I wish Jamie all the best, I really do. And I hope he finds happiness one day, even if I haven't any more of a clue than he does what form that might take.

Luke, on the other hand, is happy. Gemma has him wrapped around her little finger, so much so that he's asked her to move in with him. He's confident she'll keep the tea towels in a better state than Jamie did.

As for Mum, Dad and Julia . . . well, I have nothing to report. Nothing at all. Despite the massive, dramatic revelations that unfolded six months ago, everyone remains exactly as they always were. Julia sees Gary a lot, of course, and has built up a great relationship with him. They visit each other once a month. But that's about the only thing that's different – and she wouldn't have it any other way.

As I approach the gates to St Luke's church I feel more nervous than I have before for any date, ever. Which is silly, because it's not as though we haven't had plenty of contact in the last six months. Skype calls every other night, constant texts and emails. But they're a poor substitute for the feel of someone's skin against yours, the warmth of a strong hand.

As I enter the gates of the church, Ben is on the same bench where we sat on our first date. With blood pumping through my ears I try to keep my walk steady, calm. But when he looks up from his newspaper and stiffens, smiling, I lose my cool and break into a spontaneous giggle.

I'm in front of him in seconds with his hands clasping mine, our faces inches apart. When our lips touch, my body melts and I want to cry and laugh at the same time. Instead, I pull back, with emotion soaring through me, and whisper, 'Ben Moran, I love you too.'

Win a £1000 wardrobe from Littleblackdress.co.uk!

To celebrate our fab new partnership with Jane Costello and *All the Single Ladies*, Little Black Dress is offering Simon & Schuster readers a £1000 worth of its best designer dresses, accessories and jewellery. Once kitted out, you need somewhere to flaunt your stylish new look, so you and three girlfriends (or two couples if you prefer) will spend a fantastic two nights at the luxurious Cumberland Hotel in London, plus dinner at the Michelin-star Rhodes W1 restaurant and cocktails in the trendy Patron bar.

To enter and for full terms and conditions visit
www.simonandschuster.co.uk

Follow us on Twitter: **@TeamLBD**
Like us: **Facebook.com/yourlittleblackdress**

www.littleblackdress.co.uk